Things
I Wish I'd
Known

Linda Green

Quercus

First published in Great Britain in 2010 by Headline Review,
an imprint of Headline Publishing Group

This edition published in 2018 by

Quercus Editions Ltd
Carmelite House
50 Victoria Embankment
London EC4Y 0DZ

An Hachette UK company

PB ISBN 978 1 78648 712 4
EBOOK ISBN 978 1 78648 711 7

This book is a work of fiction. Names, characters,
places and incidents are either the product of the author's imagination
or used fictitiously. Any resemblance to
actual persons, living or dead, events or
locales is entirely coincidental.

10 9 8 7 6 5 4 3 2 1

Printed and bound in Great Britain by Clays Ltd, Elcograf S.p.A.

For Ian and Rohan

One

At first, I thought it was a joke, probably due to the unfeasibly large grin on Mark's face as we drew up outside the house. When he suggested we got out and took a closer look, a sense of unease spread over me. And at the point where I stepped on to the pavement and caught sight of the garish pink and orange 'For Sale' sign in the front garden, I realised this was definitely no laughing matter.

'Well, what do you think?' Mark said, gesturing towards the large red-brick detached house which stood in front of us.

What I was thinking was that our happy, fun, not-going-anywhere-in-a-hurry carousel ride of a relationship was about to turn into the scariest rollercoaster at the fairground, the type where you had to choose between jumping off at the top while it was still moving or careering downhill into a lifetime of joint mortgage payments.

However, I also knew that in a relationship-defining moment like this, it paid to be non-committal until the other person had explained exactly what was going on. And that the last thing I wanted to do was wipe the deliriously excited expression off Mark's face.

'I think you may be about to audition for a presenter's

job on *Location, Location, Location* and you'd like me to prac-
tise being an awkward, impossible-to-please house-hunter.'

Mark laughed and shook his head, although I was aware
I had still managed to turn the dimmer switch on his smile
down a notch or two.

'I'm going to have to spell it out, aren't I?' he said.

"Fraid so. I'm obviously being a bit dense here.'

Mark took a moment to compose himself as he gazed
down thoughtfully at his sandals. He didn't usually do
hesitation.

'I'd like us to move in together. Somewhere new, not
my place or yours. Somewhere we can be a proper couple
and not have to have toothbrushes in two different places
and dash home to get a change of clothes before work in
the morning.'

It sounded more like a proposal to merge two companies than to cement our future as a couple. But then Mark
was not a romantic candlelit-dinner type of guy (he cited
the fact that he'd once represented a client whose sleeve
had caught fire in a restaurant). He was straightforward,
practical and sometimes impulsive – as he had just
demonstrated – but he was never going to sweep me off
my feet and whisk me away to his castle on a white char-
ger. Which was probably just as well, as I was in my thirties
and still bearing the scars from two botched attempts at
broken-heart surgery and had therefore long ago stopped
believing in that sort of thing.

I glanced up and realised he was waiting for an answer.
Not just any answer. The one he was desperate to hear.

'Oh,' I said, totally inadequately, as my lips played for

time while my head tried to come up with a more appropriate response.

'Have I finally succeeded in rendering you speechless? Can I make a note of this in my diary? "Claire lost for words shocker"?'

I knew the joke was intended to cover up his disappointment. I smiled back at him, trying to make it clear that I wasn't about to blow him out. I couldn't; this was Mark, the man who had put a smile on my face for the past two years and had single-handedly restored my faith in men. It would have been unbearably cruel to extinguish the flame of optimism which burnt so brightly in him.

'Sorry. It's a bit of a shock, that's all.'

'Lucky I didn't go the whole hog and propose, then.' He was grinning, well aware of my view that it would be plain rude of me to expect my friends and family to shell out for wedding presents for a second time.

'It's just that I thought you were happy with things how they are,' I said.

'I am,' replied Mark, looking serious for once. 'But I've realised I'd be even happier if we were living together.' It was as near as he had ever got to declaring his undying love for me.

I smiled at him and kissed him on the lips. Because I wanted to and because I still wasn't sure what to say. It wasn't that I didn't love him. I did. It was simply that loving someone and wanting to buy a house together were two very different things. But now Mark had bought me a ticket for the white-knuckle ride, I was well aware that continuing on the carousel wasn't really an option any more. I put my arms around his neck and kissed him again.

'Do I take that as a yes, then?' he asked when our lips finally parted.

'Argued so persuasively, how could I refuse?' I said.

The full cheek-to-cheek grin returned to his face. His greeny-blue eyes looked like they were celebrating a hat-trick for England. Mark was happy. The panic was over. Air pressure in the cabin returned to normal. I took off the oxygen mask to find I could breathe again.

'There's just one thing I'm not sure about,' I continued.

'Here we go,' said Mark. 'You're going to add in loads of conditions now, aren't you? Some sort of prenup for living together, where you get custody of the wok if I dare to pick my toenails in bed.'

'No,' I said. 'It's, er, that.' I pointed to the house with rather less aplomb than Mark had.

'What's wrong with it?' Mark sounded put out. I decided not to tell him that if he'd been trying to find my dream house, an Identikit new-build in a sought-after cul-de-sac in Littleborough couldn't have been further from it. I took a deep breath and tried to phrase it diplomatically.

'It's, er, a bit lacking in the charm department.'

'OK, it's not chocolate-box thatched-cottage material, but if it was, it would also be cold, damp, dingy and draughty, be out in the sticks somewhere and cost us a for-tune in running repairs over the years – if we could afford it to start off with, that is. Whereas what we have here, while admittedly not aesthetically appealing, is new, warm, solid, light, easy to maintain, has straight walls and ceilings, no vermin living beneath the floorboards or in the loft, is within walking distance of the station and I reckon we can get it for under two hundred and fifty thousand, so avoiding being stung for stamp duty.'

I smiled. It was easy to see why Mark was capable of twisting anyone around his little finger in court. He possessed the true lawyer's knack of being able to paint black as white, and in such a way that you started to doubt whether it had ever been black in the first place (I was admittedly jealous of this, being the type of lawyer who somehow always got bogged down in the shades of grey in between). He was also right, of course. But as someone who had always been more head-in-the-clouds than practical, I was able to overlook that. My dream home was something older and weather-beaten, something I could fall in love with at first sight, something that oozed character from its crooked stone walls to its creaking floorboards. Something which would feel like home. My home. Not a show home.

'This is me you're speaking to, remember,' I said, poking him playfully in the ribs. 'You'll have to do better than that. I'm not going to agree to buy a house on the grounds that it hasn't got rats.'

'That's all right,' he said, pulling his sunglasses up on to the top of his head for a moment and squinting down the street. 'Here's the very man to convince you.' I followed his gaze to where a silver Saab had pulled up at the kerb and a man in his fifties, wearing an ill-fitting suit which refused to do up over his pot belly, was bounding towards us.

'What do you mean?' I said.

'That's Chris, the estate agent. He's going to show us around.' I felt the perspiration break out on my brow. And it had nothing to do with it being the hottest day of the year so far. I wouldn't even buy a pair of shoes in the first shop I looked in, let alone snap up the very first house I viewed — especially when I hadn't even known we were looking until a few minutes ago.

'What, now?'

'Yeah, is that all right? I know it was a bit presumptuous of me, but I had a *carpe diem* moment. If you want me to put him off I can do.'

Before I could answer, Chris was shaking my hand, positively foaming at the mouth at the prospect of a sale. He brought to mind a hound which hadn't been out on a hunt for weeks and had suddenly got wind of a fox. I guessed a recession did that to estate agents.

'Right,' he said when the introductions were over. 'Well, as you can see, it's a quiet but convenient location, only five minutes from the M62 and ten minutes' walk from the station. Where do you guys work?'

'Rochdale,' we said in unison, me with a distinct lack of enthusiasm.

'Well, you're ideally situated here,' he said, loosening his tie a touch as the sun reappeared from behind a cloud. 'And of course, you're near excellent primary and secondary schools. It really is a perfect family home.'

I nodded without saying anything and shifted my Birkenstock-clad feet on the pavement. The fact that he'd assumed we either already had kids or were planning to start a family made me a little uneasy. Where had he got the idea that it was a family home we were after?

I had been honest with Mark from very early on about my desire to remain 'child-free' (as I preferred to call it). I didn't announce, 'Now before we go any further, I need to make it clear that I don't want children,' as we sat down for a meal on our first date. But to be honest, I didn't have to. Because even before we'd started going out together, during the prolonged wooing phase when Mark had tried his best to charm the knickers off me every time we'd bumped into each other in the café in Drake Street, where both of our practices were based, I'd made enough references to the fact that representing a steady stream of teenage delinquents and drug addicts was the career least likely to engender a burning desire in anyone to procreate, to get the message across.

To his credit, Mark had never pushed me on the matter or tried to persuade me of the joy to be derived from seeing your offspring in a miniature Blackburn Rovers kit. But I'd long suspected he harboured a secret desire to be a father and now, suddenly, it occurred to me that this could be his first move in trying to get me to change my mind. I could see how his argument would go, something along the lines of, 'Well, now we've got four bedrooms it would be a shame to waste the space. And being so near to some good schools, we may as well take advantage of them, otherwise we're simply paying taxes to educate other people's kids.' Mark could convince anyone of anything. And before I knew it I'd have a toddler on one hip and a baby clamped to my breast.

I looked across at Mark. He gave a little shrug but made no attempt to correct Chris.

'Right, let's go inside,' continued Chris. 'This place is made for you. I have a feeling you're going to love it.'

I shrugged back at Mark and followed Chris into the small hallway, the smell of 'new' filling my nostrils.

'We'll start in the lounge,' he said, pushing the door open to reveal an expanse of laminate flooring and magnolia walls. 'Plenty of room for a big plasma screen in here.' He grinned, turning to Mark. 'Now, Claire, while Mark's watching the footie on TV, let me show you the fantastic kitchen which will make preparing meals so easy you'll have plenty of time to put your feet up with a magazine and catch up on all the latest celebrity gossip.' I raised my eyebrows.

'Should I tell him women have the vote now?' I whispered to Mark.

'Perhaps he's used to dealing with bored housewives.'

'Or maybe he's simply reading from the script,' I replied. 'In which case I'm about to get told about the state-of-the-art appliances in the beautifully appointed kitchen.'

'Now then,' said Chris, leading us into the kitchen, 'there are some state-of-the-art appliances in here . . .'

I groaned inwardly and let Chris's sales patter drift over me as I looked around. It was one of those spot-the-difference kitchens where you don't know where anything is and would forever be opening doors and accidentally putting the milk in the dishwasher and the rubbish in the washing machine.

'Mmmm, great,' I muttered unconvincingly as Chris led us back to the hallway.

'Why didn't you tell him that I hate all this hard-sell stuff?' I whispered to Mark as we climbed the stairs behind him.

'It's like telling a Jehovah's Witness you don't do religion; they simply try even harder. Anyway, some muppet showing us around isn't going to put us off, is it?'

What concerned me about Mark's reply was that it appeared to be a rhetorical question. He clearly didn't realise that I couldn't be put off because I'd never been keen on it in the first place.

'It's a beautifully appointed master bedroom, with en suite and dressing area – so plenty of room for all those designer frocks and Jimmy Choo shoes.'

I forced out a smile to be polite, realising that we would get out of the place more quickly if I went along with Chris's notion that I was Victoria Beckham in disguise.

We moved on through the next three bedrooms, inspected the bathroom (the white was at least a refreshing change from magnolia), and were finally left on our own on the landing to 'talk things through', while Chris went to open up the integral garage for our inspection.

I looked at Mark. The expression on his face suggested he would offer the asking price by the time we got downstairs.

'Well?' he said expectantly.

'You were right. The walls are straight and there's no vermin. However, I do have one concern.'

'Which is?'

'Why is he under the impression we have more children than the Waltons?'

'Ah, yes, that,' said Mark. 'He's just got the wrong end of the stick. I said it was a long-term purchase we were looking for, that we wanted to put down some roots, and he's obviously interpreted that as meaning we wanted somewhere which would cater for a growing family.'

'Right. So why do we need four bedrooms exactly?'

'Well, one of them can be a study, one room always ends up as a junk room so you may as well factor that in, and the other one can be a guest room.'

He was doing it again. Making me doubt why I had ever questioned him in the first place. I stared at him intently, looking for any visible sign that he was talking grade-one lawyer bullshit.

'And you're sure you have no desire to fill the place with the patter of tiny feet and the smell of poo and vomit?'

Mark smiled. 'I'd simply like some more space and I figured you'd feel the same way. It's the one thing neither of us has got.'

He had a point. Mark lived in a one-bedroom flat in Littleborough which had one of those all-in-one kitchen/dining/living spaces that developers trying to maximise their profits seemed so fond of (presumably they didn't think anybody would mind if their sofa permanently smelt of last night's curry). And I lived in a small (poky was the word Mark used) two-bedroom terraced house a few miles down the road in Todmorden, just over the West Yorkshire border (something Mark used to rib me about as a born-and-bred Lancastrian who had come dangerously close to reigniting the War of the Roses on numerous occasions).

I glanced across at Mark. He was obviously desperate to buy the place. I felt mean for having such a downer on it. I needed to find something positive to say.

'I guess it would be nice to have a bathroom and an en suite.'

'There speaks a woman with mildew on her over-the-bath shower curtain.'

'At least I *have* a bath.' Mark's flat only had a shower (presumably having been designed by a man who had no idea how tricky it was trying to shave your legs while standing up in a tiny shower cubicle).

'There, see, property snobbery already. Before you know it you'll be saying, "Oh, don't you have an integral garage?"'

'Come on,' I said, laughing uneasily. 'Chris'll be wondering where we've got to.'

We arrived downstairs to find Chris poised to give a demonstration of the up-and-over door.

'Obviously the garage is just as it's been finished at the moment, but if you wanted to decorate it in any way . . .'

'Great idea, I could paint it pink and do some nice floral stencilling,' I said, managing to keep a straight face.

'I can see your little lady's been reading all the latest interior design magazines,' said Chris, turning to Mark. I waited until he'd turned to lead us out of the garage before banging my head on the brick wall.

'Chin up, it's nearly over,' whispered Mark.

'And of course, the garden is wonderfully low maintenance,' said Chris, gesturing to the small square of lawn at the side of the property. 'So, what do you think?' he asked, almost quivering with anticipation. He was looking at Mark, of course, clearly being of the view that the 'little lady' would have no say on financial matters.

'It's great,' said Mark. 'Ticks all our boxes. Obviously we'll have to go away and have a think about it.' I stared at him, relieved that he hadn't said yes on the spot but already aware that it was going to be very difficult for me to back out of it.

'Sure, I understand,' said Chris, clearly gutted not to have finished off his prey. 'Don't leave it too long, though. I have another viewing arranged next week. This is the only one left and the others have gone like hot cakes.'

I was about to point out that houses were in fact about as popular as three-day-old dried-up rolls in a baker's at the moment but decided not to put the boot in when he was so obviously desperate. Instead, I glanced around at the other properties in the cul-de-sac, a couple of which were occupied. There was a man washing his 4×4 in one drive, a woman swirling a Flymo across the lawn in a side garden and two kids on their bikes, trying desperately to outdo each other's skids. It reminded me of Potters Bar where I grew up. And of why I'd been so desperate to get out. We watched as Chris waved and drove off. At which point it was just me and Mark standing on the pavement, teetering on the brink of suburban hell.

'So,' said Mark, turning to me. 'If it was *Location, Location, Location,* what would you say now?'

'Show me the next property,' I said. Mark laughed.

'How about a serious answer for once?'

I didn't have the heart to tell him that it had been. He was clearly already working out where his hi-fi and the giant yucca plant would go. The man who I loved had asked me to move in with him and had probably spent ages scouring the internet for the ideal home, which he had presented to me on a plate. OK, he couldn't have got it more wrong if he'd tried but I didn't want to appear an ungrateful wretch and I was well aware that a lot of people would have given anything to live in a house like that.

'It's not really the best time to buy a house, is it?' I said lamely. 'Are you sure we can afford it?' Mark earned considerably more than me; he was a personal injury lawyer (or ambulance-chaser as my father insisted on referring to him), contracted by one of those national 'no-win, no-fee' firms which advertised on daytime TV. Whereas I was a solicitor for a small family-owned business – and Legal Aid payments weren't all they could be.

'I'm recession-proof – people will always have accidents,' said Mark. 'Anyway, I've worked out the mortgage payments and everything. It's not a huge amount more than we both pay at the moment and we'll only have council tax and heating bills for one property. And I'll be covering the deposit and the stamp duty so you haven't got to worry about that. It actually makes huge financial sense.'

I smiled at him, knowing again that he was right and trying to ignore the churning sensation in my stomach. The ride was going too fast already. I wanted to get off. I reached out for Mark's hand and clasped it tightly.

'OK, can I sleep on it?' I said. 'Maybe a couple of nights, actually.'

He grinned, sensing he almost had me.

Standing precariously on the top rung of my rickety stepladder, I pushed the loft cover to one side, rested the torch on the edge and prepared to haul myself upwards through the hatch, reassured by the fact that if I did fall, I would at least have a personal injury lawyer on hand to try to get some compensation from the stepladder manufacturers.

As it was, the ladder – and my arms – held out and I scrambled unceremoniously on to the floorboards I'd laid across the joists to try to support the weight of the numerous boxes which were stacked there. I waited for the dust to settle and my eyes to get used to the dimness before picking up the torch and shining it around like some 1950s usherette who was a bit apprehensive about what might be going on in the back row of the cinema.

The cardboard boxes were piled high on top of each other. The building blocks of my life. They contained my DNA. Which was why they were taped shut; no one else was allowed to look at them and I would no sooner get rid of them than agree to sever my right arm. I hadn't been up there for ages, probably not since I'd moved in eight years previously. I stuck my head up there every Christmas to reach down the tree and decorations but it wasn't the same. I wasn't within touching distance. The memories were all out of reach. But not any longer. It was time. I was standing at a crossroads, wondering which way to go. Only I couldn't seem to work out where my future lay. Probably because I still hadn't come to terms with my past.

I walked over and ran my finger along the sealed top of the nearest box, which was marked 'Photos'. Making contact with the past. Acknowledging its existence while knowing I should keep it at arm's length. It was too tempting though. I peeled off the parcel tape, feeling like a kid who had discovered her hidden Christmas presents on 23 December and decided to peek inside, even though she knew it was wrong. A pile of photo albums and bulging Kodak envelopes greeted me – a reminder of the days when photographs took up half of your household storage space instead of being contained in a few megabytes of computer hard drive. I pulled out the album on top and opened it up, immediately shutting it again as I caught sight of Andy grinning back at me. Even after all this time he still had the ability to do that to me. It wasn't as if I hadn't expected to see him; most of the boxes contained cardboard-to-cardboard Andy. It was simply that I hadn't expected him to look so good. I was sure that if most women dug out the photos of the idols who used to line their bedroom walls, they would cringe in horror at why they'd ever thought Nick Berry from *EastEnders* was good-looking just because he'd had a number-one single, or wonder how they hadn't noticed Simon Le Bon's double chin at the time. But in my case I had to compliment myself on having disturbingly good taste in men at the age of fifteen. Maybe that was what had got me into so much trouble.

I opened the album again and started flicking through

it, in case I'd simply caught him on a good day, but no, whether he was standing shirtless outside the changing rooms with his arm around me on a summer's day or bent double in a baggy tracksuit doing hamstring stretches during a drizzly October half-term at the training ground, he still looked unnervingly good. Whereas I, it had to be said, looked bloody awful: all hairsprayed flick, stick arms and highly dubious outfits. That was the weird thing about the eighties – how no one realised what a sight they looked at the time. Frankie, of course, looked gorgeous in every picture, but then she always was the exception to the rule. She probably still looked gorgeous now. It was a shame the photos hadn't continued past my sixteenth birthday, when I'd emerged from my ugly duckling phase. But by that time everything had changed and taking photos had been the last thing on my mind.

I leafed through every album and photo wallet, the vast majority full of snaps taken at the United training ground. Frankie and I must have doubled Kodak's profits in 1985. By the time I'd finished, I was on a full-blown nostalgia kick and didn't hesitate in removing the tape on the next box – the one marked 'Diaries and Mementoes'. It should have had some kind of emotional health warning on the side. Inside were piles of spiral-bound notepads (normal diaries had never had enough room for my teenage angst), many of them with doodles on the front, hearts with arrows through them declaring that CS loved AP for ever. I shook my head and smiled. It had all been so innocent back then. It was as I rummaged through the diaries that I noticed the envelope poking out from the side of one of them. A sealed pale blue envelope with 'NOT TO BE OPENED UNTIL 31 JULY 2005' written on it in bold black letters. I knew what it was straight away, of course. What I couldn't work out was why I hadn't remembered it three years ago. I wondered if Frankie had opened hers then. Whether she still had it, even.

I slid my finger into the corner of the envelope and started to tear. It was like going back in time to visit a medium, armed with the hindsight necessary to know how accurate she was straight away. And, rather bizarrely, knowing that the medium had been me, aged fifteen.

I unfolded the single sheet of paper. 'Twenty Years From Now' it read boldly at the top of the page.

Love life – Married to Andy Pailes.

Holidays – Florence, Italy.

Career – Partner in big city law firm.

Looks – Kind of the same but with shorter hair and bigger boobs.

Financial status – Well off but not super-rich.

Living – In a thatched cottage in the countryside, possibly in Yorkshire.

Children – Two, Steven and Lauren.

Best Friend – Frankie.

Interests – Football (United season-ticket holder, commute to games), politics (maybe a Labour councillor), law (making the world a better place).

Are you happy? – The happiest I've ever been.

I sat with the piece of paper in my hands, unable to decide for a moment whether to laugh or cry. But within a second or two the words on the page became blurred and I realised which option I'd chosen. It was silly really. How a fifteen-year-old version of me could be capable of cutting the adult model to the quick like that. But I'd had no idea back then how life doesn't always turn out the way you plan. How all your hopes and dreams can evaporate over time. Or sometimes be cruelly squashed in an instant. And no idea that one day I would sit in a dusty attic with tears streaming down my face wondering how my life had fallen so badly short of my expectations.

I sniffed, wiped my nose with my sleeve and re-read the list, inserting the real answers where the misplaced expectations had been.

Love life – Married law-school sweetheart David at 23. Divorced at 30. Boyfriend of two years, Mark, has asked me to move in with him.

Holidays – The Lake District or Cornwall (never been to Florence).

Career – Made redundant from my first job at a big Manchester law firm. Now a solicitor with small family-owned company Barnes and Co., on rota as duty solicitor for Rochdale Magistrates' Court dealing with a succession of career criminals and small-time crooks.

Looks – Filled out a bit (boobs did at least make it to an A cup), shoulder-length hair with fair highlights. Flick gone.

Financial status – Solvent but no savings or expectations of a pay rise.

Living – In a poky two-bed back-to-back Victorian terrace. Did end up in West Yorkshire but about to move into soulless new-build in a Lancashire cul-de-sac.

Children – None. Bit of luck bearing in mind the divorce.

Best friend – Fiona, one of the clerks at Rochdale Magistrates' Court. Lost touch with Frankie more than 17 years ago.

Interests – Gardening (have my own allotment), swimming (proper front crawl in the fast lane, not gossipy breaststroke without getting your hair wet), law (though I haven't even made Rochdale a better place, let alone the world). Went off United and football in general when all the money and prima donnas came in and ruined the game. Resigned from the Labour Party after Iraq invasion, without ever volunteering for leafleting duties, let alone running for election.

Are you happy?

I stopped abruptly at the last question, imagining for a moment what my fifteen-year-old self would have thought had she known the truth back then. How disillusioned and disappointed she would have been to see what had become of her. I knew that, compared to most of my classmates, I'd done all right for myself. But all right had never been good enough for me. I'd wanted the moon and stars. I'd even got close enough to touch them before plummeting back down to earth with an almighty bump. And suddenly I felt cheated by the consolation-prize life I had instead. I realised things had gone badly off course. But maybe I still had time to put that right. Maybe I wasn't past the 'use-by' date for dreams.

Monday, 22 July 1985

As far as me and Frankie were concerned, it was nothing short of a crime. A crime which would shock the nation. A crime against humanity even.

We watched the gold BMW sweep through the gates of the training ground and park in the far corner as usual. We saw the familiar designer-tracksuited figure emerge, Rolex glistening in the bright morning sunlight.

It was only as he turned and began to stroll towards us, the other fans parting before him like that thing with Moses and the waves in the Bible, that we caught sight of it. And the full enormity of the situation became clear.

'Oh, shit,' Frankie groaned. 'Matt's had a perm.'

We smiled politely in Matt Goodyear's direction as he glided swiftly past us into the clubhouse, the mass of tight curls sticking to his head like scrunched-up pieces of tissue paper on a school collage. And then we waited, bracing ourselves for the inevitable reaction.

'Bloody hell, it's Kevin Keegan.' Gibbo's Welsh accent was the first voice we heard through the open dressing-room window above the predictable howls of laughter from Matt's teammates.

Frankie slumped on the low wall outside the dressing

room, biting what was left of her scarlet-painted nails and scuffing the toe of her stiletto repeatedly against the wall.

I stood next to her, marvelling at the way she could still stick her boobs out even when she was slouching, while racking my brain for something to say that would make her feel better. When my grandad had died, my mum had tried to soften the blow by pointing out that I did at least have another grandfather. I didn't think the same tactic would work here, though. What with Matt only having the one head.

'Maybe he did it for a dare, or for charity or something.'

I knew that twenty-eight year olds didn't do things for a dare. And I couldn't think of a single famous person who'd had a perm as a way of raising money for charity. They were much more likely to organise a big open-air pop concert and invite people like Sting and George Michael. It was less embarrassing that way.

Frankie gave me one of her looks.

'He's not Bob Geldof, you know. He hasn't done it to feed all the kids in Ethiopia.'

'I was only trying to make you feel better.'

'Well don't bother. I may as well get used to him being a laughing stock. The Arsenal fans are gonna love this, aren't they? "Can you hear us, Matt Goodyear, you sad bastard with your girlie hair?" That's what they'll sing, you know. That's what John Motson will try and talk over on *Match of the Day*.'

'So why do you think he had it done?'

'It's obvious, innit? Jane made him do it. The fat-arsed cow.'

Frankie reckoned everything was Matt's wife's fault. If Russia ever nuked Potters Bar, she'd try to pin that one on her as well.

'Why would Jane want Matt to be a laughing stock?'

''Cos she's jealous of all the attention he's been getting, you spaz. She can't stand the competition, can she? Thought she'd try and put his admirers off.'

'So have you gone off him, then?'

Frankie thought about it for a moment, pursing her full scarlet lips as she did so.

'Nah, it'll take more than a perm,' she said, tossing her own dark mane of long straight hair.

'You said you'd go off Simon Le Bon if he ever had a perm,' I pointed out.

'Yeah, well. His legs aren't as good as Matt's, are they?'

'How do you know?'

Frankie gave a dramatic sigh.

'I just know, OK?'

I hated it when Frankie gave answers like that, acting as if she had some kind of inside information – which I knew she didn't. We waited in silence outside the clubhouse for five more minutes, until at last we heard the rasping sounds of studs hitting concrete. First one, then two and finally dozens of football boots pounded over the rough path to the dry, stubbly grass beyond.

This was it. The moment we had been waiting for. The real start of our school summer holidays. United, pride of north London, were coming out to play.

The tight blue shorts, the bulging, tanned thighs, the tantalising glimpse of chest hair beneath the silky sheen of their football shirts, I took it all in, my eyes straining to absorb every detail. If Michael Rodd off *Screen Test* had appeared and started asking me questions about the clip of footage I'd just seen, I'd have got every one right. Even the bonus question about who was the only player in a long-sleeved shirt. I took a deep breath, closing my eyes. Breathing in memories I could treasure for ever, instead of ones that kept me awake at night.

'This,' whispered Frankie, 'has got to be the best place on earth.'

I nodded, still unable to believe that such a place existed. It was our first time at the training ground. Someone had told Frankie's dad that they let fans in to watch on Mondays and Wednesdays. For free as well, so my mum couldn't say we couldn't afford it. And there weren't going to be fans from any other club here, so she couldn't say there was going to be any trouble. Football hooligans weren't interested in watching players warming up and practising their half-volleys. Even my mum knew that.

We found a good vantage point on the grass banking at the side of the pitch, high enough that we could see over the crowds of fans, mostly little boys with bored-looking mums in tow, who were jostling for the best position on the touchline. The squad jogged off around the training ground, the first-team players still winding Matt up, the younger ones smirking, not daring to join in the banter but clearly smug in the knowledge that even an England star could commit a style faux pas of such monumental proportions.

I watched Matt as he jogged round, intermittently

twisting and stretching from side to side. He'd been my favourite United player since I was twelve. Not because I fancied him (he looked a bit like Tony Hadley out of Spandau Ballet; I was more of a Martin Kemp kind of girl myself), but simply because he was our best player. He wasn't my favourite any more though. Not since we'd signed Andy Pailes last season, and I'd realised that I had no wish to idolise a man who stared up at me from my cornflakes box every morning. I wasn't a kid any more. I didn't want a superstar I had to share with everyone else. I wanted a precious but as yet undiscovered gemstone. One that I could claim as my very own.

Seconds later Andy jogged past, the sunlight catching the small gold ring in his left ear. I double-checked the hair but it was still the same – thick, dark, slightly spiky and not a curl in sight. I smiled to myself, happy that I had unearthed a rare thing of genuine beauty.

As Andy edged nearer – so near that I could see the beads of sweat forming on his forehead – the corners of my mouth crept upwards and somewhere inside me a vice tightened around my internal organs. My heart was pounding. Seriously pounding, as if it might burst right out of my ribcage. For a second I thought I was having a heart attack, until I realised that was unlikely, what with me being a skinny fifteen-year-old vegetarian and my mum having switched from butter to Flora. No, my pounding heart could mean only one thing. I was in love. Big time.

Having never been in love before (fancying Jason Pike at school for six months before he'd started going out with Angela Sutcliffe didn't count, as I was only thirteen at the time; that was just kids' stuff), I wanted to keep it to myself for a little while longer. But I blew it by going bright red as Andy jogged past me. Frankie never missed these things; she was much too sharp for that.

'You fancy him, don't you? You fancy Andy Pailes,' she said, the collection of thin metal bangles on her wrist tinkling against each other as she waved her arms around.

'Shut up, will you,' I pleaded, glancing at the other fans who were milling around below us. I didn't want a public announcement. This was a very private thing.

'So is it his bum or his legs?'

I sighed, wondering how I'd ended up with a best friend who didn't know the meaning of the word subtle.

'I think he's different, that's all. There's something intriguing about him.'

'Something intriguing about him,' mimicked Frankie. 'What the hell's that s'posed to mean? You either fancy the pants off him or you don't.'

'Some of us like to go a bit deeper than that.'

'Bollocks. It's all right to admit you fancy him, you know. He's a good-looking bloke.'

'D'you think so?' I asked.

'Nah, but you obviously do. So now we've got that sorted out, you can tell me all about it.'

Frankie dragged me over to a quiet spot on the grassy bank, away from all the kids, and, with one eye still firmly on Matt, began bombarding me with questions about Andy. At first I tried to be coy, giving knowing smiles rather than detailed information as I fiddled with the badge on my canvas bag (it had one red arrow pointing in the opposite direction to lots of black arrows. I'd bought it so it looked as if being different to everyone else was a conscious decision I'd made, rather than an unfortunate turn of fate).

Eventually, under duress and in danger of losing Frankie's interest altogether, I was forced to admit I didn't know much about Andy at all.

'He's an enigma,' I explained with the same flourish of the left hand that I'd seen an art critic on a late-night BBC2 programme give when he'd used the term. The silence that followed confirmed my hunch that Frankie wouldn't want to reveal her own ignorance by asking what the word actually meant. Which was just as well, as I wasn't altogether sure myself.

'Haven't you even found a fact file on him?' asked Frankie. As far as she was concerned, fact files were the football fan's equivalent of Letts revision notes. They told you all the key stuff you wanted to know without the need for hours of research.

'Give us a chance, will you? He's only been at United a few months.'

'You mean he ain't famous enough to have one done on him.'

I didn't bother rising to the bait. Sometimes arguing with Frankie was so easy it wasn't any fun.

'Look, do you want to know anything about him or not?' I said.

'Go on, I'm listening.'

'Well, he's twenty-two, is from a place called Ponte-something in Yorkshire, started out at Huddersfield Town, played for the England under twenty-one team, signed for Leeds and had been there two years when we signed him.'

'Yeah, yeah. Very interesting. But has he got a girl-friend?' asked Frankie.

'Er, I don't know.'

Frankie gave another sigh.

'OK, let's see,' she said, pushing her shades up for a second and squinting in the bright sunlight to get a better look at Andy. 'I reckon you might be in there. He looks single to me.'

'Oh, and you can tell, can you?'

'Come on, who would go out with a guy who looks like someone out of Echo and the Bunnymen? He doesn't look like a proper footballer at all.'

'Just 'cos he hasn't got highlights and a poncey haircut, it doesn't mean he can't play football.'

'I know. All I'm saying is he's not exactly in the Matt Goodyear mould, is he?' I was going to point out that at least that meant I wouldn't find a plastic Andy Pailes in my cornflakes, when I thought better of it. Frankie was having a tough day, what with the perm and that.

'Well no, but there's room for all tastes, isn't there?'

'Absolutely. So let's work this out: he's twenty-two and you're fourteen . . .'

'Fifteen, thank you,' I said, annoyed that four months into my sixteenth year, Frankie still had to be reminded.

'OK, but that's still at least a seven-year age gap. Might be stretching it a bit.'

'Oh, like the twelve years between you and Matt isn't, you mean?'

'Course not. It's different for me, innit? I don't look . . .'

Frankie's voice trailed off as I shifted from my crossed-leg position and stretched out my long legs in a desperate but ultimately futile attempt to look less like a *Blue Peter* viewer. She didn't need to finish the sentence. The brutal truth was that I did still look like a fourteen year old. Not even my heavily hair-sprayed flick (which looked so much more grown-up than my old straight-cut fringe) could distract from the stick-insect body poking out from beneath my pedal-pushers and tea-bag tank-top.

Whereas Frankie, while only eighteen months older than me, could easily pass for nineteen, thanks to her Mediterranean looks and page-three-girl figure. Sometimes I liked having a best friend who could put Samantha Fox in the shade. Other times I worried that hanging out with Frankie didn't do me any favours. No one noticed the foothills next to Mount Everest, did they?

'Cheer up,' said Frankie, having finally noticed my bleak expression. 'Maybe this will be the year it will all kick in for you. You've got to get boobs sometime, you know.'

I wasn't so sure. Having been blessed with hormones that had forgotten the necessity for me to grow out in the right places as well as up, I was beginning to wonder if I would ever graduate from junior bras. It bothered me a lot. Every time I saw the AA sticker inside Mum's car I thought about it. And sometimes even when I changed the double-A batteries in my radio.

'Yeah, like never,' I said, turning to face Frankie.

'Hey, don't get down about it. I wouldn't mind a few of your inches in height.'

'At least you can wear high heels to make up for it. I don't fancy trying to pad my bra out. Do you remember that scene in *Little House on the Prairie*? The one where Laura Ingalls stuffed oranges down her top and they fell out in class? That would be me, that would.'

'Maybe you're gonna be one of those late bloomers,' said Frankie. 'Today a tall, skinny kid, tomorrow a catwalk model.'

'Yeah, right. And Maggie Thatcher will run off with Ken Livingstone. Dream on. Anyway, I don't wanna be a model, I want to be a lawyer, thank you.'

'Oh, whatever. I was only trying to help. But you shouldn't let it get to you. Forget about it for the summer holidays. That's what I'm gonna do. Forget about my O-level results and starting college and all the crap at home. All I'm gonna think about this summer is United.'

I liked the idea but wasn't sure that it would work for me. A lot of things that worked for Frankie didn't work for me. Like rah-rah skirts, for example. Frankie looked fantastic in hers, whereas I looked like an anaemic twiglet wearing a lampshade.

'It's all right for you. You haven't got anything to worry about.'

'Yes I have,' said Frankie. 'My family are one big problem.'

'At least you've got one. I can't remember the last time I even saw my dad.'

'There you go then. You're halfway to forgetting about him already.'

I wasn't convinced but I was prepared to give it a go.

'OK, but we'll have to come up here a lot if it's gonna work. Practically live here, I mean. I want to feel like one of the team.'

'And I wanna feel up one of the team,' Frankie replied with a smirk. She said stuff like that all the time, but I wasn't sure she actually meant it. She'd never had a boy-friend. I hadn't either but that was because I didn't look like Frankie. She didn't have an excuse.

When training was over we waited outside in the play-ers' car park. It seemed to be where everyone else was gathering, autograph books at the ready.

'Come on,' said Frankie, striding over to Matt's car. 'I'm gonna have a look inside, see if I can find out what bands he's into at the moment.' She ran her hands over the BMW's sleek bodywork before stooping to peer inside, pressing her nose against the warm glass and cupping her hands around her eyes to get a better look.

'You can't do that,' I told her. 'It looks like you're trying to break in or something.'

'I'm checking out his tapes, that's all. I wanna see what he's got; maybe I could comment on his superb taste in music.'

'I doubt it,' I said, peering inside the window as my curiosity got the better of me. 'There's a *Kids from Fame* tape in there for a start.'

'You bitch, I don't believe you,' said Frankie before her eyes settled on the offending cassette, tucked neatly away beside Elton John, the Eagles and Bread. All footballers over the age of twenty-seven seemed to list Bread as one of their favourite groups. I didn't have a clue who they were; I'd certainly never seen them on *Top of the Pops*. I wondered if they'd done the music to the Hovis advert.

'Well it must be Jane's,' said Frankie. 'I can't see Matt being into *Fame*. All that poxying around in leg-warmers and leotards and that Bruno guy with the awful perm . . .'

Frankie's voice trailed off as she heard the crunch of designer trainers on gravel. She spun round to see Matt standing there, looking at her with an irritated expression.

'Er, sorry, I was just, um, admiring your leather-trimmed interior,' stuttered Frankie as she shuffled out of the way, thrusting her autograph book in Matt's face, presumably in an attempt to divert his attention from the smeary finger-marks she'd left on the driver's window. Matt signed his name and drove off without another word. I was embarrassed for Frankie. But I couldn't help feeling kind of pleased as well.

'Well, you made an impression all right,' I said.

'Yeah, of a right joey.'

Before I could say anything, the dressing-room door opened and I felt myself being nudged in the direction of the approaching Andy Pailes.

I started towards him before stopping abruptly, realising that I had no idea what I was going to say. It was too late though. Andy had seen me and was waiting expectantly. I was trapped in no-man's-land, knowing that I'd look a right prat if I retreated now.

For a second my mouth seemed to be moving but nothing came out, as if I was in a foreign film where the dubbing was out of sync. When the words did come, they rushed like a torrent, catching up with my mouth and overtaking it within a sentence.

'Hi, sorry to bother you, can you sign this "To Claire" please, if you've got a second, that is, thank you very much.'

'Sure, no problem,' said Andy, taking the pen from my shaking outstretched hand. Everything after that was a bit of a blur, but somewhere along the line I registered him smiling at me, saying thank you, and handing the pen back before driving off, smiling at me again as he went.

I stood there for a second, wondering if I had imagined it all, before looking down and seeing Andy's signature in smudgy black biro in my autograph book.

The page wasn't even dry yet. But the impression, if not the ink, was indelible.

The wrought-iron garden gate clanged shut behind me, announcing my return home. Not that there was anyone waiting for me. Mum was at work, doing the catering for some sixtieth birthday party where she would no doubt be trying to force feed her Tuscan pâté vol-au-vents to a generation who, if my nan was anything to go by, remained sceptical about anything that wasn't a sausage roll.

I let myself in and wandered into the newly fitted MFI kitchen, all gleaming stainless steel and spotless white Formica surfaces (Mum seemed to have this weird idea that a film crew wanting a location for a Jif advert could drop by at any moment). I glanced at the note that had been stuck to the fridge with a 'Country Cousin' mouse magnet: 'Cheese and tomato sandwich in here for you. Eat it quick or the mouse will have it! Back about six. Eek, eek!'

Mum's attempts at humour were so embarrassing. I used to tell her it was why I never brought any friends apart from Frankie back to the house (actually, it was because I didn't have any friends apart from Frankie, but I wasn't going to tell her that).

I poured myself a glass of Kia-ora and took the clingfilm-wrapped sandwich cut into neat triangles out of the fridge. She'd even taken the crusts off for me, as if I was three years old and hadn't learnt to chew properly.

Laura Ashley offered her usual greeting as I went into the living room, sniggering at me from each of the purple and blue flowers on the wallpaper, taunting me from behind the chintz curtains, and mocking me from the dark recesses of the sofa. Laura had been there the day I'd come home early from school because the heating had broken down. The day Dad had left home. She had provided the stage and the backdrop. She'd seen everything, and she'd never let me forget it. Mum had been talking recently about getting a new sofa. Something with a darker pattern, that didn't show the marks so easily. I thought it was a bit late for that.

I sat down at the square glass table (Mum liked to call that end the dining room, but it wasn't really, it was just a table), pointedly turning my back on Laura, staring instead at Torvill and Dean, poised on their knees, arms outstretched, ready to begin their Bolero routine. Mum never played the record. She said the music was too dreary. She'd only bought it to put on display at the front of the hi-fi cabinet. Because their costumes matched the colour scheme in the room.

I was halfway through my sandwich when the phone rang. I still had my mouth full when I answered it.

'Hi, Claire. It's Dad.' He only ever seemed to call when Mum was working. I wondered if he had secret access to her bookings diary or something.

'Oh, hi. What do you want?'

'I just thought I'd call for a chat, if that's all right.' It was weird, because he never usually called for a chat. He always said he was too busy at work.

'Oh, right.' I decided to play it cool, not letting him know how pleased I was he'd phoned. Like women did in movies when they really liked some bloke but didn't want to show it in case he didn't feel the same way.

'What have you been up to?' Dad asked.

'I went to United's training ground today.'

'Excellent. Looked fit and raring to go, did they? Up for the new season and all that?'

'Yep.'

'What do you reckon then? Is this the year we're going to win the league?'

''Course it is. We've got the best players in the world.'

'That's what I like to hear. Healthy optimism, eh?'

No one said anything for a bit. It was always hard to think of something to say once we'd finished with United.

'How's the old revision going? Big year you've got coming up.'

'I haven't started it yet. My mocks aren't till Christmas.'

'I know. Nothing like getting ahead though, is there?'

I didn't say anything. Dad did this really weird laugh.

'Oh well, I'd better go, I suppose. People to see, places to go. It's, er, best to call me at work if you want to get in touch. I don't get home until late these days.'

The last time I'd rung him at home a woman had answered. Dad had said it was the cleaner. Like I was really going to believe that. I hadn't wanted to know her name anyway. It was enough to know she was there.

'OK.'

'I'll see you soon then. I'll have to get you tickets for a United game one of these days, won't I?' The first time he'd said that I hadn't slept for weeks. I'd given up believing he meant it now.

'Yeah, great. Bye then.'

'Bye for now. Up the blues, eh.' He did that weird laugh again and put the phone down.

I didn't think I'd ever get used to Dad not living with us. At first he'd made the effort to see me every other Saturday. It hadn't lasted long, though. When I went veggie he said there was no point him taking me to the Wimpy any more if I wasn't going to have a burger. I didn't see why that mattered. I'd have been perfectly happy with a Knickerbocker Glory.

I went upstairs. Laura Ashley was banned from my bedroom. The walls were painted in United blue, with matching United curtains, lampshade, duvet and pillowcase. Mum said it looked like a boy's room. Like that would really bother me.

I smiled up at the team poster which took pride of place above my bed. The walls were covered with pictures of the United players, cut out of *Shoot!* and *Match*. On the back of my door I had pictures of Spandau Ballet and George Michael, carefully torn out of *Smash Hits* and *Jackie* and stuck up with Blu-Tack. Although I fancied Martin Kemp (the cool one with the longish hair and the earring) I knew I didn't have a hope in hell with him. He was going out with one of the backing singers in Wham! Either Pepsi or Shirley, I could never remember which was which. I fancied George Michael as well (I used to imagine I was the rope he was holding on to in the 'Careless Whisper' video). I didn't think he had a girlfriend, so maybe I was in with a chance there.

Frankie was a Duranie, like most of the girls at school. I'd tried my best to like them. I learnt all the lyrics to 'Is There Something I Should Know?' I even wrote the line about nuclear war on my pencil case. But I lost interest when I found out Simon Le Bon hadn't meant it to be political; he'd just needed something to rhyme with 'door'.

I kicked off my trainers and flopped on to my bed, taking my autograph book out and turning immediately to Andy's page. I liked the way he'd signed his name. It wasn't one of those flashy, swirly signatures like Matt's that you couldn't read properly. It was very simple, a clear 'Andy' with a big loop on the 'y' and a little squiggle after the 's' at the end of Pailes. I traced the soft lines of his signature with my finger, holding the book up close to my face and sniffing the page as I detected the slight smell of aftershave, again very subtle, nothing flashy.

It was a nice name, Andy Pailes. Better than Claire Skidmore anyway. The other kids at school were always

Linda Green

taking the piss out of my surname. If I was lucky they called me 'Skidders', but more often it was 'Skidmark'.

I hoped Andy had a better nickname. All the players had nicknames, though sometimes it was quite difficult to find out what they were. According to the last fact file in *Match*, Mickey Squire didn't have one. But we knew he did and it was 'Nobber'. I guessed saying you didn't have one was like a code for it being too rude to print.

Rummaging in my bedside cabinet, I pulled out the United programme from the Nottm Forest game back in April. I hadn't been, of course. Mum said only hooligans and skinheads went to football matches. I'd considered having my head shaved and vandalising a phone box to try to further my cause but I'd decided against it in the end. She'd only have come up with another reason why I couldn't go. And now the Heysel thing had happened and the fire at Bradford, she had added getting trampled to death or burnt alive to the list of potential dangers. I couldn't see how she was ever going to let me go now.

I'd bought the programme from the end-of-season sale at the United shop, purely for the picture of Andy on the 'New Faces' page. I'd had to look through at least half a dozen programmes before finding it, scanning each page while a queue had built up behind me. I looked again at those dark brown eyes and the shy half-smile. 'Andy,' I said out loud. 'Andy, Andy, Andy, Andy, Andy.' I was quite sure now. Quite sure I'd got the right one.

'Did you have a nice time today then?' said Mum.

We were eating tea (one of her nouvelle cuisine pasta

38

creations, with the meat left out of my portion) when she said it. It wasn't that she was genuinely interested in my day, just that she had this thing about silence at mealtimes.

'Yeah. We got loads of autographs and one of the new players actually spoke to me.'

'That's nice, love. I was wondering if you fancied going swimming this week? Only I bumped into Kim's mum in town. She said Kim and Debbie are going to the lido on Wednesday afternoon. Perhaps you could go with them.'

Mum went to the same Tupperware parties as Kim and Debbie's mums and always made a point of saying what nice 'normal' girls they were. I had a sneaking regard for Kim's ability to do handsprings over the box in gym club and I admired Debbie's knack of keeping her over-the-knee socks up without the need for elastic bands, but I didn't think that was any basis for a lasting and meaningful friendship. The fact that they'd never even heard of Matt Goodyear was clearly going to be a problem. Besides which, I had no doubt that I would be an unwelcome addition to their previously cosy twosome.

'No thanks, I'm going down the training ground on Wednesday.'

'What, again? You've already been today. What do you want to go again for?'

'Because I like going there, OK?'

'I know you do, love, but it doesn't mean you have to go every day, does it?'

'You go jogging twice a week. I don't complain about that.'

'I do that to keep fit.'

'Well, it's a mile walk each way to the training ground. That keeps me fit. You'd moan if I sat about at home all day.'

'That's not the point.'

'What is the point then?' Sometimes I wished Mum would come straight out with it, instead of pretending like this.

'The point is you can't spend your entire summer holiday hanging around a bunch of footballers.'

'Why not?'

Mum sighed and tucked a stray strand of her highlighted shoulder-length hair back behind her ear. 'It's not normal.'

'Oh, so I'm a freak now, am I?'

'Why do you always have to twist everything I say, Claire?'

''Cos that's what lawyers have to do.'

'I'm not a criminal, Claire. I'm your mother.'

'Worse luck.'

Mum shook her head and did that thing with her lips which she did when I'd said something to annoy her.

'It's your father's fault, of course. He should never have got you interested in that football team.'

'You just don't like it that we share an interest,' I said.

Mum snorted. 'He doesn't share anything with you. He'd rather go in the firm's executive box with a bunch of blokes in suits than take you to a game.'

'They don't let under-sixteens in the boxes,' I said. 'Anyway, Dad has to entertain clients so he can improve his promotion prospects.' Mum snorted again, no doubt thinking about the career prospects she'd had until I came along. She'd told me I wasn't 'planned'. Which was a nice way of saying I was a mistake. The sort of mistake that had to be covered up under a loose-fitting wedding dress. Apparently, being a single mum hadn't been an option for her, not even at the end of the swinging sixties. She said the permissive society never got as far as Potters Bar. I guessed it must have stopped at Barnet – a bit like the travel zones on a Capital card.

We ate in silence for a while. I hadn't planned on telling her about Dad calling. But I was so mad about her having a go at him that it kind of came out.

'Dad rang today, actually.'

'You didn't tell me.'

'Yeah, well I'm telling you now, aren't I?'

'What did he want?'

'Said he was gonna try and get me some United tickets soon.'

'Well, don't get your hopes up. You know what happened last time. He's hardly got a good track record of keeping promises, has he?'

I pushed my half-eaten dinner away and got up from the table.

'Aren't you going to finish that?'

'No,' I said, heading for the door. 'Not if it means listening to you.'

I went straight up to my room, took the match programme with Andy's picture in it from under my pillow and kissed him on the lips.

Andy kisses me back. His lips are soft and velvety – just like I knew they would be.

'I came because you needed me,' he says, his brown eyes searing through me. It is like he knows me, knows everything about me, has known me all my life. I nod. My heart is about to spill over, the love bubbling out from inside me.

'I haven't got anyone, you see,' I explain. 'I'm not interested in anyone else. I only want you.' He nods. I want him to know that this isn't some silly crush. That just because I'm only fifteen it doesn't mean it's not serious.

'I'll never stop loving you,' I say. 'Not ever. This is for keeps.' He nods again. I pull him to my chest and lie there holding him until I go to sleep. Smiling in the knowledge that he is mine now. And I will never let him go.

Two

'Get me out of this fucking hole,' Daz screamed at me from behind the glass partition of the interview room at Rochdale Magistrates' Court.

Most people hate going to work on Monday mornings. But for most people the worst that can happen is that the train is late and uncomfortably overcrowded, they forget their umbrella and get wet in the dash to the office only to find the coffee machine is out of order. Whereas I, on the other hand, stoically put up with all of those things then arrived at work, descended into the bowels of the building to be greeted by a burly Group 4 Security officer, who buzzed me through two locked doors and into a small, stuffy interview room where the person on the other side of the partition was hollering at me in a barely intelligible rant while sweating profusely due to going cold turkey from spending two nights in a police cell.

I could have done without it, bearing in mind the turmoil going on in my own head. But I knew that would have to wait. My clients' crises were more important than my own.

'All right, Daz,' I said, speaking slowly and firmly. 'I'll do my best. But you need to tell me how you got in here in the first place.' Daz and I were well acquainted, of course. He was one of our regulars; a well-known heroin addict and persistent offender with a penchant for removing expensive jewellery from people's houses without asking.

Daz scraped himself off the glass partition and sat shaking in the chair as he struggled to string a few sentences together.

'Needed a fix, like. Fucking window was open. A bit of sunshine and they all lose their heads. Shocking it is, like. Should be bloody arrested for inciting a crime.'

'What happened, Daz?'

'Climbed in over the sink, didn't break any dishes or anything, mind. Slipped upstairs, stuff was out on the dressing table on view, helped myself, like. Straight into me bag, that'll do nicely, thank you very much. Didn't make no mess. Even fed the cat on the way out 'cos he was making a fuss, starving hungry he was. Oh, and I shut the window behind me so no one else could get in, like.'

Daz shook his head as if the owners of the house he had burgled should be ashamed of themselves for neglecting their cat and grateful to him for preventing any further crimes on their property, although admittedly there wouldn't have been much left to take, judging by the impressive haul of jewellery, including a particularly expensive Rolex, which the police had relieved him of barely an hour later when they'd spotted him trying to flog it on a street corner.

'The thing is, Daz, when you're out on bail, you need to keep yourself clean. The magistrates don't like it, you know that.'

'You can get me out though, can't you? You've gotta get me fucking out. I need to see Mickey, get a fix, like.'

I sighed. Although I'd long ago given up hope of Daz ever being anything other than a hardcore user, it still saddened me to hear him talk like that. The social worker within, who knew all about his chaotic childhood with his mentally ill mother, still wanted to save him from himself. But he never did anything bad enough to warrant more than a few months inside, and that was never enough to stop him falling straight back into his old ways when he came out. Mickey was usually waiting on the street corner for him when he was released, offering a free welcome-home present, knowing full well Daz would be back for more before the night was out. I ought to tell Daz to move up a league with his crimes, hold up a bank or something; that way he might earn a long enough stretch to get some proper help. As it was, he didn't stand a chance.

'I'll do my best, but no promises on this one. We'll go for an adjournment and I'll apply for bail, but it'll depend who's on the bench, OK?'

Daz nodded mournfully. He knew the score. If it was Martin 'Mother 'em' Maddox, a former head teacher in a tough comprehensive, we were in with a chance. He was the only magistrate who seemed to have any idea what it was really like on the streets out there. But if it was any of the others, in particular Joan 'Hang 'em' Silverman, we were stuffed. She was on a one-woman crusade to rid the streets of the dirty homeless, the feckless unemployed and anyone who didn't keep a clean handkerchief in their pocket or handbag.

Daz was escorted from the room, still cursing and shaking, to be replaced by another of the usual suspects. I looked up at the ceiling, trying to hide my disillusionment. It really wasn't supposed to be like this.

Daz was in luck. Maddox was sitting in the remand court. Which meant he somehow got away with bail, albeit with a pile of conditions attached which effectively kept him under curfew in his flat. Not that he would take any notice of them, mind. He grinned at me as he left court, still shaking but in remarkably better spirits.

'Thanks very much, like,' he said. 'See ya soon.'

'Not too soon I hope,' I said. He smiled again as he got out his mobile phone and switched it on. I knew who the first person on his speed dial would be.

'Mickey,' I heard him say as he went down the stairs. 'Where are you, like?'

There was just time to grab a quick coffee before my first trial of the day, which had been put back half an hour while some missing documents were brought over from the Crown Prosecution Service's building. It was par for the course, really. I'd have been worried if I turned up one day and everything ran smoothly.

I went through to the staff side of the café, where Jill poured me my usual Monday-morning black with no sugar and passed it through the hatch.

'Given up mixing with the proletariat, have we?' Nigel Foster, one of the CPS prosecutors, asked, looking up from his copy of the *Daily Telegraph* at the table in the corner. It was the sort of jibe I'd come to expect from him, as he seemed to think I preferred the company of my clients to fellow solicitors (which it had to be said in his case was probably true). Nigel was firmly in the establishment camp and of the opinion that defence solicitors were only one very small step up in the world order from the defendants themselves.

'No, that's why I thought I'd come and talk to you.'

'I do admire the fact that you retain a sense of humour despite the dreadful people you have to fraternise with,' chortled Nigel. He was forever extolling the virtues of life with the CPS but I would no more cross to 'the other side' than ask Hang 'em Silverman round for tea.

'Do I deduce that I have the pleasure of your company in court today?' I enquired.

'You do indeed. And I have to say I'm looking forward to hearing what sort of cock-and-bull story you concoct for this one. Should be most entertaining.'

Sometimes I would happily humour Nigel; on other occasions I seriously contemplated asking one of my less salubrious 'acquaintances' to wipe the smug smirk off his face. The trouble with Nigel – and all bar one of the magistrates for that matter – was that he existed in a world where he was simply unable or unwilling to contemplate the possibility that the police might occasionally lie, fabricate evidence, fit someone up or simply get it wrong. Which inevitably led him to the conclusion that all of my clients were guilty, and that therefore I spent my entire time cooking up elaborate stories in an effort to get them off the hook. I had won enough cases against him over the years to cast doubt on his theory, of course. Although it had to be

said that the case which was about to start was unlikely to
be one of them. I didn't usually go into court assuming the
worst, but on this occasion it was hard to do otherwise. I
was representing a young man called Dean Chandler, who
was known to the police, and had been arrested while
queuing inside a building society. He had been loitering
outside for some time with a carrier bag containing a child's
water pistol and a note in his pocket which read, 'Give me
the money, please.' Undeniably, this did not look good.
And on top of that, Hang 'em Silverman was hearing the
case. My only hope was to argue that the charge of
attempted robbery could not be proved because he hadn't
actually threatened anyone or demanded money. And to
hope that Silverman, who was a stickler for good manners,
was impressed by the fact that he had at least said please on
the note.

'Don't worry,' I said to Nigel, slurping down my coffee,
before standing up to leave the café. 'I'll give you a run for
your money.'

I strode into the courtroom, which was decorated in
various shades of beige and mottled brown, as if the
thought of any other colour would have been positively
frivolous.

Fiona looked up from her clerk's desk, her short, choppy
auburn hair as mad as ever and seemingly at odds with her
sombre trouser suit.

'Have a good weekend?' she enquired, her lilting Glas-
wegian accent as pleasing to my ears as ever as I sat down
in front of her.

'Eventful,' I said.

'Good events or bad?' There was a rustling from the door behind her.

'I'll fill you in at lunch,' I whispered as the door opened.

'Court rise,' said Fiona. We stood to attention and Silverman, all neat coiffure with twinset and pearls, walked in with her two cronies. She nodded her approval and lowered herself slowly and deliberately on to her chair (she'd never been the same since the castors had gone from under her on one occasion and she'd ended up on the floor. Unfortunately I hadn't been in court that morning, but Fiona's account and slow-motion action replay when the court had been empty later that day had been enough to keep a smile on my face for weeks). We sat down, Fiona introduced the case and Nigel stood up next to me.

'Your worships, what we have here is a clear case of someone being caught red-handed. Dean Chandler went to the Bradford and Bingley Building Society in Middleton to carry out a robbery. It was only the alertness of a female cashier, who had spotted him loitering outside for some time and called the police, which prevented what could have been a very traumatic incident for staff and customers.'

As Nigel droned on, trying to make out that Dean was somehow on a par with the Great Train Robbers, my mind wandered back to the Twenty Years From Now list. It had kept me awake half the night, trying to work out at what point exactly my dreams had all gone up in smoke. Some of the answers were obvious – the Andy one, for instance. But others were harder to pin down. The career dream had looked to be on course for a long time. Top marks at law school, a training contract with a large firm in Manchester and a job offer after I'd qualified, with the prospect of a partnership dangling tantalisingly ahead in the future. Until I'd been made redundant nine years ago as part of a 'restructuring programme'. I'd been out of work for six months, and when a temporary job had come up as maternity cover for a solicitor at Barnes and Co. in Rochdale, I thought I'd better take it. It was only supposed to be for nine months, but the woman I was covering for didn't return to work after having her baby so I was taken on full-time. And for some unknown reason, I'd never managed to escape.

Fiona's overstated cough and kick under the desk alerted me to the fact that the prosecution's first witness, PC Hough, was in the witness box and Nigel had come to the end of his tedious questioning. I shuffled my notes and scrambled to my feet.

'Officer Hough, when you entered the building society, can you describe what the defendant was doing?'

'He was standing in the queue.'

'Was he behaving aggressively in any way?'

'No.'

'And was he brandishing the child's water pistol which has been presented as Exhibit A?' I asked, gesturing at the orange and red toy on Nigel's desk.

'No, it was in his carrier bag.'

'And was he holding it with the carrier bag wrapped around it tightly to make it look like it was a weapon?'

'No. It was concealed in the bottom of the bag, but he hadn't reached the front of the queue when I arrived.'

'And did the defendant behave violently towards you or anyone in the building society before, during or after his arrest?'

'No.'

'Thank you, Officer Hough.'

I went through the same questions with the cashier who'd phoned the police. By the time Nigel was winding up his case I was beginning to feel I might actually pull this one out of the hat. It was all going to come down to Dean's performance. But as he rustled his way into the witness box, read the oath jauntily and chirped 'All right, miss' as I stood up, I sensed that this was going to be hard work.

'Mr Chandler, can you explain why you had a note saying "Give me the money, please" in your pocket on the day in question?'

'It was just for a dare, like. Me mate Spanner thought it would be a laugh, you know.' I glanced up at Silverman, who was clearly not seeing the funny side of this.

'And why were you carrying the water pistol?' I asked anxiously.

'Just for a laugh, like. There weren't even no water in it.'

'So, just to be clear. You had been dared to rob a building society. You wrote a note which you put in your pocket and you placed a water pistol in your carrier bag. You were observed waiting outside the building society for almost an hour before you finally went in.'

'That's right, miss.'

'But the truth is you lost your nerve, didn't you?'

'Nah, I didn't. I was well up for it.' I frowned at Dean.

He'd pushed the sleeves of his shell suit up and looked like he was about to start a fight. I realised that he had forgotten I was on his side and had taken exception to me portraying him as a coward.

'Mr Chandler, I'm simply trying to make it clear to everyone in this room that you had no intention of carrying out or even attempting any kind of robbery, did you?'

'Are you calling me a bottler?' Dean snarled at me. I groaned inwardly. Nigel would never let me hear the end of this.

'I thought the wee lad was going to run over and lamp you one,' chuckled Fiona as we sat in the café at lunchtime.

'Maybe I should start wearing a big badge in court which says "Just agree with me, I'm on your side".'

'I dare say a lad like that isn't used to anyone in authority fighting his corner. Shame though, I thought you had Nigel on the ropes until that point.' I shrugged. I'd thought that too. But Dean had managed to inadvertently shoot himself in the foot. I still thought Silverman had been harsh, though. Sending him down for two months when he'd never actually touched or threatened anyone. But it could have been worse. As she'd said herself, the sentence would have been much longer if it wasn't for the fact that he'd waited politely in the queue.

'Anyway, fill me in about your weekend,' said Fiona.

I finished my mouthful of jacket potato and took a glug of tea (I always switched to Earl Grey in the afternoon) before answering.

'Mark wants us to move in together,' I said.

'Well that's great. Congratulations,' she replied, before looking at my face and stopping. 'You don't want to, do you?'

'It's not that I don't want to. It was all a bit sudden, that's all. He wants us to buy a new place together and he took me to view a house and I felt like I had to make a decision on the spot. It was a bit like being on *Deal or No Deal*.'

'Don't tell me Mark's gone all Noel Edmonds on you and started tucking his shirt into his jeans.'

'No, I mean I led him to believe I was going to accept his offer.'

'And you're not?'

'I don't know. Part of me's wondering if I should have turned him down there and then and waited to see what was in my red box.'

Fiona raised one of her eyebrows while stirring her coffee.

'What's brought this on? I thought you two were sorted. You always seem so happy together.'

I put down my knife and fork with a big sigh.

'Did you ever have dreams, Fiona?'

'You haven't been reading one of those books that claims to interpret them, have you? Only I read one once which said that dreaming about eating chocolate finger biscuits was a sign of me wanting to escape my sexual repression. When actually it was because I went to bed bloody hungry because Neil had finished the packet himself.'

I laughed and shook my head.

'No, I mean dreams, ambitions for the future. I found this list, you see. Something I wrote when I was fifteen about what I thought my life would be like in twenty years' time.'

'And surprise, surprise, you're not the Lord Chancellor, you don't live in a palace and you're not married to a prince.'

'They weren't that daft. Well, not quite. But they weren't about working here and living in a new-build in Littleborough, either,' I said.

'What's wrong with Littleborough?' asked Fiona, who lived a few miles down the road in Wardle.

'You know what I mean. It's the whole idea of me signing up to this package deal for life. It's like an admission of failure. That I'm giving up on everything I once dreamt about.'

Fiona thought for a moment as she chewed the last of her cheese and pickle roll.

'Neil wanted to be a Formula One racing driver when he was a kid,' she said. 'He did go-karting and all that stuff, won some junior competition for the north-west. He'd been promised his first rally car and then his parents split up and everything went out of the window. Which is why he had to make do with being a copper and occasionally doing eighty around the ring road with his blue light flashing.'

'But he must wonder what could have been, if things had been different.'

'Sometimes when he's watching Formula One on TV I catch him cornering in the armchair. He's pretty good at popping champagne bottles and maybe he still fantasises about living in Monaco with some stick-thin model. But that's all it is. A fantasy. He grew up, got a proper job and me and Aidan and he's happy with his lot. A damn sight happier than that miserable bunch of F1 drivers look, at any rate.'

I smiled and nodded. Fiona was doing her usual Wise Woman of the North bit. Maybe she was right. Maybe I was being stupid, hankering after my teenage dreams instead of being grateful for what I had.

'You wouldn't gamble on what's in the red box then?' I said.

'The trouble with gambling,' said Fiona as she stood up and took her empty plate over to the hatch, 'is that sometimes you end up losing everything.'

Wednesday, 31 July 1985

The knowledge that any attempt to find something even remotely fashionable in my wardrobe was ultimately doomed never actually stopped me trying. I guess I secretly hoped that by rummaging through the assortment of undesirable items Mum had bought from Kays catalogue and the home and wear section at Tesco, I could somehow trigger a miracle of C.S. Lewis proportions in my wardrobe. Only I was hoping to discover a magical world of Madonna's cast-offs rather than the kingdom of Narnia.

I may not have been a fashion guru like Frankie, but I was acutely aware that the Delamare label didn't exactly rank up there with Nike or Lacoste. And now I had Andy to impress, creating the right image had taken on a whole new significance.

Eventually I plumped for jeans and my tea-bag tank-top again, on the grounds that they were the least naff things I possessed. Though I was conscious that even my jeans weren't the right sort. They were straight leg but they weren't stretch so they were at least two inches too wide at the bottom. They didn't exactly flap in the breeze but I could get in and out of them without too much effort, which meant they failed the test. Frankie would break into a sweat trying to get into hers, but once she had, they looked like a second skin. Mum said jeans that tight weren't healthy. As if I cared about that.

I skipped breakfast, too nervous about the prospect of seeing Andy again to even contemplate eating, and set off for Frankie's. I strolled down the street, past the rows of neat semis with their pristine net curtains and immaculate front gardens with not a begonia out of place (I suspected the flower beds had been precision designed with the aid of a giant gardening version of my school geometry set). Even the cats, sunning themselves on front steps, seemed unnaturally clean, as if they had been put through the 'delicates' cycle and left outside to dry.

I stopped off at Aspland's on the corner for my regular Wednesday-morning review of the latest *Shoot!*. I found it in the usual place under one of the 'This is NOT a public library' signs written in thick red marker pen on grubby pieces of cardboard and stuck to the racks with Sellotape. I waited until Mr Aspland was busy serving someone then began flicking through the pages, past the team poster of Arsenal and the picture spread on Bryan Robson at home with his wife and daughters, until I got to the fact file. The one on Andy Pailes.

I drew a sharp intake of breath and shut the magazine, not wanting to read intimate details about Andy in such a public place, virtually threw the money at a startled Mr Aspland and ran the rest of the way to Frankie's.

'Hello, is she ready yet?' I asked breathlessly when Mrs Alberti opened the door, letting the smell of greasy bacon and burnt toast rush out to greet me.

'Hello, love. She shouldn't be long. Come in a sec while I give her a shout.'

I squeezed past Mrs Alberti's dumpy frame into the narrow hallway beyond. It was like walking into a tiny second-hand junk shop. Bone-china figures of the Virgin Mary jostled for position with a collection of glass peacocks displaying their plumage on the crowded windowsill. The walls were lined with decorative china plates and tacky-looking mementoes of Italy. Laura Ashley would have run screaming from the house. I kind of liked it.

'Francesca, Claire's here for you,' Mrs Alberti shouted from the bottom of the stairs, struggling to make herself heard above the sound of Radio One coming from Frankie's room.

'I think you'll have to go up, love,' she said eventually. 'Tell her to turn that racket down, will you?'

'Hey, what's up with you?' Frankie was putting the finishing touches to her make-up as I burst into her room.

'Andy P-Pailes, f-fact file, *Shoot!*,' I stuttered, incapable of forming sentences.

'So, has he got a girlfriend then?' enquired Frankie, calmly dabbing her freshly applied red lipstick with a tissue before practising her pout in the dressing-table mirror.

'I dunno, I haven't read it yet, have I?'

'Here, give it to me. Let's see what this guy's made of.'

Frankie snatched the magazine from me, turned down the radio and sprawled out on her belly on the bed, crossing her ankles in the air behind her and propping herself up on her elbows as I waited for her to begin reading.

FULL NAME: *Andrew Pailes*
BIRTHPLACE/DATE: *Pontefract, Yorkshire,*
31.8.62

'Hey, that means he's twenty-three next month,' said Frankie. 'You'd better get him a card or something.'

HEIGHT/WEIGHT: *5ft 9ins, 11st*
MARITAL STATUS: *Single*

'See, told you,' Frankie said. I tried hard not to grin too much as a surge of relief ran through me. Quickly followed by the realisation that it only meant he wasn't married or engaged, not that he didn't have a girlfriend.

LIVE: *Cuffley, Herts*
NICKNAME: *Haven't got one yet*

'Likely story,' scoffed Frankie. 'It's probably Andy Pandy or something.'

MOST MEMORABLE MATCH: *The UEFA Cup Final victory last season*
MISCELLANEOUS LIKES: *Going for long walks in the country, polite people, Russian history, politics, Yorkshire*

'God, I'm nearly falling asleep,' said Frankie. 'Where does he mention nightclubs?'
'There,' I said, peering over Frankie's shoulder as I pointed to Andy's answer to the next question.

MISCELLANEOUS DISLIKES: *Racism, hooligan-ism, Margaret Thatcher, nightclubs*
FAVOURITE NEWSPAPER: *The* Guardian
FAVOURITE TV SHOW: Newsnight, Spitting Image, Blackadder
TV SHOW YOU ALWAYS SWITCH OFF: Terry and June
FAVOURITE PRE-MATCH MEAL: *Chicken and beans*

'He's a bit old to be eating from the children's menu, isn't he?' said Frankie. 'I'm sorry, Claire, the guy's got no sophistication whatsoever.'

'Just 'cos he didn't put lasagne or something fancy like Matt did. Anyway, I don't know what you're going on about, there's nothing wrong with chicken and beans.'

'Said the vegetarian,' said Frankie, throwing her head back as she laughed out loud. I hated it when she caught me out like that.

'When you've quite finished. I'd like to hear the rest of it, thank you,' I said. Frankie made a face at me before continuing.

FAVOURITE MUSIC: *The Smiths, Echo and the Bunnymen, The Cure*

I nodded approvingly. I supported Morrissey's 'Meat is Murder' stand, liked the song about the dancing horses and might have been a Goth if I'd only had the nerve to dye my hair black.

FAVOURITE FILM: *Reds*
BEST FRIEND IN FOOTBALL: *Mike Thompson at United*
WHICH PERSON IN THE WORLD WOULD YOU MOST LIKE TO MEET? *Nelson Mandela*
WHAT WILL YOU BE DOING IN 20 YEARS' TIME? *Working as a lawyer, living with my family somewhere rural, probably in Yorkshire*

The corners of my mouth curled up into a *Mona Lisa*-type smile as Frankie put the magazine down. I couldn't believe he wanted to be a lawyer too. Usually footballers either put 'running a pub' or 'being a manager' after they retired from playing. I knew for certain now. We were made for each other.

'He's absolutely perfect,' I said, sitting down on the edge of the bed to steady myself.

'If you want to lead the most boring life imaginable,' snorted Frankie.

'Come on then, what are you going to be doing in twenty years' time which is so great?'

'Lying on a Mediterranean beach, rubbing suntan lotion on to Matt's legs.'

'What, the whole time? Life's not one big holiday, you know.'

'God, you sound like my mother.'

'I'm talking about what you'll really be doing, about your whole life.'

'OK,' said Frankie, going over to a cupboard in the corner of her room and pulling out some paper and a couple of pens. 'Let's do our own Twenty Years From Now list. Five categories each and we'll both write down our answers.' She handed me a pen. I took it from her, knowing how futile it was to argue with her and liking the idea of doing it anyway. Of seeing my life planned out before me like that.

'Right,' said Frankie as she sat back down on the bed. 'My categories are love life, where you go on holiday, career, what you look like and if you're rich or poor.'

'You can't say love life, you have to put marital status like in the magazine.'

'They're my questions, just write down your answers.'

I tutted and started writing, looking up occasionally to try to glance over Frankie's shoulder.

'Come on then, your turn,' she said a few minutes later.

'OK, where you'll be living, whether you've got kids, who your best friend is, what your interests are and whether you'll be happy.'

'We're hardly gonna put we'll be miserable, are we?'

'I dunno. Morrissey seems to like it.'

Frankie shrugged and started writing. I started thinking, keen not to rush it. If I was planning out my life like this I wanted to get it right. Frankie waited in silence for a few minutes after she'd finished before she started to hassle me.

'Hurry up, we'll never get to the training ground at this rate.' I ignored her until I was certain I had it right.

'There,' I said. 'Finished.'

'Come on then,' said Frankie. 'Let's hear it.'

'You never said we were going to have to read it out.'

'What else are we going to do with it?'

'I think we should put them in a sealed envelope only to be opened in twenty years' time.'

'Why?'

The real reason was so that she didn't take the piss out of me until she knew whether it had come true or not, but I didn't want to admit that.

'Because it's what you do with stuff about the future,' I said.

Frankie rolled her eyes. 'I know what you've put any-way: married to Andy Pailes, working as a lawyer, living in Yorkshire, blah, blah, blah.' I was perturbed to think I was that predictable. But there again I had a good idea what Frankie had put too: something which involved living with Matt, being a travel rep and having loads of dosh.

'No point reading them out then,' I said. 'Have you got an envelope?'

Frankie sighed, rummaged in a drawer and pulled out an unused writing set, the sort of thing great-aunts give you for Christmas without realising that fifteen-year-old girls don't send letters to anyone – apart from thank-you notes to great-aunts for writing sets. She handed me an envelope; I tucked the folded piece of paper inside and carefully sealed it.

'I still think you've been watching too many time cap-sules being buried on *Blue Peter*,' said Frankie.

'We'd better write on the front,' I said, choosing to ignore her. 'So we don't forget what it is.' I started writing in big bold letters: NOT TO BE OPENED UNTIL 31 JULY 2005.

'Fucking hell,' said Frankie, 'that's next millennium; we'll be ancient by then.'

'You will,' I said. 'I'll always be eighteen months younger, remember.'

Frankie pulled a face and stuffed her envelope into her knicker drawer. I put mine in my bag, safe in the knowledge I had everything mapped out now.

On the way to the training ground, I stopped off at the newsagent's to buy a copy of the *Guardian*, which I arranged in my bag so it could be clearly seen.

'Aren't you gonna buy some baked beans for him too?' sniggered Frankie.

'Piss off,' I said. 'Or I'll cross you off my list as being my best friend.'

It was quiet when we arrived. The players were all getting ready in the clubhouse and there weren't as many fans as there had been on Monday. We made our way down to our vantage point on the grass banking. I'd been so excited at Andy's answers to the fact file, I hadn't stopped to think how it would go down with his teammates, most of whom read nothing more challenging than the *Sun* and the *Racing Post*. But as we watched the squad come out for the morning training session, it soon became clear that it wasn't only Frankie who thought Andy was weird.

'Are you coming with us, Trotsky, or do you fancy a nice long walk in the country?' Clubber shouted as Andy ran out. The other players started laughing. Frankie joined in too, though I don't think she understood why she was laughing. She dropped history before she did anything much about Russia.

Personally, I thought the jibe was a bit rich coming from someone who had listed *Porky's* as his favourite film in a recent fact file. Andy obviously thought so too.

'I'm surprised you've even heard of Trotsky. Did they name a racehorse after him or something?'

'Tell you one thing I wouldn't bet on,' Clubber shouted back, 'and that's your mate Mandela getting out of jail. He's got about as much chance of that as you have of getting my place in the first team.'

'He'd better start packing then,' said Andy.

I glowed with pride. Andy could give as good as he got. He didn't seem to care that he was different from all the others. I wished I could be like that.

We sprawled out in the sunshine on the grass banking, in the exact spot which Frankie had calculated gave her the best chance of seeing up Matt's shorts. Most of the players had taken their shirts off and were displaying the suntans they had acquired on various foreign holidays that summer. Frankie started trying to guess where each of them had been, as if she knew which beaches would produce a certain shade of tan (I knew for a fact this wasn't the case, as the only beach she had ever been to was Clacton).

The first strains of George Michael's 'Careless Whisper' drifted across from the top of the bank, where a girl a bit older than us was sitting with her Walkman turned up loud enough for everyone to hear. Before I knew it, I was mouthing along to the words as I gazed down at Andy's glistening chest. When the saxophone kicked in, I felt myself begin to tingle in some weird places and let out a long, deep sigh.

'What do you think heaven's like?' I asked dreamily.

'Like this, I guess,' Frankie said. 'I reckon God's the referee in one huge, never-ending football match featuring United. And the only rule is that the players have to take their shirts off.'

'I don't think the Pope would approve of that.'

'What d'ya mean? The Pope would be in goal for the other side. He used to be a goalkeeper, you know,' she said.

'No he didn't, you're having me on.'

'He did. I swear on his life. He used to play for some Polish side, I read it somewhere.'

'What, so girls like us in Poland used to fancy the Pope?'

'Yeah, I guess so. It's no more stupid than girls in Liverpool fancying Sammy Lee.'

'No, I s'pose not. I wonder what his nickname was.'

'Probably Nobber,' said Frankie. 'Now that would freak my mum out.'

An hour or so later, United manager Ken Benson led the players over the other side of the grass bank, where the pitch they used for youth team games and practice matches was.

'They can't do that,' complained Frankie, as the players disappeared from view and most of the other fans started wandering back towards the car park. 'I haven't come up here to watch grass grow.'

'They're probably practising tactics and things, stuff

they want to keep secret,' I informed her. Frankie didn't know much about that side of the game.

'Secret from who? We're hardly gonna be on a spying mission for Arsenal, are we?'

Frankie sat and fidgeted for five minutes before getting to her feet.

'It's no good, I'm going over the top to see what Matt's up to.'

'Don't be a flid,' I said, eyeing up the steep bank and Frankie's high heels and short skirt. 'You'll never get up there in those shoes.'

'Course I will. Watch me.' Frankie started teetering up the bank. The grass was short and slippery where it had been scorched brown by the sun and she had to climb on all fours, clutching on to the odd clump of longer, straw-like grass as she went. As she scrambled triumphantly to the top of the bank she popped her head up, like an inquisitive meerkat, to look for Matt, only to come face-to-groin with him as he strode up the bank from the other side with the rest of the players.

'Oh, hi,' she said lamely, craning her neck back to smile up at him before losing her footing and sliding back to the bottom of the bank, finishing in a crumpled heap with her skirt hitched up around her waist.

'They can see your knickers,' I hissed, as the players jogged down the banking, barely concealed smirks on their faces.

'It's OK, I don't mind,' whispered Frankie. 'They're my best ones.'

★

'Are you sure Matt didn't look at my arse?' Frankie asked for the fifth time, as we waited for the players to leave the clubhouse later.

'No, I told you, he kept looking straight ahead. What did you expect? He was hardly gonna jump on you after that performance, was he?'

'At least he'll have something to remember me by while we're away next week.' Frankie's family were off to Clacton on holiday, while my mum was taking me to Great Yarmouth.

'If I were you, I'd hope he's got a very short memory,' I said.

Matt certainly had very short shorts on when he emerged from the dressing room. I watched as a cluster of teenage girls, their tongues practically lolling out of their mouths, crowded round him, giving each other dirty sideways looks as they vied for his attention. Frankie turned to me and shook her head.

'Honestly, look at them,' she said. 'Have they no shame?' Seconds later she had rolled her already short skirt up at the waistband and was strutting across the car park towards him, dragging me behind her.

'Hi, Matt. Could I have my picture taken with you, please?' she said, flashing her best smile, which was nearly as dazzling as Matt's own Colgate-sponsored teeth. The crowd of girls parted grudgingly and Matt, who, if he did recognise her from earlier, was good enough not to say anything, turned to stand next to her with a fixed smile on his face. As I looked through the viewfinder I gasped as I saw Frankie's arm creep behind Matt before settling casually on his hip. A gentle breeze brought the overpowering smell of Paco Rabanne aftershave wafting through the air. Frankie's eyes glazed over and she appeared to swoon momentarily before regaining her composure just in time to smile for the shot to be taken.

'I thought you were gonna faint then,' I said afterwards.

'Nah,' replied Frankie. 'I was having one of those no-sex orgasms.'

I wasn't sure whether she was joking or whether this was actually possible. Maybe I'd missed that article in *Just Seventeen*.

With Matt departed, we turned our attention to the rest of the players. No member of the squad was allowed to get past us without signing something. It didn't even have to be a player; anyone who featured in the club handbook was deemed worthy of an autograph request. We got a 'best wishes' from manager Ken Benson and an 'all the best' from his number two Terry Dixon. Frankie even received a scrawled 'good luck' from Ray Moran, the youth-team coach, which caused great excitement at first when she deciphered it wrongly as 'good fuck'.

We were running out of people to ask when I spotted Albert Palmer, the club's balding kit manager, walking towards us with a crate under one arm. I approached him eagerly and asked for his autograph. There was a slight pause and a look of bewilderment crossed his face before it cracked into a broad smile.

'You can have it if you like, love, but I'm only Fred the baker. Still, you never know, I might make the first team yet.'

Frankie collapsed in a fit of giggles. But for me, the embarrassment of having asked the baker for his autograph was nothing compared to the realisation that the whole thing had been witnessed by Andy, who had slipped unnoticed from the clubhouse and was waiting to squeeze past the bread van to get to his car.

I wondered if this day had been sent to test me in some way, to scientifically establish exactly what degree of embarrassment a fifteen-year-old girl could withstand. Andy gave an understanding shrug.

'Don't worry, I don't know who everyone here is yet, either.'

'Yeah, but at least you don't go round asking the baker for his autograph,' I said, feeling my face turn a shade not dissimilar to something called 'pillar-box red' on the Dulux paint chart.

'True, but I might have asked the kit manager for a sliced loaf without realising.'

I smiled. I was actually sharing a joke with Andy Pailes. Not in my head but in real life. Before I knew it, I was asking to have my photograph taken with him and edging towards him, not daring to be as bold as Frankie and place my arm around his waist, but feeling drawn to the point where our bodies almost touched.

'Did you forget to deliver that one this morning?' Andy asked, pointing to the copy of the *Guardian* sticking out of my bag.

'Oh no,' I said, horrified that he should think I did a paper round. 'It's mine, I get it every day.'

'Great.' Andy smiled. 'That's two they sell round here then.'

I turned back to smile at the camera. It took me a few seconds to realise that someone's hand was resting lightly on my shoulder. And a few more for it to sink in that the hand in question could only belong to one person. Andy Pailes had his arm round me. I knew straight away that this was the most significant moment in my life so far. More important even than winning the UEFA Cup last season. I just prayed that Frankie captured the photographic evidence I needed to prove it had actually happened. A second after the camera whirred, Andy said, 'Thank you,' slipped from my side and was gone, sending me plummeting back down to earth just as the real Albert Palmer, who it had to be said was a dead ringer for Fred the baker, strolled out of the clubhouse.

'Hey, Claire. Here's your man,' giggled Frankie. 'Aren't you going to ask for his autograph?'

'Piss off,' I said. 'You're only jealous 'cos Andy put his arm round me.'

Frankie didn't say anything. But she sang 'One Albert Palmer, there's only one Albert Palmer' quietly under her breath all the way home.

The pole felt cold and slippery under my sweaty palm. I looked up and realised I was gripping it so hard, my knuckles had turned white. I hadn't felt like this since I'd been on the rollercoaster at Thorpe Park. In comparison, the number 242 bus was cheaper and the queue for it had certainly been shorter. It wasn't being on the bus that was causing the stomach-churning, though. It was what I was going to do when I got off. I suspected there might actually

be a law against it. I certainly hadn't told my mum where I
was going, or even Frankie for that matter. This was something I wanted to keep to myself. I reached up and pressed
the bell. It was a stop earlier than I had intended to get off,
but as I wasn't sure where I was going anyway, it didn't
seem to matter. The doors opened and folded back with a
hiss. I glanced at the driver's face in the mirror. He might
know, of course; I could always ask him. But it was too late
now. The doors were open. I stepped off and walked pur-
posefully in the direction the bus was going. As soon as it
passed me, I stopped and took out the fact file from my bag.

Cuffley. That was all it said. Not much to go on, but
Cuffley was a small place, much smaller than Potters Bar.
I'd brought a map with me; it was simply a process of elim-
ination. I had an idea in my head of what his home would
look like. It would be individual, of course, like him.
Something old and full of character – maybe even a thatched
roof. I remembered the picture of Matt Goodyear's house
which had featured in *Shoot!* It was big and modern and
tasteless, like it had been made out of a 'build a footballer's
home' Identikit. The one thing I knew was that Andy's
house would look nothing like that.

It smelt nice, Cuffley. Potters Bar smelt grey. But here it
smelt fresh and welcoming; it was a different class of air. I
walked on towards the village centre. Past a row of terraced
cottages and up to a wooden gate which led into a churchyard. I hesitated before pushing it open and wandering up
the cobbled path. The gravestones were the right sort. Lop-
sided and weathered with barely legible inscriptions. A few
graves were dotted with fresh flowers; others were partially

grown over with grass and weeds. But it was the church itself which I was drawn towards. It looked like the sort of church I'd painted as a child. A small stone chapel with a slate roof and stained-glass windows spaced at appropriate intervals. Towered over by a slightly crooked spire, reaching up past the treetops, oddly out of proportion with the rest of the structure. I walked around it, once in each direction. It was perfect.

I am wearing a huge dream of a wedding dress, one like Princess Di's. My mum didn't like it, of course. Tutted and said it looked like it needed a good iron. But it doesn't matter what she thinks. Not any more. I adore it. And more importantly, I know Andy will too. And that is all that matters. I gather the crumpled ball of ivory silk taffeta as I step down carefully from the horse-drawn carriage and watch it tumble on to the pavement, prompting gasps of delight from the well-wishers who have gathered outside. I smile at them and take my father's arm as I walk towards the front door of the church. I glance across at Dad's face. He is smiling broadly as if he is proud, really proud of his girl. Inside the church Andy is waiting, dressed in a charcoal-grey suit with a purple cravat, to match the colour of the tulips in my bouquet. He is thinking how lucky he is to be marrying the girl of his dreams. The girl who worships the ground he walks on. As I enter the church and the first shaky notes of the Bridal March ring out, he turns and catches his first glimpse of me. 'Beautiful,' he whispers, his eyes glistening with tears. I smile and glide on up the aisle as if I am on castors and the strength of his love is enough to pull me towards him.

'Hello. Can I help you?'

The voice was unfamiliar. I looked up. The vicar had twinkling eyes and a bushy beard. He was the right sort too.

'No, I'm fine, thanks. Just having a look round. Nice place you've got here.'

The vicar smiled. He must get this sort of thing quite often. People popping in to see if it measured up to their requirements.

'Right, I'll leave you to it then,' he said. 'Take as long as you want.'

'Thank you,' I replied. 'But I'm done now. I've seen everything I need to.'

I started back down the aisle, before turning abruptly.

'How long in advance do you need to book? For weddings, I mean.'

'Oh, I wouldn't worry for a while yet,' he said, the twinkle getting brighter. 'Come back a bit nearer the time. I'm sure we'll be able to fit you in.'

I nodded appreciatively, wondering if he was a United fan.

I left the churchyard and crossed to the other side of the street. I could see a newsagent's on the corner. It would be a good place to start. I had no idea what I was going to say. But I knew the key was to sound casual about the whole thing.

The newsagent's was cramped, bulging magazine racks down one side and a central display crammed full of everything from greeting cards to Sindy vanity mirror sets. I flicked through the birthday cards, picking out something appropriate and edging it sideways as I held the other cards in place before taking it up to the till.

'That's seventy-nine pence, love,' the woman behind the counter said. She was middle-aged and had hair which looked like it was set in curlers. I wasn't sure if she'd be any help but I handed over the money anyway before rummaging in my bag.

'Oh no.'

'What's the matter, love?' The woman looked up from the till.

'I've only gone and forgotten my address book. The card's for a friend; it's his birthday tomorrow. I need to catch the last post.'

'Does he live local?'

'Oh yeah, in Cuffley. It's just the name of the road I can't remember.'

'Do you know what letter it begins with?'

'No, I can't even remember that. My mind's gone blank. Daft, isn't it? Oh well, he'll just have to get it a day late, I suppose.'

I waited for an offer but it wasn't forthcoming. I was going to have to force the issue. Look casual, I reminded myself. I started to walk away before turning back.

'I've just thought. He probably gets his papers delivered from here. You couldn't have a look in your book for me, could you? Just in case.'

The woman looked me up and down. For once I hoped that I did look like an innocent young girl. I did my big pleading eyes thing. It worked.

'Course I can, love. Hang on a sec.'

She pulled out a large dog-eared black book from below the counter.

'Here we are, it's all done alphabetically. What's his surname?'

'Pailes,' I said, hoping the newsagent couldn't hear the sound of my heart thumping. The woman flicked forward to the Ps.

'How about that? First one on the page. Monkton Road, it is. Number nine. Owes three weeks' papers, tell him.'

The woman looked pleased with herself. But not half as pleased as I felt inside.

'Monkton, course it is. I remember now. Thanks ever so much. You've been a great help.'

As I hurried out of the shop, I prayed that Andy wouldn't go to pay the papers the next day. Or that if he did, the woman wouldn't wish him a happy birthday.

According to my map, Monkton Road was on the far side of the village. My pace quickened as I drew nearer. It had to be right. It had to be how I'd imagined. I turned the corner and a smile slid across my face. The road was straight and narrow. A row of terraced cottages stretched down one side. Opposite were a mixture of shorter terraces and semi-detached cottages, set back slightly from the pavement. Not a hint of pebble-dash or white plastic window frames in sight. I breathed a sigh of relief. I counted along the odd side of the road. Number nine was one of the semi-detached cottages. It was painted white and had stone mullion windows. The solid wood front door had a brass knocker, the front step was satin black. It was Andy's home. It was everything I had dreamt it would be.

I blinked back the gathering tears. I hadn't realised how much it would hurt, being on the outside looking in. This was where I belonged. Where I was meant to be. I crossed the road and edged closer, one hesitant step at a time. His car wasn't there. And there was no sign of life inside. But it didn't matter, I could feel his presence. It was enough to be here. I stood for a long time, a few yards from his front door. Just watching. Taking it all in. A few people went past, a woman with a baby in a pushchair, an elderly man with a plastic shopping bag. They smiled at me in a neighbourly way. It would be a nice place to live. Much nicer than Potters Bar.

I was still standing there when the silver Golf pulled up on the other side of the road and the driver got out, casually slinging his jacket over one shoulder and jangling his keys in the other hand. I started walking, forcing my reluctant legs into action. Desperate that he shouldn't see me. Shouldn't get the wrong idea. I kept walking until I was safely out of sight round the corner. Taking a couple of deep breaths, I leant on a garden wall to steady myself. It was a few minutes before I stopped shaking. When I did, I took my address book and pen from my bag and carefully wrote, '9 Monkton Road, Cuffley' in big black capital letters. I didn't write it on the page marked 'A' or 'P'. I wrote it under 'H', for home.

Three

'Fat, greedy bastard,' I said, scooping up the slug which had chomped its way through half of my lettuces and lobbing him high over the wall. The idea of getting the allotment had been to have somewhere to relax and unwind on my rare days off work. I'd envisaged ending up like Barbara from *The Good Life,* all chilled out, self-sufficient and earthily sexy. Instead I was stressed out, still having to buy most of my veg from Tesco, dirty and tired. It was hard work, this allotment lark, particularly as I'd vowed to do it all organically. I hadn't realised how mean and hungry the slugs were in Todmorden. And I suspected that the beer I'd poured into jam jars and sunk into the ground was actually encouraging them to my patch for a boozing and fast-food session, instead of drowning them in a drunken stupor.

'I've never seen a flying one before,' said a voice from behind me. I looked up to see Tomato Ted (as he was known by all at the allotments) standing there holding a large slug which looked suspiciously like the one I'd just thrown (I couldn't tell for sure, as I hadn't yet found an efficient branding or microchip system) between his thumb and forefinger. 'Hit me on the head it did while I was on my way to the water butt.'

I slapped my hand to my mouth. 'Oh, Ted. I am so sorry. I hadn't realised you were there. I shouldn't have thrown it anyway, of course.'

'It's all right. Didn't do me any lasting damage. I shan't be reporting you to the authorities.' I grinned as I imagined coming up before Hang 'em Silverman on a charge of battering a pensioner with a slug. 'I do have one request, though.'

'Go on,' I said.

'Permission to squash the blighter.' Ted was not known for his sentimentality when it came to garden pests.

I surveyed the remains of my lettuces.

'I think on this occasion I won't be offering it a defence,' I said.

'Good,' said Ted. 'And here's some advice.' I drew closer; being offered advice by Tomato Ted was generally seen as acceptance into the inner allotment circle. 'If you want rid of them, you'll have to throw them further than that. They can cover half a mile in one night, you know.'

'Really? That's incredible,' I said, annoyed at myself for not checking out the homing abilities of slugs before deciding where to dispose of them. And then I noticed Ted's shoulders shaking, and the hint of a smile on his weather-beaten face.

'Eh, I had you there,' he chuckled, winking at me before walking off in the direction of his green and bountiful plot. I smiled. The trouble with being an allotment novice was that you never knew when someone was taking the piss.

I returned to my weeding, watering and wondering.

The wondering wasn't anything to do with gardening, of course. It was about my answer. I was seeing Mark later when he'd finished work and I owed him one. Having managed to avoid the subject of the house every time we'd spoken on the phone since Saturday, I was well aware I wouldn't be able to get through a curry without it being raised. I suspected it would come up even before the pop-padoms arrived. And although I knew what Mark wanted to hear, I was still unsure about saying it. I'd made mistakes in love before. Big ones. And I didn't know if saying yes was the sensible thing to do or the surest way of waving goodbye to my dreams.

The list was still on the coffee table when I got home. It had been there since I found it. Taunting me. Reminding me of the past. And the future which hadn't materialised.

I flipped up the lid of my laptop. I needed to know what had happened to Frankie's dreams. I wasn't sure whether I wanted them to have come true or not, but I felt a sudden urge to find out. I went straight to Friends Reunited. I'd looked her up once, when it had first started. She hadn't been on it then but that was a long time ago. I scrolled through the list of names from my old school, some familiar, others who I had no recollection of at all, until I found her. Francesca Alberti. I clicked on her profile and waited, scanning the brief information she'd provided. She was married with four children, still living in Potters Bar and running her own business. I nodded. The only part which surprised me was the number of children. Frankie had never struck me as the maternal type. I was relieved about the lack of a photo, because I suspected she'd still look fabulous. I imagined her suave, handsome husband by her side, the four adorable bambinos and the business she ran, probably some sort of travel firm specialising in villas in Italy.

The fifteen year old in me, who had always been some- what in awe of her, felt a tiny bit jealous. Well, OK, a huge great bloody chunk jealous, actually. But the grown-up me was pleased for her. I also realised how much I missed her. I'd never intended to lose touch. But things had never been the same between us after what happened. And when I'd moved to Manchester to go to university we'd drifted even further apart. By the time I left, we were down to exchanging Christmas cards. And then I'd met David and everything had changed again. When I sent her the invite to my wedding, it came back to me marked 'No longer at this address'. Her family had obviously moved and I had no way of getting in touch with her. If she'd wanted to, she could have contacted me through my mum. She never did though. So I guessed she had a whole new life of her own.

And now? We could never go back to how we were. We would both have changed so much. She was a mum of four, for Christ's sake. It would be good to speak to her, though. To let her know I hadn't forgotten her. And to find out how it felt to have all your dreams come true.

I clicked on 'Send an e-mail'. I had no idea what to say, so reverted to my fifteen-year-old self.

Hi, Frankie, it's me. What have you been up to (apart from having four kids, that is)? I live in West Yorkshire now and I'm a lawyer (big surprise). Oh, and I finally made it into an A cup! Would be great to hear from you when you've got a moment.
Love
Claire
X

I hesitated before pressing send. I was making contact with the past. A past which had lain dormant for a long time but was still capable of exploding in my face. I wanted to go there though. I wanted to find out what had become of Frankie. And what had become of me.

My message winged its way to Potters Bar. Before I knew it I was on a Google search screen, and my fingers had somehow typed in the name 'Andy Pailes'. That was the trouble with uncovering the past. It was hard to know when to stop digging.

The phone rang next to me. I jumped, my fingers fumbling for the green button.

'Hi, it's me.' Mark's voice jolted me back to the present.

'Oh, hi.'

'My case has just finished and I'm starving. So if you're up for eating earlier, they open at half five. Unless you've got enough stuff from the allotment for that curry you promised to make, that is.'

I smiled. The chances of me successfully growing even a single pea now looked remote.

'No, 'fraid not. The bastard slugs have eaten it all. I'll meet you there at half five.'

'Great. See you there. I'll probably have ordered my body weight in poppadoms.'

I put the phone down, looked up at the screen, saw Andy's name, then deleted it and quickly returned to my inbox. It unnerved me, though. How close I had come.

'Hi. I take it you won,' I said as I arrived at the Bay of Bengal to find Mark sitting in our usual booth, his shirt sleeves rolled up and tie loosened, a contented look on his face as he eyed the pile of poppadoms in front of him. He grinned at me, his eyes sparkling with aliveness, stood up and kissed me. The sort of kiss which reminded me how lucky I was to have him.

'Yep, Mrs Lupton is now considerably richer and the council will be a bit more careful about how they put up their Christmas lights this year.' I laughed and shook my head. Mark's cases tended to range from the bizarre to the ridiculous. Often I felt his clients were trying their luck to cover up the fact that they'd been pretty stupid in the first place. But you really shouldn't have to worry about being hit on the head by an illuminated Christmas star while walking down the high street.

'I bet the press will have a field day with this one.'

'I know,' said Mark, breaking into the poppadoms as soon as I sat down. 'Loads of "Catch a Falling Star" headlines I should guess.' I watched as he scooped up some raita. His whole body still wired with the thrill of the win, the scent of victory practically dripping off him. He was one of those people who it was impossible to separate from his job, it was so much a part of him. I'd seen it the first time I'd come up against him in court (I'd lost, of course): the sharpness of thought, the ability to twist and turn his way out of anything, the sheer love of playing the game. I sometimes thought he was wasted being a personal injury lawyer. He could have been a top criminal barrister if he'd put his mind to it. Or some hotshot corporate lawyer. But that was where he differed from David. He loved his work but he wanted a life outside of it. And he wasn't prepared to do that whole playing golf with the boss thing and being the chair of the Rotary Club simply to work his way up the greasy pole. He'd much rather have a kick-about with the lads from the pub footie team on a Sunday morning. And, amongst other things, that was why I'd fallen for him. Because he was good at what he did but he didn't take himself too seriously. He loved life. He wasn't a slave to anyone. And his enthusiasm for whatever he did was infectious. He was a very hard man to say no to.

'So,' he said, sitting back on the plush bench seat and sweeping a stray wisp of his light brown hair back off his forehead, 'have you had enough time yet? Only if you sleep on it any longer, you'll be developing bed sores.'

I smiled. It was a fair enough point. I opened my mouth to say something but my insides were so twisted that they wouldn't let the words out. I looked up at Mark. Clouds of doubt were casting shadows over his face, his usual self-assurance momentarily obliterated.

'I do want to live with you,' I managed finally. 'I just don't want to rush into anything.'

'Two years together is hardly what I'd call rushing,' said Mark.

'I don't mean that. I mean being put on the spot about this house. I really appreciate all the effort you went to in finding it, but it just isn't me. I know you said it ticks all the boxes, but it doesn't tick any of my boxes.'

Mark's eyebrows made a desperate bid for his hairline. He clearly hadn't been expecting that. I wasn't sure if I had. But now it was out, there was no taking it back.

'I see,' he said, busying himself by trying to scoop up the last spoonful of raita from his plate in an effort to hide his disappointment. I reached out and took his other hand.

'This is not about you,' I said. 'So please don't take it personally. I'm simply suggesting that if we do this, we do it in a way that we're both happy with. That way we're not starting off with a problem, or with one of us resenting where we've ended up living.'

'Is it because it's in Lancashire?' asked Mark. 'Because if it is, I'd be willing to consider living just over the border, Walsden maybe. As long as I can see Lancashire on the horizon I should be all right. I could always get my air and water shipped in if my body can't stand the Yorkshire stuff.'

I smiled, relieved he had at least retained his sense of humour.

'I've nothing against Lancashire. Not really. It's the house. It's too new, too lacking in character. I don't want to live in a road where every house looks the same. I'm not a great fan of cul-de-sacs. Something to do with there being no way out the other end, I think.'

'OK,' said Mark, visibly brightening. 'There were some other houses on my shortlist. I'm sure there are some that aren't in cul-de-sacs. Why don't I arrange some viewings for next weekend?'

I sighed. I had tried so hard to avoid a straight 'no'. But I was going to have to put the brakes on before Mark's enthusiasm got the better of him and we skidded out of control.

'What I'm trying to suggest,' I said, choosing to look at my plate rather than Mark, 'is that we actually leave the whole house-hunting thing for the moment. It's pointless us finding something we love if we're not in a position to buy it. It would make a lot more sense to put both of our places on the market first and see what happens.'

'And what if we get an offer on one of them?'

'We move in to whoever's is left while we start house-hunting. At least that way we can see how we get on together before we commit to a whopping great mortgage.'

'So you're suggesting a sort of try-before-you-buy scheme?' said Mark, sounding a bit put out.

'It's a big step, living together. I want to make sure it's going to work.'

'Why wouldn't it work?' Mark sounded stung. I looked up at him. Sometimes he forgot that I had previous. That I was uncomfortably familiar with the house and contents splitting process.

'You might be sick of me after a few months,' I said. 'Believe me, I'm not easy to live with.'

Mark squeezed my hand, finally cottoning on to my reluctance.

'You're right. And if you change your mind about me, all you'll have to do is take me back to M and S for a refund. If you've still got the receipt, that is.'

I grinned, relieved that I had bought the time I needed and we seemed to have survived the conversation. Though I suspected Mark was putting on a brave face for my benefit.

'Are you sure you're OK about all this?' I said. 'I am sorry about the house. I know you really liked it.'

'Hey, it's not me you should feel sorry for. It's Chris, the estate agent. I'll have to break it to him very gently. He's been ringing me every day.'

We were interrupted by the waiter arriving at our table with an ice bucket and two champagne glasses. I looked at Mark. Clearly he hadn't anticipated my response.

'I wanted to celebrate in style,' he shrugged. I winced as the waiter popped the cork and poured, knowing I had metaphorically kneed Mark in the balls.

'I'm sorry. I feel really bad now,' I said, when the waiter had scuttled away. 'I know this isn't what you had in mind.'

'It's OK. We'll still get there in the end,' Mark said. 'It's just like you're taking me on the scenic route.'

I nodded. Not wanting to admit that I didn't have a TomTom to back up my lousy navigational skills.

'Thanks,' I said. 'I do appreciate you being so good about it.'

Mark smiled as our glasses collided with more of a thud

than a clink. I noticed a tiny crack in mine as I raised it to my mouth, but decided not to say anything.

We got back to my house earlier than usual. The food had been good but the conversation a little strained and neither of us had poured another glass of champagne after the first one. Mark put the recorked bottle on the kitchen table.

'Would you like some?' I asked.

'No thanks. I could do with a coffee though.'

'Sure, I'll put the kettle on. You go through.' His hand stroked my waist as he squeezed past, but he barely seemed attached to it. He was gutted, I knew that. And I felt absolutely awful for being the one who had burst his balloon. But I also knew it would have been wrong to go along with buying the house simply because he wanted to. The whole 'let's wait and see how it goes' thing really was, for me, a very sensible idea. And with the housing market the way it was, it could easily be a year before either of us had a buyer. Maybe by then I'd feel a lot clearer about everything. Maybe the list wouldn't be preying on my mind so much. Or maybe, if it was, I'd have done something about it.

I poured the boiling water into the cafetière and took two mugs from the tree. Only a few days ago I'd been swimming along quite contentedly in the slow lane. Vaguely aware that I could go faster if I wanted to but liking the feeling of not being rushed. Then someone had pulled me over into the fast lane. I'd so far managed to keep my head above water but knew I was well out of my depth.

I took the coffee through to the lounge. Mark was

sprawled out on the sofa staring into space. The list was still on the coffee table where I'd left it. I hurriedly put the mugs down and repositioned my laptop to cover the list, hoping Mark wouldn't notice.

'I just need to check my e-mails a sec,' I said, sitting down next to Mark.

There was one new message in my inbox. From someone called Francesca. I opened it up straight away, feeling the same kind of frisson I did when Frankie used to pass me notes in school.

Hi Claire,
And there was I thinking you must have emigrated! It was great to hear from you. I've got so much to fill you in on (and I'm sure you have too) that I don't know where to start and it would probably take for ever, so I've got a better idea. I know I'm springing this on you at short notice but I've really missed you and I don't want to waste any time. So come and visit us. The weekend after next would be good, the kids will have just broken up for the summer holidays. We live in Potters Bar, not far from your mum's. Would be great to introduce you to my family and we could catch up properly. Oh, and my husband's a chef, so you'll even be fed and waited on. Please feel free to bring anyone you want – it'll be a bit of a squash but we do have a sofa bed! Really hope to see you soon.
Loads of love,
Frankie
X

I didn't realise that a tear was running down my face until I looked up and saw Mark staring at me.

'What is it?' he said, putting his hand on my knee.

'It's OK,' I said. 'Just my old school friend Frankie. I haven't heard from her for years. I guess I hadn't realised how much I missed her. She's got in touch through Friends Reunited, invited me down the weekend after next. She always was a bit impulsive.'

'Great. It'll be really good for you to see her.'

'You're sure you don't mind? You can come with me if you want. She said I could bring someone.'

'What, and listen to you two going on about your school days? No, it sounds like a girl fest to me. I'll give it a miss if you don't mind.'

I nodded and stroked his hand. Relieved he'd said no. Mark wasn't part of the past. He'd feel out of place, out of time. And to be honest, it was going to be hard for me to go back. So many memories. Good and bad. And an obvious topic of conversation which we couldn't discuss with Mark there. It was probably best that I did it on my own.

'No, of course not. I'll probably pop in and see Mum while I'm there. So at least you've got out of that.'

'You make her out to be far worse than she actually is,' said Mark, sipping his coffee.

'You didn't have to grow up with her. Anyway, she likes you. You have the official Skidmore seal of approval.'

'God knows why.' The real reasons were that he was the same age as me rather than several years older. And although he was undeniably attractive, there was a certain Hugh Grant-like, clean-cut innocence about him. Unlike the rugged stubble and chest-hair types I used to go for who reeked of carnal lust when they walked into a room. Mothers don't like that. Men who are obviously having rampant sex with their daughters. But I couldn't say that to Mark.

'You charmed the socks off her last Christmas, remember? She told me afterwards you were the only decent man I'd ever brought home,' I said.

'God, shows what a lousy judge of character she is then,' grinned Mark.

I laughed and leant over to kiss him. His lips were warm and welcoming but his arms stayed resolutely by his sides. Despite all his assurances, he obviously did feel rejected. Unsure of where he stood. Of where we stood.

'I love you,' I whispered, keen to reassure him that nothing had changed, even though I knew it had.

'I love you too.' His eyes were still shut when he said it. As if he couldn't bear for me to see the hurt.

I snuggled into him on the sofa, folding his arms around me. Letting him know it was still OK. We sat like that for a long time. Talking about nothing of importance. Neither of us wanting to reveal how we were really feeling. I knew that Mark wasn't going to stay the night long before he said it.

'Anyway, I'd better be going. You've got a long day tomorrow.'

I nodded, deciding not to try to persuade him to change his mind. He had a right to go away and lick his wounds. And I needed some time to work out where we went from here.

He got up from the sofa and we walked through to the kitchen together.

'I'll call you tomorrow,' I said.

'Sure.' He kissed me on the lips, started to open the door and turned back to me.

'It'll be weird, won't it? Seeing the "For Sale" sign outside here.'

I nodded again, knowing he was looking for reassurance that I was at least going to go through with Plan B.

'Bet you I sell mine first,' I said.

'I hope so,' he said. 'That way I get to stay in Lancashire.'

'Away with you,' I said, smiling. He waved and I shut the door. Wondering how long the champagne would last before it went flat.

Saturday, 3 August 1985

'Honestly, the face on you. Anyone would think I was taking you to a concentration camp not a holiday camp.'

It was the first day of the new football season and I was on my way to Great Yarmouth. And for some reason, Mum expected me to be happy about it.

'Sorry for not jumping up and down in excitement.'

'There's no need to be sarcastic, Claire. I don't ask for much, just that you don't sit there with a face like a wet weekend for the entire journey.'

'But it is a wet weekend.' The rain hadn't stopped since we'd left home. The windscreen wipers were in serious danger of overheating. 'Anyway, I'd rather spend the week at the training ground.'

'You could have told me before I booked.'

'You didn't ask. You never do.' It was easy arguing with Mum. I always seemed to win, sometimes on points, sometimes with a knockout blow. I was already ahead on points.

'So you didn't want to go on holiday at all?'

'Not to poxy Great Yarmouth.'

'Ah, so where should I have taken you then?'

'Florence. It's in Italy.'

'I know where it is, thank you. Why do you want to go there?'

' 'Cos Andy Pailes has been there.'

Mum shook her head. 'I might have known it would be something daft like that. Well, you'll have to make do with Great Yarmouth.'

'Can't wait.'

'It's not that bad, Claire. You always used to enjoy our holidays there.'

'Yeah, well, it was different then, wasn't it?'

'What do you mean?'

'Dad was with us.'

Having delivered the knockout blow, I immediately wished I'd settled for a points win. We drove the rest of the way in silence. Apart from the hypnotic sound of the windscreen wipers swishing back and forth.

The woman in the red jacket who greeted us could hardly talk for smiling. We were shown into a chalet which looked identical to every other one we passed on the way from reception. The only good thing was that I did at least have my own little bedroom (Mum was sleeping on a sofa bed in the main living area). I took the photo of me and Andy out of my bag. It was my favourite picture of us together. Not the original, of course, that was in my photo album. This was a reprint. I had five more at home, each one hidden in a different place. You could never be too careful with photographs. I kissed the top of his head through the plastic wallet.

'Miss you already,' I whispered. I stood the photo up against the lamp on the bedside table. Hoping the cleaner would think Andy was my boyfriend.

Mum was being all cheery at breakfast the next morning. This was generally a bad sign. And it particularly pissed me off because United had lost 1–0 away to Forest.

'How about a nice game of tennis this morning?' she said.

I was good at tennis. Dad had taught me when I was younger. We used to play together in the park. I'd kept practising after he'd left. Though it hadn't been the same on the Swingball in the garden.

'You don't play tennis.'

'I didn't mean with me. There's a Teen Scene Club here.'

'Yeah, right. I can really see myself teaming up with some zitty thirteen-year-old boy.'

'There might be girls your own age around.'

'I doubt it. Most people my age wouldn't be seen dead here.'

Mum sighed, chased the last spoonful of Special K around her bowl and went off to the pool without saying another word.

I walk into my bedroom. Andy is lying in my bed.

'Come here,' he says, pulling back the duvet. I slide in next to him and he wraps his muscular arms around me, holding me tight, protecting me, keeping me safe from harm.

'I've missed you so much,' I say.

'I know, but I'm here now.' I smile as he kisses the top of my head. We are on holiday together; everything is all right now. It doesn't matter where we are, as long as we are together.

The front door of the chalet burst open. I jumped up and pulled my clothes on quickly. I heard the clank of a bucket and the tap whooshing on and opened my bedroom door to find the chalet maid standing there in her Marigolds. I gave her a dirty look for not knocking first as I slipped out the front door. I wandered down to the pool. Mum was lying on a sun-lounger at the far end.

'Oh, so you've decided to grace me with your presence, have you?'

I think she was trying to be sarcastic. Adults are crap at being sarcastic.

'Didn't have much choice. The cleaner kicked me out.'

Mum looked at my jeans and T-shirt.

'You could have put your cossie on, at least tried to look the part.' I had packed my swimming costume under duress. I had no intention of wearing it in public.

'I'm OK as I am, thank you.' I sat down on the lounger next to her, staring out across the pool, my face set to 'I don't want to be here' mode. Everywhere I looked there were people enjoying themselves. Small children screaming excitedly as they splashed about on inflatables, parents laughing at their antics, couples lazing next to each other, rubbing sun cream into each other's backs. It was the worst bit of being a teenager. Having to watch everyone else being so bloody happy.

Mum looked across at me and sighed. 'At least take your trainers off if you're stopping. They look ridiculous.'

I looked at her. She was wearing a turquoise floral-print swimsuit, matching eye shadow and clip-on dolphin earrings. And she was calling me ridiculous.

'Can I have the key, please?' I said. 'I'm going back to the chalet to get my book.'

When I returned five minutes later with my signed copy of United captain Dave Orton's autobiography tucked under my arm, there was a man sitting in the lounger next to Mum. He had slightly greying hair and a deep suntan and was wearing red swimming trunks that looked a size too small. Mum was leaning on one side, listening to him. I noticed that she was sucking her tummy in. When he finished talking, she threw back her head and laughed. It wasn't her normal laugh, either. It was deeper, dirtier. I didn't like it. As I approached, she looked up and immediately stopped laughing.

'I thought you were going back to the chalet?'

'No, you should try listening. I said I was gonna get my book.'

I looked at the man on the lounger, who showed no sign of moving.

'Er, this is Brian, love. He only lives in Waltham Cross. I always say it's a small world, don't I?'

'Hello,' said Brian, briefly acknowledging me before turning back to continue the conversation with Mum. I hovered above them for a few moments, but as soon as the laughing started again I headed back to the chalet. The cleaner had gone. Andy had gone too. I went straight to my room and picked up the photo of him.

'I wish I wasn't here,' I said, kissing his forehead before clutching the photo to my chest. 'I wish I was with you, where I belong.'

When Mum came back at lunchtime she didn't mention Brian. She took a Jackie Collins book outside with her in the afternoon. It was called *The Bitch*. I didn't see Brian talking to her again.

'So, how bad was Clacton then? On a scale of one to ten.'

We were sitting in Frankie's bedroom on the Sunday morning after United had beaten Watford 3–1 (Goodyear, Orton and Dodds). Neither of us usually got up in time to see Sunday mornings. But after a week with our families, I guess we were both desperate for some meaningful conversation.

'About a hundred,' said Frankie, doing her usual drama-queen bit. 'Aunt Josie kept going on about Connie's wedding preparations and saying things like, "And when are you going to find yourself a nice Catholic boy, Francesca?"'

'What did you tell her?'

'When the Pope screws Madonna.'

'You didn't.'

'No. I didn't. Wish I had though. Stupid interfering cow.' Frankie stabbed her pillow repeatedly with her hair-brush. She'd be scary if she was armed.

'So where's the virgin bride?' I asked, nodding in the direction of Connie's half of the room, which was suitably pink, prim and spotless. The Alberti sisters were a bit like rival animals, marking out their territory. Only instead of peeing on her land, Frankie had stuck up pictures of Matt, Simon Le Bon and John Taylor to keep Connie at bay.

'Oh, she's downstairs somewhere. Probably sucking up to Mum by helping with the dinner. Proper little housewife she's turning into.' Frankie went back to stabbing the pillow.

'Great Yawnmouth was fun,' I said.

'I bet. What d'ya do all week?'

'Stayed in my room mostly.'

'Yeah, I can see that.' Frankie put her arm next to mine. She looked like she'd been grilled to a golden brown while I'd been put in the microwave on defrost.

'Well, I only burn, don't I?' I said. 'Anyway, Mum was by the pool most of the time. I was trying to avoid her.'

'Did she cop off with anyone?'

'She is thirty-nine, you know.'

'Oh yeah. What about you, then?'

I stared at Frankie, unable to believe what I was hearing. I'd spent the entire week pining for Andy. Crying myself to sleep every night because I wanted to be with him so much it hurt. I wondered if she'd even thought about Matt while she'd been away.

'In case you've forgotten, I'm only interested in one man.'

'I know, but he's not interested in you, is he?'

'How do you know?'

'Well he hasn't invited you round for his birthday yet, has he?'

'No, but I'm still gonna see him. I'm going to the United centenary do on the thirty-first.'

'Yeah, in your dreams.'

'No, I'm gonna turn up outside the front gates so I can give him his card when he goes in. It'll be my last chance to see him before I go back to school. And I don't know why you're laughing, because you're coming with me.'

'Now you are talking crap,' said Frankie. 'How the hell am I gonna wangle that one?' She had a point. Her mother's fear of her being murdered, raped or abducted by a marauding mob of tattooed skinheads meant that she wasn't allowed out of the house at night on her own, not even to pop down the road. Frankie had to suffer the ultimate indignity of living in a permanent exclusion zone, which began two yards outside her house. If she dared to instigate an unauthorised incursion she was immediately shot down in flames. It was like the Falklands all over again.

'I have a cunning plan,' I said in my best Baldrick voice.

'Oh God,' said Frankie.

'Look, do you wanna see Matt in his tuxedo or not?'

'Course I do,' she said.

'Right then, you'd better come downstairs with me.'

Mrs Alberti was doing the ironing when we marched into the lounge. According to Frankie, her mum always got up at four a.m. the day after they got back from holiday, so she could get everything washed, dried and ironed in one day. I thought it was taking the Catholic guilt-trip thing a bit far.

She looked up and smiled at me as we sat down. Frankie said her mum liked me. That she thought I was a good influence. Which goes to show what crap judges of character parents are.

'Hello, Claire love. Did you have a nice holiday?' she said.

'Yes, great, thanks. How about you?'

'Oh, smashing. My sister always makes us feel very welcome. And she was a great help with the wedding arrangements, wasn't she, Conchetta?'

Connie looked up from her copy of *Bride* magazine, gave a sickly-sweet smile and confirmed that Aunt Josie had helpfully pointed out the need to ensure the napkins at the reception were the same colour as the bridesmaids' dresses. Frankie rolled her eyes. I couldn't help wondering what odious sin she must have committed in a previous life to have been saddled with a sister who made Julie Andrews look positively depraved. I had suggested to Frankie that if she wanted to make some dosh she should grind Connie down into tiny granules and sell her as some kind of sugar substitute.

I looked at Mrs Alberti but she wasn't paying any attention to what was being said. She had stopped ironing and was staring at Frankie's T-shirt with a quizzical expression.

'Why didn't you get them to put "Hello"?' she said.

'You what?' said Frankie.

'On your T-shirt. Why couldn't you have asked them to put "Frankie says Hello" instead of "Frankie says Relax"? Come to think of it, you could have got them to put Francesca instead of Frankie as well. I'll never understand why you don't use your proper name; you'd have complained if we hadn't given you one.'

I turned to look at Frankie, who didn't seem to know

whether to laugh or cry. 'See what I mean?' she whispered. 'They're all on another fucking planet in this house.' As if to illustrate the point, a jingly rendition of 'Pop Goes the Weasel' blared out from across the road, announcing the return of Frankie's older brother.

'Hello, love,' said Mrs Alberti, visibly brightening as Alberto entered the room. 'How was business?'

I thought the term 'business' was stretching it a bit. Alberto had a dilapidated pink ice-cream van which sold Mr Whippies. And according to the rumour going round our school, he spent more time in his 'ice-cream love machine' messing around with a box of 99 Flakes and a couple of slags from the sixth form than actually selling any ice creams.

'Bit quiet for this time of year,' he said.

'Never mind, love, you go and get yourself cleaned up. Dinner will be ready soon.' She smiled lovingly at him as he headed upstairs. I decided to take my chance.

'Mrs Alberti, my nan and grandad are having a golden wedding anniversary party next Saturday. And they've said I can bring a friend, so I wondered if Frankie could come.'

'Oh, it's very nice of you to ask, Claire.'

'It's only a quiet family do, see. It won't be late and my mum'll drop her off afterwards.'

'Well, maybe just this once, seeing as it's a family thing.'

'Thanks very much,' I said. 'I'll make sure they send some cake home for you.'

Frankie came out to the front door to see me off. 'You lying cow,' she laughed as soon as we were out of earshot.

'Sometimes, when you're a lawyer, you have to use your powers of persuasion,' I said. 'And anyway, Andy's worth lying for.'

It had to be the right place. The Tesco near the training ground in Potters Bar would be far too busy, more chance of being stopped by a fan and asked for an autograph. I couldn't imagine him wanting that. The Co-op in Cuffley was nice and quiet. And it was right on his doorstep. But this was the sixth time now and still no sighting. It was costing me a fortune in bus fares. I was beginning to wonder whether he went shopping at all. Or whether someone else did it for him.

The shopping basket, already weighted down with orange juice, pineapple chunks, three tins of baked beans and the biggest block of mature Cheddar I'd been able to find, bashed awkwardly against my legs as I stopped to consult the crumpled shopping list my mum had left before dashing off to work (she hadn't questioned my new-found willingness to run shopping errands. She'd simply said how nice it was that I was pulling my weight at home these days). PG Tips it said on the list. But the Yorkshire Tea looked far more appealing. The chance to drink tea produced in Andy's birthplace was too good an opportunity to miss. Frankie took the mickey about the Yorkshire thing. Said that eating two Yorkshire puddings a day didn't turn you into a Yorkshire person, just like eating lots of Madeira cake didn't mean you could claim to be from Madeira, it just made you fat. I popped the Yorkshire Tea into the basket anyway, deciding Frankie was only jealous because she couldn't pin her colours to Matt in the same way. Nothing much came from Harlow in Essex.

Anything which could make me feel closer to Andy. That was what I wanted. If I could surround myself with him, eat the same food, drink the same tea, breathe the same air, I could shut my eyes and be with him whenever I wanted to. And one day I would wake up and it would be real. I wouldn't be in Potters Bar. I would be in Cuffley, in Andy's house. And he would be smiling down at me, bringing me breakfast in bed, kissing me softly on the top of my head. Telling me I was his special girl. That I meant the world to him.

I glanced down at the list. Only one thing left to get. I knew where everything was now. Had developed an encyclopaedic knowledge of the layout of the Co-op. But I chose to take the long way round, revisiting favourite haunts, lingering near the baked beans in the tinned goods aisle, browsing at the array of chicken breasts in the chiller cabinet, fingering the cans of Tetley's on special offer this week, all the time glancing around me, peeping down each aisle as I went.

Eventually I came to what Mum referred to as the 'women's bits' and reached up for the large box of slightly perfumed Vespre sanitary towels. I presumed they were for me, as Mum still used the chunky, old-fashioned type that looked like they could absorb the contents of Lake Superior. Frankie said it must be like putting a brick in your knickers. But then Frankie was far more sophisticated in the sanitary provision department. She used tampons. I wanted to use them too but Mum had been horrified when I had suggested it, saying tampons were for when I was older. I wondered just how old you were supposed to be to use them. After all, Mum was thirty-nine but she still used towels. I had images of women skipping off to the chemist on their fortieth birthday to buy their first packet of tampons.

I started to work out how many sanitary towels I'd have to use over the next twenty-five years. I was still doing the calculation in my head as I approached the checkouts. Two women were on this afternoon. The dark-haired one with the boil on her chin and the young blonde girl with the wonky ponytail. Sometimes it was only one of them. It all depended how busy they were. They probably had all three tills working in the mornings. I was only guessing. I never came that early because I knew he'd be at training.

The queue for the dark-haired woman was shorter. I started towards her but stopped abruptly as something caught my eye in the other queue. It was the glint of gold from his earring I noticed first, followed, as my gaze dropped to the floor, by the flash of blue on his Adidas trainers. At last, I felt my hand tighten on the basket handle and a frown spread across my face as I struggled to work out how I could possibly have missed him in the aisles. But now was not the time for inquests. If I moved quickly, I could still sneak in behind him.

I turned on my heel and darted forward, narrowly beating an elderly lady with a blue rinse to the checkout. My hands were shaking as I began emptying the contents of my basket, so much so that a tin of baked beans slipped from my hand on to the conveyor belt with a thud. My gaze shot upwards, just as Andy turned and caught me staring at him. There was a flicker of recognition on his face before he smiled and said, 'Hello. I know you from the training ground, don't I? It's Claire, isn't it?'

My eyes widened. He had noticed me. He knew who I was. He'd even made the first move.

'Hi,' I said, smiling back at him. 'Sorry, you took me by surprise.'

'Even footballers have to go shopping sometimes,' he said.

I nodded. Andy was still smiling. Still looking at me. I was caught between gazing into his eyes and trying to catch a glimpse of his shopping. To memorise each item on the conveyor belt as if I was a contestant on *The Generation Game*. And to see if the lasagne served one or two people.

'Excuse me, are you two together?'

The voice belonged to the checkout girl with the wonky ponytail. She was looking at us. At me and Andy. Together. That was what she thought. That the two of us belonged together. That we were an item. I felt a glow of warmth inside me.

'No,' said Andy.

'Oh, so are, um . . . are these things yours?'

She was pointing to my shopping. To the cheese, the pineapple chunks, the tins of beans. And the box of Vespre. I clapped my hands to my face, my fingers cold against my hot cheeks.

'I'm so sorry,' I said to Andy. 'I was miles away. I forgot to put the bar thingy down. They're mine. All those things are mine. I'm really sorry.'

'It's OK,' he said. 'No need to apologise. It's an easy

mistake to make. Here, they won't be much use to me.' He passed me the box of Vespre, which I realised were now of huge sentimental value and would be worth a fortune in years to come when he was an England star.

'I'm so sorry about that,' I said.

'No problem,' Andy said. 'But next time you try to get someone else to pay for your shopping, at least pick someone of the right sex.'

I started laughing. Andy was laughing too. I watched as he packed his shopping away. The lasagne was for one. And the pizza wasn't really big enough to share.

'See you then,' he said, turning to say goodbye. 'Thanks for brightening up my shopping trip.'

'That's OK,' I said. 'Any time. See you soon.'

I watched him walk out of the door and across the car park before disappearing from view. I had brightened up his day. It was only a matter of time now. Before I brightened up every day for him. I hadn't dreamt of it starting this way, with a mix-up over sanitary towels. But it didn't matter how these things started. It was how they ended that was important.

Four

The train pulled in to Potters Bar station. My life, not the station platform, flashed before me. The times I'd waited here, huddled up on one of the benches with Frankie when we were on our way to the United ground. And later, when I was a student, struggling down the steps with all my worldly goods, desperate to escape to my new life in Manchester.

I walked down the subway and squinted in the bright sunlight as I came out the other side. The bus station had been redeveloped but was still disturbingly familiar. Mum had said to ring when I arrived and she would come and pick me up. But now I was here I didn't want her to. I wanted to walk. I felt the need to acclimatise, like I'd just stepped off a plane somewhere in South America, thousands of feet above sea level.

The last time I'd been here, with Mark, the previous Christmas, we'd driven, arriving under cover of darkness and leaving at dusk the next day without having left the house. It was a long time since I'd walked these streets. I didn't get down much these days. I had the excuse of being on the duty rota to cover the police cells at weekends. But to be honest I think even my mum knew that it wasn't that which kept me away. It was a house full of memories. Most of which I'd rather forget.

I dialled Mark's number on my mobile as I walked along. Things were better between us but still not back to how they had been. The 'For Sale' signs outside our homes a reminder that the market, like us, had stalled and we were waiting for things to start looking up.

'Hiya, I'm here,' I said when he answered.

'Great. Journey all right?' I could hear the sound of water splashing in the background.

'Yeah, fine. Where are you?'

'I'm having my hair cut.'

I frowned. The usual barber Mark went to was a confirmed dry-cut man.

'But Nathan doesn't wash hair.'

'No, I'm, er, somewhere different. In Manchester, actually. Thought I'd have a look round the shops afterwards.'

'Oh,' I said, knowing Mark would usually balk at paying city salon prices or going anywhere near a shopping centre. 'Well, I'll ring you tomorrow, when I'm on the train home.'

'Sure,' said Mark. 'Have fun.'

I put my phone back in my pocket. As I looked up I realised that I was only fifty yards away. The automatic pilot had clearly taken over. The front garden appeared the same as ever. I would no doubt be told there was a different variety of fuchsia or the crazy paving had been redone, but it looked the same to me. I stood on the doorstep and rang the bell. Remembering a time when I had a key and could let in anyone I liked. Anyone at all.

My mother opened the door. She was a reluctant pensioner, her hair dyed the same shade of golden brown as I could always remember. It was worn pinned up now, her concession to the expectation that ladies of a certain age should have short hair. Although she still retained her dangly earrings and hid the wrinkled skin around her neck with a brightly coloured silk scarf.

'Claire, why didn't you ring?'

'I was halfway here by the time I remembered.'

'It's silly struggling with that heavy bag on your own.'

'Never mind, I'm here now, aren't I?' I always had to remind myself to continue being an adult, not to regress into that whole antagonistic mother and teenage daughter routine. We'd moved on from there. Not particularly far, but we had at least moved on.

'Yes,' she said, kissing me on the cheek. 'And it's lovely to see you. Come in and I'll put the kettle on.'

I put my bag down in the hall and walked through to the kitchen. Mum chatted away about people and places I could barely remember, as if I had only left yesterday and was desperate for news of the machinations of the Potters Bar set. I followed her through to the lounge, cup and saucer in hand (my mother still resolutely held out against the onset of mugs). The Laura Ashley sofa had long disappeared, as had the wallpaper, but still the room held on to its secrets. Still it was uncomfortable for me to sit there, knowing what it had been a witness to.

'So, how's Mark?' said Mum, stirring her half-spoon of sugar around the cup with a dainty teaspoon.

'He's fine, thanks.' I stopped myself saying we had some

news because I knew my mother would leap to the wrong conclusion. As it turned out, she didn't even need prompting.

'I really like him, you know,' she said, patting me on the hand. 'I was wondering if you two had got any plans for the future?'

I smiled, knowing that a mention of the possibility of a fortnight's holiday somewhere warm next spring wasn't what she had in mind.

'We might be moving in together, actually.'

'Why only might?'

I decided not to mention the possibility of buying somewhere new at this stage. I wanted to keep it as simple and low key as possible.

'Well, we've both put our places on the market; just depends how long it takes to sell one of them.'

'Oh, well that's great. And it makes sense not to rush into anything.' She might have omitted the words 'this time' but I knew exactly what she was getting at. My propensity to fall hard and fast had got me into trouble before. She remembered only too well. Because she'd been there to help pick up the pieces.

'Good. I'm glad you approve,' I said, deciding not to go into the whole business with the list and all the feelings it had brought up about the past. She didn't like to be reminded of any of that. And I knew full well what she'd say about it all.

'And how's Malcolm?' I asked instead, deciding it was safer to change the subject. Malcolm was, as my mother had once described him, her 'man friend'. He was a permanent fixture at Christmas and other family gatherings. I couldn't remember quite where he'd come from but equally it was getting hard to remember him not being there. She saw him most weekends, and often in the week now, since he'd retired. They were, to all intents and purposes, a couple. Except for the fact that they retained their separate houses and their own lives. And that was how it would stay, of course. For one simple reason. Because he wasn't Dad.

'Oh, much the same as ever. His back's playing him up at the moment. He won't bother the doctor with it though. Says you have to expect things like that at his age. He never complains about anything, you know.'

I nodded. It was true. Malcolm was a salt-of-the-earth kind of guy. I liked him. Primarily because there was nothing about him to dislike. And because he was obviously devoted to Mum. There was a pause in the conversation. I knew what Mum was going to ask next way before she actually asked it. It always took her a few minutes to build up the courage. To steel herself for whatever news I might have.

'Have you heard from your father?' she asked. She didn't say seen him, of course, because he no longer lived in this country. He and his second wife had been running an English pub for ex-pats in Spain for about five years now. In the most recent photo he'd e-mailed he looked particularly bronzed and relaxed, one arm draped around the much paler Denise (her classic redhead complexion had remained stubbornly un-Mediterranean). She still looked

good for her age, mind. Though I wasn't going to tell
Mum that, of course.

'Yeah, I had an e-mail from him a couple of months
back. Saying that business is good and he's still enjoying
the laid-back life over there.' I knew better than to mention Denise. It was the fact that she'd now been married to
Dad longer than he'd been married to Mum which really
galled her. I remembered the look Mum had given her at
my wedding. And the way she'd sucked her stomach in
when she'd been asked to stand next to Dad for the family
photographs. It was sad, really. How much she obviously
still loved him. And ironic that I, the one who had once
berated her for constantly attacking him, was the one who
now had to remind her she was better off without him.

Mum nodded.

'I'm getting a new sofa delivered on Monday,' she said,
changing the subject.

'Oh, great.'

'From that SCS place. You know, the ones that adver-
tise on the telly with that chap with the nice smile.'

'You mean Martin Kemp?'

'I think that's him. Lovely eyes he's got.'

I shook my head, unsure whether to laugh or cry.

'I used to have his picture on my wall. He was the bass
guitarist in Spandau Ballet.'

'No, it's not him. This is the fella who used to be in
EastEnders.'

'Yeah, I know, it's the same guy.'

'No, it can't be. He was scruffy with long hair and an

earring. This chap's much more presentable. It must be a different Martin.'

I opened my mouth to say something, decided against bothering to argue with her, and took a Bourbon biscuit from the plate she offered me instead.

'What time are you expected at Frankie's?'

'In about an hour,' I said, glancing at my watch.

'It's a wonder I haven't seen her if she lives near me.'

'Maybe you wouldn't recognise her now.'

'Of course I would. She always stood out a mile. She wasn't exactly a plain Jane, was she?' It was strange to hear my mum say that. At fifteen I hadn't realised that she'd registered how stunning Frankie was. Although maybe that was why she'd always disapproved of her.

'Still, having four kids must have changed her a bit,' I said, more in hope than expectation.

'Four, you say? Her mum must be thrilled. That's the thing about these Catholic families, there's never a short-age of grandchildren.'

I smiled weakly, knowing it was a not-so-subtle dig at my failure to procreate. My cup clattered down on to my saucer.

'So,' I said, keen to move things on again, 'have you iced any good cakes lately?'

From the outside, Frankie's house looked like any other semi in Potters Bar. Certainly not as modern or swish as I had imagined. A selection of toys lay abandoned in the front garden: a battered tricycle, a bigger bike with foot-ball stickers plastered all over it and one of those rather evil-looking plastic baby dolls in a toy buggy. If Lloyd Grossman had been peering through the keyhole asking 'Whose house is this?' I certainly wouldn't have guessed it was Frankie's.

I rang the bell and waited. The sound of children screaming and shouting came from inside. After a while the noise subsided slightly and I rang again. A young boy's voice called, 'Someone's here,' and seconds later footsteps approached and the door opened.

The woman who stood there was big. I mean seriously big; only politeness would have stopped me using the F word. She was clothed in black, stylishly so, her top cut to show off a little cleavage and her wide trousers skimming over her rounded hips. The body was entirely foreign but the face which was smiling at me was undeniably Frankie: fantastic cheekbones, full lips and dark, playful eyes, all exquisitely made up, shown off in a flawless complexion and framed by the same long dark hair she'd always had.

'Hi,' said Frankie. 'It's OK, you have got the right house. I guess I should have warned you that I'm twice the woman I used to be.'

'No, I wasn't thinking that,' I said, embarrassed that I must have let my surprise show.

'It may have been nearly twenty years, but I can still read your face like a book, you know,' said Frankie. 'And you were thinking, "God, Frankie's turned into a fat cow," or words to that effect.'

I grinned at her, relieved to have instantly fallen back into the old banter.

'Actually, I was thinking about how you and Dawn

French both prove you don't have to be a size zero to look gorgeous.'

'Thank you,' said Frankie. 'Flattery will get you everywhere. Now come in and give me a hug, if you can still get your arms around me, you annoyingly skinny thing.' I stepped forward and embraced Frankie. It felt weird to be holding her again. But a nice kind of weird, so nice that when we let go and grinned at each other I could see her eyes had welled up like mine.

'You're looking good, girl,' said Frankie, touching my shoulder-length highlighted locks. 'Relieved to see you got rid of the big hair.'

'Ah, but I still have the tea-bag tank-top and pedal-pushers somewhere,' I said.

There was a scream followed by a wailing sound from somewhere inside the house.

'Come on,' said Frankie. 'I'd better introduce you to the children before they kill each other.'

I slipped off my sandals and followed her through to the lounge, where a small girl with long dark hair was lying on the floor bawling her eyes out, watched over by a similar-aged boy with glasses. An older boy with slightly spiky hair was looking daggers at her from the sofa.

'Paulo snatched the DS from me,' screamed the girl.

'I did not. She snatched it from me,' shouted the older boy, who presumably was Paulo.

'Right,' said Frankie, clapping her hands, 'someone's not telling the truth here.' The small boy, who had so far kept out of the spat, ran up to Frankie, tapped her arm and when she bent down, whispered something into her ear. Frankie nodded, patted him on the head and said, 'Right, Sophia, give the DS back to Paulo. Paulo, next time don't hog it for so long and if she snatches it from you, don't snatch it back, come and tell me, OK?' Paulo and Sophia scowled at each other then turned to scowl at the younger boy, who had obviously grassed them up. I couldn't help thinking he had excellent witness potential.

'Claire, I'd like you to meet my delightful children, Paulo, Sophia and Roberto. Kids, this is Claire, my old school friend I told you about who's come to visit.'

'Has she brought us presents?' asked Sophia. 'Most people who come bring us presents.'

I winced, knowing I should have thought to get them something when I'd picked up the wine and chocolate truffles on the way. Although as I hadn't even known their ages it would have been hard to know what to get.

'They could share the chocolates I got you, if you like,' I whispered to Frankie. The look she gave me in return made it quite clear that was not going to happen.

'Sophia, you know it's rude to ask people that. Besides which, it's not Christmas or your birthday. Claire's a guest and you guys love having people to stay. Though if you carry on behaving like this, she might turn around and go straight home.'

I smiled, hoping to illustrate that this was not going to happen, but the children still looked suitably chastened. I crouched down next to Roberto.

'Hi, so how old are you?' I asked.

'Five and a half,' he replied in a whisper.

'I'm five and a half too,' chimed in Sophia. 'But I'm older than him because I came out first.'

Frankie nodded at me. 'Twins,' she said. 'Although you'd never think so. They couldn't be more different.'

'Hi, Sophia. Was that your doll I saw in the buggy outside?'

'Yes, but I'm getting a new Bratz one for Christmas.'

'If she behaves herself,' said Frankie.

'And you must be at least twenty-one,' I said, turning to Paulo, who grinned back at me.

'I'm nearly eight. You support United, don't you? Mummy told me.'

I glanced up at Frankie.

'Paulo's United's number one fan. He was very impressed when I told him you'd seen them play at Wembley.'

'It was the old Wembley though, wasn't it?' said Paulo. 'So you must be really old.'

I laughed.

'Not so cheeky, you,' said Frankie.

'Do you still go to the games?' asked Paulo.

'No, I haven't been for years, I'm afraid,' I said, deciding not to add that the Wembley match had been my first and last United game.

'But you still support them?' asked Frankie.

I shook my head. 'Not really. I could probably only name a handful of their players these days. I lost interest when they all turned into prima donnas and football became big business.'

'What's a prima donna?' asked Paulo.

'Someone who's full of themselves, a bit of a show-off,' said Frankie.

'A bit like Matt Goodyear,' I laughed, digging Frankie in the ribs.

'He was Mummy's favourite player,' said Paulo, turning to me. 'Who was yours? Mummy said she couldn't remember.'

I looked at Frankie and smiled, letting her know I appreciated her discretion, although it hadn't been necessary.

'Andy Pailes,' I said. 'The best left back we ever had.'

'Never heard of him,' said Paulo. 'He can't be very famous.'

'No, he wasn't,' I replied. 'Not really.'

'Anyway,' said Frankie, 'I'm going to stick a DVD on for you kids so Claire and I can have some peace. What's it to be?'

'*Ben Ten.*'

'*Fifi and the Flowertots.*'

'*Bob the Builder,*' came the replies from Paulo, Sophia and Roberto in turn.

'You see,' said Frankie, turning to me. 'There's just no pleasing them.' She rummaged in a cabinet, pulled out a copy of *Lazy Town* and stuck it in the DVD player. 'You can all sit together on the sofa; any arguing and it goes off. And guys . . .' the children looked up as Frankie pressed play, 'enjoy the show!' She picked up Roberto and placed him strategically between Paulo and Sophia on the sofa.

'I take it he's the family mediator,' I whispered as we left the room.

'The nearest I've got to one,' said Frankie. 'Joe calls him

Supergrass but he's just naturally honest. He doesn't like it when the other two get away with stuff they shouldn't.'

'Sounds like you've got a lawyer in the making.'

'Well he's certainly not going to be a footballer. Joe named him after Roberto Baggio but I've never seen a child with less ability with a football. Which is weird, because Paulo, who's named after Paulo Maldini, is a complete natural. He can't stop scoring goals.'

'So I guess you got to name Sophia after your favourite film star.' I smiled.

'Yep, although as you may have noticed she doesn't appear to possess an ounce of Miss Loren's elegance or style. Maybe by the time she's a teenager she'll have stopped thumping boys and having tantrums.'

'Can't think where she gets that temperament from,' I grinned.

'Come on,' said Frankie, leading the way upstairs. 'There's one more to meet yet.' She knocked on the door at the end of the landing, the one from where loud, whining music was emanating. 'Can we come in?' she called.

'What?' came the reply.

'If you turned it down a bit, you might be able to hear me ask if we can come in,' Frankie shouted. I smiled, remembering how Frankie's own mother used to say much the same thing.

The music stopped abruptly and the door opened to reveal Frankie standing there aged fifteen. It wasn't, of course. But I did have to do a double-take. In actual fact the girl standing before us was even more stunning than Frankie had been. She was taller and thinner for a start and she wore her long dark hair twisted round and tied to one side at the front, with a wispy fringe falling flatteringly over her forehead. I was doing the maths quickly in my head. Frankie had a teenage daughter, in which case she must have had her about the time we'd lost touch. When, as far as I knew, she hadn't even been going out with anyone. Certainly not Joe. It was weird to think that such a big thing had happened to her and I knew nothing about it. The girl's dark eyes looked up at me, her dangly hoop earrings jingling as she flicked back her fringe.

'Hi,' she said. 'I'm Emily.'

'Pleased to meet you, Emily,' I said, kissing her on both cheeks as Frankie's family used to do to me. 'I expect you'll be wanting all the dirt about what your mum got up to as a teenager.'

'Oh God, yeah. That'd be great. Then next time she tells me I can't do something, I can say "But you used to do worse than that." '

'Hey,' said Frankie, turning to me. 'Some friend you are.'

'Don't worry,' I said. 'I won't tell her the story about you tricking your mum with the golden wedding cake.'

'That was your idea,' said Frankie. Emily giggled.

'So what were you up to, Emily, before we interrupted you?' I asked.

'Oh, nothing really.'

'She was probably re-reading *Twilight* for the hundredth time and swooning at the pictures of the vampire fellow on her wall,' said Frankie.

Emily's face flushed. 'His name's Robert Pattinson,' she

said to me. 'He plays Edward Cullen from the book in the new *Twilight* movie. My best mate Alia and me are going to the premiere in London in December.'

'In her dreams,' mumbled Frankie.

'Mum doesn't approve,' said Emily, rolling her eyes.

'Let's see a photo of him then,' I said.

Emily threw open the door behind her and I walked in. The first thing that struck me was how the room was split down the middle, just like Frankie and her sister's bedroom had been. On one side was a pink princess four-poster, which I took to be Sophia's, even though she didn't appear to be the slightest bit pink and princessy to me. On the other side was a cast-iron bed with a white duvet set, which I assumed was Emily's. The walls above the bed were adorned with a mass of posters and photos printed out from the internet, mainly of one particular man. Lean, dark, with heavy eyebrows, piercing eyes, a come-to-bed smile and hair which varied between floppy, spiky and plain wild.

'Wow, he's gorgeous,' I said. 'If I was twenty-odd years younger . . .'

'You'd be a geeky, flat-chested teenager with a flick from hell and he wouldn't give you a second look,' cut in Frankie. I made a face at her.

'I've got no idea why she was my best friend,' I said to Emily. 'She always had rubbish taste in men as well.' Emily giggled.

'Anyway,' said Frankie to Emily, 'we'll leave you to your vampire gazing. Make sure you're ready to go out in half an hour, and no bathroom hogging, Claire'll want to freshen up and get changed.' Frankie shut the door behind her. I started laughing.

'What?' said Frankie.

'It's good to know that nothing's changed. You always used to do that, think I hadn't got dressed for wherever we were going when I actually had.'

'Oh,' said Frankie, looking at my frayed jeans and crumpled vest top. 'It is Joe's restaurant we're going to, you know. Not Pizza Hut.'

'I'll see if I can find something more suitable,' I said, grinning as I followed her downstairs and picked up my overnight bag.

Frankie looked me up and down when I arrived back in the kitchen ten minutes later wearing cropped trousers and a square-necked top.

'Will I be allowed in?' I asked.

'I suppose so. Times are hard, they can't afford to be as choosy as normal,' smiled Frankie, reaching for the kettle. 'Tea or coffee?'

'Tea, please, milk, no sugar,' I said, sitting down at the kitchen table as directed. 'The kids are great. Emily's gorgeous.'

'She's the fifteen year old from hell sometimes.'

'She can't be harder work than you were.'

'I never had a vampire fixation. She hardly ever leaves her room, you know. She looks bloody anaemic to me. And she's always complaining about being tired when all she does is lie there swooning at Robert what's-his-name or reading that bloody book.'

'But isn't that what all the teenage girls are into these days?'

'To an extent, but she's more obsessive than the rest of them. She never goes out with other girls, no one apart from Alia, anyway, and she's as bad as her if not worse.'

I grinned at Frankie. 'You sound just like my mother used to.'

'Yeah, well, she had a point, didn't she?'

'Maybe, but I didn't think that at the time. What does Emily say when you suggest she leaves her bedroom?'

'That vampires don't like sunshine.'

I smiled, wishing I'd come up with a line that good when I was Emily's age.

'There you go then, you're fighting a losing battle. Give up and let her indulge it. She'll probably grow out of it soon.'

'Like you did, you mean?' Frankie turned to look at me seriously for a moment.

'Is that what the problem is? You're worried she's going to do something daft?'

'You can't blame me, can you? For worrying about her. When I remember what happened to you . . .'

'That was me, not Emily. She appears to have her head screwed on a lot better than I did.'

'I hope you're right,' said Frankie, putting two mugs of tea on the table. 'For all our sakes.'

By the time we arrived outside Joe's restaurant in Waltham Cross, courtesy of Frankie's erratic driving in the people-carrier, we were running considerably late (Emily did hog the bathroom) and were all rather frazzled (the younger kids argued about whether Stephanie or Sportacus was the best character in *Lazy Town* all the way there).

The restaurant was on the high street, not far from the station. I seemed to remember a carpet shop, a newsagent's and a dry cleaner's being there before, but the whole parade had now been taken over by convenience stores and fast-food outlets with neon lights. The London creep into Hertfordshire had become an onslaught. The restaurant itself had a stylish black and silver frontage. I looked up at the sign: Ristorante Ricotta.

'Was it named after your favourite cheese?' I asked Frankie as she got the younger children out of the car.

'Oh, I haven't told you that, have I? Ricotta's our surname.'

I managed to hold my composure for a second before a snort, followed by a snigger, came out.

'Sorry,' I said. 'Very juvenile of me.'

'It's all right,' said Frankie. 'I guess I gave you enough stick about being called Skidmore over the years. Time for you to get your own back. We've heard them all, mind. Joe's known as the big cheese at work and I've been called Mamma Ricotta on occasions.'

I shook my head, imagining how horrified she'd have been at the prospect of the name change at sixteen. Joe had to be some guy for her to saddle herself with that surname. I imagined a Marco Pierre White type figure, a brooding mix of charm, temperament and dark Latin looks.

Frankie herded the children into the restaurant. We were eating early, it was mainly other families there, but somehow I suspected our table was going to be noisier than anyone else's.

'Daddy,' Sophia shouted and ran over to a man standing

in the kitchen doorway, dressed in black and white checked trousers and a white top and hat. He was big, bigger than Frankie. On the short side, virtually bald and wearing dark-rimmed rectangular glasses. He couldn't have looked less like Matt Goodyear if he'd tried. Or less like the sort of man I'd imagined Frankie would marry. He bent down, scooped up Sophia in his arms and gave her a huge kiss before putting her down and coming over to greet Frankie with a kiss on the lips.

'Claire, this is my husband, Joe,' said Frankie.

'Delighted to meet you, Claire,' said Joe, kissing me on both cheeks. 'From what I hear, you two were as thick as thieves when you were teenagers.'

'Yeah, we were quite a double act.'

'You'll have to fill me in later,' said Joe, tapping his nose. 'I pay good money for information, you know.'

I laughed and looked over at Frankie. She was gazing at Joe with a look so warm, so loving on her face that it brought tears to my eyes. I wasn't sure if I'd ever loved anyone like that. Not even Andy.

The children clustered around Joe. He spoke to each in turn and gave them a wink or ruffled their hair. Sophia gazed up at him in utter adoration. Emily kissed him fondly on the cheek. Emily who, I guessed, was not his own but clearly regarded him as a father. He was indeed the big cheese. Frankie had found someone very special indeed.

Joe ushered us to a table. The children began arguing over who was going to sit next to him. 'As soon as the food's ready I'll come and sit with you,' he told them. 'All of you in turn. We'll play musical chairs.'

I leant across to Frankie. 'I doubt if the Pope would get a better reception,' I said.

'They all worship him,' said Frankie. 'Paulo even boasted in the playground once that his dad cooked better pizzas than anyone else's dad. He's a real hero. I'm just the one who shouts at them all the time.'

'Hey, I'm sure they're proud of you as well,' I said.

'Maybe, but you can't boast about your mum selling bras that are bigger than anyone else's bras.'

'Is that what you do?' I laughed.

'Yep, I run an internet company selling luxury lingerie for larger ladies. Sexy stuff, not belly-warmers.'

'What, peephole bras and crotchless knickers?'

'The works.' Frankie winked. 'Including stuff you certainly can't find in M and S.'

'You'll have to show me later,' I said.

'They won't fit you, I'm afraid. Cup sizes start at DD. We're not called Ample Bosoms for nothing.'

I laughed and shook my head.

'You'll have to watch it,' I said. 'I might just launch a lingerie company of my own for the less well endowed.'

'What will you call it?' asked Frankie.

'Fried Eggs,' I replied.

'Now,' said Frankie when she finally came downstairs later, having put the younger children to bed and left Emily reading by a nightlight, 'what was that you said about wine and chocolates?'

'I thought you'd still be stuffed,' I said, reaching into my overnight bag and passing Frankie a bottle of Cabernet

Sauvignon and the truffles. The food, unsurprisingly, had been fantastic. Joe's house speciality spinach and ricotta cannelloni was the best I'd ever tasted. And the slice of wood-fired pizza which Emily had passed me (none of the other kids would give any of theirs up) had made me vow never to go to a pizza chain again.

'Thanks,' said Frankie, ripping open the cellophane. 'The thing is, chocolates aren't food, they're soft drugs for mums.' She took a couple, passed the box back to me, grabbed two wine glasses from the kitchen (the large sort which lull you into thinking you can't be drunk when you are), plonked herself back down on the sofa next to me and filled the glasses almost to the rim.

'And don't worry if I get pissed, because Joe will be able to carry me upstairs when he gets back from work.' She raised her glass. 'Cheers. So what are we drinking to?'

'Old times?'

'Nah, let's go for new beginnings,' said Frankie, clinking her glass against mine and taking a large gulp. 'The past's overrated if you ask me.'

'What do you mean?'

'I only went on to Friends Reunited because I was nosy and wondered what you were up to. I'm not into all this looking back through rose-tinted spectacles lark; it wasn't that good as far as I can remember.'

'We had some laughs, didn't we?'

'Yeah, but there was some pretty crap stuff as well. Or have you forgotten how horrible it was being a teenager?'

I took a sip of the wine. I hadn't forgotten the bad bits. But I hadn't forgotten the good parts either.

'I hated some of it. But I liked the hopes and the dreams. The idea that you could do anything, be anyone you wanted to be.'

Frankie snorted a laugh. 'Only it didn't turn out that way, did it?'

I hesitated, eyeing her over the top of my glass. Wondering if she still had hers.

'Have you read the list?' I asked.

'What list?'

'The "Twenty Years From Now" list we did.'

'Oh, that old tosh. I found it when I was having a clearout before the twins were born, had a good laugh and threw it away.'

'You haven't got it any more?'

'No. Why would I keep it?'

'I wanted to know what you put.'

Frankie laughed. 'What, so you could take the piss?'

'No. Well, maybe a little bit. I was just interested. I found mine, you see. Only a couple of weeks ago. I'd forgotten all about it, and when I opened it . . .'

'You thought, "What a sad, deluded teenager I was" and chucked yours in the bin too,' finished Frankie.

'Well, er, no, actually. It made me think.'

Frankie rolled her eyes and shook her head. 'You haven't changed a bit, have you? You always did think too much. Analyse everything, worry yourself stupid.'

'It was just weird, seeing this life I'd imagined for myself.'

'Don't tell me, you said you were going to be married to Andy Pailes, living in some picture-book cottage with two adorable mini-Andy and mini-me kids while running

129

the country and bringing the tyrants of the world to justice.'

I shrugged. Put like that it did sound faintly ridiculous. Well, OK, highly ridiculous.

'Nothing seems to have turned out how I planned, that's all.'

'Do you think I planned this?' Frankie said, gesturing around her. 'Living in some chaotic semi with four kids and having to buy all my clothes from Evans.'

'I guess not,' I said, smiling. 'But you're happy, aren't you?'

'I'm the happiest I've ever been. Joe's wonderful, he treats me like a princess and he's my best friend. I love being a mum – even if the kids do my head in at times. And I'm happy with myself – I wouldn't mind dropping a dress size or two but I'm not beating myself up about it, and I'm certainly not going to stop eating chocolates,' she said, helping herself to another.

'And you don't ever think about what could have been?'

'I tried it, Claire. When I worked as a travel rep. I was living it up in the Costa del Sol. I fell in love with a tall, dark, handsome Spanish rep who made Matt look positively ordinary. I thought I'd found my dream man. Had my dream life.'

'So what happened?'

'Emily's what happened.'

'Oh.' I nodded sympathetically. 'I take it he didn't stick around?'

'Did a runner the morning after I told him I was up the duff. Never saw or heard from him again.'

130

'What a bastard. That must have been so tough for you.'

'It was. I came back here with my tail between my legs. Mum disowned me and kicked me out of the house.'

'But that's awful. How could she do that to her own daughter?'

'I'd sinned, hadn't I? Gone against the Pope. Therefore I had to be excommunicated.'

'What did you do?'

'Declared myself homeless and got a council flat in Cheshunt.'

Something clicked inside my head.

'That must have been when we lost touch. I sent you an invite to my wedding . . .'

'Your wedding?'

'Yeah, David, the guy I was seeing.' I noticed Frankie looking down at my left hand. For the ring which wasn't there. 'Oh, we split up about eight years ago. Irreconcil-able differences as us lawyers say. Anyway, the invite came back marked "No longer at this address". I thought your whole family must have moved. That you didn't want to stay in touch for some reason.'

'No. Just my mum's way of sticking the knife in. It was like I no longer existed.'

'Bloody hell. I'm so sorry. If I'd had any idea, I would have come and hammered on her door, demanded to know where you were.'

Frankie shrugged. 'Oh well, at least you've found me now.'

I smiled and leant over to give her a hug. She stayed holding me for a long time.

'What about your dad?' I asked, when she eventually looked up.

'He couldn't stop her; you know how she ruled the place. He was caught in the middle. He made secret visits to the flat. Bought me stuff for Emily whenever he could spare the cash without Mum noticing. He doted on her but he died when she was one. Heart attack. Not surprising really, considering the stress it all caused him.'

I reached out and squeezed her hand, remembering how she'd always adored her father.

'And that wasn't enough to make your mum see sense?'

'Nope. She blanked me at the funeral. Connie said she blamed me for him dying. Wouldn't even so much as look at Emily.'

'You must have been in bits.'

'I was. Until Joe put me back together again. I met him at the funeral. He'd taken his father, who'd been an old friend of Dad's; they'd worked together at the council. He stopped to offer us a lift when he saw me and Emily waiting at the bus stop in the rain afterwards and that's where it all started. Well, how the friendship started. The rest just grew from there. And I know what you thought when you first met him because I thought that too. He wasn't the sort of guy I'd look twice at. But when you've been that low and someone comes along and treats you like you're the most amazing woman on earth, well, you start to believe it. And that's when you realise that looks count for nothing at the end of the day; it's what's inside that counts.'

'You're right,' I said. 'But I never thought I'd hear you say that.'

'I guess it's one of the lessons life teaches you. And here's another one,' said Frankie, giggling as she leant closer. 'The good-looking guys are crap at sex; they don't have to try, you see. But Joe, well, he's found places I never knew I had.' We cracked up laughing on the sofa together, me nearly spilling my wine, Frankie almost dropping the chocolates.

'And I suppose you're going to tell me you couldn't possibly comment because you've only ever had the good-looking ones,' Frankie grinned. 'Your ex, David, what did he look like?'

'Pretty damn good, I guess. Dark hair, dark eyes, stubble, sporty body.'

'You've just described Andy.'

I hesitated, having always been in denial that David's physical similarity to Andy had been the attraction.

'Not really. David was a bit taller and his hair was different.' Frankie looked unconvinced.

'Where did you meet him?'

'He was a solicitor at the firm I did my training contract with. A real hotshot corporate lawyer. He was nine years older than me, incredibly intelligent. I guess I was a bit in awe of him.'

'Sounds familiar,' said Frankie.

'Yeah, well, I couldn't believe it when he made a move for me. And I fell hook, line and sinker as usual. It was all very intense: he proposed six months after we got together and we were married within a year.'

'So what went wrong?'

'He was a workaholic. Should have seen the warning

signs really. We had a registry office wedding and only a weekend away for a honeymoon because he had a big case on at work. He got a partnership at another firm not long after we married and I never saw him. He worked crazy hours, evenings, weekends, the lot. As Princess Di would have said, "There were three people in our marriage and it was a bit crowded", only in my case it wasn't a person, it was his work which got in the way. And there's not much you can do to fight that.'

'How long did it last?'

'Seven years. I was made redundant when we'd been married six years and it was downhill all the way from there. He was too busy to be supportive and it was like we were moving in different worlds. By the time I got the job where I am now, it was too late. He didn't even show up for the celebration takeout I'd ordered for us because he'd been too busy at work to go out for a meal. He phoned me from the office to offer me a divorce, like it was some kind of plea bargain.'

Frankie shook her head. 'I hope you took him to the cleaners.'

'Not really. The only thing of his I kept was the surname. I'd put up with being a Skidmore for that long I couldn't face going back to it. Which is why I'm plain old Cooper now.'

'So you're still single?' asked Frankie.

'Yeah, but I've been seeing a guy called Mark for two years. He's a solicitor too but he couldn't be more different from David. He's great. Makes me laugh, easy to talk to, doesn't mess me about and doesn't take work too seriously.'

'What's the catch?'

'There isn't one. He wants us to buy a house together, actually.'

'So why don't you sound very enthusiastic?'

I hadn't been aware it was so obvious. My finger traced the rim of my wine glass.

'I'm just not sure about it, that's all. Having already made a hash of things once, I want to make sure it's the right decision. And then when I read the list . . .'

'Fucking hell, Claire. You can't turn the guy down because he's not Andy Pailes.'

'No, it's not that.'

'So what is it?'

'It just feels like I'm kissing goodbye to all those hopes and dreams I had. Mark arranged for us to view this new build in a cul-de-sac, and I know he meant well but it scared the life out of me. I could see this future where we had net curtains and stayed in the same jobs for ever and had two point four children and a Volvo and . . .' My voice turned squeaky and trailed off. It was Frankie's turn to put her arm around me.

'You're a funny onion, you are. We grew up, Claire. We're nearly forty. It's time to get your head out of the clouds.'

I nodded although I wasn't entirely sure I'd be able to breathe the air down below, so long it was since I'd been there.

'Anyway,' I said, doing my best to pull myself together, 'I bet you still get a tingle every week when you see Matt on Sky Sports.'

'Not really. Joe and the kids just have a good laugh at him at my expense.'

'You can't blame them, can you? Some of the things he wears . . .'

'It's not his fault. Jane always did have lousy fashion sense. I bet she buys all those shirts for him.'

I gasped, about to berate her for still being on the hapless Jane's back, when I saw the grin spread across her face.

'Now who needs to grow up?' I laughed, reaching for another chocolate.

Saturday, 31 August 1985

The train pulled out of Potters Bar station. Jerking forward, taking me closer to Andy. I'd hardly slept the night
before. Tossing and turning. Thinking about seeing him
again. Praying he'd remember me.

Frankie settled back in her seat, crossing her miniskirted
legs so exaggeratedly I could see her knickers and suspend-
ers. It reminded me of that 'all in the best possible taste'
woman Kenny Everett did on TV. Except Frankie made it
look sexy. I saw her gaze drop to my hands, which were
fiddling with the handles of my bag.

'So, did you get Andy a birthday card then?' she asked.

'Yeah, but . . .'

'But what?'

'I dunno whether to give it to him. He might think I'm
desperate.'

'You are.'

'I don't want him to know that, do I?'

'Show us what you've written inside, and I'll tell you
whether it sounds desperate.'

'I can't. I've stuck the envelope down now.' I hadn't
really. But I knew that if I showed Frankie the card and

she held it up to the light she would see the indentation of three kisses (which I'd decided had looked too familiar) beneath the Tipp-Ex.

'Suit yourself,' Frankie said, turning to stare out of the window, her leather jacket squeaking with each jolt of the train. She looked good in that outfit. If she had been going to my nan and grandad's golden wedding she would probably have given Grandad a heart attack dressed like that. Sex appeal seemed to ooze from her pores. The only thing that came out of my pores was sweat.

'D'ya reckon Matt'll take Jane to the do?' I asked.

'S'pose he'll have to. She'll probably look a right state, mind. All lumpy thighs and fat arse.'

'You shouldn't say that, it's not nice. She is nearly thirty.'

'If I look like that by the time I'm thirty, you have permission to shoot me.'

'OK,' I said, laughing. I knew I wouldn't have to though. I couldn't imagine Frankie ever looking less than perfect.

'What'll you do if Andy has someone with him?' Frankie asked. 'Some leggy model with big tits.'

'He won't.'

'How come you're so sure?'

' 'Cos I know him. He's got more class than that.'

By the time the train pulled into Hornsey station I had an unshakeable image in my head of Andy arriving with Sam Fox on one arm and Linda Lusardi on the other.

I loved Hornsey High Road. It was dirty and smelly and tatty. It was how London should be. I imagined how it would look on a match day, the crowd moving in one great swell, a sea of royal blue. The sound of fans chanting, of turnstiles clicking. One day, when I had my mum off my back, I'd be part of all that.

We didn't go to the main gates first. It was only five o'clock and the do didn't start till seven thirty. So we wandered down to the club shop. It was like stepping into Santa's grotto when you were a kid. Only the presents weren't wrapped up, they were displayed right in front of your eyes. Wall-to-wall United. You couldn't ask for anything more. Except maybe Andy Pailes in a little room somewhere, asking you to sit on his lap.

I had a fiver of saved pocket money with me, which I knew wouldn't go very far. So it was important to get as much of Andy as I could for my money. The shop was full of Matt stuff. Posters, Matt Goodyear fan club pencil cases, notebooks and key rings. I was glad Andy didn't have a fan club. I didn't want him cheapened like that. Eventually I found a programme containing an interview with Andy and a postcard-sized photo of him in action. Which just left me enough for the new team poster.

Frankie was still gazing at the array of Matt goods on offer.

'Are you getting anything?' I asked.

'Only that,' she said, pointing to a baseball cap with Matt's picture on the front. It was last season's so the photo was pre-perm. I guessed that was why she was getting it.

We approached the counter. I recognised the woman serving from the training ground. She was in her thirties and wearing a high-necked cream blouse with a ruffle and a velvet bow and sporting a mousy Princess Di hairstyle that only served to accentuate the fact that she wasn't

nearly as pretty or young as Princess Di, and also happened
to be at least six inches shorter and a good six inches wider
(apart from which, the likeness was uncanny).

'Hello there,' she said, nodding in recognition. 'What
can I get you two?'

Frankie asked for the cap.

'Oh, you're a fan of Matt's, are you?' she said. 'He was
in here with his wife only a couple of days ago, buying
some of our United baby clothes they were.'

'Baby clothes?' repeated Frankie.

'Yeah, Matt's going to be a dad. Right chuffed he seemed
about it.'

Frankie's face appeared to slip off her head and slide on
to the floor, like something out of a cartoon. For a minute
I thought she was going to burst into tears. Until I remembered that Frankie was much too stylish to cry.

'Well, thanks for breaking the good news,' she snapped
at the Princess Di look-nothing-like. 'Remind me to spoil
your day sometime.' She picked up the cap, threw the
money down on the counter and flounced out of the shop.

'She's Italian,' I said by way of explanation as I paid for
my stuff and hurried after her.

'Are you OK?' I said, when I caught up with Frankie
outside.

'Never been better,' she said, scraping her stiletto heels
across the concrete.

'Nothing much you can do about that, is there?'

'Except hope Jane gets so fat she explodes,' Frankie said
over her shoulder as she set off back up the road.

When we got to the main gates, we saw another woman

we recognised from the training ground leaning casually against the wall, fag in hand. She was called Dawn (if her gold name pendant was to be believed, and I'd never known anyone wear a false one) and she looked about twenty. She had long, peroxide-blond hair, which needed the roots doing, and a heavily made-up face. The first time we'd seen her, Frankie had said that she looked as if she worked on the make-up counter at Boots, had taken the wrong turning and ended up at the training ground by mistake. Dawn eyed us both up and down without saying a word. I gave her a half-smile. Frankie scowled at her.

By seven o'clock there were a dozen or so fans waiting outside the gates. Mostly kids apart from us and Dawn. We were looking out expectantly for the first car when the woman who had served us in the shop came round the corner.

'You two still here?' she said. I wondered if she had some sort of affliction where she kept stating the obvious. 'My name's Susan, by the way,' she continued.

'I'm Claire,' I said, deciding I might as well talk to her if she really did know the players.

'You calmed down yet?' she asked, turning to Frankie.

'I've had better days,' Frankie replied.

'You were wasting your time there anyway, love,' said Susan. 'Matt's devoted to Jane, he'd never mess her around.'

'How come you know all this?' said Frankie.

'You get to know all sorts, working at the shop.'

'Like what?' I asked, wondering what she knew about Andy.

'Well,' said Susan, lowering her voice, 'Nobber went out with her over there.' She nodded in the direction of Dawn.

'How long for?' I asked.

'Oh, only a few weeks. This is Nobber we're talking about.'

A few minutes later Nobber swung round the corner in his black Escort XR3i. There was a woman sitting next to him. Long curly blond hair, kind of pretty but tarty with it. My mum would have made some comment about her running out of material for her dress. The driver's window was down but as soon as Nobber caught sight of Dawn he wound it up and drove straight through with no more than a wave at the waiting fans.

I saw Dawn mouth the word 'bastard' before turning on her heel and strutting off up the road, biting her bottom lip. I felt a bit sorry for her. But there again I couldn't understand anyone falling for Nobber in the first place.

The rest of the players started arriving in quick succession: Skip, Gibbo, Clubber, Thomo, each one accompanied by a glamorous wife or girlfriend. I wondered if there was some kind of designer footballer's girlfriend/wife shop in London that supplied all the players. Every model came with long legs, big tits, big hair, nice teeth and a little black dress. I could just about qualify on the long legs criteria but failed dismally on the others. I pictured myself in the reject basket outside the shop. Waiting for some non-league player from Barnet to come along.

'Hey, look,' said Frankie, 'here comes the birthday boy.'

I looked up to see Andy's silver Golf edging towards us. I didn't look at him straight away. I looked at the passenger seat. It was empty. I gave a huge sigh. Andy was a vision in black. He even looked good in a bow tie, where most of the others had looked like complete dicks. He stopped just out-side the gates. I let the kids go first. I didn't want them around cramping my style. As he signed the last autograph he looked up and flashed me a smile good enough to die for.

'Hi, Claire,' he said. 'How are you?' He'd remembered my name. We were on first-name terms. It was only a matter of time now.

'Fine, thanks,' I said, holding out the photo of us; the original, not one of the reprints. 'Could you sign this, please?'

'Sure. It's a nice photo is that.'

'Thanks,' I said, wondering if the compliment was meant for me, Frankie who'd taken it or Kodak who'd developed it.

'And, er, um, this is for you,' I said, pulling the card from my bag and handing it to him. 'Happy birthday.'

He hesitated for a moment, as if he wasn't quite sure what to do.

'Oh, thanks very much. That's doubled my tally in one go.'

I grinned, wondering who the other card was from, as Andy took the envelope, opened it, made a suitable 'aahh' sound at the picture of the puppy in football boots on the front of the card, and thanked me again before putting it on the passenger seat. If he did notice the Tipp-Ex he was good enough not to say anything.

'Hope you have a good night,' I said.

'Thanks, I'll do my best.'

He flashed me another smile and was gone, sweeping through the gates into the car park, out of sight.

I strode back to Frankie triumphantly.

'See, I told you he was different.'

'He's different all right,' chipped in Susan. 'Only one without a wife or girlfriend.'

'So?' I said.

'Well, you've seen the earring, love. Work it out for yourself.' Susan winked at me and walked off.

I turned to find Frankie laughing. 'She's got a point,' she said.

'Piss off,' I said. 'You're only jealous.'

And she was, I knew that. Because I had Andy all to myself and Matt belonged to someone else. Someone who, far from looking a 'right state', as Frankie put it, actually looked the best I'd ever seen her when she arrived with Matt a few minutes later. Frankie knew it too. She went up and got an autograph from Matt, but he didn't even bother to look up and see who he was signing for. He only had eyes for Jane.

We waited until we'd seen all the players arrive. I didn't want to leave. I wanted to stay all night, so I could feel close to Andy. Could say I'd spent his birthday night with him. We had to go though. Frankie had told her mum she'd be back by nine.

My mum picked us up from the station as we'd arranged.

'Have you got the cake?' I asked.

'Yes,' she said, handing over a brown paper bag with the grease from the buttercream filling coming through it. 'Though I wish I knew what you two are up to.'

'Thanks,' said Frankie, taking the bag. 'It's just that Claire said you still had some of the golden wedding cake left, and you know how much my mum likes your baking.'

Mum looked at us in the rear-view mirror. 'Mmm,' she said, sounding unconvinced. 'I'd better get you home.' We clambered into the back of the car and Mum drove off.

'Oh, I meant to tell you,' she said as we were waiting at the traffic lights in the High Road. 'My friend Rachel's doing the catering for that do at United tonight. Some last-minute job when it turned out the usual firm was double-booked.'

I looked at Frankie and we both rolled our eyes at the same time. 'Now she tells us,' I hissed, rueing the lost chance of a ticket to the ball.

The room begins to fill with guests, mostly office staff and members of the supporters club. I self-consciously pull my skirt down and straighten my blouse. It is a simple uniform, black skirt and white top. I am relieved I don't have to wear an apron or a ridiculous hat like the waitresses in the Little Chef. I've had to wear my hair up but I don't mind that. It actually makes me look older, more sophisticated even.

I thread between the guests, smiling, tray of canapés in hand. Looking, searching everywhere. But still no Andy. The wives and girlfriends gather at one end of the room. Greeting each other with kisses on both cheeks, then laughing as they rub the lipstick marks off each other. They all stand in a certain way. One hip slightly out, the other leg (always the one with the split up the skirt), pointing diagonally outwards. Occasionally they throw back their heads and laugh, or toss their hair. They all look immaculate, they all look the same. A blur of black and blond and gold, tinkling and shimmering. Knowing they have what everyone else in the room wants. A piece of United to call their own. I am not one of them yet but I will be soon. I want it more than anything else in the world. And if you want something badly enough it will come to you. I know that.

The guests are asked to take their seats. I return to the kitchen to collect the first of the starters. I am given tables three and four to look after. As I approach table three at the far end of the room I see Andy at last. He doesn't have anyone with him. He looks absolutely gorgeous in his dinner jacket. I reach over to give him his starter.

'Thanks,' he says, looking up at me. He continues looking for several seconds before his face breaks into a smile.

'Hello again. I didn't know you worked here.'

'I don't usually,' I say. 'I'm just helping out for the night.'

'Well I'm glad you're here,' Andy says. 'I was dreading turning up to this on my own. But I'm not on my own now, am I?'

I blush and look down before hurrying away, smiling to myself. Every time I go back to the table Andy smiles at me. He can't say much, not with all the others there. But he doesn't need to. I can see it in his eyes.

I stand attentively behind his table during the after-dinner speeches. It is only when the dancing starts and the other players clear off to the bar that I finally get to be alone with him. 'Move Closer' by Phyllis Nelson comes on. Andy reaches out for my hand.

'May I have the pleasure of this dance?' he says.

I smile and let him take my hand and lead me across to the centre of the dance floor. Other couples move out of the way. I hear whispers; one of the players' wives asking what he's doing dancing with a waitress. I don't care though. Because he has his arms around me. And I am not a waitress now. I am one of them. They just don't know it yet.

Five

'Will you represent me, Miss Cooper?' My heart sank as I recognised Jake Dennison's voice. I turned around to see him standing there in his familiar Manchester City shirt and a pair of jeans which defied the laws of science by staying together despite the fact that there were clearly more holes than denim left in them.

'Hi, Jake,' I said. 'It only seems like five minutes since I last saw you.'

'It was. I'm up for a breach of probation.'

I let out a deep sigh. I had a soft spot for Jake. He had never hurt anyone; he'd just been brought up to believe that if you wanted something you simply went out and nicked it. This from his mother, only it turned out she was actually his grandmother. His real mother, who he'd always believed was his older sister, had got pregnant with him at thirteen. Coming from that sort of background, he'd done remarkably well to stay clean, sober, relatively sane and be nothing worse than a serial thief and occasional burglar.

'Oh Jake, it's not that I don't like you, but I was kind of hoping it might be a bit longer this time.'

'I know. It was like one of those impulse purchases you

ladies have. Only it wasn't in a shop, of course. And I didn't pay for it.'

'What did you take, Jake?'

'A turkey,' he said. I considered this statement for a moment before asking the obvious question.

'Dead or alive?'

'Alive.'

I nodded. Jake's list of 'previous' was fairly eclectic by Rochdale standards. But livestock was, as far as I was aware, a new venture for him.

'I feel quite a story coming on, Jake. I think I'm going to need a strong cup of coffee and a croissant. Can I get you anything?'

'How much is toast?' asked Jake.

'It doesn't matter, I'm buying. And I take it you'd like your usual cup of sugar with some tea thrown in?'

Jake grinned. 'Nice one, Miss Cooper.'

Jill did the honours and we settled down at a corner table in the public part of the café.

'Come on then,' I said. 'Let's hear it. From the beginning if you don't mind.'

'I was walking along Catley Lane Head, minding me own business, like, when I saw this bird. A feathered one, like, I'm not being funny. Anyway, it was in a field, not tied down or anything. I didn't even know what sort of bird it was at first, but then it came nearer the fence and started making this gobbling noise and I realised it was a turkey.' Jake took a break for a mouthful of toast and a slurp of tea. I braced myself for the next instalment.

'So, I looked around and I couldn't see any other turkeys

or a farmer, like, and I wasn't even sure if it belonged to anyone.' I decided against pointing out that wild turkeys were not common in that part of Rochdale. 'And then I noticed some sort of sack in the corner of the field. And that's when I had the idea of nicking it.'

'So it wasn't stolen to order?'

'Oh no. I was just using me head, like. What with Christmas being not too far away and that.'

'Right,' I said, nodding. 'So what happened next?'

'Well, I caught it and put it in the sack. Only trouble was, it was flapping around inside and I kept having to stop. And I'd only been walking about five minutes when a bloody cop car came past.'

'And I take it that as you know the local cops pretty well, they stopped and asked what you had in the sack?'

'That's right. So I just said nothing, but the bloody bird started screeching and flapping its wings. That's when one of them got out the car and asked to have a look inside. I pretended I was surprised at first, that I hadn't realised there was a turkey in there, like. But I'm not sure they bought it.'

I gazed down into my coffee, trying to keep a straight face as I imagined how anyone could inadvertently pick up a sack with a live turkey in it and carry it along the road for five minutes without realising it was in there.

'OK,' I said. 'I'm going to have my work cut out on this one but I'll give it a go. The first thing you'll have to do is apologise for trying to cover it up. And we'll need to stress that it was an opportunistic crime rather than a premeditated one and that you were not intending to do the bird any harm. That is right, isn't it?'

'Oh yeah, I wouldn't have killed it myself. I don't like turkey anyway. We usually have a KFC bucket for Christmas dinner.'

I nodded and watched Jake drain the last dregs of tea from his mug. Somehow, I sensed this was going to be a long day.

'Is that a turkey roll you've got?' Fiona grinned when I joined her table at lunchtime. 'Only don't gobble it all up at once.'

'News travels fast round here,' I said, sitting down with my cheese salad roll. Fiona hadn't even been in the same courtroom as me.

'Yeah, well I heard you did a bootiful job getting an adjournment.'

'Am I going to get this for the rest of the year?' I asked.

'I suspect so. I'll certainly be putting my turkey order your way in the run-up to Christmas.'

'You've got to hand it to the lad, he's nothing if not enterprising.'

'I know. And I've got to thank you and your young friend for brightening up my morning. Boy, did I need it.'

'Why, what's up?'

'Oh, just Aidan again.' Fiona's fifteen-year-old son was going through some sort of rebellious stage and had fallen in with the wrong crowd. 'He was out till one a.m. on Friday night after they broke up from school. Wouldn't tell us where he'd been or who he'd been with.'

'He's a teenager. That's what they do.'

'No, this is different. It's this new bunch of kids he's been hanging out with. There was graffiti on some of the walls near us on Saturday morning. And the bus shelter had been smashed.'

'Aidan wouldn't do anything like that, would he?'

'I don't know. His so-called mates could be putting him up to it. Goading him to get into trouble because he's a copper's son.'

'What does Neil think?'

'He told Aidan to be big enough to tell his mates to fuck off if they tell him to do something he doesn't want to. But I don't think he's strong enough to do that.'

'I wasn't when I was his age,' I said.

'Did you get hassle from other kids at school then?'

'Yeah. Doesn't everyone?'

'I didn't,' said Fiona.

'Yeah, but I bet you were a mouthy cow.'

'Was that meant as an insult?'

'No, compliment actually. I can't imagine you taking any crap. And that's a good thing. I wish I'd been able to give as good as I got at that age.'

'Trouble is I want to be Aidan's mouthy mum minder, but unfortunately I don't think that'd go down too well. I guess he'll have to sort it out for himself. I just worry he's going to end up in here one day. Give it a few years, he could be one of your failed criminals from hell.'

'No, he'll sort himself out. You'll see. Just keep him well away from any untethered farm animals in the meantime.'

My next case after lunch was adjourned – some cock-up with getting the right papers by the CPS – which meant I had a rare hour or so to myself.

I knew exactly what I was going to do. Something I should probably have done a long time ago. But the time was right now. The turkey case had tipped me over. I set up my laptop in a quiet corner of the café and went to the *Guardian*'s legal jobs website. It felt good simply to do it. Taking myself by the scruff of the neck and hauling myself towards the life I was supposed to be living. And maybe still could.

The first disappointment was how few jobs there were under the north-west and Yorkshire and Humberside sections. Five in total. And when I looked more closely, a couple of those were for legal secretaries and a couple more for legal caseworkers. There was only one job for a qualified solicitor. At a large corporate firm in Manchester. They wanted someone to specialise in employment law, which I'd had plenty of experience in at the previous firm I'd worked for. It was a proper job with a proper salary. And it wasn't in Rochdale. And I wouldn't be dealing with people who stole turkeys or were dared to rob a bank with an unloaded water pistol. I saved the page to favourites and opened up a Word document. 'Curriculum Vitae' I typed at the top. Because I was actually going to do this. I was taking back control of my life.

My mind was still full of my job application when I got to Mark's after work. I pressed the intercom for flat number 7. Silence for a few seconds and then a click.

'Hi, come on up,' said Mark.

'You're supposed to check who it is first. I could be a crazed bunny-boiler hitwoman for all you know,' I said.

'OK,' said Mark. 'Tell me something about me that nobody else knows.'

'You farted the first time we had sex,' I said. Laughter from the other end of the intercom – and a cough from behind. I turned round to see a young man standing there with a broad smirk on his face.

'Beam me up, Scotty,' I mumbled feebly into the intercom. I was still squirming in embarrassment when I arrived at the top of the stairs (I hadn't been able to face joining the smirking man in the lift). The door to Mark's flat was ajar, the smell of garlic and onions wafting out on to the landing.

'Hiya. You may want to avoid one of your neighbours for a while,' I said as I walked in and shut the door behind me.

'Why?' asked Mark, turning around from the cooker to face me. It was his hair I noticed first. It had gone. Well, some of it anyway. The wispy, floppy strands shorn much closer to his head. It was only then that my gaze dropped to his clothes, none of which I'd ever seen before. In place of the usual jeans, T-shirt and trainers was an expensive-looking grey shirt with oversized cuffs and collar, a pair of baggy black trousers with a twisted seam and some smart suede shoes with a large buckle on the front.

'Why?' I repeated.

'Yes, why avoid the neighbour?'

'Oh, he overheard my end of the conversation on the intercom. Must have sounded pretty weird. Er, what's the occasion?'

Mark shrugged as if it was no big deal that he'd entirely

changed his appearance since the last time I'd seen him three days ago.

'I told you I went to a new hairdresser's on Saturday; fancied a bit of a change, that's all. Don't you like it?'

'Yeah, I do. At least I think I do. It may take me a while to get used to it, that's all. What about the gear? Where did you get that?'

'King Street.'

I nodded, although still not quite understanding. Mark had spent a small fortune in shops frequented by Premiership footballers. The same Mark who usually balked at the idea of buying a new pair of trousers from Next unless they were in the sale.

'So what brought this on?'

'Just thought it was time I updated my image a bit,' he said. 'Made more of an effort. Though if I look like a complete prat, please tell me.'

I put my briefcase down and walked over to him, noticing the smell as soon as I did so. Mark had aftershave on. He never wore aftershave.

'You look great,' I said, running my fingers through what was left of his hair. 'It suits you, reminds me a bit of Daniel Craig.'

'Well, I'll settle for that. Still got a bit of work to do on the six-pack, mind,' he said, sliding his arms around my waist.

'Don't worry, I'll make sure I don't take any photos of you emerging from the water in your Speedos.'

'Thank you. Although I might be able to do my own stunts soon,' he said.

'What do you mean?'

'I've joined a climbing club.'

A laugh spilled out of my mouth before I could stop it.

'What?' he said.

'I'm sorry, but you were the one who famously said, "I hate stairs", that time the lift was broken. You even talked about getting a ground-floor flat so you could avoid them altogether.'

'I'm not climbing stairs. It's a climbing wall. A massive place in Rochdale. I did a taster session on Sunday and signed up on a beginners' course. Then when I get good enough they do trips out rock-climbing and abseiling. That sort of thing.'

'Oh, right. Great,' I said, trying desperately to be encouraging and supportive while wondering what the hell was going on. 'Only I didn't think you had a head for heights?'

'Well, sometimes you have to push yourself a bit. Go outside your comfort zone.'

I nodded again, convinced this wasn't Mark talking and he'd been brainwashed by some sort of trendy extreme-sports sect while I'd been at Frankie's.

'Sure, well as long as it's not a ploy to pick up clients when they fall and break their neck.'

'I hadn't thought of that. Maybe I'll take some business cards with me next time,' he grinned, brushing the hair out of my eyes. 'Anyway, you chill out for a bit, you've had a long day. The lasagne's nearly ready.'

I kissed him on the lips and went to sit down on the sofa. I kicked off my heels and put my feet up. It was then that

I saw it. The book lying slap bang in the middle of the coffee table. *Gangs* by Ross Kemp.

'Why have you got this?' I said, holding it up in the air.

'A guy at the climbing club recommended it. There's some interesting stuff in it about gang culture around the world.' If I'd compiled a list of 'books least likely to be found on Mark's coffee table', the complete works of Ross Kemp would have been up there. The hair and the clothes and the rock-climbing I could put down to a rare weekend on his own with money to burn. But this took things to a whole different level.

'You're going to tell me you've joined the Territorial Army as well, aren't you?'

'Don't be daft,' said Mark, walking over and sitting down next to me. 'It's only a bloody book.'

'I'm simply trying to get my head around why you've acquired a whole new look, wardrobe and set of hobbies and interests while I was away.'

Mark looked stung. It occurred to me that this could be something to do with the house. With him feeling I'd rejected him. I reached out and stroked his hair. 'You haven't done all this on my account, have you?'

'No, of course not. I simply fancied trying something new. Didn't want to get stuck in a rut.'

'OK,' I said, still unconvinced. 'That makes two of us, then.'

Mark looked worried for a moment.

'Have you taken up macramé on ice?' he asked.

I laughed, although I could see the potential for a celebrity version on Saturday nights.

'No. But I am applying for a new job.'

Mark nodded as if he'd been expecting it, which surprised me. 'So where is it?'

'A firm called Smith MacGuire in Manchester. They want an employment law specialist, corporate stuff I think. But it's got good career prospects and it's serious money as well.'

'That'll come in handy with the new house then.'

I was thrown for a second, aware that I was agitated because this wasn't supposed to be about the new house. It was about me doing something with my life. Besides, as neither of us had even had a viewing yet, the new house thing still seemed a very long way off.

'I've just got to the point where if I don't get out of Rochdale soon I'll stay there for ever.'

'You're bloody good at it, though. Your regulars would really miss you. Having someone they can trust. Someone to fight their corner.'

I hadn't really thought of it like that. But now I did I felt bad for even contemplating deserting them.

'I've done my time though, haven't I? It's been the longest maternity cover on record. Surely I'm allowed to move on at some point.'

'Of course you are. And I know you have to put up with a lot of crap, but I do think you'd miss it more than you realise. And that this is more about what you think you should be doing than what you really want to do.'

'Why do you say that?'

'I don't know. All this business with seeing Frankie again seems to have unsettled you. Made you want to change things.'

He was right, of course. Unnervingly so. But I didn't

want to admit that. Partly because I was embarrassed about how fixated I had become with the list and partly because I didn't want him to worry about where he stood in all this. I'd never told him about Andy. And I certainly didn't want to go into it all now. Me turning down the house had undoubtedly caused a wobble in our relationship. I didn't want to make things any worse.

'It just got me thinking, that's all. About how sometimes we can lose sight of what we want to do. End up drifting. Feeling a bit rudderless.'

'Is that how you feel?' he asked, stroking my hair.

'I guess so. I always used to be so clear about where I was going, what I was going to do.'

'But you said Frankie's life was nothing like you'd expected either.'

'It isn't, but—' I broke off, realising I was about to say that she was happy. And that wouldn't sound good at all. 'Are you sure you don't mind me inviting them up?' I'd suggested a return visit to Frankie, with the whole family. Now I'd found her again I wanted to make sure we did more than just send Christmas cards.

'Of course not. I'm looking forward to meeting her. Just as long as you don't both regress to your teens and start singing Spandau Ballet and Duran Duran songs.'

'Don't worry,' I said. 'I am so over Martin Kemp.'

I kept glancing at Mark all through dinner. Trying to get used to the new look as he explained the basics of rock-climbing to me. And wondering what the real reason behind his transformation was. Even when we snuggled up on the sofa afterwards, the aftershave was disconcerting. It was like I was with a new man. Only the old one was still with me as well. He leant over and started kissing my neck. Seriously kissing it, not simply a nuzzle.

'Steady on,' I said. 'Have you been watching those vampire films again?'

He smiled, but there was a distinctly odd look on his face, half excited, half frightened to death.

'Come on,' he said, taking hold of my hand and pulling me up from the sofa. He led me past the bedroom to the front door.

'Where are you taking me?' I asked as he opened it and ushered me through.

'Out,' he said.

'But *Newsnight*'s on in half an hour.' It was kind of our week-night ritual. Curling up together on the sofa to watch Jeremy Paxman tearing some hapless politician to pieces with both of us point-scoring and seeing if we could come up with a better defence than they could for whatever it was they were alleged to have done wrong. I always insisted on staying up to see tomorrow morning's front pages at the end of the programme before we adjourned to the bedroom. Mark didn't know why. I simply told him that I didn't like getting surprises when I woke up.

'I know,' he said now. 'That's why we're going somewhere else.'

'Don't I need my jacket and bag?' I asked as he pulled the door shut behind us and pressed the button for the lift.

'Nope,' he said. 'Not unless you're planning to make a run for it afterwards.'

I looked at him, still not understanding, as we stepped inside the lift. And then a minute later the door shut, the lift stayed still and Mark started unbuttoning my shirt. Suddenly I understood all too well.

'We can't do it here,' I said as he kissed my shoulders and let the shirt fall on to the floor. I wasn't sure whether it was a climbing instructor or Ross Kemp who had advocated sex in an unusual/exciting setting. But there was no way this was something Mark would do of his own accord.

'Why not?' he asked breathlessly as he moved down to kiss my breasts.

'It's a bit *Fatal Attraction*,' I said as he pushed me up against the lift wall.

'Well you're the one who started talking about bunny-boilers, putting ideas in my head,' he replied, unclasping my bra in one deft movement and circling and flicking with his tongue.

'Now, if you're quite finished,' he said, looking up for a second with a wicked smile on his face, 'I should very much like to ravish you.' He hitched my skirt up and slipped his fingers inside my knickers. I let out a moan. He was good with his hands. Always had been. My eyes were shut, my breath rapid. Despite my initial reluctance I was actually getting turned on by this. Maybe a new man was just what I needed.

Some time later – and I mean some time – we sank down on to the floor in a damp, breathless heap.

'Jesus,' I said. 'Did you forget to mention the tantric sex course as well?'

'Yeah,' said Mark with a grin. 'Sting sends his regards.'

I laughed, and as I did so I had the sensation that the earth was moving. Mark was good but not capable of that from where he was sitting.

'Fuck,' I said. 'Somebody's called the lift.'

We scrambled to our feet as the lift descended to the ground floor. Mark pulled on his trousers. I stepped into my knickers, tugged my skirt down and, unable to locate my bra, threw my shirt back on and started buttoning fast.

The doors slid open at the bottom. A slim woman in her fifties in a buttoned-up cardigan was standing there. Mark nodded and smiled at her. She stared at us for a second. I glanced down to check I didn't have a boob hanging out before realising she was waiting for us to get out. I nudged Mark and we shuffled out, Mark smiling and nodding so much that even if she hadn't suspected anything at the beginning, she probably did by now.

'Oh God,' he said when the doors had closed behind us. 'That was Miss Watson from upstairs. She does the Christian Aid collection for the local church.'

'She's probably too prim to even suspect anything then,' I said.

We walked back up the stairs to the third floor, giggling like a couple of teenagers. The lift was waiting outside Mark's flat. The doors open. A hand protruding from inside, holding between thumb and forefinger my missing black lacy bra.

'Yours, I presume,' came a voice from inside.

I reached out and took the offending article.

'Thanks,' I muttered. The hand disappeared, the doors

shut again. 'Oops, sorry,' I said, turning to Mark. 'I guess that's another neighbour you'll have to avoid for a while.'

'Don't worry, it could have been worse.' Mark grinned. 'It could have been your knickers. Anyway, we'd better get back to the sofa.'

'You're not up for it again, are you?' I said.

'No, but Jeremy Paxman will be wondering where you are, and you might just have made tomorrow morning's front pages.'

Monday, 21 October 1985

I climbed out of bed, padded across the bedroom floor and went straight to my dressing-table mirror, pressing my face as close to it as I could while slowly curling back my top lip. The steel bar that ran across my top row of teeth gleamed menacingly back at me. I hated it, hated it more than I had ever hated anyone or anything in my life. Which was particularly worrying as I'd only had it for a few days. I couldn't help wondering how much I would hate it by the time I finished wearing it.

Six to nine months, the orthodontist had said. It might as well have been a life sentence as far as I was concerned. It was going to be a nightmare. I had decided that before I'd even got it. And nothing that had happened since had made me change my mind. The first day of wearing it at school last week had been even worse than I'd imagined. It hadn't exactly been going well before the brace. The downside of my best friend being in the year above me was that now she had left school and gone to college, I was Johnny-no-mates at break and lunchtime. It was tough getting used to not having her around. Throwing in a mouth full of metal to contend with was beyond a joke.

I'd tried to hide it at first, managing to smile with my

mouth closed at the few people who said 'awright' to me as I arrived. My vow of silence survived registration, due mainly to the fact that nobody had spoken to me, but finally succumbed to Mrs Osborne's persistent questioning in biology.

'Come on, Claire. The process by which plants turn sunlight into food. I'm sure you know the answer; perhaps you'd care to share it with us?'

The whole class had turned to look at me then, as if sensing there was some reason for my reticence.

'Photothynthethith,' I'd lisped finally, the resulting 'thank you' from Mrs Osborne drowned out by the laughter of my classmates.

By break time the news had spread. 'Oi, Metal Mickey, give us a smile.' 'Hey, Skidmark, you shouldn't eat coat hangers for breakfast, they get stuck in your teeth.' The jibes had come thick and fast. Each one making me clench my jaws ever tighter shut, until I'd begun to feel they had been wired together like my teeth.

I grimaced at my reflection in the mirror. And now today I was supposed to wear it to the training ground. Andy would never fancy me with it on. Not in a million years. It would be like asking someone to go out with the Elephant Man. And however nice he was, I couldn't expect him to do that.

'Do you want a straw for that orange juice, love, would it make it easier?' Mum asked as we sat in silence at the breakfast table. I glowered at her from under my flick.

'It just takes a bit longer than usual. I can't feel my mouth any more, it hurts so much.'

'Never mind, it will get better.'

'How do you know? You never wore one.'

'The orthodontist said so, didn't he? You've just got to get used to it. The more you wear it, the easier it will get.'

'I'm not wearing it to the training ground, if that's what you're getting at.'

The very thought of turning up to see Andy with half of Sheffield steelworks in my gob was making me feel sick.

'I've told you already, Claire. If you don't wear it, you're not going. It's a brace, not a fashion accessory. You don't realise it now, but you'll thank me for making you wear it one day when you've got lovely straight teeth.'

I couldn't imagine ever thanking my mum for anything. At that particular moment, I viewed her as nothing short of evil for having delivered me at the feet of Satan the orthodontist in the first place.

'Anyway,' continued Mum, obviously not about to give up, 'if it's a problem, don't go up there. Half-terms are supposed to be for doing things with your friends and family. Not mooning over some footballer on your own.'

'It's not my fault Frankie's got her bridesmaid's dress fitting. Anyway, there's nothing wrong with me going to places on my own; it's called being independent,' I said, glancing up from the back page of the *Daily Mirror*.

'It's because you want to do such strange things that no one else wants to do them with you,' said Mum.

'Says the woman who goes to Tupperware parties on her own.'

'That's completely different. It's to do with my work.'

'So how come you get all done up before you go?'

'Oh, so I can't even make the effort to look my best now, can I?'

'I dunno why you bother. You're not going to meet any men at a Tupperware party, are you? Not unless you're planning to pin the organiser's husband to the settee.'

It was only when I saw Mum's expression that I realised what I'd said. I opened my mouth to say sorry but nothing came out. The word remained stuck in my throat, in the exact place it had been for years. Threatening to choke me if I tried to dislodge it.

'Listen, young lady, I've had to sacrifice my personal life to work all the hours God sends to bring you up. So don't start making smart remarks like that, OK?'

'I'm gonna go up and get ready,' I said. 'I don't wanna miss them arriving.'

I sat staring forlornly into the mirror. I'd been so busy looking at my brace that I hadn't noticed the huge zit which had appeared on my face overnight. I suspected Mum possessed secret powers, a bit like the wiggly-nosed woman in *Bewitched*, and must somehow be spiriting blemishes on to my face at crucial points in my life as a penance for my sins. I had no doubt that if Andy saw it, it would put him off me for life. The question was how to get rid of it. Squeezing it was not an option. Frankie did that and I considered it particularly gross.

Instead I reached for my medicated skin tonic, trying not to think about Frankie's assertion that it contained radioactive material. The liquid was blue, the same blue they used for National Health glasses. I wondered if they were linked in any way. I pressed the damp cotton-wool pad hard against my chin, feeling the tingling sensation radiate across my face. When I removed the pad, the spot momentarily appeared to have diminished. But within seconds the fresh supply of oxygen had breathed new life into it, enabling it to return to its former splendour before my very eyes.

I resorted to the concealer stick I had bought for just such emergencies. It was shade 001, which the lady in Boots had assured me was the palest one available. But after applying a liberal covering I concluded that I must be anaemic, such was the difference between its colour and that of my skin. I tried dabbing some talc on top of the concealer to help blend it in, but only succeeded in creating an unsavoury looking growth that appeared to be in dire need of medical attention.

With a sigh, I wiped the mixture off, deciding that the original spot was less obtrusive than my botched attempt to conceal it, and opted instead for a diversionary tactic. Beads.

Beads were not really my thing. But I had noted how good they looked on Madonna, so when I'd spotted a long string of luminescent peach beads on sale in the market for £1.50, I'd decided to give them a go.

I had even practised dancing to 'Into the Groove' with them on. Admittedly they didn't jangle about as much as Madonna's did (though neither did my boobs, for that matter), but they did look reasonably trendy. And if I teamed them up with my new short peach skirt, peach and cream vest top (bought after Frankie had informed me that horizontal stripes were the answer for the flat-chested) and cream jacket, I had what I considered a more than passable outfit. With a final twist of my beads in front of the mirror, I was ready. I hurried downstairs and out the front door before Mum had a chance to see me and make any comments about it being October and the need to dress sensibly. Yes, I'd be bloody freezing but that didn't matter. What mattered was looking good.

It felt strange, going to the training ground on my own. But I supposed I would have to get used to it. Frankie was always busy these days. Busy with preparations for Connie's wedding, busy with college work, busy with a whole new set of friends. All she ever talked about now was her mate Tara at college. I was thinking of getting her a T-shirt to replace her Frankie Goes to Hollywood one. Something with 'Tara says . . .' on it.

And she kept on saying things like 'You wouldn't understand' or 'When you leave school'. I was left feeling like some little kid who wasn't tall enough to go on the biggest ride at the theme park. Except that in my case I was plenty tall enough. I just couldn't seem to attract the attention of the man who was selling the tickets.

It wasn't until I was tottering down the garden path that I remembered how difficult it was to walk in proper heels. I'd had no choice but to wear my best white shoes; my usual blue pumps hadn't gone with the outfit, and on this occasion trainers were clearly out of the question. I knew Frankie would be proud of me though. For wearing such high heels.

'Nice legs, darling.'

I was vaguely aware that the gruff voice and wolf whistle that had preceded it had come from a group of workmen to my left. I waited for Frankie to shout her usual colourful riposte. It was only after several seconds that I remembered Frankie wasn't with me. Which meant the comment, and whistle, had been directed at me.

I spun round.

'Sexist pig,' I shouted at the nearest of a group of middle-aged workmen who were presiding over a large hole in the pavement.

'Give over, you love it really.'

'In your dreams, Grandad,' I yelled over my shoulder. But he'd hit a raw nerve. Deep down inside, way beyond the feminist pretensions, a tiny part of me was turning cartwheels of joy. For the first time in my life, someone had treated me as a sex object. A hint of a smile crossed my face as I walked on confidently to the training ground, occasionally sneaking a quick look down at my legs.

When I arrived, I was introduced to the novel experience of being disappointed not to see Susan from the club shop. Without Frankie, any familiar face would have been welcome. With no one I knew to talk to I tried to blend discreetly into the background. It was only when Andy pulled into the car park ten minutes later that I realised I didn't mind being on my own. Because it meant I could concentrate all my efforts on him.

I let the kids go up first. A dozen or so of them clustered around his car. He never used to get all that attention before. It was only because he was playing regularly in the first team now. He didn't seem to mind the fuss though.

He looked as if he was enjoying it. Clubber didn't look so pleased, mind, when he came in and only one kid bothered to ask for his signature. He glared at Andy as he walked past. Andy was so busy signing autographs he didn't see it. I did though, so I gave Clubber a dirty look back on Andy's behalf. After what seemed like an age, the last of the kids scuttled off clutching his autograph book. Andy looked up, a smile lighting up his face.

'Hi, Claire, long time no see,' he said. He remembered my name. Even after all this time. We were like old friends now. Me and Andy.

'I know. I've been busy.'

I didn't want to say I'd been at school. It would have spoilt everything.

'You're looking great, anyway.'

'Thanks,' I said as he stopped in front of me. 'Must be down to you guys being top of the league.' I smiled at him and noticed his gaze drop to my mouth. I checked discreetly with my tongue to see if I'd got a bran flake stuck to my teeth, but there was nothing there – only my brace.

I snapped my mouth tight shut, cursing myself for being so concerned with covering up my spot and then getting the wolf whistle that I'd forgotten to take my brace out on the way as planned. I had mutated into Jaws with the metal teeth from the James Bond film and Andy was about to run screaming in the opposite direction. He didn't, of course, just smiled back politely before walking off towards the clubhouse.

As soon as his back was turned, I rushed to the Ladies,

where I yanked the brace from my mouth and rinsed it under the tap, hating the feel of the slippery plastic between my fingers. I briefly contemplated flushing it down the loo and telling my mum it had accidentally fallen out. But it would be pointless. The dentist had casts of my mouth and would simply make another one, possibly even more hideous than the first. I wrapped the brace in toilet paper, stuffed it into my bag and went back out to watch the training.

Even in the practice match, Andy played in the first team. Clubber didn't look very happy about playing with the reserves. But it was his own stupid fault for getting himself sent off and suspended in the first place. He couldn't expect to walk back into the first team, not with Andy playing as well as he had been.

'Hi. Where's your friend today?'

I looked up with a start to see Dawn, the girl who'd gone out with Nobber, standing next to me.

'She's busy. It's her sister's wedding on Saturday.'

I still wasn't sure if that was the real reason Frankie hadn't come. But it sounded plausible enough. I wondered why Dawn didn't have a job to go to but felt it would be rude to ask. And remembered it was equally rude not to introduce myself.

'Oh, I'm Claire, by the way.'

'Pleased to meet you. I'm Dawn.'

'I know.'

'Don't tell me, that Susan told you. And probably told you all sorts of other stuff about me as well. She's the worst gossip I've ever met, that woman.'

'She didn't say anything bad. Only that you'd gone out with Nob . . . I mean, Mickey Squire.'

'Don't worry, you can call him Nobber, everyone else does. It doesn't bother me. I knew his nickname before I went out with him so I s'pose it was my own stupid fault.'

'Do you wanna get back with him?' I asked. Dawn snorted, obviously finding something amusing.

'Yeah, but it's not up to me, is it? It's up to him. Anyway,' she continued, 'you didn't come here to hear my sob story. Who've you got your eye on?'

'Oh, no one in particular,' I said, immediately averting my eyes from Andy. 'I like them all. It's the football I'm interested in actually.'

Dawn looked doubtful but didn't push the point any further. I felt bad about lying to her after she'd walked away. But I didn't think it was right to tell her about me and Andy. It would be like rubbing her nose in it, because I had something she didn't. A United player who cared.

Nobber was the first to leave after training. I watched as Dawn checked her lipstick in her compact mirror, brushed a loose strand of hair from her eyes and strode across the car park towards him. He walked straight past her, without so much as a nod, let alone a kind word. Dawn stopped in her tracks and looked up at the sky for a second, before turning and marching out of the car park, lips pursed and head bowed.

I couldn't see the point of loving someone who treated you that badly. I gave silent thanks that I had better taste in men than Dawn. As if to prove the point, Andy came out and greeted me with a warm smile.

'Hiya, you still here? I thought you'd have had enough of us by now.'

'Nah, you can never get too much of a good thing.'

Andy laughed. 'Is that right? So how come you're on your own today, then?'

'Oh, Frankie, my friend, she's having a bridesmaid's dress fitting.'

'Whose wedding is it? Not yours, I hope.'

I stared at him for a second, unable to believe what he'd just said. He was flirting with me. He'd practically asked me out. In fact he'd only just stopped short of proposing.

'No,' I said, giggling as I tried not to blush. 'It's her sister's. Big do she's having on Saturday. Three o'clock kick-off, same as you.'

'Are you going?'

'Yeah, worse luck. I'd rather be listening to the commentary on the radio. I'll have to try and smuggle my trannie into the church.'

'I'll tell the lads not to score in the first half then; we don't want the vicar throwing you out for cheering.'

I laughed. It felt so normal, sharing a joke with him. As if we'd known each other for years. We were standing next to his car now. But he wasn't making any attempt to get in. He hadn't even opened the door. He was too busy talking to me.

'So what are you up to for the rest of half-term?'

I was mortified that my schoolgirl status was still so obvious.

'Oh, not much. Studying mainly. It's my final year. O levels and all that.'

'God, don't remind me. My dad still hasn't forgiven me for flunking my maths.'

'How many did you get then?' I asked.

'Oh, I managed eight, I think. Which isn't bad for a footballer, I guess.'

I nodded. It was probably more than the rest of the team had put together. 'So what are you planning to do afterwards?'

'I'll be off to college to do my A levels, then uni. I want to be a lawyer.'

Andy grinned at me. 'Fantastic. That's what I'm planning to do when I'm too old for this game.'

'Really?' I said, deciding not to let on that I already knew in case he thought I'd just copied him.

'Yeah, it's what I was going to do before Huddersfield Town offered me a contract and football got in the way. I reckon I'd be a damn sight better at that than running a pub. I've just started an Open University law course so I don't get left behind by bright young things like you.'

I grinned, chuffed that he considered me bright. 'It'll be ages before you have to give up playing though. You're not that old.'

'Well thank you. Flattery will get you everywhere. Now, what can I sign for you today?'

'Um, I've got the Everton programme in here somewhere,' I said, rummaging in my canvas shoulder bag before triumphantly producing it. I looked expectantly at Andy, who was staring down at the programme, seemingly reluctant to take it from me. I couldn't think why until I looked down and saw what had caught his eye.

There, stuck rigidly to the picture of Dave Orton on the front, was a familiar-looking pink object with protruding wires and a decorative toilet-roll covering.

I stood, mouth wide open, eyes fixed firmly on my brace, as I rued the fact that I hadn't flushed it down the toilet when I'd had the chance.

'They're horrible things, aren't they?' said Andy, breaking the awkward silence. 'Don't worry, I used to wear one, I know what it's like.'

'Yeah, but I bet you never took it out to show people. I don't usually carry it around in my bag like this, honest,' I said, prising the brace off the programme and taking a bit of Dave Orton's left knee with it as I did so.

'Are you sure you don't want me to sign it for you?' he asked.

I was already thinking how cool it would be to have Andy's autograph permanently in my mouth when I looked up at him and realised he was joking. A smile spread slowly across my face and I started laughing. Andy was laughing too. We were laughing together.

'How long did you have to wear yours for?' I asked eventually.

'Oh God, over a year, I think. I had awful fangs that stuck out here,' he explained, pointing to the top corners of his mouth. 'The kids at school used to call me Dracula, it was horrible. Still, believe it or not, it is worth it in the end.'

'Right. I guess you just don't think that at the time.'

'Anyway, don't worry about it. I'll pretend I never saw it. Now let me sign that programme of yours.'

As I waited for Andy to drive off, I noticed him adjusting his rear-view mirror. For a second I thought he was looking at my legs. I shook my head and smiled to myself. The wolf whistle must have gone to my head.

Frankie had told me Connie's dress was awful but I still gasped when I caught sight of her coming down the aisle looking for all the world like a crinoline lady toilet-roll holder. Frankie didn't look much better, mind, trussed up in an unflattering pink taffeta creation chosen by Connie, presumably because it was so hideous that she would find it impossible to upstage the bride on her big day.

A ripple of approving 'aaahs' ran from the back of the church to the front pews as Connie made her way down the aisle. I couldn't decide whether the other guests were being polite or whether they genuinely had as bad taste as Connie. Frankie looked across at me as she trailed past. I grinned, so she thought I was being supportive. But actually it was quite funny, seeing her looking awful for a change.

The ceremony itself was tedious to the point of being painful. I shifted uncomfortably on the hard wooden pew, the words of the priest droning on fuzzily in the background like an irritating bluebottle. All I could think about was Andy and how he was doing. It was a big match today against Liverpool. A real test for him. I knew he'd pass it, I had every faith in him. But I wanted to help him through it, every minute, every second. Mum had said I couldn't take my radio into church. That it would be disrespectful. So all I could do was wait.

'Conchetta looks a picture, doesn't she, Claire?' Mrs Alberti said afterwards, brushing a tear away with a lace-edged handkerchief as we stood in the confetti-strewn churchyard, watching the official photographs being taken.

'Mmm,' I replied, trying not to laugh. 'She certainly does.'

I looked at my watch. They'd be into the second half by now. These Catholic dos took so bloody long. I scoured the churchyard, sure I couldn't be the only one on tenter-hooks. I was right. Mr Alberti was over in the far corner, trying to hide behind a tree, transistor radio pressed against his ear. He'd always been a big United fan; that was where Frankie had got it from. Every summer he created an entirely blue flower display along the central promenade in the park. Most people thought he had a thing about lo-belias. Only me and Frankie knew it was a civic tribute to United. Such loyalty deserved to be rewarded. I'd told Frankie that should Percy Thrower ever forget to put a plastic cup on the top of one of his garden canes and acci-dentally poke his eye out, she should write in to *Blue Peter* nominating her father as his replacement.

'What's the score?' I whispered, sidling up to him.

'Nil–nil,' he said. 'But we're on top, should be two–nil up by now. Goodyear and Orton both missed sitters in the first half, apparently.'

I smiled, remembering what Andy had said about telling the lads not to score before half-time. It was the first time I'd ever been pleased that United weren't winning.

'Can we have the bride's family now, please?' the pho-tographer shouted.

'Here,' said Mr Alberti, thrusting the radio into my hand. 'You'd better listen for me. Else I'm in big trouble.'

I took the radio from him as he hurried off to join the rest of the family. When Matt scored a few moments later they must have seen me jumping up and down, because when the photographer took the next shot, Frankie (who had been looking decidedly pissed off) was actually smiling. And Mr Alberti's arm was raised aloft triumphantly.

'Isn't it lovely to see a man so proud of his daughter?' I heard a guest next to me say. I couldn't help thinking how much prouder Mr Alberti would look at the final whistle.

We won 1–0. Andy played a blinder, according to Alan Green on the radio. 'A performance of considerable poise and maturity which will give the watching England manager Bobby Robson something to think about.' That was what he actually said. I could have broken the school high-jump record at that moment. All the way through the speeches I kept thinking about it. My Andy playing for England. When we had to toast the bride and groom I said, 'Andy for England' instead. Nobody heard me though. I only said it quietly.

When all the speeches and that were over, Frankie was finally allowed to leave the top table. She hurried over to join me, ignoring the smiles and greetings from other relatives who lined the route. She still looked uptight about the whole thing.

'Matt scored the goal,' I said.

'Excellent.'

'You don't seem very pleased.'

'Course I am. I'm just fed up with having to wear this poxy dress and my dad going on about what a wonderful daughter Connie is. It made me wanna puke.'

'You should have. It would have given you an excuse to take the dress off.'

Frankie laughed. I liked it when she laughed at stuff I said. She hadn't done it so much lately. She usually only laughed at things Tara had said. Tara hadn't been invited to the wedding though, because Frankie had met her after the invites had gone out. I don't think Frankie wanted her there anyway. She wouldn't have wanted Tara to see her in that outfit.

'Hello, Francesca, how are you, love?'

A woman with a face that looked like a well-used piece of silver foil bent to embrace Frankie, almost falling out of her sequinned top as she did so, and planted a ring of mauve lipstick on her cheek. Frankie pulled away. The colour seemed to have drained from her face. The woman looked familiar but I couldn't place her.

'Have you got a kiss for your Uncle Tony, then?' she said, edging sideways to allow a small man with a sun-tanned face and wire-rimmed glasses to step forward. It was only when I heard his name and saw a flash of unnatur-ally white teeth that it clicked. The Maria Bellini School of Dancing in Potters Bar. Frankie had been a star pupil when she was younger; she'd won medals for it and every-thing. I'd gone to see her once in a show. She'd been brilliant; everyone had been talking about how good she was. Auntie Maria (the woman with the tinfoil skin) had marked her out for big things. Only Frankie had chucked it all in when she was twelve. Said it was kids' stuff. Her mum had never forgiven her.

Uncle Tony was still standing there flashing those teeth, his moustache twitching as he waited for a kiss. Only I could tell Frankie wasn't going to give him one. She'd taken a few steps backwards and her jaw had tightened. Her eyes seemed to have turned from brown to black.

'Excuse me,' she said to Maria. 'I've just got to show my friend to the toilets.'

Frankie took hold of my arm and led me into the ladies' bogs. I was sure I could feel her shaking.

'Are you OK?' I said.

'Yeah, I'm fine.'

'What was all that about?'

'He's not my real uncle.'

'I know.'

'Well he's got no fucking right, has he?'

'No,' I said, having no idea what she was on about. Frankie disappeared into one of the cubicles, peed loudly, emerged without flushing and washed her hands twice under the hot tap.

'Are you all right now?' I asked. She didn't answer. Just wiped her hands on her dress and headed back into the hall.

'Francesca, I've found someone who wants to say hello to you,' Mrs Alberti called from across the room as she spotted us making our way towards the bar. Frankie pretended she hadn't heard. A few moments later Mrs Alberti was tottering towards us, dragging a spotty-faced lad of about our age behind her.

'Who's that?' I asked.

Frankie rolled her eyes. 'Oh God, it's this boy called Salvatore; he used to live next door when we were kids.'

Mrs Alberti and Salvatore arrived in front of us, both of them grinning inanely.

'Go on, son,' said Mrs Alberti, giving him a gentle poke in the ribs. 'Don't be shy.'

Salvatore took a deep breath and, in a shaky, out-of-key voice began to sing the opening lines from 'Frankie' by Sister Sledge.

Mrs Alberti clapped her hands and the flap of skin hanging from her chin wobbled in delight.

'Well?' she said, looking at Frankie expectantly, when at last he had finished. 'What do you think?'

Frankie didn't hesitate. 'I think Sister Sledge are crap and he's a complete wanker,' she said, before turning on her heel and flouncing out of the hall.

Mrs Alberti was still standing there, her mouth gaping open, when the first notes of 'Tonight, I Celebrate My Love for You' brought Connie and Maurizio out into the centre of the dance floor. An appreciative audience gathered around them, cooing and taking photos. I decided to get some fresh air. Peabo Bryson and Roberta Flack always had that sort of effect on me.

I found Frankie sitting on the steps outside, like a dollop of dropped candyfloss.

'I can't believe you said that.'

'She's always trying to fix me up with Italian boys. I'm sick of it.'

'You should have seen that Salvatore's face. I thought he was gonna cry. Mind you, I'd cry if I had a voice like that.'

Frankie started to laugh. We sat there for ages, just laughing and talking. She didn't mention Tara once.

Six

Mark pulled up outside my house just as I arrived back from the allotment. I sensed from the way he winced as he got out of the car and hobbled over towards me that his rock-climbing had not gone too well.

'What happened?' I asked.

'Just turned my ankle a bit on the way up. Nothing too serious.'

I took hold of his hand and he winced again.

'Rope burns,' he explained, holding up his palms. 'Slipped a bit on the way down.'

'What about the bit in between going up and coming down?'

'That was fine. I seem to be OK at the hanging around at the top bit. Just need to brush up my technique on the rest.'

I nodded and kissed him. Despite his apparent enthusiasm, I still wasn't convinced that he was actually enjoying it. I liked the new hairstyle and had got used to some of the clothes, but I couldn't get my head around the idea of someone who had been known to drive a couple of hundred yards to the newsagent's suddenly becoming some kind of action hero.

'Come in and stick your foot up on the sofa. I'll see if I can find some frozen peas.'

'No, it's OK. I've eaten at the café, thanks.'

I pulled a face at him.

'I hope you've got better lines than that if you're going to be the pre-meal entertainment tonight.' Frankie and her family were due in an hour or so. I'd decided to cook a curry rather than take them to an Italian restaurant which wasn't anywhere near as good as Joe's. Although as I'd never cooked for a chef before, I was feeling slightly anxious about it.

'Don't worry, I'll do my utmost to charm and entertain your guests. I'll have to get back home tonight though. I've got a viewing for the flat first thing tomorrow morning.'

I was thrown for a second. I hadn't expected either of us to get any viewings for months.

'Oh,' was all I could manage.

'Does the prospect of me moving in fill you with that much excitement?'

'Sorry, I didn't mean it to sound like that. I was surprised, that's all.'

'Well, you never know, we could be first time lucky.'

'Yeah, let's hope so,' I said, bending down to take off my muddy wellies. And secretly hoping that whoever was viewing Mark's flat wouldn't like it. Because if they did, we'd be back to looking at houses and the whole panicky 'my life is turning into a cul-de-sac' thing would start again. I thought I'd bought some time with the 'let's sell ours first' idea. But now the only person actively looking to buy in Britain was going to sniff around Mark's flat, I realised the sand might run through rather quicker than I had expected.

We heard Frankie's family arrive long before they actually knocked on the door. Sophia's high-pitched scream was recognisable even from inside, and was followed by some sort of shouting match over who had been worst behaved on the journey. Mark looked up at me from the kitchen table.

'I never promised you a quiet weekend,' I said.

'No, but you didn't tell me to bring my ear-protectors either.'

'The kids are great. Just don't expect shy, retiring children.'

Finally, the knock came. It was on the front door which was bolted and I never used. Southerners really had no idea how things worked north of the Watford Gap. I went out the back door and dashed around the end of the terrace to the front. They were standing huddled together on the pavement, all looking rather travel-weary.

'Hey,' said Frankie, as she caught sight of me. 'It's our friend up north. You never told me you lived in the hills. Or that you don't have proper summers up here.'

I smiled, glancing up at the low grey clouds as the wind whipped my hair across my face.

'Well it's lovely to see you,' I said, giving her a hug on the pavement. 'And you're lucky it's not raining. Todmorden's the third wettest place in England. Usually it's chucking it down.'

'Hi, Claire,' said Joe, stepping forward to kiss me on both cheeks. 'Good to see you again.'

'And you. How was the journey, or shouldn't I ask?'

'Long,' said Joe. 'We resorted to telling the kids to look out for polar bears when we got to the M62.'

'Can you see the Northern Lights from here?' asked Paulo. 'We learnt about them at school.'

'I'm afraid not,' I said. 'But I am planning tomorrow morning to take you to a fab children's museum where you can run around and touch everything.' Paulo, Sophia and Roberto's faces lit up.

'Sorry,' I said, turning to Emily, who was looking particularly trendy in a long layered dress and Aphrodite sandals. 'I know it's not going to be much fun for you.'

'It's OK, I'm used to it,' she said with a shrug. 'And at least it will keep them quiet so I'll get a chance to read.'

'*Twilight* again?' I asked.

'No, the next one. *New Moon*. I read some of it on the way up and I can't wait to finish it.'

'Anyway,' interrupted Frankie. 'Is the door broken or is there any chance of actually going inside to warm up a bit?'

'Sorry,' I said. 'Follow me. We use the back door, it's a northern thing.' I led them round the side of the house and down through the back-to-back houses.

'Why do you put your washing up in the street?' asked Paulo.

'Because we don't have gardens. Just a back yard.'

'Is that a northern thing as well?' asked Paulo.

'I guess so,' I laughed.

It was only as I got to the back door that I noticed the clenching in my stomach. I was about to show Frankie my life, to hold it up for her scrutiny. And I couldn't help wondering what she'd make of it: Mark, the house and all my worldly goods. It was crazy, really. All those years I'd tried to impress Frankie, to measure up to her. And here I was at thirty-eight still doing the same thing.

Mark looked up from *The Times* sports section as we walked in and rose from his chair at the kitchen table.

'Hi,' he said, smiling as the Ricotta clan shuffled inside. 'I'm Mark, pleased to meet you all.'

I looked at him hard as I did the introductions, trying to view him through fresh eyes, to see him as Frankie would. He looked good, actually. Somehow better than I remembered.

'Hi,' said Frankie, stepping forward to kiss him. 'Tough luck, eh? Ending up with Claire.' Mark burst into laughter, glanced at me to check I was laughing too, then carried on.

'Watch it, you'll be sleeping in the shed if you're not careful,' I said to Frankie.

'Is that a northern thing too?' asked Paulo.

'I think Claire was just joking,' said Joe. 'Anyway, good to meet you, Mark,' he said, shaking his hand. It was weird seeing them standing there together. The two men in our lives. Two men who couldn't have been more different from the prototypes that were Matt and Andy. Frankie was obviously perfectly OK with that. So why did I still imagine Andy standing in this kitchen? Why did I wonder what he was doing now? And whether he ever, in some quite unguarded moment, wondered about me.

'I'll stick the kettle on,' I said. 'You guys go through and chill out.'

'Have you got biscuits?' Sophia asked Mark, tugging at the sleeve of his jumper.

'Loads,' he said.

'Chocolate ones?'

'Are there any other kind?' replied Mark. Sophia grinned and followed him through to the lounge.

By the time I made it in there with a tea tray laden with drinks and biscuits (chocolate ones, of course), Sophia and Paulo were squabbling over who got to sit on the sofa next to Mark.

'Is he usually this popular?' asked Frankie, who had Roberto sitting quietly on her lap.

'No, usually people run a mile,' I said, putting the tray down.

'It's not that I have a personal hygiene problem,' said Mark. 'It's because I'm a lawyer; scares people off.' At which point Sophia and Paulo both jumped up and made a beeline for the biscuits.

'See?' he said.

'I think it was the lure of chocolate, actually,' said Frankie, as she dived in to grab a biscuit before the children had scoffed them all.

'Paulo's is bigger than mine,' whined Sophia.

'She's had more than me,' said Paulo, squaring up to Sophia. There was a crash as Roberto held up an arm to defend himself against the flailing arms and legs of his brother and sister and knocked an ornament off a shelf.

'Sorry,' said Frankie, checking it wasn't broken before putting it back. 'Do you have parks up north?'

'Yep, there's one ten minutes' walk away.'

'Good. I think after being cooped up in the car so long they need to let off some steam.'

'Can I take my football?' asked Paulo.

'Only if you let me go in goal,' said Mark.

We all walked together down to the town centre, apart from Emily who'd said she was too tired to come and had opted to stay at home and read. Roberto was on a fold-up scooter he'd brought with him, Paulo had his football tucked under his arm and Sophia was being swung along by Joe and Mark.

'Are you sure your ankle's going to be OK?' I asked Mark. Joe had volunteered to take the children to the park so that Frankie and I could have some time to ourselves, and Mark had nobly offered to go with him.

'Yeah, I think it will hold up for a gentle kick-about.'

Joe laughed. 'Aah, you've never played football with Paulo before, have you?'

'Mark's not playing with Paulo, he's playing with me,' said Sophia. Frankie rolled her eyes.

'See you back at the house, then,' I called, as we stopped at the crossing and they carried on up towards the park. 'Have fun.'

I turned to Frankie, who was looking around as she pulled her silk scarf up around her neck.

'I don't suppose you've got an indoor shopping centre, have you?' she asked as we crossed the road.

'Nope, we have an indoor market but I guess that's not exactly what you had in mind.'

Frankie laughed. 'Not quite. I was thinking something more like the Trafford Centre.'

'Twenty-five miles that way, I'm afraid,' I said, pointing

in the direction of Manchester. 'You know, it's a shame you didn't end up with Matt.'

'Why's that?'

'You would have made such a good WAG. The original and best. Victoria Beckham would have been a pale imitation of you.'

Frankie grinned. 'Yeah, and I could have had liposuction and a gastric band fitted after having the kids to lose weight. And let someone film it for reality TV.'

I chuckled at the thought of it.

'I don't know why you're laughing,' she said. 'You'd have been the one they'd have done "worst-dressed WAG" photo montages of in the Sunday magazines.'

'Oh, cheers.'

'Hey, it's a compliment. Most of them haven't got two brain cells to rub together. A lawyer WAG on a crusade to save the world and no interest in fashion would have been ripe for taking the piss out of.'

'Bit of luck it didn't happen then,' I said.

'Do you mean that?' asked Frankie.

I shrugged and pointed to the Bear café further down the road.

'That's a great place for coffee and cake,' I said.

'Come on then,' said Frankie. 'Sounds much better than perusing hardware stalls and haberdasheries in the market.'

We climbed the stairs to the first-floor café and approached the counter where a tempting array of cakes were on display.

'Hi, Pam,' I said to the tall, dark-haired woman behind the serving hatch.

'Hiya, Claire, I'm glad you're here. I've been meaning to tell you, Incredible Edible Todmorden is having a harvest festival on the twenty-eighth of September. Wondered if you'd like to bring some stuff from your allotment?'

Frankie looked up from the cakes and started sniggering.

'I'll do my best,' I said. 'Although I think the word "harvest" is a bit grand for two carrots and a couple of green tomatoes.'

'That bad?' said Pam.

'I'm afraid so. Anyway,' I said, turning to Frankie, 'what are you having?'

'Don't tell me you're growing vegetables now,' said Frankie as we sat down at a table by the window with our coffees and two large portions of chocolate cake.

'No, I'm not actually. Only slug food.'

'It all sounds a bit like *The Good Life* to me.'

'Oh, I thought it was quite trendy. Kim Wilde does that gardening programme and people think she's really cool.'

'That's because every bloke had fantasies about her when she did the "Kids in America" video. It's got nothing to do with gardening. WAGS definitely don't garden.'

'Well, like I said. Bit of luck I'm not a WAG then.'

Frankie stirred her coffee and took a bite of her cake.

'Do you still think about him?'

'Who?'

'Come on. This is me you're talking to.'

I rubbed a hole in the steam on the window with my sleeve and looked down to the street below. The people and cars passed by in a blur.

'He was everything to me,' I said.

'I know,' said Frankie, reaching out to squeeze my arm as I bit my lip hard. 'You were so young, though. I look at Emily now and I can't believe you were the same age. It's scary.'

I shrugged and went back to looking out of the window.

'What's he doing now, do you know?'

I shook my head. 'It was always all or nothing with me and Andy. So I figure it's best to leave it at nothing. What I don't know can't hurt me.'

'Still,' said Frankie, 'it doesn't matter now, does it? You've got Mark. He's great. I really like him.'

I nodded and smiled, trying to pretend that I was fine with that. To give no sense that I still lay awake at night thinking about Andy. About what could have been if things had been different.

'So are you any closer to moving in together?'

'I guess so. He's got a viewing on his flat tomorrow.'

'Don't sound so excited.'

'That's what Mark said.'

Frankie put her coffee mug down on the table. 'So, what's the problem?'

'I don't know. Things have been a bit awkward since I told him I didn't want to buy that house with him.'

'I'm not surprised. He probably felt rejected.'

'I know. I've told him so many times it was about the house not him, but I don't think it's got through. And now he's gone all weird on me.'

'What do you mean, weird?'

'He didn't used to have his hair like that or dress trendily. He had a sort of fashion makeover when I was down at yours.'

Frankie giggled. 'Well, one of you has to be dragged into the current millennium.'

'It's not just that. He's taken up rock–climbing. And bought a book by Ross Kemp.'

'Jesus. That is serious. Have you lusted after someone macho in front of him?'

'No, not at all. And he's well aware that I still fancy George Michael, even though I understand now why he was never going to be interested.'

'Such a disappointment for us girls,' tutted Frankie, shaking her head. 'If only it had been Andrew Ridgeley.'

'One of those things I wish I'd known when I was fifteen.'

'What are the others?'

'That Martin Kemp would end up doing sofa ads and my mum would say he had nice eyes.'

'Your mum fancies Martin Kemp?'

'I know. I went off him straight away. Nothing worse than your mum fancying the same guy.'

'So all we need now then,' said Frankie, 'is for your mum to confess she had the hots for Andy.'

'Why do you say that?'

'Well that's what this is all about, isn't it? You've never really got over him. You married someone who reminded you of him and now you don't want to move in with Mark, simply because he's not Andy.'

I sighed, not knowing what to say. And fearing she was getting uncomfortably close to the truth.

'It's not that. It's just all been a bit sudden. I feel I'm being pressured into it. Mark can be impulsive like that.

He comes up with an idea and gets totally carried away with it.'

'Sounds rather romantic.'

I shook my head.

'He couldn't be less romantic if he tried. The living-together speech sounded more like a business plan.'

'There's a lot to be said for being practical and sensible.'

'Says she who was never either,' I laughed. 'Anyway, I bet Joe's a real romantic. He strikes me as a big softie.'

'He is actually. He cried most of the way through our wedding service. Poor Emily kept asking what was wrong. She was only three, she didn't understand.'

'He's great with the kids too.'

'So is Mark. I bet he'd make a fantastic dad.'

I looked out of the window again.

'Don't you want children?' asked Frankie.

'No, I never have.'

'Yes you did. I bet it was on your list.'

'I thought you said that was a load of old tosh?'

'It wasn't to you when you wrote it. Why did you change your mind?'

'David didn't want children. I guess I just got used to the idea of not having any. And when we split up, I was relieved we hadn't. I'd have hated to put my kids through what I went through when Mum and Dad split up.'

'What about Mark?'

'I think he'd probably like to be a dad. But it's not a big issue for him. He knows how I feel.'

'But things have changed. You and Mark might stay together for ever. Not everyone breaks up.'

'Even if we did stay together, I'd be scared of screwing them up. Look at what our families did to us. They're hardly good role models, are they?'

'I know, but you have to break the chain somewhere, don't you? Be brave enough to give it a go, try to do things differently.'

'When you found out you were pregnant, the first time, with Emily, did you ever think about—' I broke off, concerned from the look on Frankie's face that I shouldn't have asked. It was her turn to look out of the window

'I did, but not for very long. All that Catholic guilt stuff, I guess. I was terrified of giving birth and being a mum but I knew I couldn't get rid of it. And I'm so glad I didn't, even though it's still scary as hell being a mum. Especially when you know what teenagers are capable of.'

'Well it looks to me like you're doing a great job. I don't think our mums had a clue, really. They were from a different generation, weren't they?'

'I guess so. But that doesn't stop me being concerned about Emily.'

'How is she? She seemed a bit quiet.'

'I'm really worried about her,' said Frankie. 'She's always tired and under the weather, picks up anything that's going around. And she's lost weight. Quite a bit, I think, although it's difficult to see under those baggy clothes she wears.'

'You don't think she's got an eating disorder?'

'I don't know what to think. But I do know that with me and Joe being the size we are, she could get a hang-up about it. They get this whole body-image thing rammed down their throats these days.'

'Have you spoken to her about it?'

'Not directly. And if she did have anorexia or something she'd only deny it anyway. But I have made an appointment for her to see the doctor next week. Told her it's just to find out if there's a reason for the weight loss. And why she always seems to be tired and going down with something.'

'And what did she say?'

'She didn't protest. I think she quite likes the idea of them taking a blood sample. Thinks it will boost her vampire credentials.'

I laughed as Frankie wiped the chocolate cake crumbs from her mouth.

'Well, hopefully it will put your mind at rest.'

'Either that or I'll get a mouthful from her when she finds out the doctor isn't Robert Pattinson.'

I watched Emily during the meal that evening. She did pick at her food but no more so than any other teenager. And she certainly rivalled Mark in her ability to demolish a pile of poppadoms. She was quieter than the last time I'd seen her, though, saying very little apart from thanking me for the meal at the end. At which point Joe declared that I must be a better cook than him because she never thanked him for his meals.

Frankie put the younger children to bed; Paulo and Roberto in the spare room and Sophia in my room, where she and Joe were going to sleep.

We stayed up talking for a while, Emily with her head still in *New Moon*, the rest of us sharing a bottle of wine and reminiscing about eighties TV shows and films. Until it was time for Mark to go home and Frankie and Joe turned in, knowing they'd get an early wake-up call from the kids in the morning.

Emily stifled a yawn and grinned at me as we were left alone in the room together.

'Come on, let's get ready for bed,' I said. 'I don't suppose we'll get a lie-in in the morning either.'

Emily went to the bathroom first while I set up the sofa bed. It was only when she returned in her nightshirt that I noticed how skinny her legs were. And that they were covered in bruises.

'Have you been playing football with Paulo?' I asked. 'Because if you have, I suggest you get some shin pads.'

Emily frowned for a second before glancing down at her legs.

'Oh, those,' she said. 'I've got no idea where they all came from. I seem to collect them. A bit like spots, I guess.'

I smiled and headed for the bathroom. By the time I returned, Emily was snuggled up under the duvet.

'Are you sure you don't mind sharing the sofa bed with me?' I asked. 'I'll happily sleep on the floor if you'd rather.'

'No, course not,' said Emily. 'It'll be fun. Like a sleepover.'

'Except with a boring grown-up like me,' I said, sliding in next to her. 'You'll have to teach me what you talk about on sleepovers.'

'I haven't been on that many really. Only at Alia's.'

'So what's she like, Alia?'

'She's great. Really funny and a bit wacky. She's scene.'

'Seen what?'

Emily laughed. 'No, I mean she's a scene kid.'

I looked at her blankly. 'Go on, you'd better fill me in,' I said.

'Scene kids like emo music but dress more colourfully and are quirkier. From what my mum says, if Cyndi Lauper were around today, she'd be scene.'

'Right,' I said, feeling positively ancient and uncool. 'And what's emo music?'

'Emo means emotionally unstable. Emos dress a bit like goths did in your day and listen to depressing music, stuff by Paramore, Avenged Sevenfold and My Chemical Romance.'

I nodded again, not wanting to admit that I'd never heard of any of them.

'So what are you?'

'That's the problem, I don't really fit into any one group. I like emo music, I dress like a bohemian, I'm a bit of a geek and my best friend's scene. The only things I'm definitely not are a plastic or a chav.'

'I've heard of chavs,' I said, triumphant to have scored at least one point on the 'Are you cool enough to be a teenager?' scale.

'Plastics are obsessed with looks, like Girls Aloud,' explained Emily.

'I've heard of them too. And seen them on telly, and I know that Cheryl Cole is married to Ashley Cole who plays for Chelsea.'

Emily grinned. 'Mum would have been a plastic.'

I laughed. 'God, she would, wouldn't she? I wonder what I'd have been.'

'What were you like?'

'Swotty and uncool.'

'A geek then, I guess. What music were you into?'

'Spandau Ballet.'

'I've heard of them,' laughed Emily, getting her own back.

'They were new romantics but I didn't wear frilly shirts or make-up like them.'

'So what were you into?'

'United,' I said. 'Well, Andy Pailes really.'

'Was he the guy on your bedroom wall?'

'Yeah, he was,' I said, aware that it was the understatement of the year but deciding not to elaborate any further.

'Got any pictures of him?' asked Emily. I hesitated, embarrassed to admit I had enough pictures to fill an entire box.

'Just a few.'

'Can I see them? I did show you my pics of Robert.' This was true. Although she, of course, had no idea of the real reason for my reluctance to pass photos around.

'They're in the loft, I'm afraid. I'll have to dig one out for you another time.' I reached out and turned the lamp off. Hoping Emily would recognise the signal but forgetting that she was fifteen.

'Were you totally and utterly in love with him?' she asked dreamily.

'Yeah, I was.'

'Did you ever get to meet him? I've seen Mum's photos of her and that Matt guy she liked.'

'Yeah, I've got some like that of me and Andy.'

'And was he gorgeous in real life as well?'

I smiled, glad Emily couldn't see my pink cheeks in the dark.

'Yeah,' I said. 'He was.'

'Robert will be gorgeous when I meet him at the premiere.'

'You're still planning to go, then?'

'Me and Alia wouldn't miss it for the world. Just think, I might actually be able to touch him.'

I shut my eyes for a second. Still feeling Andy's touch. And the ache it had left behind.

'It doesn't matter if you don't, though. Sometimes it's better that way. You won't end up disappointed.'

'Robert will never be a disappointment to me. I know that.'

'Night, Emily,' I said, turning over on to one side so she didn't see the tear running down my cheek. And I didn't have to tell her that I had known that too.

Tuesday, 10 December 1985

I held the Immac bottle at arm's length and peered again at the instructions. It was the bit on the label that read, 'Do NOT leave on for longer than 10 minutes' which particularly worried me. I couldn't help wondering what would happen if I did. Would my skin peel off with it? I had visions of looking like a napalm victim for the Junior Blues Christmas Disco. And that wasn't the idea at all.

The idea was that my stubbly legs, which had responded well to the ideal growing conditions under my thick over-the-knee socks during the winter, would be instantly transformed into super-smooth ones, enabling me to wear my shiny black ten-denier tights without any fear of the hairs sticking through.

That in turn would allow me to wear the black mini-skirt I had bought for the occasion from Chelsea Girl. It wasn't that short. Only a couple of inches above the knee. But having long legs made it look shorter than it actually was. I hoped that the overall effect would be to make me look as sexy and sophisticated as the woman in the Immac adverts. I had decided that sexy and sophisticated was the image I needed to cultivate.

Sitting precariously on the edge of the bath, I undid the

cap and squeezed the lotion out, smearing it thickly over my legs with the spatula provided. It didn't seem to go' very far. I ended up using the entire bottle, which pissed me off because it had cost nearly three quid.

There was nothing to do then but sit there shivering in my bra and knickers, wishing Frankie was coming with me and wondering whether Andy would be there.

Frankie had been deemed too old to go. Under-sixteens only, they'd said. Not that she'd have gone even if she'd been allowed. She'd probably have said it was too childish for her. That was what she said about everything. Unless it was her college disco, of course. Which, as she kept telling me, was for adults only. Still, as long as Andy was there. That was all that mattered. I'd got him a card and a present. It was a pen – not a grotty old Bic or anything; a proper Papermate one in a box that had cost me ten quid. I'd decided it was personal enough without being over-familiar or too expensive. I didn't want him to feel bad that he hadn't got me anything.

Glancing at my watch, I realised I had daydreamed nine minutes away. My legs would be starting to fry. I scrambled to wet a chunk of cotton wool, and was about to begin the major deforestation exercise when I heard the phone ringing in the hall.

Ignoring it was not an option. A ringing phone always engendered a sense of urgency in me. It was the realisation that it could be a matter of life or death (I had never actually received a life-or-death phone call, but had seen plenty of them on TV and in the movies). Either that, or Andy offering me a lift to the disco.

I slithered off the edge of the bath and hurtled down-stairs as quickly as my Immac-covered legs would allow.

'Hi, it's me.'

'Oh, hi, Frankie.'

'Don't sound so pleased.'

'No, I was in the middle of doing my legs, that's all.'

'What for?'

'The Junior Blues disco, it's tonight.'

'Oh yeah, I'd forgotten. Do you want me to come round, do your make-up or anything?'

'I thought you were seeing Tara tonight?'

'Yeah, well I'm not now. Do you want me to come or not?'

'Yes please. Just give me half an hour to get myself sorted out.'

As I turned to race back upstairs to the bathroom, fear-ing my legs might spontaneously combust at any moment, I was confronted with a telltale trail of Immac down the centre of my mum's much-loved red stair carpet.

I swore out loud, knowing the carpet would be scarred for life, even if I wasn't. I managed to salvage my own legs and was trying to mount a carpet cleanup operation by colouring in the stains with a red marker pen when Frankie arrived.

'It wouldn't wash off. It was the only thing I could think of. Mum'll do her nut if she sees it like this,' I explained as I let her in.

Frankie started laughing, then stopped abruptly and caught her breath as she looked at me properly for the first time.

'Wow, your hair,' she said. 'It almost makes you look grown up.'

'Thanks,' I said, taking it as a compliment even if it was a sarky one. I'd forgotten that Frankie hadn't seen my new hairdo. It had been my mum's idea to get it done, which meant I now had to accept that she had made one worthwhile contribution to my teenage years. Initially, I had been reluctant. But when the hairdresser had shown me the finished look in the mirror I had been pleasantly surprised. The kid with the flick and the straggly split ends was gone, and in her place was a young woman with big, Farrah Fawcett style layered hair. The hairdresser had said I wouldn't have looked out of place on *Dynasty*. I had gone straight home and written that in my diary. In case no one ever paid me such a compliment again.

'So why aren't you seeing Tara then?' I asked Frankie.

'Oh, she's back together with her boyfriend. She's going out with him instead.'

'Some friend she is.'

'She did ask. I said I didn't mind.'

I would never muck Frankie about like that. She knew it as well. I think that was why she was so touchy about it.

'Do you wanna see my outfit?' I asked, changing the subject to one I hoped she would be more comfortable with.

'Yeah, OK. Go and put it on.'

I returned a few minutes later wearing a black top with a square neckline, the short black skirt, and slingbacks which Mum had lent me (the only decent thing she had in her wardrobe). Frankie stared at me without saying a word.

'Oh God, you hate it, don't you?'

She shook her head. 'No. It looks great. I just hadn't noticed before, about you getting a figure, I mean.'

I spun round to look in the mirror. Two pert mounds were visible where my washboard chest had once been, and my skirt curved in a soft arc around my hips. The top half could be put down to the padded bra I had bought with my savings especially for the occasion. But I could only conclude that the hips must have crept up on me overnight.

I turned back to Frankie and shrugged.

'You're gonna knock him dead,' she said.

'I hope not. He's not much good to me or United dead.'

'Come on, you daft cow,' she said. 'Let's get your face done.'

Frankie spent ages applying my make-up. Pencilling the eyeliner as close to my lashes as she could get it, then smudging a deep copper tone across my eyelids, bringing the shimmering pools of blue below to life.

'There,' she said when she'd finally finished. 'Take a look at that.'

I stared at the mirror. At the stylish young woman with the flawless complexion and a brace-free smile (for tonight at least) encased in honey-coloured lips. I wanted to give Frankie a huge hug. The sort of hug we used to share together all the time. But I wasn't sure if that was a bit childish.

'Thanks. Thanks a million,' I grinned instead.

The huge black-and-white photographs of past United teams and triumphs towered over me as I made my way, wide-eyed, up the main staircase at Priory Park. I would have knelt and kissed the royal-blue carpet if there hadn't been anyone else around.

Inside the suite where the disco was being held, rows of blue and silver foil decorations hung from the ceiling and a giant glitterball twirled high above the makeshift dance floor. The DJ, a bearded man sporting a Pringle jumper worn over a silky lemon poloneck, was thumbing through a box of singles, no doubt putting aside anything by Frankie Goes to Hollywood deemed inappropriate for his audience. Most of the other guests were younger than me. Much younger. I imagined what Frankie would say if she was here. Wondered if I should slip out quietly now before anyone noticed. But I couldn't go – not without seeing Andy.

Matt was the first player to arrive. He was met by a surge of Junior Blues members, all squealing in excitement as they battled for his autograph. I stayed exactly where I was, relieved I was above that sort of thing.

'Hello, stranger.'

I knew straight away who the voice belonged to. The faint smell of aftershave confirmed it if I'd had any doubts.

'Hiya,' I said, turning to face Andy.

'I hardly recognised you,' he said. 'Your hair looks great. Really suits you.'

I blushed. I'd hoped that he would notice my hair but hadn't for a moment thought he would actually comment on it.

'Oh, thanks. I didn't even realise you were here.'

'Ah, I slipped in quietly through the back door. Didn't

want to risk a stampede like that,' he joked, gesturing towards Matt.

'I thought you'd be used to it by now, being our star player.'

'I don't know about that. I'm sure Clubber will get his place back at some point.'

'Not the way you're playing. You're gonna get an England call-up soon, that's what they said on *Saint and Greavsie* last Saturday.'

'Oh, I wouldn't take too much notice of them.'

'They said it in the *Daily Mirror* as well.'

'OK, you win. I'm not going to argue with someone who thinks I'm the world's greatest footballer. Would you like to join my fan club?'

'I didn't know you had one.'

'I didn't until just now. You're the first member. Congratulations.'

I laughed. Aware that things seemed different between us tonight. Although I wasn't quite sure why.

'Do I get free membership then, for being the first?'

'You drive a hard bargain, you do. How about honorary life membership, will that do you?'

'Yeah, I guess so. But make sure you carry on playing for a long time. I want to get my money's worth.'

Andy laughed again.

'Where's Thomo tonight?' I asked, looking around.

Andy hesitated before replying.

'He's not coming. His wife's not very well.' He looked down, seeming thrown for a moment. 'Where's your friend, anyway?' he said after a pause.

'What, Frankie? She's too old to come to Junior Blues events now. This is my last one, too.'

'You're joking, over the hill at sixteen? That's really depressing. You're making me feel ancient.'

'Sorry,' I said. 'Anyway, it's all right for you. You'll still be able to come to this next year.'

'So I will. That's one date in my social calendar, then. Mind you, I'm not sure if I'll go, it wouldn't be the same without you.'

'What do you mean?' I looked up, hardly daring to think about what Andy might say next.

'Well, there'd be no one to take the piss out of me for a start.'

The disappointment lasted all of a few seconds. Then I started laughing. Andy was laughing too. Huge belly aching laughs. The sort that made other people wonder what the joke was. I noticed Clubber and Nobber, who had just arrived, looking over at us. As soon as Andy saw them he stopped laughing.

'Anyway,' he said, 'I'd better go and sign some autographs. I'll catch up with you later. Come and rescue me if it looks like I need it.'

'OK,' I said. 'I'll keep my eye out.'

I stood at the edge of the room, watching a group of girls about my own age who were dancing round their handbags, tossing their hair and laughing hysterically at nothing in particular. They looked good, I could see that. But it didn't bother me. Because for once I knew I looked better. I had no desire to dance myself, particularly as 'The

Reflex' by Duran Duran was playing, I never knew what to do with my feet to the 'fle-fle-fle-fle-flex' bit.

Every time I glanced over at Andy, he was surrounded by a cluster of fans. I hated having to share him with other people, wanted to shout at them all to leave him alone, that I had seen him first.

'OK, everyone, it's time for some fun,' said Kay, the Junior Blues organiser (who looked like she truly had just stepped off the set of *Dynasty),* some time later as she announced that the promised party games were about to get under way. 'First up is the balloon game. Can I introduce your team captains: Dave Orton, Barry Gibbons, Matt Goodyear and Jamie Kane.'

A cheer went up as the players came forward and Kay began to explain the rules. You had to pass the balloon down the line between your teammates without using your hands or arms or letting it touch the ground. The DJ put on 'Agadoo' and I started edging towards the door at the far end of the room, imagining what Frankie would say about it all.

'Hey, not so fast. Don't think I'm doing this if you're not.'

I turned to look at the owner of the hand which had just grabbed my arm.

'Come on,' said Andy. 'You're on my team.'

My heart was racing as I took my place in front of him in a long column of Junior Blues members and players who had lined up behind Dave Orton. Andy had picked me for his team. Without me even asking. I was desperate to know what it meant. Whether it was some kind of sign that he was interested or he was just being friendly.

'I'm not sure I'm going to be any good at this,' I said. 'I've never done it before.'

'Good,' said Andy. 'That should make it more fun.'

I turned to the front as Kay blew the whistle. We were squashed close enough together that I could feel the warmth of Andy's breath on the back of my neck. I daren't turn round in case he caught me looking. So I stood, eyes fixed forward, like a blinkered racehorse in the stalls, oblivious to everything going on around me.

'Quick.' The squeal came from the little girl in front. She was standing facing me, a large red balloon wedged between her knees. I squatted down and, as instructed, inched the balloon from her. I shuffled round to face Andy while trying to prevent the balloon riding up towards my hemline.

'Here, let me help you,' he said, taking hold of my hips to steady me and pulling me nearer. His thighs rubbed against mine as he grappled for the balloon, our bodies pressing against each other. I wondered if this counted as foreplay. I could feel a letter to *Just Seventeen* coming on. Nobody else seemed to realise what was happening; they all thought it was part of the game. Even Andy was acting like there was nothing going on, smiling and laughing as if it was all a bit of a joke. Maybe it was to him; maybe whatever it was I was feeling, he wasn't feeling at all. Or maybe he did feel it but he simply didn't want to let on in front of everyone else. Our foreheads were almost touching. I kept my eyes lowered because I knew that if I looked up, if my eyes met his, I might not be able to stop myself.

'There,' he said, as he finally wrested the balloon from me. 'That wasn't too bad, was it?'

He let go of me and turned to pass the balloon on. The beads of perspiration on my face turned to hot red blotches. I didn't know what to do, how I should react. I wasn't even sure what he'd meant about it not being that bad. All I did know was that I'd had a close encounter of the Andy Pailes kind. And I didn't think I'd ever be the same again. I straightened my skirt and stood waiting for the game to end. Our team came last, which was no surprise considering how long me and Andy had taken. As Kay called for volunteers for the next game, Andy whispered, 'See you later,' and slid out of the line behind me. I needed a minute to myself to get my head together. I headed straight for the toilets, shut the cubicle door behind me and leant heavily against it, taking long, deep breaths as I tried to stop myself shaking. My body still seemed to be in shock; nothing was functioning as it should be. My head was buzzing with it, the sight, the smell, the feel of him. I didn't understand why anyone bothered taking drugs when you could get a high like this from a man. But one fix wasn't enough. I needed to sort myself out and get back out there. I had to be near him, to touch him again. To give him a chance to say anything he might want to say.

I touched up my make-up, trying to powder over my flushed cheeks, and headed back out to the function suite. The next game had ended, 'The Birdie Song' was being faded out and the DJ, seemingly forgetting the junior status of his audience, announced that he was going to 'slow things down' for the final dance.

Whitney Houston started crooning about needing a few more minutes to get herself ready. I scanned the room for Andy. Eventually I found him, on the far corner of the dance floor, locked in the tight embrace of a chubby twelve-year-old girl, who was clinging on to him as if her very life depended on it. I was smiling to myself when Andy caught my eye.

'Help,' he mouthed silently.

I didn't need asking twice. Putting my handbag down on a chair, I strode boldly across the dance floor, pausing only to consider how best to unlock my rival's vice-like grip.

'Excuse me, please,' Andy said to the girl. 'I think it's this young lady's turn now.'

The girl looked up with a mean scowl on her face. For a second I feared I would get my face smashed in after school for this. Then I remembered I wasn't at school. I was at Priory Park and Andy Pailes had just asked me to dance. For real, not just in my head. I stood my ground, letting it be known that I wouldn't take no for an answer.

'Thanks,' said Andy, as the girl reluctantly let go and I slipped smoothly into her place. 'I could feel my circulation beginning to cut off there. You may have just saved my life.'

I felt Andy's hands on the back of my waist. I had an overwhelming desire to throw my arms around him and squeeze him tight, even tighter than the fat girl had done. I didn't though. I placed my hands lightly on his sides, barely touching his shirt at first, before slowly allowing my fingers to close around him. Although our bodies weren't quite touching, I could tell they fitted perfectly together, like interlocking parts of a jigsaw.

'So, have you recovered from all that excitement?' he asked.

I hesitated, unsure what he was getting at, whether he'd noticed my prolonged absence.

'Yeah, I just got a bit hot, that's all.'

An awkward silence hung in the air.

'What'll you be doing for Christmas then?' Andy asked just as Whitney boomed her intention to make love the whole night through.

I tried to pretend I hadn't heard her. 'Oh, nothing much, just the usual family stuff at home.'

'You don't sound too keen.'

'My mum does my head in.'

'My dad's hard work as well,' said Andy. 'To be honest, it's a relief not to have to spend Christmas with him.'

'So what'll you do on Christmas Day then?'

'I'll be with the rest of the lads at the training ground for a bit in the morning. Then Thomo's invited us round for Christmas lunch.'

'What, the whole team?'

'No. I meant Ann . . . just, er, me and a friend, actually.'

'Oh.'

I flinched as if I'd been slapped across the cheek. He had a girlfriend. As much as he'd tried to cover it up, it was obvious. I'd been stupid enough to think he was flirting with me and all the time he had a girlfriend. My hands loosened their grip until I was barely touching his shirt. My feet felt like I was wearing huge, heavy football boots.

And the studs were somehow sinking into the wooden dance floor. I looked up at the glitterball above us as I tried to blink back the tears. It didn't seem to be twirling any more. It was the rest of the world that was spinning. I tried to steady myself, scared I was about to keel over. I didn't even notice that the music had stopped. Neither did Andy.

'Party's over, Trotsky,' said Clubber as he walked past. 'And it's way past her bedtime.'

Andy pulled away sharply, leaving us standing awkwardly together on the empty dance floor.

'Are you going to be OK getting home?' he said after a while. A few minutes ago I'd have thought he was making a move on me, but now I knew he was simply being polite.

'Yes thanks, my mum's picking me up.'

Andy nodded and looked down at his feet. He seemed flustered. I wanted to get my handbag and give him the card and present but I knew I couldn't do that now. It wouldn't be right.

'Have a great Christmas then,' he said as he started to walk away.

'Yeah, you too,' I said.

I didn't mean it though. I hoped his girlfriend would choke to death on the five pence hidden in the Christmas pudding.

I stand at the end of my road waiting for him. I stamp my feet, kicking out against the cold, and blow a plume of warm breath into the air.

I recognise the car as soon as it appears round the bend on the main road. I wave a gloved hand as it glides to a halt in front of me and he leans over to open the passenger door.

'Merry Christmas,' he says, the warmth from his smile shattering the brittle air.

I get in and turn to greet him. 'Merry Christmas, you,' I say, so overcome with emotion I can barely get the words out.

He leans over and kisses me on the lips. Just the once. But it is enough to chase the last vestige of coldness from my body.

We pull up outside his house and I step from the car like a princess, lifting my long skirt so it doesn't drag on the ground.

'Shut your eyes,' he says as we step into the hall.

'Why? What are you up to?'

'Trust me,' he says. 'Just shut them.'

I do as I am told. Trusting him more than I trust myself. He takes my hand and leads me through to the lounge. I can smell vanilla; warm and velvety. Hear the fire purring and popping, feel it radiating heat.

'OK, you can open them now.'

I do it slowly. Letting my lids rise like a theatre curtain, revealing the scene inch by inch. I see the present under the tree first. A small box wrapped in shiny silver paper, the corners neatly square. Behind it the trunk rises tall and straight from the pot, the lowest branches dipping towards the floor as if weighed down with snow. Further up they shoot in all directions, the ends splaying out like fingers drawn by children on stick people. A helter-skelter of silver tinsel encircles the tree, with sparkly silver baubles dotted in between and on top a silver star, not too big, nor too small. Behind the tree, on the windowsill, a row of candles light the stage.

'It's perfect,' I whisper, squeezing Andy's hand. 'Absolutely perfect.'

Linda Green

'Aren't you going to open it then?' he asks, nodding towards the present.

'What, now?'

'It'll be Boxing Day if you leave it much longer.'

I bend down to pick up the present. It is light, and something rattles and moves inside as I turn it over and prise open the Sellotape before sliding out a velvet-covered box. I look up at Andy; he is smiling at me, willing me on. I lift the lid and peek inside. Hanging from a silver chain is a single sapphire, twinkling in the reflection from the lights. I take a sharp intake of breath.

'Thank you. It's beautiful.'

'Good, just like you. Here, try it on.'

He takes the necklace from me. I lift my hair up while he fastens the clasp and steps back to admire it.

'It goes with your eyes,' he says. 'I knew it would.'

'I don't know what to say.'

'You don't have to say anything.'

We sit on the floor next to the fire. Andy wraps his legs and arms around me like tentacles, hugging me to his chest. I feel the softness of his jumper enveloping me, the roughness of his stubble against my face. It feels so good being held like this. I don't ever want him to let go. Nothing can happen to me while I am in his arms. I am safe here.

'I love you,' I say, lifting a hand to stroke the side of his face.

'I know,' he says. 'I love you too.'

I let the words seep into me. And smile as my tears blur the lights on the tree.

This is where I will spend every Christmas from now on. Next year I will wake up here on Christmas morning. Will pad downstairs in my bare feet before Andy has even stirred, to put his *present under the tree. Then slip back into bed beside him, nestling up against his warm body, watching him breathing. Smiling as he sleeps.*

By the following year the Christmas cards on the mantelpiece will say 'To my Husband' and 'To My Darling Wife'. And one Christmas, not too long after that, it won't just be the two of us any more. There'll be a baby, the cutest face you've ever seen, sleeping soundly in a cot next to the Christmas tree. Lauren if it's a girl, Steven if a boy. With a 'v' not a 'ph'. A little Pailes for me to love and cherish. A part of Andy and a part of me.

Seven

'The thing is, Danny, I don't really think pleading not guilty is an option.'

'Why not?' said Danny, who was slumped on a plastic chair in front of me in an interview room at court.

'Well, the fact that you signed your full name on the graffiti makes it very difficult.'

Danny frowned and stared up at the ceiling.

'We could say someone else wrote it to get me into trouble.'

'We could, if that was the truth, but it isn't, is it?'

Danny shook his head.

'In which case, I suggest you plead guilty. Admit you did it, apologise and hope they'll take your plea into consideration when sentencing.'

Danny shrugged and went back to picking at a scab on his arm.

'And as much as I hope there won't be a next time, can I make a couple of suggestions?'

'If you like.'

'There's a graffiti wall at the youth centre, a few streets away from where you were. You can do stuff all over that, you're allowed. And if, just supposing, you did fancy doing a bit of spraying somewhere else, don't use your full name next time. Make up a nickname for yourself.'

'What like?'

'There's a famous graffiti artist called Banksy. He just signs that. Everyone admires his work but no one knows his real name.'

'So I could call myself Dan the Man?'

'Something that hasn't got Dan in would be better.'

'But then no one will know it's me.'

'I know, Danny. That's the point. The police won't know it's you either.'

A smile spread slowly over Danny's face.

'Nice one, miss. Thanks for the tip,' he said with a wink.

I sighed as he left the room. This was what I'd been reduced to. It was a lousy, low-down job but I guessed someone had to do it.

Fiona was sitting down with her lunch when I made it through to the canteen.

'Have a good morning?' she asked.

'Not really. How about you?'

'Oh, the usual, adjournments, delays, chaos and confusion.'

'You look wiped out,' I said.

'Aidan didn't come home until the early hours again. Wouldn't say where he'd been this morning. If he carries on with this when they go back to school next week, he'll be falling asleep in the classroom.'

'I seem to remember being able to function on a few hours' sleep at that age.'

'Well I certainly can't. I used to worry about him when

he was little, all the usual paranoid new-parent stuff. But I'd give anything to have that back again now. Teething and potty training were a breeze compared to this.'

'At least he won't be a teenager for ever.'

'True. Don't suppose I'll ever stop worrying though. Which reminds me, what happened to your Mark?'

'What do you mean?'

'I saw him this morning on my way to work. Had a real shiner around his left eye.'

My stomach clenched as I had visions of him being caught up in some kind of brawl. Perhaps the interest in gang culture had gone too far. Ross Kemp had a lot to answer for.

'I've got no idea,' I said. 'He hasn't mentioned anything. Though I haven't seen him since the weekend. I'm on my way to meet him for a quick bite of lunch now.'

'Well, you'd better fill me in when you get back. If there's gossip and scandal around, I want to be the first to know.'

I hurried off in the direction of the town centre, wondering what on earth had happened to him. What I couldn't understand was why he hadn't told me. The legal world in Rochdale was very small. Someone would have been bound to notice. When I arrived at Costa Coffee, he was sitting on one of the high stools facing the wall, as if anxious to go unnoticed. Yet even from the side profile I could see why Fiona had been so alarmed. It really was quite a shiner. The best approach would be to try to use humour to disarm him. A straight question would be sure to be met with a denial. He was a laywer, after all.

'Are you looking for legal representation?' I asked. 'Only if you are, it's your lucky day. I know all the right people.'

Mark grinned sheepishly at me.

'A snowboard did it.'

'I've heard stories like this before,' I said. 'Far too many of them.'

'No, really. You know I said I was going snowboarding at that Chill Factor place?'

I nodded, vaguely remembering a mention of the latest extreme sport he was going to try.

'It was great, I was doing really well until the point I went over a ridge and the board came up and smacked me in the face.'

I looked at Mark and shook my head. 'If one of my clients said that I'd think they were lying through their back teeth.'

'If it's any help, I have a guilty plea from the snowboard,' Mark joked.

'I think Daniel Craig will be doing his own stunts for a while longer, won't he?'

'I guess so.'

'Does it still hurt?'

'Just a bit sore. I put some ice on it last night.'

'Good. Well, lunch is on me. What are you having?'

I sat down on the stool next to Mark with our baguettes and coffees. Aware that I was irritated, not by him getting injured but by his insistence that he was enjoying something which I knew damn well he wasn't. I wanted to shake him, to shout at him to stop this pretence. But at the same time I couldn't help feeling it was my fault, that he was doing all this because I had made him feel insecure over the whole house thing. The immediate pressure had eased. The viewing on his flat had come to nothing and I still hadn't had any interest in mine. But sooner or later someone would put in an offer. And when they did, I needed to be ready to move in with Mark or have Mark move in with me while we started house-hunting. The trouble was, I didn't feel ready at all. If anything, seeing Frankie again and talking with Emily had brought everything to the surface. All the old memories and feelings. I was thinking about Andy more than ever. Thinking about the list.

'What case are you working on?' I asked, keen to break what felt to me like an awkward silence.

'Oh, a woman who cut herself opening a tin can at some council day centre.'

'So who does she reckon's to blame for that?'

'The council, of course. For not providing her with training in opening cans correctly or putting up a warning notice that tins can be sharp when opened.'

'Jesus. Does she have learning difficulties or anything?'

'Nope.'

'Just plain stupid then. And trying to make a quick buck out of it.'

'As her legal representative I couldn't possibly comment.'

'You're never going to win that one though, are you?'

'I don't know. I won that other case where the guy complained that the council hadn't put a sign up warning that the fire could be hot.'

I shook my head.

'What?' asked Mark.

'Don't you ever wonder what it's all about? If this is what we went through years of legal training for?'

'Sometimes. And then I remember that life doesn't always turn out how you planned and you just make the best of it. And that working for some big corporate company would be a nightmare, full of suits who are up their own arses.'

'You don't think I should have applied for that job then?'

'No, I didn't mean it like that. I wasn't talking about you. Of course you should have applied if you feel you need a change. I know exactly how you feel. That's why I've done something about it too.'

'Applied for something, you mean?'

'I've got it, actually.'

'What, a new job?'

'No, not a paid one anyway. I've volunteered to do some casework for LawWorks in Manchester. They do free advice for people who don't qualify for Legal Aid.'

I was gobsmacked. It wasn't quite up there with buying Ross Kemp books but it wasn't far off. Although in a totally different direction this time. To be honest, it was something I'd thought about doing myself, although never managed to get round to. The fact that Mark had beaten me to it not only perplexed me but also made me feel bad.

'But I'm the one with the social conscience.' I realised as soon as I said it how bad it sounded. Mark started laughing.

'And you've got a monopoly on having one, I take it.'

'I didn't mean it like that. I'm just surprised.'

'You always seem to be surprised lately.'

'That's because you keep doing surprising things.' I lowered my voice as I glanced around the café. Aware that this was starting to sound like an argument.

'Aren't I allowed to try new things, broaden my horizons and all that?' asked Mark after a while.

'It's the reason why you're trying them that bothers me,' I said.

'What do you mean?'

What I meant was that it felt like he was trying to please me or impress me. But I knew I couldn't say that without it sounding mean and ungrateful. Most women complained that their men weren't making enough effort. And here I was complaining that he was trying too hard.

'I don't want you to do stuff because you feel you should.'

'I'm not. I'm doing it because you're right: sometimes this whole no-win-no-fee stuff does feels pretty hollow, even when I win the case. So if I can find a way I can use my legal skills to help people who really need it, well, that's great.'

'So what's involved?' I asked, trying to sound more positive.

'Probably only a few hours a week, depending on what cases get referred to me. They do a lot of employment stuff, so I might have to pick your brains sometime.'

'Of course, just let me know if I can help.'

'So that's fine then?'

'Yeah,' I said, deciding it was the only reasonable thing to say. 'Any more surprises up your sleeve?'

'You'll have to wait and see,' said Mark.

★

I gave the front door a good shove with my hip; the rain had made it stick again. A small pile of post lay on the doormat inside. I picked it up and flicked through: bills mostly, the odd circular. And a thick white envelope with a Manchester postmark addressed to Ms Claire Cooper.

I threw the rest of the post down on the kitchen table and tore open the envelope. As soon as I saw the Smith MacGuire letterhead I knew. I had an interview for the job in three weeks' time. I might not spend the rest of my life at Rochdale Magistrates' Court after all. I let out a whoop and did a little jig around the kitchen. It felt good to be wanted. And it made me think that maybe there was still time to turn my life around. That perhaps I could make a through road out of a cul-de-sac. But if that was the case, if there really was nothing stopping me apart from my own doubts, where did I draw the line? Because if I could find my way to getting at least one tick on the list, what was to stop me trying for more? Even the one which seemed the most distant, the most out of reach. But which, like a glittering far-off jewel, held the greatest attraction.

It was only as I jigged back around the kitchen that I noticed the flashing light on the answering machine. It wouldn't be work, they always called my mobile. It occurred to me that it could be something to do with the interview. I pressed play and picked up a pen and pencil. It was Frankie's voice I heard. Although it wasn't her usual voice at all. It was a voice so empty, so devoid of any life or joy that it stopped me in my tracks.

'Claire, it's Frankie. Can you give me a call as soon as

you get this.' A pause, which although silent conveyed far more than the words. Then she left her phone number. Slow and deliberate, as if each number pained her. Followed by a click.

I called her back straight away. The phone rang several times. Her voice was flat when she answered, but as soon as I said hello it went high and squeaky.

'What's the matter? Are you OK?'

'It's Emily,' she said. 'The blood tests came back from the doctor. We had to go to hospital for some more tests. She's got leukaemia.'

I shut my eyes and bit my lip as the sobs came from the other end of the phone. Frankie had been right to worry. Maternal instinct was obviously not to be doubted. Although the truth was far worse than even she had feared.

'Oh Frankie, I'm so sorry. How awful.'

'I wish it had been anorexia now. I think I could have coped with that. But this . . .' Her voice trailed off. I heard her blow her nose. Could picture her red-rimmed eyes.

'What do the doctors say? How bad is it?'

'It's bad. Something called acute lymphoblastic leukaemia, which progresses quickly. And she's got a high leukaemia cell count, which means it's already well advanced.'

'So she'll have to have chemo?'

'Yeah. She's starting it tomorrow, but they've also found she's got something called a Philadelphia chromosome, which means there's a high risk of relapse. She could die, Claire. My beautiful Emily could die.' The sobs came again.

From both ends of the phone this time. I felt so helpless, so small and pathetic in the great big horrible world that had landed such a brutal blow.

'Try not to think that,' I said. 'You have to shut that out and believe she can get through this. Be strong for her.'

'I know. And I try really hard when I'm with her, but it's so hard. Do you know what she said when the consultant asked if she had any questions? Would she still be able to go to the *Twilight* premiere? As if that's the only thing worth living for.'

I smiled a watery smile. Remembering when I had thought like that. Unable to see anything more important than Andy.

'Where is she now?'

'In her room. She only got back from hospital this afternoon and she's going in first thing in the morning. I don't know what she's doing. She's very quiet but she says she wants to be on her own.'

I knew she'd be talking to Robert. Praying to him, no doubt. Because he was the closest thing to a God she had.

'What have you told the little ones?'

'Just that their big sister's very ill. That she needs to go to hospital. Sophia asked if the doctors would make her better so I said yes. I didn't see how I could say anything else.'

'And Joe?'

'He's putting on a brave face but inside he's in bits. He had to walk out the room at the hospital when they took the bone marrow sample. They gave her a local anaesthetic but she still cried out with the pain. It was horrible.'

'Oh Frankie. You poor thing. I don't know what to say. I just wish I could make this all go away for you. If there's anything I can do, however small.'

'There is one thing. If I give you her e-mail address, will you drop her a line? She won't speak to anyone at the moment but she really took to you. She's been talking about you, a lot. Said you weren't like other grown-ups. You seemed to understand about her and Robert. Didn't make her feel silly about it.'

I smiled and sniffed at the same time. Honoured to be thought of in that way. And desperately sad that we weren't communicating in different circumstances.

'Of course I can. It's the least I can do. Although I don't know if I'll find the right thing to say.'

'You will,' said Frankie. 'I know you will.'

'I'll do my best. But listen, if you need to talk. Or just cry down the phone at me. Any time, day or night. I'm on call, OK?'

'OK,' said Frankie. There was a high-pitched scream and crying from somewhere in the house. It was a comforting sound in a way. Showing that life, in part of the Ricotta family at least, was continuing as normal. 'I'd better go,' she said. 'You know what they're like.'

I replaced the handset and sat down heavily on the chair. Feeling empty and winded and sick. The interview letter lay open on the table where I'd left it. Except, of course, it didn't seem nearly as important as it had done ten minutes ago. I put it back in the envelope and pulled my laptop out of my briefcase.

I sat for a long time before I wrote anything other than 'Dear Emily'. But when the words did finally come, they came in a flourish. Pouring out on to the screen. Full of Robert. Full of hopes and fears and dreams.

Friday, 10 January 1986

I gazed down at the latest picture of Andy in an England shirt in my United scrapbook. Even now, three days later, I still bristled with pride as I re-read the glowing newspaper testimonies to his impressive display on the hallowed Wembley turf. I had bought all the newspapers the day after and stuck each report firmly into place in my scrapbook, smoothing down the corners to ensure they didn't buckle or come unstuck when I turned the page. It was my way of paying homage to Andy, and, at the same time, reminding myself that good things did still happen – even if they were becoming increasingly few and far between.

The list of bad things in my life was getting pretty long and had now been extended to a second sheet of ruled A4 paper. The top one was, of course, 'Andy going out with someone else'. I'd found out what her name was. Annie, as in 'Annie, I'm Not Your Daddy'. That was how she introduced herself, apparently. Susan from the club shop had told me. I didn't see why anyone would resort to a Kid Creole and the Coconuts song when a simple 'Annie' would do. But Susan said people in promotions were funny like that. Turned out that was what she was. A fucking United promotions girl. Just to rub it in, there was a photo of her

with Andy and the rest of the team in the United programme most weeks. Advertising the new range of leisure
wear. She was dressed in a United vest top and shorts cut so
high you could see her arse. And she was wearing ankle-
warmers and stilettos. Like you'd really do a workout in
high heels. She had big tits and big hair as well, of course
(Susan reckoned you had to, to work in promotions). And
the players were holding her up, like blokes used to do to
dancing women in those old films. Skip, Gibbo and Matt
were holding her shoulders, Nobber was by her feet and
Andy was somewhere in the middle, near her arse. Susan
said that was when they'd met. That she fell for him because
he was polite and didn't try to chat her up like the others
did. I couldn't work it out though, what Andy saw in her
(apart from the obvious, I mean). Susan said she was as
thick as shit. The sort of woman who thought the Gaza
Strip was a club in Soho. I didn't get it. Andy was a *Guardian* reader; he watched *Newsnight*. I doubted if Annie could
keep up with *John Craven's Newsround*.

I kept playing 'Is She Really Going Out With Him?' at
full volume over and over again, shouting out the words so
loudly that I drowned out Joe Jackson.

I wished I'd never seen the photo or knew who she was.
Whenever I closed my eyes, all I could see was her and
Andy together. Holding hands, kissing, going for long
walks in the country. All the things I'd dreamt of doing
with him. That was the worst thing. Not that she was
going out with him but that she'd stolen my dreams.

The most recent addition to the bad things list was Thomo's departure. It had all been very sudden. One minute

he'd been talking about looking forward to a possible Wembley appearance with United in the Milk Cup Final. The next he'd been pictured in the papers proudly wearing an Aston Villa shirt and shaking hands with his new manager. I still couldn't get my head round it. I'd always imagined the team would stay together for ever. That Andy, Thomo and the rest of them would see out the remainder of their playing days at Priory Park before retiring to some home for ex-United players in the Hertfordshire countryside where I could go and visit them and reminisce about the good old days. Thomo's departure had forced me to confront the possibility that it wasn't going to be like that.

I kissed the picture of Andy and flicked through the scrapbook, counting the number of blank pages remaining. There were fourteen. I would be very happy indeed if fourteen pages' worth of good things happened between now and the end of the season.

'How do you fancy being taken out for a slap-up meal tonight?'

If it had been Andy asking me, I'd have jumped at it. But it wasn't, it was Dad on the phone. There had to be a catch.

'Why would you want to do that?'

'I don't need a reason to take my own daughter out, do I?'

'No, I s'pose not.'

'So I'll take that as a yes then?'

'I'll have to ask Mum first but it should be OK.'

'Good. I'll pick you up at seven thirty, on the corner as

usual. Wear something nice, we're going somewhere a bit better than the Wimpy.'

I enjoyed a couple of hours idly fantasising that Dad was going to announce he was moving back home, or at the very least getting me tickets for the Milk Cup semi-final, before Mum came home and brought me back down to earth.

'What's he done wrong then?'

'What d'ya mean?'

'Well he must be trying to soften you up for a reason. He wouldn't offer to take you out otherwise, would he?'

'He doesn't need an excuse to take his own daughter out, does he?' I said, repeating Dad's line with even less conviction than he had been able to muster.

'He's hardly made a habit of it in the past, has he? Don't you think it's strange that he should suddenly push the boat out like this? You're sure he's not emigrating to Australia or anything?'

'That's right, go and spoil it for me. You can't bear him making me happy, can you?'

'I just don't like him building up your expectations like this in case he lets you down, like he usually does.'

'Oh, like you've never let me down.'

Mum shook her head and walked a few steps towards me.

'I've always been there for you, Claire. I do at least try to make you happy.'

'You won't even let me go to United matches, that's how much you care about my happiness.'

'I don't want you getting caught up in the trouble, you know that.'

'Well, if anything happens to me you can always get Gerry Marsden or your mate Buddy Holly to make a charity record to raise some money for you, OK?'

'Buddy Holly's dead, Claire.'

'Don't tell me, he was killed by hooligans at a football match.'

'Don't be so facetious. I didn't bring you up to say things like that.'

I wasn't sure what facetious meant, but guessed from the tone of Mum's voice that it was something bad.

'I must have got it from Dad then, mustn't I? Everything I do or say that's wrong is down to Dad.'

I turned to walk out the room.

'Enjoy *Dempsey and Makepeace,* won't you?' I called back over my shoulder.

By the time I trotted down the road to meet Dad, I was so convinced he was about to emigrate to Australia that I expected to see him sitting in the car wearing a wide-brimmed hat with corks hanging from the rim and sipping a can of Foster's.

So, in a strange way, the fact that there was no hat and no can of Foster's but the passenger seat was occupied by a red-haired woman came as something of a relief at first. It was a good few seconds before I realised that Dad hadn't brought the woman along for decoration or to make up the numbers. She had to be there for a reason.

'Claire, I'd like you to meet Denise.'

The introduction may have contained the bare minimum of information, but it was still more than I had wanted to know. The woman now had a name. And it was much harder to pretend someone didn't exist when you knew their name.

'Hiya, Claire, nice to meet you at last. Your father's told me a lot about you.'

While aware that I was supposed to reply jovially, 'All of it good, I hope,' I did not feel inclined to observe social etiquette simply in order to put Denise at ease. Nor did I wish to let Dad off the hook by giving his girlfriend my seal of approval.

'What did he say?'

'I'm sorry?'

'What did he tell you about me?'

Denise was clearly thrown by such a direct question and looked to Dad for assistance.

'Honestly, Claire, what do you think I told her, that you were a raving lunatic or something?'

'No, I didn't think you knew much stuff about me, that's all.'

'Well, I told her that you were a big United fan and a vegetarian and that you want to be a lawyer when you grow up. You do still want to be a lawyer, I take it?'

I resented the patronising tone in his voice, which implied that my desire to be a lawyer was as far-fetched as wanting to be an astronaut or a racing driver. I also resented the phrase 'when you grow up', which missed the fact that I already had.

'Yes, I do still want to be a lawyer. I'm doing work experience with the Crown Prosecution Service at Hornsey Magistrates' Court next month, actually.'

'Good for you,' Dad replied, obviously sensing this was going to be a very long evening. 'At least we've got that one sorted out.'

When we arrived at Valentino's, I forgot my animosity towards Denise and my anger at Dad for a few moments in the excitement of entering an establishment frequented by United players. I gazed at the three framed photographs which took pride of place in the plush reception area. They showed Matt Goodyear, Barry Gibbons and Dave Orton shaking hands with a rotund, slightly balding Italian man. Each photograph had been inscribed with a suitable message such as the 'Thanks for a great night, Luigi' which Matt had written in black felt-tip pen. I hastily scanned the ranks of other diners, in case I could see any familiar faces amongst them.

'Hey, how about that then, Claire?' said Dad, following my gaze. 'You might end up sitting next to Matt Goodyear.'

'Is he your favourite player?' asked Denise, fiddling with the spaghetti-like straps of her red dress.

'No, Andy Pailes is, actually. Didn't my dad tell you that?'

Luigi seated us at a table by the window. I gathered from the conversation that Dad and Denise were regular clients. I couldn't remember him ever taking Mum out to restaurants. Certainly not to ones that had proper tablecloths anyway.

'I expect this is all a bit of a drag for you, isn't it, Claire?' said Denise. 'I bet you're usually out with your friends on a Saturday night.'

I stared blankly at her, wondering why she was trying so hard to be friendly.

'Yeah, sometimes I am.'

'So where do you go?'

I wished I hadn't lied now. It meant I would have to lie again.

'The pictures, things like that.'

'Oh, I love the cinema. What was the last thing you saw?'

I hesitated. I wanted to say something cool like *St Elmo's Fire* or *The Breakfast Club*. But I didn't want to get caught out by any further questions from Denise which might expose the fact that I hadn't seen either of them. I decided to play it safe.

'*Gremlins*, I saw *Gremlins*. That was good.'

'Oh God, yeah, I loved that. Weren't they cute at the beginning? I'm a sucker for kids' stuff like that. *Bambi* is my all-time favourite film, you know. I cried buckets when his mother got shot.'

I had no idea why adults tried to pretend they liked kids' things. None of my classmates would be caught dead at anything less than a 15 certificate.

Luigi came back to take our order. We agreed to skip the starters, deciding to have desserts instead. I asked for the Napolitana pasta dish (mainly because it was the only vegetarian thing on the menu), Dad ordered the chicken and Denise plumped for the venison.

'She can't have the venison,' I said.

Dad looked at me. He had one of those fixed smiles on his face.

'Why not? It's what she wants.'

'Two minutes ago she said *Bambi* was her all-time favourite film. She said she cried when his mother got shot. And now she says she wants the venison.'

'I'll have the fish if it's going to upset you,' offered Denise, clearly embarrassed. Dad rolled his eyes and told Luigi to stick with the original order.

'For heaven's sake, Claire, there's no need to create a scene,' he said, as Luigi returned to the kitchen scratching his head. 'Just because you choose not to eat meat, it doesn't mean to say other people can't. Denise wants the venison and that's what she's having.'

'Why did she say all that stuff about *Bambi* then? She's a hypocrite.'

Dad gave me a look which meant 'shut up'. Denise started fiddling with the straps on her dress again. We sat in silence until the main courses arrived.

'Do you reckon they'll win the semi-final, then?' Dad asked as he tucked into his chicken breast.

'Yeah, easy. It's only QPR, isn't it?'

'They need to win something this year, even if it is only the Milk Cup. Doesn't look like they're going to win the league now, does it?'

'We're only six points behind Everton,' I said.

'No chance of them slipping up, though. Not the way Lineker's playing. Still, now Roy Brown's come in as chairman we might be able to buy another decent striker ourselves. Best thing that's happened to United for years, that Brown is.'

'How can you say that? He's a Tory MP. He's a complete fascist.' I was still recovering from the shock of United's recent boardroom coup. I had visions of Maggie Thatcher being appointed honorary chairman of the club before the season was out.

'He could be Hitler's long-lost son for all I care; he's putting two million quid into the club, that's what matters.'

'Money isn't everything, you know.'

Dad laughed. 'Are you sure you're a teenager?'

'What's that supposed to mean?'

'Oh, it doesn't matter. Money might not be everything to you, Claire, but it's pretty important to the rest of us. And it'll come in handy to buy a replacement for Thomo, won't it?'

'That's different. They should never have sold him in the first place.'

'They didn't have much choice, did they? Not with that business with his wife.'

'What did his wife have to do with it?'

'She had cancer, didn't she. That's why he went to Villa, so she could be near her family in Birmingham. Only they kept it all hush-hush because they didn't want it getting in the papers. That's what they were saying at the match last week anyway.'

I pushed my half-eaten bowl of pasta away and stared out of the window. It all made sense now. I hated myself for ever having doubted Thomo's commitment, for thinking he had let me down. My bottom lip started to tremble.

'Hey, come on, don't upset yourself,' said Dad. 'This is supposed to be a celebration.'

'Is it?' I looked blankly at him. 'What are we supposed to be celebrating?'

'Well, Denise and I have got something to tell you, actually.' He paused for a second, shifting uncomfortably in his seat. 'How do you fancy going to a wedding in September?'

'Depends if United are at home. And whose wedding it is.'

'Ours, silly. It's going to be our wedding. We got engaged on New Year's Eve.'

I felt as if a nuclear missile had exploded inside me, rendering all my vital organs useless and severing all communication links. My father was going to marry a hypocritical Fergie lookalike. I could only presume he must be having some kind of mid-life crisis, like the men in sitcoms.

I stared at Denise, who was looking down at her plate, chewing the same piece of food over and over again to avoid having to say anything. I couldn't believe that this woman was going to be my stepmother. She wasn't even wearing a bra, for Christ's sake. For all I knew she didn't have any knickers on either.

'Well, aren't you going to say anything?' Dad asked, clearly seeking my blessing.

'Actually, I've changed my mind,' I said. 'I don't want any pudding, thank you. I've kind of lost my appetite.'

It wasn't until I got home that I was able to cry properly. The sound of the front door shutting behind me seemed to trigger my tear ducts back into life. A blurry vision of Mum appeared at the far end of the hall.

'What's he done now?'

'It's not his fault; it's hers.'

'Whose fault, Claire? You're not making any sense.'

'Denise, that's who. The stupid tart that Dad's gonna marry.'

'Marry? Your father's getting married?'

'Yeah, in September. He wants me to go to the wedding. That'll be it then, I s'pose. He'll never want to see me again. Not once he's got her.'

'Hey, don't be silly. Of course he'll want to see you.' Mum went to put her arm around me but I pushed her away.

'How can you say that? You thought he was going to emigrate a few hours ago. That's how much you think he's bothered about me.'

'You know I didn't mean that.'

'Why bother saying something if you don't mean it?'

'I told you, love. I didn't want him building your hopes up, that was all. I didn't want him hurting you, like he obviously has done.'

'You're as bad as her, you know. You say stuff you don't mean and you make things up 'cos you think it's what I want to hear. Why can't you tell the truth for once?'

Mum walked a few steps closer towards me.

'Because sometimes the truth hurts, love. Sometimes I think you need protecting from it.'

'Is that why you never admit that you hate Dad?'

'I don't hate your father.'

'There you go again, see, lying to me and saying stuff you don't mean. Just leave me alone, will you?'

I pushed past Mum and ran upstairs to my room, hurling myself on to my bed. The two men I loved most in the world had both deserted me for other women. I wished I could either rewind to being a little girl, so I could be the apple of Dad's eye again, or fast forward so I could have a chance of getting Andy back. I hated this awkward bit in the middle, where the tape machine appeared to be stuck on pause.

I popped out to the bathroom and pulled a string of sheets from the toilet roll. As I crept back across the landing, I heard Mum crying downstairs. I felt bad about what I'd said to her. I wasn't going to go down and tell her that, mind. Because I knew it wouldn't make any difference. She'd still hate me. Like she still hated Dad.

Eight

'OK, you have fifteen minutes to get ready,' announced Mark when he arrived at my house after work on Friday evening three weeks later. He had that look in his eye. He was up to something. And I had no idea what it was.

'Get ready for what?' I asked. 'This doesn't involve getting rude in a lift by any chance, does it?'

'No,' laughed Mark. 'Not that I'm aware of. I'm taking you away for the weekend.'

My instinctive reaction was to be thrilled. I couldn't remember the last time I'd been whisked off for a weekend away. In fact, when I thought about it, I realised it was because it had never actually happened before. Certainly Mark had never done it. And although David and I had managed a few odd nights away, he'd never spared the time off work for an entire weekend. And then I remembered Mark's behaviour of recent weeks. The words 'odd' and 'unpredictable' came to mind. Along with the realisation that his idea of a good weekend away might not necessarily be mine.

'Where are we going?' I asked.

'Aahh, that would be telling,' he said, grabbing me around the waist and kissing me.

'But you have to give me some idea so I know what to pack.'

'Three questions then,' said Mark. 'But only three, mind.'

'OK, do I need my passport?'

'No.'

I tried not to show my disappointment that the romantic weekend in Florence was out of the window.

'Formal or casual clothes?'

'Do I look like a guy who'd choose formal?' This was true. Even after his fashion makeover he could only be said to be in the smart-casual camp.

'You're right,' I said. 'Wasted question on my part. City or countryside, then?'

'Countryside.'

'Should I be worried?'

'You've had your three. Not my fault if you wasted one.' It wasn't the reassuring answer I'd been looking for. Still, the possibility of some gorgeous old country hotel with a roaring fire and four-poster bed had not been ruled out. And I was in need of a break. The whole thing with Emily had really got to me. I was emotionally drained, worried sick about her and could think about little else.

'OK,' I said. 'Can you give me twenty minutes?'

'Is this what you're like at plea bargaining?'

'I want to drop Emily a quick line first. Let her know that I'm going to be away for a couple of days.' We'd been e-mailing back and forth on a regular basis. I didn't ask much about the chemo. Just left her to tell me what she wanted to. Mainly her worries that she wouldn't be able to go to the premiere. And I, of course, wasn't able to tell her that her mother was worried she might not even be alive by then. I'd told her bits about Andy to try to help. About me always getting spots when I was due to see him. And how much he'd liked my hair when I had it cut. All designed to make her laugh or give her hope that she'd look great with short hair while it grew back.

'Go on, then,' he said. 'And say hi from me.' Mark had been upset when I'd told him. Though it was different for him. He didn't have the bond I had with Frankie. Or with Emily for that matter.

I went upstairs to the bedroom and bundled a variety of clothes into my suitcase. A pair of jeans and some combats, a couple of jumpers and a fleece. A nice outfit for dinner, some heels, jewellery and my best lingerie – just in case that country hotel turned out to be the secret destination. Then I sat down at my laptop to write to Emily. It felt wrong somehow, me going off to enjoy myself while she was going through a round of high-dose chemotherapy. But Frankie said she liked to hear about normal things, stuff that I was doing. That she got sick of everyone asking her how she was all the time. She wanted to hear about good things, happy things. Anything that could make her forget. Even for a moment or two.

'Ready,' I said five minutes later as I arrived downstairs with my bulging suitcase.

'Come on, then,' said Mark, ushering me outside. 'Your chariot awaits.'

We headed north to Burnley, then west, I crossed off potential destinations at each turn. By the time we got to the M6 I was pretty sure (although I did, admittedly, give a small sigh of relief as we passed the turning for Black-pool). We'd been to the Lake District together once before, the first holiday we'd had together if I remembered rightly. Just for a week, a village called Hawkshead, near where Beatrix Potter had lived. I remembered tea shops, the odd stroll around a lake, lock-ins at country pubs, a lot of sex (we were still in the honeymoon stage of our relationship) and a visit to the football museum in Ambleside (this after I'd told him I used to be a big United fan). We'd stayed in a nice hotel too, although I seemed to remember I'd booked it myself to make sure.

'Are we nearly there yet?' I asked as we approached junction 36.

'You're worse than a kid,' laughed Mark.

'I'm not very good at surprises. I like to know. Do I get any clues?'

'It's not Scotland.'

'OK, my guess is still on, then.'

'What's your guess?'

'I can't tell you, can I? Otherwise if it's not there you'll think you've chosen the wrong place and worry I'll be disappointed.'

'I'm worrying already now you've piled the pressure on like that.'

'Well don't,' I said. 'I'm sure it'll be lovely, whatever it is. It's just nice to get away.' What I didn't tell him was that I had my fingers crossed under my leg as I said it.

We left the motorway at junction 36 and headed west for some time. I was tired by now. It had been a busy week at work and I was still recovering from being on police cells duty rota the previous weekend. I had a disturbing knack of being called out at two a.m. the night before a big trial. I was looking forward to a long hot bath, soft fluffy towels, a lie-in and maybe even breakfast in bed.

Mark turned off towards Grizedale Forest. He was heading up towards the hotel we'd first stayed at together, I was sure of it. But ten minutes later he took a sharp left and we started down a bumpy track. It was pitch black and had started to rain. All I could see in the headlights in front of the swishing windscreen wipers were trees.

'Are you sure this is the right way?' I asked.

'Pretty sure, yeah.'

'It's not the way to Hawkshead.'

'We're not going to Hawkshead.'

'Oh. Well there don't even seem to be any buildings down here.'

'I know. I wanted to find somewhere you could really get away from it all.'

A feeling of unease spread over me. A sense that this was not going to be what I'd expected. We followed the track round to the left and pulled up sharply in a small gravelled car park.

'Come on,' said Mark, leaping out of the car like some kid desperate to get to the beach. 'Let me show you.'

I quickly pulled on my waterproof jacket before he grabbed my hand and led me along a gravel track to a clearing in the woods. For a second I wondered if this was all an elaborate plan to have sex with me in the forest; if it was the next unusual venue to cross off after 'lift'. And then through the darkness I caught sight of a circle of soft lights. And in the middle, the tents. Half a dozen of them spaced out around the clearing. Large canvas bell tents. I glanced across at Mark to see if it was a joke, but the look on his face was one of pure unadulterated excitement.

'Camping,' I said. 'You've brought me camping.'

'No,' he said. 'This is glamping.'

'And what's that?'

'Glamorous camping. Luxury tent provided, complete with wooden floor, futon to sleep on and a wood-burning stove to keep us warm.'

I nodded slowly, letting the information sink in. Deciding how best to react.

'Right, but no, er, bathroom facilities, I take it?'

'Yeah,' said Mark, producing a torch from his jacket pocket and shining it across to a small hut at the edge of the clearing. 'They've got a hot shower and a toilet. In there, I think.'

I struggled for a moment not to burst into tears. His intentions, as always, were honourable. It was a really sweet thought to take me away, and no doubt this place sounded great on the internet. I could see why he was so enthusiastic about it. But the reality of turning up in the pitch black and pouring rain on a freezing-cold night at the end of September and being shown to a tent, however glamorous, rather than an en-suite room with four-poster and whirlpool bath, was undeniably glum.

'You'll love it,' Mark said, filling the awkward silence. 'Just wait until morning when you wake up to birdsong and the wind rustling through the trees.'

I smiled and nodded at him. Trying desperately not to let my disappointment show.

'You didn't tell me to pack my wellies,' I said, looking down as my shoes started sinking into the mud.

'It's all right. I threw them in the boot while you were upstairs packing. And I've brought a double sleeping bag so we can keep each other warm. Not that it will be cold. There's a stove, like I said.'

'So which one's ours?' I asked, trying to show willing.

'Er, I'm not too sure. The woman who runs it just said she'd leave the breakfast basket in it ready for the morning.'

I was getting breakfast in bed after all. Or breakfast in futon at least. I felt myself start to soften, sensing how desperate Mark was for me to like it.

'Thank you,' I said. His eyes lit up in relief.

'I knew you'd love it. I'll nip back to the car to get our wellies, then we'll go and find our tent.' I stood there, rain dripping down my face, shivering in the cold. Concentrating hard on keeping the smile on my face.

I awoke in the early hours to what sounded like foxes fighting and the rain beating on the canvas above. It was still dark and the fire had gone out, leaving a distinct chill in the air. To which, as I was only wearing a flimsy camisole and shorts set (I hadn't wanted to be the passion killer who went to bed in a jumper), you had to add a buttock and nipple chill factor, in order to truly appreciate it. Mark, who had brought pyjamas, was sleeping soundly next to me. As much as I wanted to get back to sleep, I was aware I needed the toilet. It was just unfortunate that the only one in question was on the other side of the field. Quietly I unzipped my side of the sleeping bag and slid out. I fumbled around on the floor, feeling for the torch, then flicked it on to search for the waterproof to throw over me. I unzipped the flap to the tent and stepped into my wellies, like some mixed-up lingerie model who had gone to the wrong venue for the photo shoot. When I got to the hut I couldn't find a light inside and ended up squatting in the dark with the torch shining up at me as if I'd been caught in the act by a patrolling security guard.

I made my way gingerly back to the tent. It was only as I shone the torch around to establish the exact location of the futon that I noticed the man sitting bolt upright looking at me. The man who was not Mark.

'Sorry,' I muttered. 'They all look the same in the dark.'

'Fine by me, love,' he said, his eyes appearing to adjust to the torchlight in time to give my bare thighs a quick once-over. 'I'm very happy to oblige.'

I slunk back to the correct tent next door. Even on a weekend away, it seemed, we now had a neighbour to avoid.

'So what's the plan today then?'

We were sitting on the futon, huddled under the sleeping bag, having polished off our breakfast in record time in order to provide fuel for our freezing bodies. Mark hadn't admitted that, of course. Just said that having gone to the effort of making it on our two-ring camp stove, he didn't want to let it go cold. But I suspected his reason for shovelling the eggs and hash browns down so quickly was the same as mine. I was hoping that there was no plan. That we could have one of those lazy, wandering-around-doing-nothing kind of days. But the excited expression on Mark's face indicated otherwise.

'Ahh, that would be telling.'

I groaned inwardly, aware I was beginning to suffer from surprise fatigue.

'At least make sure I'm properly dressed for whatever we're doing this time.'

'OK,' said Mark. 'Trainers, jeans, a fleece and your waterproof should do the job.'

I nodded, resisting the temptation to ask whether my nice dress and heels were actually going to get an outing at any point.

'So we're going to be out in the elements. Will there be any pain or embarrassment involved?'

Mark considered the question for a moment.

'Hopefully no pain. Difficult to say on the embarrassment front due to it being uncharted territory.'

'OK, not very reassuring, but as long as the guy in the next tent's not involved, I'll take a chance.'

Mark looked at me, clearly waiting for an explanation.

'We had a night-time rendezvous,' I said. 'Of the unwanted and unexpected kind.'

Mark shook his head and laughed. 'Honestly, I can't take you anywhere, can I?'

An hour later I was standing in another clearing in the same forest, peering skywards as directed by Mark, unsure about exactly what I was supposed to be looking for.

'I can hear something in the trees,' said Mark. 'Keep your eyes peeled, I think it's coming.' It wasn't a bird, or a plane, or Superman for that matter. It was some poor bastard hurtling through the trees hanging on to a zip-wire looking absolutely terrified. It was only a nanosecond after seeing him that it occurred to me that Mark hadn't brought me here to enjoy a spectator sport.

'That's what we're doing, isn't it?'

'Yep,' said Mark, a huge grin on his face. 'I've booked us on a three-hour hire-wire forest adventure.' He said it in the same tone of voice you would say, 'I've booked us on the Orient Express', or 'I've booked us on a luxury cruise.'

'And what gave you the impression I'd enjoy swinging through the trees like a monkey?' I said.

'Come on, it'll be great fun. You'll get a real kick out of it.'

'I thought this was supposed to be a relaxing weekend away from it all?'

'It is. We'll relax later.' Quite what was relaxing about going back to a tent in a muddy field I wasn't sure.

'Promise me you have no more surprises up your sleeve.'

'Scout's honour,' said Mark. 'Now come on. We've got a safety session with an instructor before we set off.'

Which was how, shortly afterwards, I came to be standing on a small wooden platform in the treetops, a harness around my body, being encouraged to jump by a young Australian woman with far too much energy and zest for life.

'Go, go, go,' she whooped. The rest of our group were

clapping and cheering. I felt like a kid at the top of the slide who desperately wanted to go back down the steps but didn't want to lose face with his peers. I shut my eyes and stepped off the platform. My stomach lurched, my hands gripped the rope for dear life and a few seconds later I swung into the cargo net which had been strategically placed to stop us on our short practice run. I could hear Mark and the instructor whooping. I waited for the sense of elation to wash over me but it didn't come. Probably because I knew that half an hour from now I was going to be standing on a much taller platform about to hurtle more than 275 metres through the trees with no cargo net at the end of it.

'See, I told you it was fun,' said Mark, as we made our way to the start of the course proper. He appeared to be buzzing with the thrill of it all, unaware that the smile I had forced on to my face was only there for his sake.

Somehow or other I managed the first zip-wire. Mainly because I'd stumbled off the platform by accident and had my eyes shut for most of the way. I waited at the bottom for Mark to come down, ready to capture his descent on the video camera as instructed. He whizzed along, legs 'running' while he sang the walking in the air song in his best Aled Jones voice and landed gracefully in the wood-chipped landing pit. I, of course, had forgotten to do the running bit with my legs, which might have explained why I'd landed bottom-first in an unceremonious bump-and-drag action.

I watched Mark as he dusted himself down and unclipped his harness from the wire. I still wasn't sure whether he was actually enjoying himself or simply putting on a brave front for me. What I did know was that there was no way I was going to let him turn the video camera on me.

'So what's next?' I enquired through gritted teeth.

'That thing up there,' said Mark, pointing to a precarious-looking set of huge metal stirrups suspended high above our heads. I blamed Ant and Dec for this. Giving people the impression that putting someone through sheer terror in a wilderness hellhole was actually amusing in any way. Although I supposed I should be relieved that so far there had been no mention of eating creepy-crawlies.

The rope ladder up to the platform was the first challenge. An annoyingly agile teenager went first, powering his way up and practically leaping across the stirrups with barely a downward glance.

'Bastard,' Mark whispered to me. 'I hate it when the kids make it look easy.'

Mark followed on behind. I watched him going up; he looked good, actually. Rather professional. No doubt the rock-climbing training had paid off. He clipped his safety harness on to the wire at the top and made his way steadily across the swinging stirrups, nowhere near as fast as the teenager but still managing to look assured. Which was the one thing I knew I didn't look as I clambered up the ladder behind him. Oddly, when I got to the top, I quite missed the Australian whooping woman. I could have done with a bit of that energy and enthusiasm washing off on me. Gingerly I reached out my left foot. 'Harness,' called someone from the ground. I smiled sheepishly and clipped myself on before trying again. Maybe I had a small stride, though how someone with long legs can have a small stride I'm not sure; something to do with my hips not working properly perhaps. But once I had one foot on the stirrup, all I could do was wobble wildly in the air as I tried to make contact with the next one.

'Try and go faster. You need to build up a bit of a momentum,' yelled Mark from the far platform.

I grimaced at him, not wanting to have a domestic in the middle of this but feeling inclined to knee him somewhere soft and spongy when I got to the other side. Finally I managed to get my other foot in the next stirrup, only to find that as I tried to bring my rear leg forward I lost my footing. I gasped as I felt myself falling but a second later the safety harness pulled tight and I was left dangling in the air, one foot in a stirrup, the other flailing around in no-man's-land.

'Someone get the instructor,' bellowed Mark from the platform. I heard footsteps below as a young lad ran off down the track.

After what seemed like an age (but was probably barely a minute or two), someone strong and reassuringly ape-like was reaching out to me, telling me to keep calm as he hooked me on to his harness, instructed me to cling on to him and brought me back down to ground level within a few seconds.

'Thank you,' I said feebly. 'I'm obviously one of those rare people who appears not to have descended from apes.'

'Are you OK?' asked Mark, who had climbed back along the stirrups and down the rope ladder to get to me.

'I guess so. Just a bit shaken.'

'Perhaps you should skip this section,' said the instructor.

'Yeah,' I said, looking up at Mark. 'And the next three as well, I think.'

We sat in the tent drinking tea. The rain, which had mercifully eased off during our hire-wire adventure/disaster, was back to beating down on the canvas. Mark had the triumphant air of someone who had conquered Everest (he had offered to quit when I had but I'd told him to carry on, seeing that he really wanted to). I was, however, lacking anything like a shared sense of achievement. Having been bubbling quietly for much of the weekend, the volcano was in danger of erupting.

'Maybe we could come again another time,' said Mark. 'So you can get to finish the course.' I looked at him wondering what planet he was currently inhabiting. Because it certainly wasn't mine.

'No thanks.'

'You were just unlucky, that's all. It could have happened to anyone. I'm sure if you'd carried on you'd have really enjoyed it.'

'Mark, I didn't enjoy it, OK? I could go back a hundred times and I still wouldn't enjoy it. A high-wire forest adventure is not my idea of fun. The only reason I never entered *The Krypton Factor* was because I knew I'd hate the assault course.'

'You should have said.'

I shook my head. 'What chance did I have? It was all booked. I turned up and was told that was what I was doing, like I turned up here and was told we were camping—'

'Glamping,' Mark interrupted.

I glared at him.

'The thing is, you never stop to think, do you? Or to ask what I'd like to do. You get totally carried away on some whim and assume that I'll like it simply because you do.'

'That's not fair. I wanted to surprise you.'

'Surprises aren't always good, you know. There are nasty ones too.'

'But I did think about this. I booked it because you like the countryside.'

'When have I ever said that?'

'It's on the list.'

'What list?'

'Your list. The twenty years from now one. You said you wanted to live in the countryside. You said a lot of things.'

I put my mug down on the floor and stared at Mark. It was like he'd knocked over the first domino and set a whole line of them toppling, splaying out in different directions. Revealing a pattern at the end which solved some cryptic puzzle. Or, in this case, explained everything about what had been going on over the past couple of months.

'When did you see it?'

'At your place, the night you said you didn't want to buy the house. You tried to hide it when you came in with the coffee but I'd already read it.'

'Why didn't you tell me?'

'Guilt, I guess. It was like reading someone's secret diary without knowing what it was. By the time I realised, it was too late. I knew stuff I wasn't supposed to know.'

'But you still should have said. It's not like you went rummaging through my drawers. It was my stupid fault for leaving it there on the bloody coffee table.'

'To be honest, I didn't know what to say. It was pretty obvious why you'd been looking at it. Your life hadn't turned out like you'd planned and you wanted to get it back on track. I figured I'd be first on the list to go. That's why I kept quiet.'

'Oh Mark,' I said, leaning over to stroke his arm. 'I wouldn't do that.'

He shrugged. 'Well I'm not Andy Pailes, am I? I never played football for England for a start.'

I flinched as I heard his name. Coming from Mark's mouth it sounded cold and unfamiliar. I felt like the two halves of my life were about to collide.

'I'm surprised you've even heard of him.'

'I only had a vague recollection. Probably had his sticker in my Panini album when I was at school. I had to look him up on the internet to find out more.'

I heard the sound of car brakes screeching in my head. It was too late though to avert the full impact. All I could hope was that Mark hadn't got close enough to see the carnage. I decided to work on a damage limitation exercise in case there was still time.

'I'm surprised you found anything. He only played for England once.'

'There wasn't much. Only a biography and photo on the United old boys page.'

I breathed a silent sigh of relief, sure that United wouldn't have mentioned anything untoward.

'What did it say about him?' I asked, trying to appear casual.

'Just listed his appearances, goals and stuff. And a bit about what he's doing now.'

I nodded. I wanted to ask what he was doing but I knew that would be one question too many. I needed to play it down. Feign lack of interest.

'He wasn't one of their star players or anything. Not really,' I said.

'He must have been pretty special though, to be your favourite. Wasn't Matt Goodyear the big heart-throb in those days?'

'Yeah, well. I never like to follow a crowd, do I?'

'So were you some kind of groupie then?' Mark was smiling but my skin crawled. I still hated the word.

'He was my favourite player, that's all. It was no big deal.'

'He was important enough for you to want to marry him.'

'I was fifteen, for Christ's sake. I wanted to be prime minister as well.'

'That was a narrow escape for Britain then.'

I smiled at Mark and squeezed his hand, relieved at the first light moment in the conversation. He couldn't know. He would surely have said if he did. Certainly wouldn't have cracked a joke.

'You said you wanted kids as well,' Mark continued.

'I guess I've changed my mind about a lot of things.'

Mark nodded, his face serious again.

'Does it bother you?' I asked.

'Not enough to matter,' he replied.

'So your trip to King Street,' I said, deciding to take the opportunity of moving the conversation on. 'You were trying to look more like a footballer, weren't you? That's why you did it. You were trying to be what I wanted. Or what I wanted when I was fifteen, anyway.'

Mark looked down at the floor, the brave face crumpling, the confident façade cracking to reveal the inner child who I'd always known was inside.

'I was so scared you were going to leave me. I didn't want to lose you. I was prepared to turn myself into whatever it was you wanted me to be. Which I figured must be the opposite of me. Some adventurous, sporty, outdoor type.'

'You didn't need to do that.'

'I did, though. Because you're everything to me, even if I have never said it.'

I rested my forehead against his, kissing him lightly on the nose. 'You have now,' I whispered. 'And I don't want you to be someone you're not. I want you to be Mark.'

He nodded and kissed me back. Although he still didn't seem convinced.

'But when you were looking at that list, you must have been thinking about Andy. Wondering what your life would have been like if you'd ended up with him.'

I shook my head vehemently then stopped abruptly, aware that I was protesting too much. And I didn't want

Mark to have any idea how much I still thought about Andy. Wondered what could have been.

'Only in the same way you might wonder what it would have been like being married to Madonna.'

'I don't think I'm her type.' Mark smiled.

'I don't know. I think you could be exactly what she needs.'

'Look,' he said, 'if you do want out, now or at any point, please tell me. I'd rather know than have to face you slipping away gradually.'

'The only thing I'm leaving,' I said, 'is this bloody campsite.'

'I thought it would be romantic.' He shrugged.

'Maybe it would, in June when it was twenty degrees warmer. And if you'd told me where we were going so I could pack the right kind of clothes.'

'Sorry,' said Mark. 'I guess I wasn't thinking.'

'Or maybe trying too hard.'

'I want you to be happy.'

'I am.'

'So why do you seem to be so restless? Why are you applying for jobs and getting in touch with old friends and poring over lists you made twenty years ago?'

It was a fair point. And one which I wasn't really sure of the answer to myself.

'I found the list in the attic. It threw me, that's all. It was like a blast from the past. Knocked me off course, for a while.'

'But you're back with me now? Full steam ahead and all that?'

'Yes. Yes I am.' I wanted to believe it. And maybe if I said it enough it would become true.

'So are you going to cancel that job interview then?'

I shook my head. 'No, because that's something I need to do. To see if I can still cut it out there.'

Mark didn't appear to be convinced. I took his face in my hands and kissed him softly.

'But you can quit the worthy volunteering Law Works stuff if you want to.'

'No,' he said. 'That was the one good part of all this. Your list did make me think about where my life was going. And the fact that everything I do is for money. I've discovered I like helping people for the sake of it. I'm really enjoying it.'

'More than you're enjoying the extreme sports?'

Mark looked up and smiled. 'Is it that obvious?'

'It's just not you.'

'I've never been so bloody petrified in my life, the first time I went up that climbing wall. Oddly enough, I am kind of getting used to it now. I actually enjoyed that today. Certainly more than the snowboarding. But I'd still rather go back to a lie-in and a kick-about with the lads on a Sunday morning.'

'Good,' I said. 'And in that case, I request permission to donate *Gangs* to Oxfam.'

Mark laughed. 'There were a few good bits in it, honestly.'

'That may be so. But I never could stand Grant Mitchell in *EastEnders*. He'd have been a natural out there today, you know. Swinging through the trees like an ape man. Now, can we start packing?'

'Do you want to go home?' Mark asked.

'No. We've still got one night left, and I know a really nice hotel in Hawkshead.'

Friday, 14 February 1986

I hated February the fourteenth. It was the worst day of the year not to be going out with anyone. Even worse than Christmas. At least at Christmas you got cards from other people. It didn't matter that they were people you didn't give a stuff about, kids in your class who didn't bother speaking to you the rest of the year, and distant relatives you never even knew existed. You had something to put up. Something to hide your disappointment about not getting a Christmas card from someone special. But on Valentine's Day, if you didn't get a card from the person you wanted one from, there were no consolation prizes. No hiding place.

And it was worse than ever this year. Because I knew Andy would have sent one to her. To bloody Annie. And I still couldn't understand why and what the hell he was doing with her. I wanted to write to him, to bring him to his senses. Tell him he wasn't like the other players and that was no bad thing. He didn't have to try to be like them. Andy Pailes was different. At least he was supposed to be.

I don't know why, but I still dashed downstairs as soon as I heard the postman. A couple of envelopes were lying on the doormat. A large white one, which could have been a card, and a slim brown one which looked like a bill, both with the addresses face down. Taking a deep breath, I picked up the white one and turned it over. It was addressed to Mrs Maureen Skidmore. So was the bill. I went into the kitchen, grunted a greeting to Mum and sat slumped over the kitchen table.

'Are those for me?' Mum asked, pointing to the envelopes I had tossed on to the table.

'Well they're not for me, are they?'

Mum sighed before opening the bill, shaking her head and picking up the white envelope. She tore across the top with her finger, started to pull out whatever was inside then stopped halfway, flushed bright red and pushed it back inside.

'What is it?' I said.

'Oh, nothing important, I'll look at it later.'

She was lying through her teeth. I knew what it was. It was a Valentine's card. My forty-year-old mother had got a fucking Valentine's card. I finished my breakfast as quickly as I could and slunk off to school.

Kim and Debbie had got two each. If you asked me, that was being greedy. Not that I wanted one from some poxy kid at school. But at least if I'd got one it would have shut everyone else up. I told them I didn't believe in St Valentine's Day. That it was a commercial scam by card companies to boost their post-Christmas sales. That's what my mum used to say. Until she got one.

I went round to see Frankie after school. She had a half-day on Fridays. She'd got three cards from lads at college. But they didn't really count because it wasn't like she was bothered about them. To be honest, she seemed annoyed they'd sent them. Which was weird when you thought about it.

'My mum only went and got one, didn't she?'

'Who off?' asked Frankie.

'I dunno. Some perv down our road who gets off on middle-aged joggers, probably.'

'That's really gross.'

'Yeah, I know. So don't you fancy any of these lads then?' I asked.

'No, I told you. They're all stupid pricks. They go round trying to touch up half the girls in college.'

'Have any of them asked you out?'

'What's it matter? I'm not interested.'

I decided to let the subject drop.

'Oh God, I meant to tell you. Jane's had the baby. It was in the paper yesterday.'

Frankie went quiet. I wondered if I should have broken the news more gently.

'I know,' she said after a while. 'They had a picture in ours today.' She reached down by the bed and picked up a neatly folded copy of the *Daily Mirror*. On the back page was a big photo of Matt kissing the forehead of a tiny baby with a shock of dark hair. A little girl called Emma.

'Crap name,' I said. 'I bet Jane chose it.'

'I like it,' said Frankie. 'I think it suits her. She's gorgeous, isn't she?'

I nodded. Aware that I always seemed to say the wrong thing to Frankie nowadays.

'So do you still like him, even though he's got a kid?'

'Course I do. Andy's screwing some tart at United but it hasn't put you off, has it?'

'That's different. I've still got a chance.'

'Yeah, right.'

'What do you mean by that?'

'Well he's hardly gonna dump her for you, is he?'

'You don't know that. You didn't see what he was like at the Christmas disco. I told you what he said to me.'

'You probably imagined it. Heard what you wanted to hear.'

I suspected Frankie was jealous of me and Andy. Because she knew nothing would ever happen with her and Matt now he was a dad. But I still didn't like the way she was making me out to be some little kid.

'Are you calling me a liar?' I demanded.

'No. I'm just saying grow up. Get real.'

'That's not what you said last summer.'

'Yeah, well. That was a long time ago.'

We sat in silence for a while. I couldn't believe what she'd just said. I guessed she must have given up on Matt because of the baby. But I didn't see why she had to make out that I was being stupid for still loving Andy.

'I'd better go,' I said. 'Do you wanna come round and listen to the match with me tomorrow?'

'Nah, sorry. I can't. I've got a Saturday job.'

'You never told me.'

'It's only down the Little Chef.'

I laughed. Frankie was the only person I knew who had failed her hostess badge in the Guides.

'What's so funny?'

'I just can't imagine you wearing that crappy uniform and serving people cups of tea and fry-ups.'

'Yeah, well. I need the dosh, don't I? Tara and me wanna go on holiday in the summer. Abroad like.'

'Your mum'll never let you go.' I didn't mean for it to sound nasty. But I was hurt that she hadn't told me. And that I obviously wasn't invited.

'She'll have to get used to it. I'll be going abroad on my own next year.'

'How come?'

'It's part of my course. You have to do a week's work experience, somewhere foreign.'

Frankie was doing travel and tourism at college. She reckoned she was going to end up working as a travel rep in Florida, sipping cocktails with Matt Goodyear. One of my mum's friends was a travel agent. She worked in the Co-op, booking old biddies' day trips to Bognor.

'Oh, right,' I said. I'd always imagined that me and Frankie would go away together when we were older. Only to somewhere in this country. But I guessed that wasn't going to happen now.

'Right, then. I'd better go,' I said.

'See ya. Hope they win.'

'Yeah,' I said, wondering why she'd said they instead of we.

'And Pailes is down and this looks serious.'

The words sliced through my history revision like a cut-throat razor. I tossed the textbook to one side, the ser-iousness of the drama unfolding on the radio immediately

taking precedence over the Russian Revolution. I sat rock-
ing to and fro on the edge of the bed as I pictured the scene
being described by LBC's commentator. The physio kneel-
ing attentively over Andy, the United supporters chanting
'off, off, off', Robson protesting his innocence over the
tackle and the referee seemingly happy to take his word for
it. Just because he was the bloody England captain. I winced
as the stretcher came on and Andy was lifted on to it, his face
apparently etched with pain, and I burst into tears as he was
carried off, applause ringing from the Old Trafford stands.

The rest of the match passed by in a blur. I was only
vaguely aware that Manchester United went on to win 1–0.
All I cared about was how badly Andy had been injured.
The verdict came a few minutes after the final whistle.

'And the news from the visitors' dressing room is that
Andy Pailes has torn his ankle ligaments and could be out
of action for several weeks. That must make him doubtful
for the Milk Cup Final next month. Now, other scores
coming in from around the country . . .'

I thumped my pillow, a single blow first, followed by a
volley of uppercuts and left hooks. I hoped Robson felt
every punch. Three days ago I'd been celebrating us getting through to the Milk Cup Final. Now Andy probably
wouldn't be able to play. The thought of him missing out
on that was too much. I wanted to go to him and comfort
him, but I knew that would be impossible. Because Annie
would be with him. Fussing around and pretending that
she cared, when I knew full well she didn't.

An hour went by and still I sat there, deep in thought and
determined to maintain my bedside vigil. It didn't matter

that it wasn't Andy's bedside; it was the gesture that was important. Shortly after six, Mum knocked on my bedroom door.

'Go away,' I said, knowing that such a response was guaranteed to bring her into my room, where she could witness the full extent of my misery.

'What's the matter, love?' She sat down on the edge of the bed.

'Andy's been stretchered off. He's done his ankle ligaments in. He'll be out for ages; he'll probably miss the final.'

Mum appeared to be unaware of the significance of this information.

'Never mind, it's not the end of the world. Try and cheer yourself up for tea. It's spaghetti tonight, your favourite.'

I stared at her, wondering how she could possibly be so insensitive as to think a bowl of spaghetti was going to make everything better.

'I'm not hungry, can't you see that?'

'You've got to eat, Claire. There are starving children in Ethiopia who would be grateful for the food you waste.'

'Well send my spaghetti to them, then. And stop making out that you care about them more than me. You didn't even buy the Band Aid single.'

Mum stood up again.

'Listen, Claire, I haven't got time for this nonsense. I'm trying to cook a proper meal as well as sort you out. Do you want spaghetti or not?'

'No. I told you, I'm not hungry.'

'Fine. Well I'll be in the kitchen. You're staying up here, are you? Only I've got a friend coming round later.'

'OK.'

'And I don't want to be disturbed.'

'I'm staying up here. Just leave me alone, will you?'

Mum walked silently out of the room. I lay there brooding for the rest of the evening, until it was time for *Match of the Day*. Part of me couldn't bear the thought of seeing Andy in pain but another part of me felt a duty to be there for him, to share in his suffering.

I crept downstairs to the kitchen and stuffed a couple of digestive biscuits into my mouth, not wanting Mum to see that I was hungry after all. Still wiping the crumbs from my lips, I stood for a moment outside the living-room door. I couldn't hear any voices so presumed her friend must have gone home. He hadn't though.

I walked in to find Mum sitting on the sofa next to a tall man with a moustache who had his arm draped around her shoulder. For a second I thought it was happening all over again. I was about to run from the room and dash full pelt down the road, to fling myself into my mother's arms, when I remembered that I couldn't do that. Because this time Mum was the one on the sofa.

'Who's he?'

'Oh, er, Claire.' Mum's face was flushed. 'This is my friend Malcolm. Malcolm, this is my daughter, Claire.'

Malcolm looked decidedly awkward about the introductions and immediately withdrew his arm from Mum's shoulder.

'What's he doing here?'

'Honestly, have you no manners at all? Malcolm's here because I asked him round to dinner.'

'You never said.'

'I did, love.' Mum was smiling one of those fake smiles. 'I told you earlier I had a friend coming round.'

'You didn't tell me it was a man though.'

'For goodness' sake, does it make any difference?'

'Yes, it does. You don't normally have men round.'

Mum turned to Malcolm. 'I'm so sorry about this.'

'It's OK. Maybe I should leave.'

'No, please, there's no need for that. Claire's going back to her room now, aren't you?'

'But I want to watch *Match of the Day*.'

'Well I'm sorry, you'll have to miss it for once. It won't kill you.'

'That's not fair.'

'I don't mind watching the football,' said Malcolm, obviously trying his best to be accommodating. I eyed him suspiciously. I didn't like the shirt he had on. Or the way that he'd made himself so at home on the sofa. In fact I didn't like anything about him at all.

'It's OK, I know when I'm not wanted.'

'Claire, please don't be like that.'

But I was already heading for the door. I stopped to listen once I had slammed it behind me.

'I am so sorry about that. She's at an awkward age at the moment. To be honest, she's been at an awkward age for most of her life.'

I heard Malcolm and my mother laugh. Both of them, together. Laughing at me. Laura Ashley was laughing too. I ran upstairs to my room and sat on the bed with my hands over my ears.

It was no good though. I could still hear the laughter. I took my Walkman from the bedside table, fitted the headphones snugly over my ears, and pressed the rewind button. I counted the seconds out in my head as the tape rewound, knowing exactly how long it took now. And sure enough when I pressed the play button Andy was there.

'Well, obviously, it was a great thrill for me to play for England. I didn't expect it at the beginning of the season but I'm determined to seize my chance . . .'

I knew the words off by heart now, I had replayed the radio interview so often. But I still loved listening to it, hearing Andy's voice so close to me. I shut my eyes, automatically hitting the rewind button every time the interview came to an end. When I finally drifted off to sleep, it was with Andy talking to me, whispering sweet nothings into my ear.

Nine

'The thing I don't get, Kaz,' I said, turning to the young skinny woman sitting across the table from me twiddling her hair, 'is why you not only made no attempt to avoid the security cameras but seem to be positively smiling into them at one point.'

Kaz shrugged and looked away. She was one of my regulars who I found particularly hard work. She had a drug habit, cocaine mainly, and a penchant for shoplifting. She was in this whole revolving-door thing of being in and out of prison on a frequent basis. From what I could gather her life was pretty chaotic; boyfriends coming and going, hassle from her family, moving about all the time. She was also rather uncommunicative, which wasn't a great help when I was trying to dig her out of holes she had got herself into.

'Kaz?'

'You never know, do you? Might get talent-spotted, like, if you're looking your best. For some modelling agency or a reality TV show.'

'I don't think talent scouts tend to monitor CCTV pictures.'

'Well, all sorts of stuff gets on to the internet. It could

end up on YouTube. So I thought I'd do my hair and make-up and give it a go, like.'

I shook my head. I didn't actually buy it. Despite her best efforts to appear otherwise, Kaz was a bright girl. Not academically so, but street-savvy and sharp. She certainly wasn't stupid. So I couldn't work out why she was pretending to be. I decided it was time to try to get to the bottom of it.

'How do you think that will go down in court, Kaz? Do you think it'll make you look good? Give the right impression?'

'Yeah, I think it'll give them a laugh.'

'Or more likely send you back to prison.'

'Good,' she muttered.

'What did you say?'

'You heard me.'

'You want to go to prison?' She shrugged and stared up at the ceiling. I could see her bottom lip trembling. 'Why, Kaz?' I asked, my voice softening.

'If you must know, it's because it's better than my fucking life outside.' She bit her lip, struggling to maintain the hard-girl act now she'd opened up.

I blew out and shook my head. It was a humbling thing to hear. I didn't want to believe that anyone's life could be worse outside than in jail. And I knew it wasn't because prison was cushy. I'd been to the women's establishment Kaz usually ended up at and it certainly didn't strike me as pleasant.

'So you got caught on camera on purpose, to go back inside?'

'Yeah. Seemed like the best option at the time. If I go in for a decent stretch I get help, see, with trying to come off. So I thought if I piss them off by smiling and laughing at the cameras it might even get in the papers and then they'd have to make an example of me.'

'Are things really that bad?' I asked.

Kaz nodded and bit her lip again.

'Tell me,' I said. 'Tell me about all the crap in your life.'

'Why, so you can have a good laugh?'

'No, Kaz, so I can help.'

'Why would you wanna help me?'

'Because you're a fellow human being and no one should have to try to get sent to prison for a better life.'

The dam wall burst and Kaz started to sob. I wanted to give her a hug but was worried she'd take it the wrong way, think I was pitying her. I delved into my bag and handed her a couple of tissues.

'Take your time,' I said. 'I've got all the time in the world.'

She blew her nose, took a deep breath and started to talk. I listened intently, scribbling notes down as she spoke. She owed money. Lots of it. Her dealer was after her. Had threatened her. Suggested she could pay it off by letting him be her pimp. Her boyfriend was a user too. Stole off her, what little she had, and went missing for days on end. She suspected he was screwing around. She felt like a prostitute anyway when he turned up. That was all he used her for. Although instead of paying her, he took from her instead. She owed rent on her council flat. Had been threatened with eviction. And she spent every minute of every day worrying about where she was going to get her next fix

from. And how the hell she was going to pay for it. Apart
from that, it seemed, everything was hunky-dory.

'OK,' I said. 'I'm going to go for an adjournment.'

Kaz rolled her eyes.

'I'll be out on bail, won't I?'

'Not if I ask them to remand you.'

'Can you do that?'

'I can try. I can say there's a risk of you absconding if
you're bailed due to your chaotic lifestyle.'

'And then what?'

'I'm going to try and get you a rehab place. Residential.
Somewhere out of the area.'

'There aren't any. That's what they always tell me.'

'I'll be a pain in the arse then. Keep knocking on doors
and hassling people until they get sick of me.'

Kaz gave the faintest glimmer of a smile.

'Thanks,' she said in a voice which was barely audible. 'I
still don't know why you're bothering for me.'

'What is it that Jennifer Aniston says, in those adverts for
the shampoo you keep nicking?'

'Because you're worth it.' Kaz grinned.

'There you go then.'

As soon as I got home I checked my e-mails. Emily managed to send one most days – even if it was just a quick
one-liner. But it had been three days now since I'd heard
from her. I'd texted Frankie to ask if everything was OK.
Not OK in the normal meaning of the word, but rather a
euphemistic way of checking Emily was at least still alive.
The reply had come late at night. Frankie was staying with

Emily in hospital while she underwent a particularly gruelling round of chemo. It was all taking its toll now. The sickness, the nausea, the constant stream of injections and blood tests. Emily was struggling to remain positive. And it was breaking Frankie's heart to watch her go through it all.

I felt so helpless being up in Yorkshire. I'd offered to go down the weekends I wasn't working to help out, but Frankie had been adamant that they could cope. Especially as Joe's family were doing a sterling job of looking after the younger children.

I was relieved to find something in my inbox. I opened up the message.

Hiya, Claire. It's OK. I am still here. Just had a really crappy few days spewing up and having loads of blood tests. Been like something out of a vampire movie – except without Robert, of course. I'm glad he can't see me at the moment, mind. I look like a right minger. Alia's gonna get me a Halloween witch's wig with long black hair – in case I need it for the premiere. Not that I'm robsessed you understand!
L8ers.
Emily Pattinson (I wish!)

I smiled as I read it. It was her optimism which always got to me. That and her failure to complain about what she was going through. To do the whole 'why me?' bit. Maybe she did it inside her head. Or when she was talking to Robert. The way I used to do with Andy.

★

I looked at myself in the full-length bedroom mirror the next morning. What was good enough for Rochdale Magistrates' Court might not be good enough for Smith MacGuire in Manchester. I'd invested in a new pair of shoes for the occasion, but the suit still seemed to say 'Rochdale' to me. Maybe I should have followed Mark's example and gone shopping in King Street for something new. It'd have to do for now though. The train was due in twenty minutes. I had an interview to go to.

I stood on the platform at Todmorden wondering why so many significant moments in my life involved railway stations. Maybe it was something to do with the sense that everyone else was moving on. That if I didn't jump on board a train to somewhere I'd get left behind.

The Manchester train pulled in, only a few minutes late. I found myself a window seat in a quiet part of the carriage. It was so much more pleasant travelling by train mid-morning rather than in the rush hour. I got a notebook out of my briefcase and re-read my questions and the answers I could give to theirs. Or what I thought theirs might be, at least. It was a long time since I'd been for an interview. I suspected I lacked the sharp edge of the type of go-getting career lawyers who probably clocked up several interviews a year. I knew the interview panel would probably ask me why I'd stayed in my present job so long. And I wasn't sure what to say. Loyalty didn't seem to be a desirable quality in an applicant any more. Only ambition.

By the time the train pulled into Victoria station I was convinced they'd only granted me an interview due to some bizarre quota system. Maybe they didn't have enough stuck-in-a-rut lawyers on the duty solicitor rota. I decided not to bother with the tram and walk instead. It was one of those beautiful crisp autumn mornings with the sun hanging low in the sky. Manchester bustled on around me: mums with runny-nosed kids in buggies, students hanging out because they had nothing better to do and no money to spend, and an army of grey shoppers intent on bagging some bargains while the younger, fitter crowd were at work. I cut through St Ann's Square, past the ever-hopeful buskers, who were definitely of a much higher quality than those in Rochdale. I could get used to this, I thought. An altogether more pleasant place to work (and shop if I happened to get the odd lunch hour).

I turned the corner into John Dalton Street. Smith MacGuire's offices loomed large in front of me, the imposing frontage doing nothing to quell my nerves. I opened the heavy glass door, walked up to the reception desk and stated my name and business.

'Lift B, third floor,' the receptionist answered robotically as she slipped my name into a visitor's pass and handed it to me. 'Please wear at all times and return before leaving.' I was tempted to ask what the penalty was for not returning the pass and whether I'd require legal representation if I forgot but thought better of it. As far as I could remember, most people who worked for corporate law firms had undergone humour by-pass operations.

When I got out of the lift there was another reception desk, someone else to announce my arrival to.

'They're running slightly late,' said the receptionist, 'and you are early.' Her tone suggested this was almost as big a crime as being late. 'Please do take a seat while you wait.'

I glanced around me at the swish waiting area with leather-upholstered seats and a water cooler. I decided to go to the toilet first to reduce the amount of time I would have to sit there pretending to be interested in glossy life-style magazines.

I followed the sign for the toilets to the end of the cor-ridor. There were two doors, one with a picture of Barbie on and the other with Ken. Maybe someone here did have a sense of humour after all. I pushed the Barbie door and went through into a huge room, all black and steel with mirrored walls (someone had at least had the good sense to draw the line at a mirrored ceiling). I went through to a cubicle and shut the door. On the back was a sign saying 'Are You Dehydrated?', below which was a colour chart depicting different shades of urine and the relevant med-ical assessment from 'Optimum health' through 'You need to drink at least two litres of water a day' down to 'Seek an urgent medical assessment'. My anxiety levels, which were already high, shot through the roof as I sat and peed, won-dering if this was all part of the interview process and some machine was secretly extracting a sample from the toilet bowl which was to be shown to the interview panel for assessment before I even entered the room.

Flustered, I turned to flush, only to be greeted by a sign reading 'Which level of flush do you require?' over two buttons, one marked 'Two litres' and the other 'Four litres'. I was panicking now; the simple act of relieving myself had turned into some type of aptitude test. I had no idea how much water a normal flush contained but pressed 'two', suspecting the 'four' button would have triggered a black mark on my card for failing to conserve water. I walked over to the long trough-like washbasins, but as I finally worked out which of the several taps and dispensers contained the soap, a pair of large hairy hands appeared from the other side of the trough. I gasped and jumped back, fearing a spy for the interview panel was about to arrest me on suspicion of crimes related to personal hygiene.

'It's all right,' said a male voice from behind the mirrors. 'Just takes a bit of getting used to.' It was only then I realised that this was where the Kens and Barbies came together on either side of the troughs to wash their hands. It reminded me of the communal toilets in *Ally McBeal*, which would have been enough to put me off working at Cage, Fish and Associates, despite the appeal of regular song-and-dance routines to break up the working day.

I dried my hands quickly and hurried back to the reception area, checking before I sat down in case the chair had a sign about optimum weight for height ratios and advice on a calorie reduction and exercise programme.

By the time I was called into the interview room, I was convinced Big Brother had been watching me and I was about to be voted off at any moment. The chair of the panel introduced himself as Ryan Kellerman, the MD. I recognised his voice instantly, and one glance down at his hirsute hands confirmed the worst. He was washbasin man. And I was dead in the water. He was flanked by two colleagues, a younger woman who looked unnervingly like the Barbie picture on the toilets and an older man with sophisticated streaks of silver in his hair. Kellerman started outlining Smith MacGuire's 'raison d'être', using phrases such as 'expanding corporate capabilities' and 'streamlining management systems'. He was so smooth I was surprised his clothes didn't simply slide off him. His first question to me was the obvious one.

'So, Claire, you work out of Rochdale Magistrates' Court, where you've been for, now let me see, yes, seven years. It must be interesting work, dealing with some rather difficult clients, I imagine. So what experience and qualities could you bring to Smith MacGuire?'

I was sorely tempted to shout, 'Piss off, you patronising bastard' and leave the room. But I didn't want to give him the satisfaction. It was quite clear that what he was actually saying was 'Why does a jumped-up duty solicitor from lowly Rochdale think she can make any sort of valid contribution to a slick, swanky corporate set-up?' So that was the question I decided to answer.

'Well,' I said. 'One of my clients yesterday was a low-life cocaine addict from a sink estate with an attitude problem and not a hope in hell of getting off.' The Barbie woman exchanged anxious glances with Kellerman. 'But I talked to her, tried to get under her skin. Found out what had prompted her to do it, what she wanted and how I could help her achieve it. She left me with a smile on her face and a belief that I could make a difference. I'm sure as a top-ranking corporate company you understand that you can't put a price on that sort of client satisfaction.'

The Barbie woman raised an eyebrow, the silverhaired

man nodded; even Kellerman was silenced for a moment. And I sat there, ready for the next question and trying not to think about what would happen to Kaz if I wasn't there.

'So, how did it go?' asked Mark when he arrived at my house after work.

'You were right,' I said, giving him a kiss before letting him in. 'They were a bunch of suits up their own arses.'

Mark laughed. 'I hope you gave as good as you got then.'

'I think I did. Which means it could go either way. They'll either tell me where to go or be impressed by the fact that I put up a bit of a fight.'

'But would you want to work for them if you did get offered the job?'

'I don't know,' I said, sitting down at the kitchen table. 'The money's good, career prospects excellent, very swanky offices.'

'But you're Claire Cooper.'

'What do you mean by that?'

'None of those things matter to you. You care about real things, real people. You always have.'

'Some of the work would be useful, the employment rights stuff.'

'You'd miss your clients, though. You know you would. You might complain about them sometimes but I've seen you when you've come home after getting someone off who the police had been trying to fit up. You're buzzing with it. That's what job satisfaction is for you.'

I shrugged. He had a point. But this wasn't about what I

enjoyed doing. It was about what I was capable of doing, what I should be doing.

'This is all about your list, isn't it?'

'I just think it's time I moved on.'

'You're feeling you haven't fulfilled your destiny.'

'I want to know if I can do it.'

'It's getting in the way, Claire.'

'What is?'

'This obsession with the way you wanted your life to be.'

'It's not an obsession.'

'It feels like it to me. You need to break it. Confront it head on and decide exactly what it is you want from your life.'

I was taken aback by Mark's comments. He wasn't usually this perceptive. Or this assertive, come to that.

'And how am I supposed to do that?'

'You can start with this.' He reached into his pocket, pulled out a folded piece of white paper and put it on the kitchen table.

'What's that?'

'Andy Pailes's address.'

I stared at him, my eyes bulging, my lower jaw almost hitting the table.

'I don't understand.'

'I want you to go and see him.'

'Why?'

'To put the whole thing to rest. To see if that life you wanted for yourself is better than the one you've got.'

'I've told you, he wasn't that important. I want you.'

'And I've known you long enough to know when you're

lying. I don't want to be second best, Claire. Someone you've settled for because you can't have the person you really want.'

I shook my head, unsure how to react. Aware that it was the biggest gesture anyone had ever made to me. And that Mark was doing an incredibly brave thing.

'You don't have to do this.'

'I know. But I want to. I want to get you back. Despite what you say, I don't feel you're with me at the moment, and I don't think you will be until you put this whole thing to rest. And the only way to do that is to go and see him.'

'But that's a crazy thing to do.'

'I'm hoping he'll be fat and bald and you'll wonder what you ever saw in him and come running back to me.'

I smiled. The whole thing still felt surreal. I looked down at the piece of paper lying there between us.

'How did you get it?' I asked.

'A little bit of detective work. It wasn't hard. I had enough clues to go on from the United website.'

I nodded. He knew more about Andy than I did. At least about what he was doing now, where he was. I wanted to know but still didn't feel it was right to ask or pick up the piece of paper. It would feel disloyal to Mark. Even though he had offered it to me on a plate.

'It might not be a good idea to go. I don't really want to rake up the past.'

'It's not raking up the past, it's putting it to rest so you can concentrate on your future.'

It was easy for Mark to say. He had no idea about what lay beneath if I disturbed the surface. And once I had, I might not be able to put things back how they were. Because I was scared that if I so much as caught a glimpse of him, I might lose control. Like I had done before.

'I'm asking you to do it for me,' said Mark. 'I'm prepared to live with the consequences, whatever happens. You have my permission. I want you to go and see him. What you do after that is up to you.'

He got up from his chair, kissed me on the top of the head and walked out of the door. I sat looking at the piece of paper for a long time before I picked it up and unfolded it. When I did, I caught my breath as I read the address. All this time. And he was so close. Close enough now to be able to touch.

Monday, 7 April 1986

I peered down anxiously at the scuffmarks on the heel of my shoe and the metal rod poking through underneath where the plastic cap had come off. It hadn't mattered until I had arrived at court and noticed that all the sophisticated, professional women who hurried by, bulging briefcases at their sides, had immaculate shoes. Not a mark on them. I worried that mine were betraying my efforts to fit in, declaring to the world that the feet inside did not belong to a well-heeled lawyer but to a schoolgirl whose mother had said, 'What do you need a new pair for? There's nothing wrong with the ones you've got.'

It was a shame, because in all other respects I had brushed up fairly well. The neat black suit (which even had a proper lining) looked particularly impressive. The lady in the shop had said so when I'd tried it on. Even Mum had been forced to agree, saying it was classic and versatile and would come in handy for funerals. Quite whose funeral she'd had in mind, I hadn't liked to ask.

My hair was swept back off my face in a businesslike fashion, my make-up application skills had improved no end (I now understood that streaks of burnt-orange blusher applied liberally to my cheeks only succeeded in making me look like a fading new-romantic pop star), my teeth were almost straightened and were brace-free for the occasion and if I squeezed my shoulders in a bit you could even see a hint of cleavage.

It was quite ironic really. That at the point a few weeks past my sixteenth birthday where everything on the outside was finally coming together, inside everything was falling apart. Only my shoes gave the game away, affording a glimpse of the mess going on inside if you peeled back the outer layer.

'Miss Skidmore?'

I scrambled to my feet and grasped the outstretched hand of the tall, efficient-looking woman standing before me.

'Yes, that's me.'

'I'm Miss Jenkins from the Crown Prosecution Service. You'll be shadowing me for the next week while you're with us. Now, if you'll come with me, I'd like to show you round the courtroom before the magistrates arrive.'

I nodded and trotted obediently after Miss Jenkins, who had set off across the foyer before she'd even finished speaking. It was the smell of Court One that struck me first. Slightly musty, with an underlying aroma of leather-bound books and a hint of floor polish. The sort of smell that made you whisper without realising it. I marvelled at the austere surroundings, the oak-panelled walls, the coat of arms, the imposing magistrates' bench. I could start afresh here, be anyone I wanted to be. Could stop being Claire Skidmore, the lonely misfit who wandered the school corridors in constant fear of being noticed, and become Claire Skidmore, budding lawyer with the world at her feet. All I needed was the shoulder pads. And the shoes, of course.

The court rose as the magistrates entered the room. I followed Miss Jenkins's example and bowed my head solemnly before sitting again. The clerk called the first defendant and a timid-looking woman clutching a Superdrug carrier bag shuffled into the courtroom to face a charge of shoplifting eight pounds' worth of toiletries from Superdrug. I wondered if she had brought the carrier bag with her to prove that she did usually pay for her shopping. I smiled supportively at the woman. Miss Jenkins showed no such mercy.

The morning passed in a whirl of adjournments, fines and stiff sentences; the chairman of the bench sternly telling a succession of defendants that they were a burden upon society.

'Finding it interesting?' asked Miss Jenkins when we broke for lunch.

'Oh, definitely. You can't help feeling sorry for some of them, can you? He seems a bit mean.'

'Well, it is a magistrates' court, not a holiday camp. There's no room for sentiment.'

'No, of course not. I'm sure you're right.'

'Good. Well, you go and grab something to eat and meet me back here at one fifty sharp.'

For once, I didn't mind eating on my own. Real lawyers would never bring a bright orange lunchbox bearing the slogan 'Chill Out' to court – I was quite sure of that. I sat on a bench outside the court building, munching my sandwiches and idly daydreaming about trying Maggie Thatcher for crimes against humanity.

'Are we ready for action then?'

Miss Jenkins was standing in front of me, with a shorter, jolly-looking man at her side. I slid my lunchbox discreetly behind me.

'Er, yes. Of course. I'm coming now.'

Miss Jenkins's lunch companion followed us into the courtroom.

'Hi, I'm Gary Hurst, defence solicitor,' he informed me as we settled into our places. 'You'll have some company this afternoon. I've got someone shadowing me as well. You never know, you might even recognise him.'

Before I could work out the reason for his cryptic comment, the door opened and Andy walked in, still limping slightly following his injury. The first thing that came into my head was that it was a late April Fool's joke. I was convinced the magistrate would walk in and reveal himself as Jeremy Beadle from *Game for a Laugh* at any second. But when I saw the equally surprised look on Andy's face, I realised that it wasn't a set-up at all.

'Andy, this is Miss Skidmore,' said Mr Hurst. 'She's going to be with the CPS this week.'

'Pleased to meet you,' said Andy with a mischievous grin on his face as he reached out to shake my hand. 'You do look very familiar; are you sure we haven't met somewhere before?'

I had to stifle a giggle as the magistrates came back in and we all stood to attention.

'What are you doing here?' I whispered to Andy.

'I met Gary through the Open University. After I got injured I asked if I could shadow him one afternoon a week. Give me something useful to do while I'm out of action. What about you, is this your first day?'

'Yeah, I'm with her,' I said, pointing to Miss Jenkins. 'She's dead good but a bit mean. I think your Mr Hurst fancies her.'

Andy raised his eyebrows and smiled. I noticed him look me up and down again.

'Nice suit,' he said as he settled down next to me on the wooden bench. 'You really look the part.'

'Thanks,' I said, positively glowing. 'Sixteenth birthday present. I think I'll try for the briefcase for Christmas.'

Andy stared hard at me, then broke into a smile, nodding to himself as if he'd finally solved the last clue in a particularly difficult crossword puzzle.

The steady stream of defendants came and went in a blur. It was impossible to concentrate on the cases with Andy sitting there, inches away from me. Within touching distance but still out of bounds. I wondered if he could sense the atmosphere. It didn't feel like a one-way thing, though after what had happened at Christmas I couldn't be sure. But I did know he'd looked differently at me just now. Like he was seeing me through new eyes. It was as if Annie didn't exist in the courtroom. As if there was no one in the world apart from me and Andy.

'Any questions?' Miss Jenkins asked as she packed away her briefcase at the end of the afternoon.

'Er no, I don't think so. It all seemed pretty clear.'

'Good, I'll see you tomorrow. Nine thirty prompt,' she said before dashing off with Mr Hurst in hot pursuit.

Andy flashed a smile at me.

'So, how are you? How's it all going?'

I knew I couldn't possibly tell him the truth. I didn't see how I could explain how bad everything was. Not without mentioning Annie. And I didn't want to even say her name in case it broke the spell.

'Fine thanks,' I said, deciding to swiftly change the subject. 'What about you? How's your ankle? Are you gonna be fit for the Milk Cup Final?'

'Well, it's touch and go, but the physio thinks I'll make it.'

'Really? That's fantastic. I can't wait. I've never seen us play at Wembley.'

'Are you going?' he asked.

'No, couldn't get tickets. I'll watch it on telly, though. And I'll be shouting so loudly you'll be able to hear me at Wembley.'

'I'd better play well then, if I've got you to answer to.'

'Too right you had. A good performance should book your place in the World Cup squad.'

'God, you've got it all worked out, haven't you? I wish I could be as confident as you are.'

'What do you mean? Robson's bound to pick you, especially after the way you played last time.'

'Tell you what, if I do get picked, I'll take you on as my agent.'

'Great. I'm available from the end of June, soon as I've done my history O level.'

'Right you are then, that's sorted,' he said, grinning.

'Can you clear the courtroom now please, ladies and gents,' the usher called.

I looked around the empty room and realised he must

mean us. 'Ladies' he'd said. I'd never been called a lady before. We made our way to the door, Andy holding it open for me. Like I really was a lady.

'How are you getting home?' he asked.

'I'll get the train. It doesn't take too long.'

'Don't be daft. You live near the training ground, don't you?'

'Yeah, about a mile away.'

'That's settled then, I'll give you a lift. As long as you don't mind me stopping off at the club on the way. I need to pick some post up.'

'No, that's fine. If you're sure it's no trouble.'

'It will be a pleasure,' he said. 'Come on.'

I followed him out of the courtroom in a daze, praying that I wouldn't revert to my schoolgirl self the second I stepped outside the building.

'I'm sure that last defendant recognised me,' Andy said as we walked together to the car park. 'I thought for a moment he was going to ask for my autograph.'

'I know, I don't think he could believe it. It could have been worse, mind. If he'd been an Arsenal fan he'd probably have tried to thump you.'

Andy laughed as he unlocked the passenger door and held it open for me.

'All I need now is for one of our lads to come up for drink-driving while I'm there. Then I would be rumbled.'

'The others don't know about you doing this then?'

'No,' he said as we set off. 'They wouldn't understand. I'd get some serious stick from them. You know what it's like.'

I wondered how he knew that I got lots of stick too. It

was as if he understood everything without me even having to tell him.

'Don't you get sick of them having a go at you all the time, just because you're a bit different?' I asked.

'I usually try and ignore it. Part and parcel of the game, that's what the gaffer would say. A bit of banter never hurt anyone.'

'It does though, doesn't it?'

'Yeah,' he said after a second. 'Sometimes it does.'

I smiled warmly and found myself reaching out to touch his hand, giving it a reassuring squeeze as we waited at the traffic lights.

Andy turned to look at me. I pulled my hand back. Neither of us said a word.

The lights turned to green and the car behind beeped its horn, cutting the silence in two. Andy dropped the handbrake and moved off.

The silence continued until we came within sight of Priory Park.

'You must miss having Thomo around,' I said.

'Yeah, it's not the same without him. It was only him and Skip I could really talk to, to be honest.'

'How's his wife?'

'Not too bad. She's still having chemotherapy; they think she's responding to it, but it's too early to say for sure.'

'I was so upset when I heard. I didn't think it happened to people her age.'

'Well it does. And it always happens to the good ones, people like Sarah. Thomo loves her so much, you know. I mean really loves her, not just . . .' His voice trailed off.

'It must be so scary for him,' I said. 'I don't know how I'd cope if something like that happened to someone I loved.'

I could only think of one person I loved. I was sitting next to him.

'It's not easy,' said Andy, pausing for a second. 'My mum died of breast cancer when I was twelve.'

'Oh God, I'm sorry, I'd no idea.'

'That's OK, you weren't to know. I haven't told many people about it.'

'Were you close, you and your mum?'

'Yeah, we were. Very close. She was lovely.'

I tried to picture Andy's mum in my mind. I saw her with soft dark hair and warm rosy cheeks. The sort of mum who made big apple pies with lots of sugar sprinkled on top, not Tuscan pâté vol-au-vents.

'I bet she was. I bet she would have been very proud of you as well.'

Andy smiled at me.

'I hope so,' he said.

I wondered exactly how many other people Andy had told about his mum. Whether 'not many' meant two, or twenty. I hoped it was more like two.

A few minutes later we were driving through the main gates at Priory Park, the security man nodding to Andy as he raised the barrier. It felt like he was nodding to me too. That I was part of it all. Part of Andy.

'Do you want to come in with me?' he asked. 'You can wait here if you'd rather, it's up to you.'

'I'll come in, if you're sure it's OK.'

'Course it is. I don't think even Roy Brown charges for entry on non-match days.'

'What's he like, Brown? Is he as bad as he comes over on telly?'

'Worse. I can't stand him. He's like something out of the dark ages, full of all this "traditional family values" crap he's heading up for the Tories at moment.'

'Does he have a lot of say, though, about the football side of things?'

'Most of the time he leaves it all to Ken. But every now and again he sticks his oar in, just to prove who's in charge.'

Andy broke off as he held the glass door open and I slipped inside. The receptionist looked up, smiled at Andy and stared at me. The security man next to her followed my progress across the foyer. I felt like the mystery girl on the arm of someone famous in those Sunday magazine photographs. Everyone wondering who I was and what I was doing with him. I was so relieved I was wearing my little black suit and not my school uniform.

I looked up and caught Andy grinning at me.

'What?' I said.

'Just you. Turning heads without even realising it.'

I hadn't imagined it this time. He was flirting with me. Andy Pailes was actually coming on to me. I floated up a flight of stairs and along a corridor, trying not to let the grin slip any further across my face. Andy paused in front of a panelled door and turned to me.

'Fancy a quick look at the UEFA Cup? Could be your last chance; it goes back in a few weeks.'

I nodded, not needing convincing. Andy reached out and

took my hand, his fingers curling around mine. It was like one of those science experiments at school, where the static electricity makes your hair stand on end. Only this wasn't some poxy physics lesson. It was me and Andy getting together. Like I always knew we would. My heart was in danger of overheating it was beating so fast as he led me into the room and I caught sight of the huge silver trophy which took pride of place in the long glass cabinet. He seemed to like it. Seeing my reaction. Making all my dreams come true. I looked down. He still had hold of my hand. I squeezed it to make sure it was real. He squeezed back.

'Let's get you a closer look,' he said, disappearing for a minute before returning with a security man, who unlocked the cabinet.

'Cheers, Ted.'

'No problem. Just give us a shout when you're done,' he said, jingling the keys in his hand as he shut the door behind him.

Andy lifted the UEFA Cup up and passed it to me, laughing out loud as I buckled under the weight.

'Heavier than you thought, eh? Here, let me give you a hand.' He moved closer to me, supporting the base. His left hand touching mine. I could see our elongated reflections on the side of the cup, blurring into one.

'Can I kiss it?' I said.

'Sure, go on.'

I turned my head sideways and kissed the cup, the shiny surface cold against my lips.

'My turn,' said Andy.

'Haven't you kissed it already?'

'No,' he said. 'Never.'

Andy leant over and kissed me. Right on the lips. They fizzed for a second like I'd just taken a mouthful of moon dust. He tasted so good, better than anything I'd ever tasted in my life. I let the sweetness seep into me, trickling down my throat like lemon and honey, soothing everything inside. Kissing it better. I couldn't take it in. Andy Pailes had just kissed me. For real, not in my head. My whole body had gone limp. If Andy hadn't been holding the cup as well, I would have dropped it.

'Did you like that?' he asked. I nodded, still unable to speak.

'Let's put this down,' he said, taking the cup from me and placing it back in the cabinet. He turned round to face me. He had a look in his eyes, like he was possessed or something. No one had ever looked at me that way before. I took a step backwards, unsure what was coming next. My stomach was churning like a cement mixer. It was all happening so fast, and I wasn't sure where it was leading. I realised I'd never stopped to think about that. All the times I'd imagined our first kiss, it had always gone on for ever. Now it had happened for real. It had been and gone. We were on to the next bit. Something I hadn't dared think about in my dreams.

He moved towards me, his body colliding with mine and the momentum carrying me backwards until I hit the wall. He was kissing me hard, his chin like sandpaper, the rough edges scratching my skin. I didn't mind though. Not really. His hands were all over me, squeezing and rubbing, moulding me into shape. I could feel his thighs pressed against mine, his pelvis pushing into me. Like he couldn't get close enough. And I was gone, completely gone. Andy Pailes was doing this. Not to anyone else. To me.

'What about your girlfriend?' I said, when we broke for a second to breathe.

'I haven't got a girlfriend,' he said. 'Not any more.'

It was like someone had turned off the hurt inside. Pulled the plug and let it all drain away. He had dumped Annie. For me. A huge smile spread across my face and we started kissing again. More frantic even than before. My arms were locked around him. My clothes sticking to me. The back of Andy's shirt was damp with sweat.

'I've got a confession to make,' he whispered. 'I'm getting turned on.' Before I could say anything he unzipped his fly and slid my hand down. 'Take hold of it,' he said.

I didn't look down, just did as I was told. Taking hold of his prick, wishing I knew what to do with it. He put his hand over mine and started moving it up and down.

'Like this,' he said. 'That feels good.'

I carried on. My fingers sliding over the ridges, feeling him getting harder. Hearing him groaning in my ear. Praying he was enjoying it as much as he seemed to be.

'Use your mouth,' he said.

I wasn't sure what he meant for a second, until I felt his hand on my shoulder, pushing me down towards the floor.

'What if someone comes in?'

'They won't,' he said. 'Trust me.'

I did trust him. I'd have done anything he asked. Anything to please him. I sank down on to my knees. I'd never seen a man's prick before. Not even on TV. I felt embarrassed just looking at it. I didn't dare look up and remind myself who it belonged to.

'Go on,' he said. 'Make me come.'

I closed my eyes and took a deep breath before taking it in my mouth, trying to remember anything I knew about blow jobs. All I could think of was a girl at school mucking about with a cucumber in cookery, saying she was sucking it off. My lips closed around him and I started moving up and down, trying not to catch him with my teeth. I felt like I was going to suffocate; there was no room to breathe. Right at the point where I thought I might pass out, he came, warm slimy liquid spurting into my mouth. It tasted disgusting, and I worried I was going to gag. I needed air. I did the only thing I could think of. I swallowed. The taste was still there afterwards. Like a medicine you couldn't get rid of. But at least I could breathe.

I leant back against the wall and discreetly wiped my mouth with the back of my hand. I didn't know where to look. The UEFA Cup was in the cabinet only a few feet away. It was all so weird. Ten minutes ago we'd never even held hands. Now I'd had his prick in my mouth. It was like I'd gone to the fair to go on the carousel and ended up being spun on the waltzer.

Andy did himself up and pulled me up towards him. He looked knackered, like he'd just finished extra time in a football match. He kissed me on the lips. I hoped he didn't mind the taste.

'Come on,' he said. 'We'd better get out of here. Ted'll be wondering what we're up to.'

I didn't want to go. I wanted to stay and talk. To find

out how long he'd felt like this. What it was that had made him fall in love with me. But I barely had time to tuck my blouse in and straighten my skirt before Andy ushered me along the corridor.

'I need to pop in here,' I said as we came to a ladies' toilet.

'OK,' said Andy. 'I'll go and find Ted. I'll meet you back here in a couple of minutes.'

I closed the door, grateful for a moment of privacy, and slid a pubic hair from my tongue. I held it up to the light, unsure what to do with it. The Claire who kept an Andy Pailes scrapbook would have saved it, framed it perhaps. The Claire who'd just given Andy Pailes a blow job dropped it in the bin. I had him for real now. I didn't need mementoes.

Andy was waiting for me outside. He didn't say anything. Just led me up the corridor to the post room. I stood in the doorway as he went in.

'Now then, Andy. You'll be getting as many as our Matt soon,' the post lady chuckled, handing him a large bundle of letters before turning to me. 'He's ever so popular, you know, your fella here. I hope you don't get jealous of all this.'

I blushed and looked at my feet.

'Oh no, it's nothing like that,' Andy said quickly. 'Claire's just a friend.'

The words tore at me like a knife in the back. I looked at Andy to see if he was joking but he wasn't. I didn't understand what was going on. It was as if he was embarrassed about what had just happened. Which was weird because he hadn't seemed embarrassed at the time. And half an hour ago he'd loved all the attention I was getting. I'd felt like he was showing me off as we'd walked in. But now it was like I had shown him up and he couldn't get me out of there quick enough.

He ushered me back along the corridor, down the stairs and out the main doors without a word. We got to the car park just as Clubber arrived.

'Weh-hey. School outing is it, Trotsky? Has she brought her lunchbox? Or are you providing that?'

'Leave it out, Clubber.' Andy looked flustered.

'What's the matter? Can't she come out to play tonight? Annie's gonna love this. You taking up with a groupie. Wait till I tell her.'

'I said drop it.'

'Bit touchy today, aren't we? Must have a guilty conscience.'

Andy glared at him as he walked past but said nothing more.

'I'm sorry about that,' he said as we got into the car. I wasn't sure which bit of it all he was apologising for. The confusion must have shown on my face. 'Clubber. He's a complete prat. Just ignore him.'

'It's OK,' I said. 'It doesn't matter.'

It did though. It mattered that Clubber had called me a groupie and that Andy didn't want to be seen in public with me. I wondered if my blow job had been crap. Or if he'd been lying about Annie and had a guilty conscience.

'Why did Clubber say he was going to tell Annie?' I said as we set off. 'You said you're not going out with her any more.'

'I'm not,' Andy said. 'But he is.'

Neither of us said much on the way home. I wondered if Andy minded about Annie going out with Clubber. It must be weird, your ex going out with one of your team-mates. I hadn't expected things to be this complicated. It was making my head hurt just thinking about it. Andy dropped me off on the corner of my road. I wanted to ask when I could see him again, but the look on his face stopped me. He seemed to be pissed off with me already. I didn't want to make things any worse.

'Bye then,' I said.

'Yeah,' he said. 'See you around.'

That was it. That was all he said. He didn't even ask for my phone number. It was as if the whole thing had been no big deal. But it had. It had been to me.

I walked down the road, the taste still lingering in my mouth. I felt like crying, which was stupid. This should have been the best day of my life. I tried to remember that first kiss, how good it had felt. But all I could think about was what had happened afterwards. I felt different. More grown up. I wondered if other people could see it, if my mum would be able to tell what I'd been up to as soon as she opened the door. And whether she'd be able to smell the evidence on my breath.

Andy squeezes my hand as we wait on the doorstep of Skip's house. I look up at him.

'You look gorgeous. Relax, they're going to love you.'

I nod, trying to convince myself as much as anything. It's such a big step, being invited round for dinner. And by the club captain no less. It means we are officially a couple now. Andy and Claire, said in the same breath. Not a whisper but a statement of intent.

Skip's wife Gill opens the door. She's wearing a strappy red dress in a flimsy, expensive-looking material. Her hair and make-up are immaculate.

'Hi, Andy,' she says, kissing him on both cheeks. 'And you must be Claire,' she adds, gripping my shoulder tightly as she kisses me. 'Lovely to meet you. Now I know why he's always got a smile on his face these days.'

I feel myself blush. 'Hi, these are for you,' I say, handing her the wine and flowers.

'They're lovely, thank you. Come in. Let me take your coats.'

I follow Gill through into the hall, my heels tapping across the polished black-and-white tiles, and hand over my jacket.

'Dave won't be a minute, he's just putting the kids to bed,' Gill says.

Seconds later Skip comes downstairs holding a little girl wearing pink pyjamas.

'Hello, mate,' he says, nodding to Andy. 'Hi, Claire, nice to meet you properly at last. Sorry about that, I had my hands full.'

'I can see that,' I say. 'What's her name?'

'Holly, we call her trouble for short. Her big brother's gone straight to bed but she seems to have different ideas.'

I start playing peek-a-boo with Holly, laughing exaggeratedly every time she pops her face out from behind her hands.

'Holly, time for bed now,' says Gill.

'I want the Cinderella lady to read me a bedtime story.' She points straight at me. Everyone starts laughing.

'You are honoured,' says Skip. 'She's usually shy with new people.'

'That's Claire, love,' says Gill. 'And she's come here to relax.'

'It's OK, I'd love to read to her,' I say.

'Please, Mummy.'

'OK. But straight to sleep when Claire's finished, mind.'

Holly claps excitedly and kisses Skip and Gill good night before running over to grab my hand.

'Looks like you're in demand,' says Andy.

I grin. 'Come on then,' I say to Holly. 'How about you take me up to your bedroom? What story are we going to read?'

'Cinderella.'

'Fantastic, my favourite.'

As we climb the stairs together, I hear laughter coming from the living room, and Gill's voice saying, 'She's charming, Andy. A real breath of fresh air.' I smile to myself, knowing I have been accepted.

'Can I take your dish, Claire?' Gill says later, when we've all finished.

'Yes thanks. That was lovely. Can I help at all?' I ask.

'You can give me a hand with the coffees if you like; save you listening to these two going on about the match.'

'Claire knows more about football than I do,' says Andy.

'Right, well she can explain the offside rule to me while we make the coffee.'

I follow her out into the pine fitted kitchen.

'Andy can't take his eyes off you, you know. He's completely smitten,' she says as she fills the kettle. I flush pink and look down at my shoes. 'And I can see why. You're perfect for him. You make a great couple, you really do.'

'Thanks,' I say.

'I was only sixteen when I met Dave, you know.'

'So you've been together since then?'

'Yeah, twelve years in August. I don't know where the time's gone.'

'I hope we can be as happy as you two.'

Gill pours the boiling water into the coffee percolator and turns to face me.

'You will be,' she says. 'I've seen the way he is with you. He's yours for life.'

Ten

I got off the train at Saltaire station. It hadn't taken much over an hour. Crazy really. That you could travel so far in such a short journey. Somehow as I'd walked between Bradford Interchange and Forster Square to catch the train the years had slipped away, each day torn off a calendar and thrown to the ground until I was wading knee-deep through dates from the past, feeling them crunch under my boots, watching the faded yellows and browns of my previous life. Until I'd emerged from the train here, a village rich in a past of its own. Salts Mill, looming large above everything, rejuvenated now as a trendy shopping, art gallery and dining venue for the chattering classes but once the employer of the mill workers who lived in the patchwork of terraced houses, built by Sir Titus Salt, which still surrounded it. I stood there feeling small and inconsequential in its shadow. And suddenly I was fifteen again, a piece of paper in my pocket, a house to find, an idol to locate. The word had been ruined now, hijacked by TV talent shows, cheapened and sullied. But I still remembered its true definition: an image of a deity, used as an object of worship, a person or thing that is the object of excessive or supreme adulation. That was what he had been to me. And now I was going to find him. To see the future I never had. To see if it had turned out to be glittering and golden. Or whether the passage of time had rendered it dull and tarnished.

I started walking. Over the canal bridge, down the steps and on to the towpath. I put my hand into the pocket of my long chocolate-brown coat. The piece of paper with his address on was still there. It was all so much simpler now, of course. Google had taken all the fun out of finding your way somewhere. Removed the need for demonstrating initiative or communicating with your fellow human beings. Press print and you were there. I supposed it was just as well really. At least on this particular occasion. Because it gave me time to try to sort out the maelstrom inside my head. Had I driven Mark to do this by pushing him away? Why did I feel so disloyal to him for being here, when it was his idea in the first place? I'd left it a couple of weeks. Going any sooner would have demonstrated indecent haste; any longer would have been unkind to Mark by prolonging his agony. It was only now I was here that my questions moved on. Was Andy going to be here? Would he recognise me? Would he shut the door in my face? Or invite me in? And if he did, what was going to happen then? Could I trust myself? Or him?

I walked on, my legs unable to decide whether to be heavy and full of trepidation or to bounce with a spring in them and break into a trot. I pulled my woollen cap down firmly on my head as the wind swirled the autumn leaves in ever-increasing circles around my boots. The fields on the other side of the canal gave way to a wood. A lock was in front of me, the point where I had to turn right, away from the canal.

I made my way up a small lane past a row of cottages on one side. It was only at this point that I realised I had no idea what to say. I tried to remember how our last conversation had ended, but all I could recall was the lump in my throat and the tears which had followed it. I could hear water now, coming from a different direction to the canal. In front of me were two large mill buildings which appeared to have been turned into apartments. And standing on its own to one side of them, a low, sprawling stone building with a slate roof and mullion windows. On the wall next to the front door – a proper wooden door with a large black knocker – was a sign, 'Mill Race Cottage'.

This was it. This was where he lived. In my dream home. I shook my head. It was so bloody typical. If I'd drawn a picture of where I would be living in twenty years' time to go with the list, this was what it would have been. With Andy standing at the front door, of course. He was making it difficult for me already and I hadn't even seen him yet. It was a mistake. I shouldn't have come. It was all going to be too much. I stuffed my shaking hands into my pockets and walked on past the cottage, fifty yards or so to where the sound of roaring water was emanating from. I looked down over the stone wall to see the River Aire tumbling down a weir, the white foam crashing against the boulders. I couldn't do this. The ache I had carried around inside me for more than twenty years had reverted to the sharp pain it had once been. The hurt was being reawakened. And I couldn't bear to feel its claws tearing at my heart again.

I turned and started walking. I even made it past his front door without so much as a sideways glance. I would have carried straight on and back the way I'd come to the train station. Told Mark he hadn't been in or maybe hadn't wanted to see me. Drawn a line under it for good. But then the dog came bounding up to me. A gorgeous black and white Border collie with mud-spattered fur and a lolling tongue. I smiled at it, the stupid way people do, before looking up to see its owner rounding the corner, one of those long ball-throwing sticks in his hand. I knew instantly, even at that distance. Something in his gait and the sound of his voice as he called to the dog.

'Titus, come here. Leave the lady alone.'

I stopped, unable to walk another step. My legs feeling weak beneath me, my heart battering against my ribcage, trying desperately to escape as it remembered what had happened to it last time.

He carried on walking towards me, calling to Titus, who raced back to him only to dodge the attempt at putting him on a lead, perform a dog's equivalent of a handbrake turn and return to run circles around me, wagging his tail before stopping to have a good shake in front of me, sending mud flying everywhere.

'Titus.' The tone of voice changed sharply. Titus's tail dropped and he stood solemnly still as the lead was clipped on to his collar.

'I'm so sorry,' Andy said, finally arriving in front of me. 'I hope he hasn't ruined your coat. I'll pay for you to get it cleaned if it needs it.'

I stared at him, unable to speak or move. Slowly, silently,

taking everything in. The hair was slightly sleeker and shorter than it used to be and flecked with grey now, as was his stubble. But he was still unmistakably Andy. The same chiselled features; only his face was weatherworn, his eyes heavier somehow. A slight frown creased his brow as he finished speaking and continued looking at me. As if peering at someone in the street who he knew he recognised but couldn't quite place. He looked for a long time before he said anything.

'Claire?' he uttered finally.

I nodded. 'Hello, Andy.'

Another silence. I couldn't work out whether he was pleased to see me or petrified. Maybe both.

'What are you doing here?'

'I needed to see you.'

He nodded, as if that was a perfectly acceptable reason for turning up unannounced on his doorstep after twenty-odd years.

'Well you'd, er, better come in then.' He smiled for the first time. A smile so achingly familiar that I found myself smiling back without even realising. Then rummaged in the pocket of his wax jacket and produced some keys. Titus was already jumping up at the door.

'Let me open it then,' he said, squeezing past to unlock it and turn the handle. The door opened on to a flagstoned square hall with low oak beams. Andy held out his hand.

'After you,' he said.

'Thanks.' I stepped inside. Knowing that I was on his territory now. And under his spell. I watched him take off his boots on the doormat and bent to slip off my own.

'Here, let me take your coat,' he said. 'Is it OK? I meant what I said about getting it cleaned.'

'It's fine, honestly. The mud'll brush straight off when it dries.'

'He's just a bit excitable, I'm afraid. Not used to having house guests.'

I glanced at the coat rack and down at the mat. Only men's jackets. And only men's boots and shoes. Andy lived on his own. I wasn't at all surprised. In fact, I realised I hadn't even considered the possibility that he would have a wife, or children. If I had, I wouldn't have come. Thinking about it, it was crazy to simply turn up like this. What would I have said if a woman had answered the door? How could Andy have explained my arrival to two inquisitive teenage children? I felt stupid. I'd been reckless, not stopping to think of the consequences of my actions. I was indeed sixteen again.

'I'm sorry,' I said. 'I shouldn't have turned up unannounced like this. Look, if you'd rather I go . . .'

'Don't be silly,' said Andy. 'It's good to see you. You're looking really well.'

I was aware of his gaze on me as I took off my cap and scarf and hung them on the coat peg. And aware of the colour rising in my cheeks.

'Thanks,' I said. 'You're not looking too bad yourself.'

'Considering I'm getting on a bit, you mean.'

'Hey, I didn't say that.'

We smiled at each other. Whatever it was that had been there, it hadn't gone away. Simply lain dormant all these years. Waiting to be ignited again.

'Have you come far?'

'Only Todmorden.'

'Really? How did you end up there?'

'It's a long story,' I said.

'How did you find me?'

'That's a long story too.'

'You'd better come through then. I'll put the kettle on.'

He led me into the kitchen: quarry-tiled floor, oak units, more beams, a butler's sink and an Aga, which Titus made a beeline for, curling up on the tiles underneath. My ideal kitchen. In my ideal home. Belonging to someone who, twenty-two years ago, was my ideal man. Was he my ideal man now? Lookswise he'd give George Clooney a run for his money. I'd never for a minute thought he would be fat and balding but nor did I think it was possible for him to get better-looking with age. As it stood, there was no sense of disappointment. And the lack of a wife and children meant there were no obvious 'Warning: Keep Out' signs. Only the guilt I carried inside for even thinking about it when Mark was sitting at home, having been big enough and brave enough to ask me to do this.

'My boyfriend gave me your address,' I said, feeling the need to draw a line between us very clearly in the sand.

'Oh, I see,' said Andy, his face shielded from view as he filled the kettle and flicked it on. Only he didn't see, of course. It made no sense at all.

'I found a list I'd written when I was fifteen. About what I'd like to be doing in twenty years' time. Being married to you was number one.'

'Looks like you had a lucky escape there then,' Andy

said, turning round to face me. I took it that he was joking, although it was hard to tell from his face. He was testing me. In the same way I was testing him.

'Maybe you're right,' I said. 'Mark just wanted me to make sure. Before we took things any further.'

'Are you planning to get married?'

'No, just live together. Once bitten, twice shy and all that.'

'You were married before?'

'Yeah. For seven years. Didn't work out though.'

'I'm sorry,' said Andy.

'No need to be. He was a workaholic lawyer.'

Andy pursed his lips and blew out as he shook his head.

'Tea or coffee?'

'Coffee, please, white no sugar.' It was only as I answered that I realised how absurd it was. Everything that had happened between us and he'd never even known how I took my coffee. It reminded me that we'd never had a grown-up relationship. Not really. Only in my head.

'So what does your boyfriend do?' Andy asked as he scooped some ground coffee into the cafetière.

'He's a lawyer too.'

He turned to me and grinned.

'You're a sucker for punishment, aren't you? I take it you're a lawyer yourself?'

'Yep.'

'Well that must be one thing ticked off on your list.'

'I guess so. Though I don't think I envisaged working at Rochdale Magistrates' Court somehow.'

'Obviously the work experience made quite an impression on you.' He stopped short as soon as he said it, as if realising it had come out wrong. Sounding like a reference to what had gone on between us. He poured the coffee quickly, splashing some of it and having to wipe the surface down with a cloth. 'I bet you're a defence solicitor,' he continued.

'How did you guess?'

'I remember what you said about feeling sorry for the defendants. And about how hard-nosed that CPS woman was.'

I smiled, wondering what else he remembered.

'Come on,' he said, picking up the coffees. 'Let's go through to the lounge.' Titus jumped up as Andy opened the kitchen door. 'I wasn't talking to you,' Andy said. 'Back in your basket. You're not going anywhere until you've had a good clean.'

The lounge was just as I'd imagined it: oak floors and a fully beamed ceiling, some Hockney prints on the walls, including one of Salts Mill, a row of mullion windows and an open fire set in a stone fireplace.

'I love your house.'

'Thanks. It's a former mill building. Used to be two cottages until they converted it into one before I bought it.'

'How long ago was that?'

'About fifteen years now.'

I nodded, starting to piece together Andy's post-me life in my mind.

'So you didn't stay down south for long?'

'No,' he said, gesturing to me to sit down on the sofa. 'As soon as the old knee gave way and I had to stop playing, I was back up here like a shot. West Yorkshire's my home. I wouldn't want to live anywhere else.'

I nodded as I sat down, sinking into the plump cushion behind me. Andy sat in the armchair opposite, as if knowing that sitting next to me would have been pushing things a step too far.

'So come on,' he continued. 'How did you end up in West Yorkshire then?'

'I'm an adopted northerner.' I smiled. 'It kind of feels where I belong. I went to law school in Manchester and lived and worked there when I was married. After the divorce I moved to Todmorden. It was near enough to Rochdale where I work but I wanted to be out in the sticks a bit. I love the hills, the way you notice the colours changing during the seasons.'

'You don't miss Potters Bar then?'

I shook my head. 'I went back recently. My mum's still there. And my friend Frankie.'

'The girl with long dark hair you used to come to the training ground with?'

'Yeah, that's her. She's got four kids now. She's happy living there. But I could never go back.'

We sat for a moment without saying anything. I could hear Titus scratching at the door in the kitchen.

'Have you got any kids?' asked Andy.

'No. My husband didn't want any. Bit of luck, the way things worked out. What about you?'

Andy shook his head. 'No. I did want them. That was the problem, I guess.'

'What do you mean?'

'I lived with a woman for five years. Jennifer her name was. She was the first really serious girlfriend I'd had for a long time. I thought we were going to get married and have a family but it turned out she had other ideas. Went off to work in Abu Dhabi. Said she didn't want to be tied down or to live in Yorkshire for the rest of her life. So that was that. She was a lawyer too. Bloody unreliable bunch, aren't they?'

I nodded. All the times when I'd thought about him, wondered what he was doing, who he was with, I'd never for a moment imagined him being dumped. Idols were for ever. You didn't walk away from them. At least not in my case.

'And there's no one else?' I asked. I cringed as soon as I said it. Hoping he didn't take it the wrong way. Think that I was prying. Trying it on even.

'No, it's just me and Titus. Named after the man who built Salts Mill, by the way, not Titus Bramble the Wigan footballer.'

I smiled. He still had the ability to make me laugh.

'Do you regret it?' I asked. 'Not having a family, I mean.'

'I guess so. Though not as much as I regret other things.'

I shifted on the sofa, made a point of rearranging the cushions behind me. Anything to deflect from what he had just said. And what he might have meant.

'What, like voting for New Labour?' I said, hoping to swiftly change the subject.

Andy grinned.

'It's crazy, isn't it? There we were moaning about Thatcher and Reagan, little knowing that we'd end up with Blair and Bush.'

'Just another of life's disappointments, I guess.'

'Yeah,' said Andy. 'There seem to have been quite a few of those.'

We sat in silence as we drank our coffee. The air heavy with things that hadn't been said.

'So what are you doing now?' I asked as I put my mug down.

'I'm a bloody lawyer too. Only a sports one, mind.'

'Why do you say only?'

'It's all corporate and commercial stuff. Lining the pockets of football club chairmen mostly. Not really what I wanted to do at all.'

'What did you want to do?'

'Criminal stuff. Helping people who really need it. Who appreciate what you're doing for them. Like you do, I guess.'

I smiled.

'What?' he said.

'If you could hear some of the things my clients come out with you'd know why I was laughing.'

'But it must have some rewarding moments.'

'It does,' I said, 'but a lot of frustrating ones as well. That's why I'm trying to get out.'

'To do what?'

'Employment law, corporate stuff at a big firm in Manchester. I've had an interview, I'm waiting to hear.'

Andy shook his head. 'It's funny, isn't it? Both of us wanting to do what the other one's doing.'

'Didn't you try to get into criminal work?'

'No. I couldn't really, could I? Too many people remembered my name.'

I nodded slowly. Embarrassed that I hadn't thought it through. There was an awkward silence. Now Andy had brought up the subject, it hung over us like a thundercloud waiting to burst.

'Does your boyfriend know what happened between us?'

I shook my head. 'Not the sort of thing you can just drop into a conversation, is it?'

'I didn't think he did. He wouldn't have given you my address if he'd known.'

I shrugged. 'Maybe not. I don't know. He wants me to confront things head on. To see what could have been and walk away from it.'

'It's not that easy, though, is it?'

'It is if you're happy with what you've got.'

'You're not, though, are you? Otherwise you wouldn't be here.'

I stared at him, the expression on my face hardening at his assumption.

'Maybe I'm only looking for closure.'

It was Andy's turn to look stung. I hadn't realised I had the ability to hurt him. Now or ever. I gazed down at my feet, wishing I hadn't said it. But knowing his hurt didn't run as deep as mine.

'I've thought about you a lot, over the years.'

I looked up to make sure it really was Andy's mouth the words had come out of. That was going to be my line.

'I thought you'd want to forget me.'

'Don't be daft. You meant a lot to me, Claire. It wouldn't have happened otherwise.'

'It didn't feel like that at the time.'

Andy sighed. 'Things were awkward for me. Professional footballers aren't supposed to do things like that. At least they weren't back then. I'd probably get away with it now. It would have been nothing compared to what most of them get up to.'

I looked up at the ceiling, my bottom lip beginning to tremble. Hating the fact that he had cheapened it like that. Reduced what had happened between us to a minor misdemeanour.

'Sorry, that came out wrong. What I meant was that it was simply a case of being the wrong time for us. You were too young. I couldn't let things go any further.'

I shrugged, wondering exactly how much further we could have gone.

'Look, if you'd have been five years older it might have been entirely different. Who knows, maybe we'd still be together.'

I raised my eyebrows. He was making it hard for me now. Telling me I could have had everything I wanted. That my life could have been here with him. I felt the tears pricking at the corners of my eyes. I so didn't want to cry in front of him again.

'I'm sorry, Claire. I seem to be making things worse,' he said, walking over and sitting down on the sofa next to me. I saw his hand reach out to squeeze mine. Felt his fingers on my skin. Caught the scent of him in my nostrils. I knew I had to put a stop to this. Couldn't risk letting him touch me a second longer. Because already my resistance was ebbing away. I was slipping down some deep, dark time-warp tunnel and if I got to the end I would be sixteen once more. And I would let it happen all over again.

'I think I should go,' I said, pulling away and standing up in one swift movement.

'You're scared of how you're feeling, aren't you?'

'It was a bad idea to come here. It's stirred up a lot of emotions.'

'That doesn't necessarily have to be a bad thing.'

'It does in my case.' I started walking towards the door. Andy followed silently, a few steps behind. Perhaps unsure of his next move, of which Claire he was dealing with. Which wasn't surprising because I wasn't sure either. The sixteen year old wanted him to grab me, to pin me up against the wall and start frantically kissing me. The thirty-eight year old, who still bore the emotional scars from last time, knew that would be wrong and could only lead to trouble.

'Maybe we could meet up again sometime,' I heard Andy say from behind. He hadn't lost it. The ability to bring me down one minute and up the next.

'Why?' I asked, swinging around to face him.

'Because I like you, Claire. I liked you then and I still like you now. And I remember how well we used to get on. Before all the shit happened, I mean.'

'I don't know if that would be a good idea.'

'It just seems a shame, after you've taken the trouble to come here and see me. To think that we'll never see each other again.'

The pain was sharp this time. Maybe he'd known. Maybe that was why he'd said it. 'Never' was a word I struggled with. It brought to mind the hurt of our last meeting. Of resigning myself to spending the rest of my life with nothing but painful memories.

I stopped with my hand on the doorknob. The hesitation was fatal. Showed him I wasn't so sure about walking away for good.

'Here,' he said, handing me a piece of paper and a pen from the table in the hall. 'At least give me your mobile number. Then if I ever need someone to tell me what a git I am, I know how to get hold of you.'

I turned and smiled at him, successfully disarmed. I took the pen and scribbled down my number, my hand shaking as I did so.

'Thanks,' he said, handing me a hastily scrawled mobile number in return. 'That's so you can check to see if I'm in first before you come round next time.'

I hesitated. Wanting to tell him that there wouldn't be a next time. That Mark's offer had only extended to the one visit. But something stopped the words coming out. The same thing which made me take the piece of paper and stuff it quickly into my pocket.

'It's been good to see you,' he said, handing me my coat. 'I'm really glad you came.' He leant forward to kiss me. I turned away but it was too late. He still caught me on the cheek. The merest touch of his lips. But it was enough to let me know what had gone unsaid. That he was there if I wanted him. And now only a phone call away.

He saw me out to the pavement. My steps unsteady. My head light.

'Where's your car?' he asked.

'I came by train.'

'Can I give you a lift to the station?'

'No thanks,' I said. 'I could do with some fresh air.'

Somehow I got back home. I didn't remember any part of the journey. I must have switched to automatic pilot due to the numerous malfunctions in my head. Andy was back in my life. Part of me wished his wife had opened the door, two children playing behind her in the hall. In which case I would have apologised for having the wrong house and fled back home. Knowing it was not only over but dead and buried. A real sense of closure. Of putting the past to rest. Presumably that was what Mark had been hoping for. Certainly not this. All I could think of was that *Friends* episode. The one where they all put their idols' names on a laminated card on the understanding that if they ever got the opportunity, their partner would not stand in their way. And then Ross had been sitting in Central Perk when Isabella Rossellini walked into the room. Except in my case, Andy hadn't blown me out. He'd made it very clear what was available. And as Mark had given me his address, told me to go and see him in the first place, he couldn't complain if I took him up on the offer. He probably wouldn't either; he'd probably go so far as to wish us every happiness. Which was what made it even harder. You didn't take advantage of nice guys like that. It simply wasn't right.

I sat and sweated and stewed. I had a bath, feeling guilty enough to remove even the faintest whiff of Andy from my person. And then sat at the kitchen table staring into a knot in the wood so hard I expected it to split in two. Until seven thirty. When the knock on the door I had been expecting came.

Mark looked as if he was undergoing the most agonising wait of his life. His face was pale and drawn. His eyes implored me to put him out of his misery, one way or another. I felt his pain like a stab to my heart. I stood to one side to let him come in. Wanting to at least do this in private. And then before he could say a word I burst into tears, throwing my arms around him. Needing the warmth of him, the strength of him, the solidness of his love.

He held me close to him, until the point where there was a pause in my sobs and I looked up.

'You came back then,' he said.

'Did you really think I wouldn't?'

'I didn't know what to think, to be honest. Did you see him?'

I nodded through my tears.

'But I take it he wasn't quite as you'd remembered.'

I nodded again, unable to bring myself to dim his unfailing optimism.

'Can you throw away that list now?' said Mark. 'Can we go back to how things were?'

I nodded once more.

'Thank you,' I said. 'For doing that for me.'

'That's OK,' he said. 'It needed to be done. And I knew we'd both feel better afterwards.'

He held me tighter than he'd ever held me. I didn't have the heart to tell him I felt far worse than I'd been before.

Friday, 11 April 1986

It was in the middle of the Hornsey riot case that Andy walked into court. It hadn't been a full-scale riot like the one last year, more a skirmish with baseball bats and one home-made petrol bomb which hadn't worked. But I liked to think of it as a riot. It sounded far more dramatic.

He simply strolled in and sat down next to me. As if it was a perfectly normal thing to do. No one in the court-room would have guessed that the last time we'd seen each other I'd had his prick in my mouth. Gary Hurst turned round and nodded to him, very matter-of-fact. The magistrate gave him a quick glance and then turned his attention back to the unsavoury-looking collection of yobs standing before him. And everything carried on as it was before.

Apart from in my head, where Andy's unexpected arrival had caused some sort of malfunction. He wasn't supposed to be in court on a Friday, only on Monday afternoons. He could have changed his routine in order to witness the Hornsey not-quite-a-riot trial but it seemed unlikely. So he must have come to see me. Which, bearing in mind how we'd parted on Monday, didn't make sense at all

The possible explanations for Andy's behaviour that day

had been spinning around in my head like some kind of manic Rubik's Cube. No matter how hard I tried to unscramble it, I couldn't get the pieces to fit. Presumably he must have liked me to come on to me like that. But if he did like me, I didn't see why he'd been so off with me afterwards. Unless my blow job had been totally crap. But if it had been, surely he wouldn't have come in my mouth. Unless men could fake that stuff. I wasn't sure. I was beginning to feel out of my depth. All I did know was that the Andy I used to chat to at the training ground had never been off with me like that. That was who I wanted back, the Andy I used to know, not this new version. But I didn't know if he still existed. Or even if he ever had.

I could smell his aftershave; it was stronger than usual, freshly applied. He was turning me on without even trying. Or maybe he *was* trying. I looked across at him sitting there, only inches away from me. His hair still wet from the shower. He looked so good, I wanted him all over again. Wanted to show him I was better than Annie. That I could make him happier than she ever had. If only he'd give me another chance.

A commotion at the front of the court alerted me to the fact that the case had collapsed, the defendants grinning cockily and congratulating each other as they left the court. Miss Jenkins was standing over me, explaining about some legal technicality and the fact that things didn't always go to plan. Muttering something else about how impressed she'd been with me. And how I should get in touch next year to see about doing some more work experience.

I nodded and smiled and said something suitably appreciative, all on automatic pilot. I just wanted to get to the point where me and Andy could be alone. I watched as Miss Jenkins strode towards the door, not even waiting for Mr Hurst, who gathered his things and scuttled off after her, clearly having blotted his copybook by scuppering her case. He wasn't going to get anywhere with her now.

And then Andy was standing in front of me. Asking if I was OK. Smiling, as if everything was fine again, and offering me a lift home. It felt like it was happening all over again. Only I couldn't be sure because I'd got it so wrong before. It could be some kind of game. One I didn't know the rules to. And I couldn't learn because they were written in a foreign language.

'What are you doing here?' I said.

'Something's come up next Monday, so I thought I'd come this afternoon instead.' He sounded about as unsure of the whole thing as I felt. 'And anyway,' he continued, 'I wanted to give you this.'

He handed me a small white envelope with my name written neatly in block capitals on the front. I looked at him blankly, wondering if it was a belated birthday card, before prising it open. Inside were two tickets for the Milk Cup Final at Wembley. My jaw dropped and my eyes bulged wide. I looked up at Andy. He was smiling at me expectantly.

'I don't know what to say.'

'You do want to go, don't you?' he said.

'Course I do, I just can't believe that you'd do this for me.'

'It was no trouble. Anyway, I felt bad about Monday. I wanted to say sorry.'

'What for?'

'For putting you in an awkward situation. Afterwards . . . you know.'

'It didn't matter.'

'You were pretty quiet on the way home.'

'I was worried, that was all. I felt like I'd done something wrong. Shown you up or something.'

Andy stood for a moment, not saying anything, shaking his head slowly from side to side.

'You haven't done anything wrong, Claire. I just wasn't expecting any of that to happen. I hadn't thought things through.'

The Rubik's Cube unscrambled in my head.

'So everything's fine between us?'

'Sure it is. I got you the tickets, didn't I?' He was laughing as he said it. Like the old Andy would have.

'Thank you,' I said. 'Thank you very much.'

I tucked the tickets safely inside my bag and walked with Andy to the car park, feeling as though my shoes had developed huge air-cushioned soles. I still didn't understand exactly what was going on. Whether we were going back to how we were on Monday, or how we'd been before that. I wasn't even sure which I wanted. All I knew was that I had to be with Andy. Whatever that involved.

'So, how's it been going? Had any good cases since I saw you?' he asked.

'Oh God, loads. I don't know if good's the right word though; some of them have been pretty awful. The thing is, I get so angry about it when people aren't treated fairly. Sometimes I want to stand up in court and shout at the magistrates. Miss Jenkins says that if I want to be a lawyer, I've got to stop letting my heart rule my head.'

'And what do you think?'

'I think that's crap. It's just a lousy excuse for not getting involved when you know you should do.'

Andy nodded. Very slowly.

'It's like that last bloke,' I said. 'The one who was up for hitting his wife. I don't know how your Mr Hurst could have defended him. Going on about him being in the Rotary Club, as if that made it all right.'

'I know. Gary says it's all part of the job, that he's there to give people the best defence possible, regardless of what he thinks of them.'

'I dunno,' I said, 'I'm not sure if I'm cut out to be a lawyer.'

'Nonsense,' said Andy. 'You've got years to go before you qualify. There's plenty of time for you to become hard and cynical like the rest of us.'

I looked at him, unsure as to whether it was a joke or not.

'But I don't want to get like that.'

'Then don't.' He smiled gently. 'Be yourself, Claire Skidmore, the lawyer with a conscience. You never know, it might even catch on.'

'But what if it doesn't?'

Andy shook his head.

'You worry too much, you do.'

'I can't help it, there's so much to worry about. Didn't

you watch *Threads*? Thatcher and Reagan will probably nuke the world to pieces before I get the chance to become a lawyer.'

'True. Worse things could happen, mind.'

'How d'ya mean?'

'Well, Arsenal could do the double.'

I elbowed Andy in the ribs as I started laughing. 'Now you're taking the piss.'

'Would I?' he said.

When we got to his car, he came round and unlocked the door for me. His body brushed against mine. I thought for a moment he was going to kiss me. He didn't though. It was only then that I knew for certain I wanted him to. I wished I knew what I had to do to get him to do it again. But the truth was I still didn't know what had made him kiss me in the first place.

Andy got in and turned the radio on. We didn't say much at first. It felt a bit awkward again, being back in the car with him. A few minutes later 'Don't Stand So Close To Me' came on. Andy turned the radio off. Which was weird, because I was sure I'd read somewhere that he liked The Police.

'So, is it back to school for you next week?' Andy asked as we headed towards Potters Bar.

''Fraid so. I wish I didn't have to but I've got my O levels to do before I can escape. At least it's only for a few months. I'll be going to college in September. It should be better there.'

'A more adult environment, you mean?'

'Yeah, I guess so. I've never really fitted in at school.

It's a bit like you and Clubber's lot, I s'pose. It's like I'm on a different planet to everyone else. I don't really belong there.'

'So where do you belong?'

With you, Andy. With you. I looked at him in alarm, waiting for his reaction. And then realised I hadn't actually said it out loud. Only in my head.

'Oh, I dunno. I don't seem to belong anywhere right now, certainly not at home.'

'Family giving you grief, are they?'

'You could say that. My dad's remarrying in the summer and my mum's started seeing some bloke called Malcolm. They don't care about me any more.'

'Hey, come on. I'm sure that's not true.'

'It is.'

'Have you tried talking to them about it?'

'There's no point. I hardly ever see my dad, and my mum still treats me like I'm twelve years old.'

'I know what you mean,' said Andy. 'My dad's like that. Sends me birthday cards with footballers on. Doesn't seem to realise that I'm one myself now.'

I smiled at him.

'That's better. Just think of all the good things you've got to look forward to.'

'What, like you playing in the World Cup?'

'No.' Andy seemed irritated. 'Your own stuff. Things you're going to be doing. I bet you've got holiday plans, you and Frankie.'

I opened my mouth to say something but nothing came out. I didn't know how to explain that Frankie had better people to go on holiday with. Or that I'd kind of hoped he might ask me.

'Your road's next left, isn't it?'

I looked out of the window with a start. Aspland's news-agent's was looming large in front of us on the next corner. I bit my bottom lip to try to stop it trembling and clenched my fists, digging my nails into my palms so hard I thought they were going to bleed. I couldn't cope with this. Going back to being friends with Andy again. If that was what this was. Things had moved on and I couldn't pretend nothing had happened between us, even if he could. I knew that if I let him drive off now, that would be it. Nothing else would ever happen between us. I wouldn't even see him again for months. And I couldn't cope with that. Not on top of everything else.

My breath caught as the first sob arrived. The noise that came out was pitiful. A sharp, choking cry, like that of an animal, snared in a trap.

'Hey, what's the matter?' Andy turned in to my road and ground sharply to a halt as the tears began streaming down my cheeks. My head was bowed and my hair hung limply over my face, my shoulders shaking as I sobbed.

He undid his seat belt, leant over and brushed a soggy strand of hair back from my face, tucking it behind my ear. His hand went back to brush a tear away from my cheek. And back again, only this time there wasn't even a tear. He stroked my face softly, as if I was a porcelain doll.

'It's all right,' he said. 'Come here, it's all right.'

I flung my arms around him, burying my head in his shoulder.

'I'm sorry.' My muffled voice drifted up from between the sobs below. 'I was trying so hard not to cry. It's just I'm going through a rough time right now. And I don't think I can cope without you. You're the only one I can talk to.'

I sniffed loudly. I didn't have any tissues. Andy reached over to the back seat and handed me a United shirt.

'I can't use that.'

'Yes you can. I've only worn it once; it shouldn't be too smelly.'

'Are you sure?'

'What, about it being smelly?'

'No. About me using it.'

'Course I am. There's plenty more where that came from.'

I took the shirt and blew my nose gingerly on the sleeve, apologising as I did so.

'Oh God,' he said. 'I didn't realise you were going to do that with it. I'd never have offered it to you if I'd known.'

I smiled up at him, a thin, watery smile.

'So how come I'm the only one you can talk to?' asked Andy. 'Why can't you talk to Frankie?'

'We had a row. She doesn't want to be my friend any more. She thinks I'm . . . Oh, it doesn't matter.'

'No, come on, she thinks you're what?'

I hesitated, fearing it would sound ridiculous. But I knew I had to tell him, in case I never got the chance again.

'She thinks I'm stupid . . . for loving you so much.'

I waited. Waited for Andy to start laughing. To tell me

Frankie was right, I was being stupid. I should grow up. Get a life. Get real.

But he didn't laugh. He didn't say a word. He lifted my head towards his, looked at me for a moment and kissed me. Deep and hard and long. Drawing out the doubts and confusion, injecting pure ecstasy in their place. He loved me. He really did. It wasn't just a one-off, it was a real relationship. The whole thing on Monday must have been some kind of test. And I'd passed it because I hadn't given up on him or had a go at him or demanded to know what was going on. And now I was getting my reward. Everything I'd ever wanted. Andy. All to myself. In years to come I wouldn't even remember these past few days. The wobble in between. The first kiss and this one would melt seamlessly into each other. The start of our relationship. Of our life together. The tears dried instantly and a smile lit up my face.

'Don't ever stop smiling,' Andy whispered. 'You've got a beautiful smile.'

I wished I'd had a tape recorder going. I would be able to replay it in my head over and over again. But it would have been nice to be able to play it back to Frankie.

'Is there anyone inside?' he asked, nodding towards the house. I hesitated for a moment, feeling my stomach clenching. It was what he wanted though. And it was the grown-up thing to do.

'No,' I said. 'No one at all.'

Andy nodded. We scrambled out of the car and hurried up the front path. I fumbled with the key in the lock and led him into the lounge without saying a word. Andy threw his jacket down and yanked his tie off. Pulling me over to the sofa and laying me down. One by one he undid the buttons on my blouse, kissing me frantically as he did so. I was looking at him, staring into his eyes, trying to make myself believe that this was really happening. I wondered what Frankie would think if she could see us now. Whether she'd be jealous that it wasn't her and Matt. Andy slid my blouse off my shoulders.

'Your go,' he whispered.

Andy Pailes was asking me to undress him. I had no idea what to do. I started to unbutton his shirt. But my hands were shaking so much I couldn't do it. He put his finger to his lips as I started to apologise. I watched as he pulled his shirt over his head and tossed it on the floor. The ache deep inside me got a whole lot worse.

Andy lowered himself on top of me. I flinched as his bare skin touched mine. Confirmation that he existed in the flesh, not just inside my head. I'd thought the hairs on his chest would tickle me but they didn't. Not really. He was breathing heavily now. Pushing against me, rubbing his hand up and down my thigh, getting closer and closer to the ache inside. I felt his fingers touch me, stroking me through my knickers, then slipping inside. I heard myself moan out loud. Laura Ashley started laughing.

I closed my eyes, trying to shut it out. But the laughter got louder. I could see myself now. Twelve years old, my hair tied in bunches, my dirty white socks sagging around my ankles, a bruise on my left knee. We'd been sent home early from school; the central heating had broken down. It was on at home though. I felt the warmth hit me as I let myself in and stepped inside the hall.

The laughter was the first thing I heard. It was a deep, throaty laugh, belonging to a woman. It wasn't my mum's laugh though. The laughter turned into a moan. A rhythmic, repetitive moan, which grew louder by the second. It was coming from the lounge. Slowly I pushed open the door. Pauline from next-door-but-one was lying on the sofa, her skirt hitched up around her waist, her legs splayed apart. She didn't have any knickers on. Dad was lying on top of her, or in between her, it was hard to work out which exactly. His trousers were lying in a crumpled heap on the floor. He still had his socks on. Pauline was still moaning. Writhing and wriggling, while Dad was thrusting into her, harder and harder each time.

'Stop!' I shouted.

They both looked up, startled. Pauline swore, Dad called my name. But I was gone, I was running; out of the house and down the street, all the way to the baker's where Mum worked. Where I threw myself at her, crying into her floury apron and beating my fists against her sides.

I opened my eyes with a start. Andy was looking at me in alarm. I realised I must have shouted out loud.

'Are you OK?' he said. 'Do you want me to stop?'

'No,' I said. 'I want you to carry on. Not here though. The sofa's not comfortable. Can we go upstairs?'

Andy nodded and I led him hurriedly up to my room and shut the door behind us. I turned to face him. But he wasn't looking at me. He was staring at the pictures of himself which lined my bedroom walls. I stood, feeling naked and exposed in just my bra and skirt, waiting for him to carry on where he'd left off. He didn't move, though. Just kept staring at the pictures. I couldn't understand what the problem was. I thought he'd like them.

'Is everything all right?' I asked.

'Yeah,' he said eventually. 'Come here. Let's do this properly.'

He slipped my skirt off and unfastened my bra. He knew now that it was padded. I froze for a second, bracing myself for the look of disappointment on his face. But he didn't falter, simply cupped what there was of my breasts in his hands as he kissed me hard on the neck. I knew he had done this before. Probably more times than I'd care to know about. But today he was doing it with me. And that was all that mattered.

He took his trousers and pants off. I noticed the lines where the suntan stopped, where his shorts usually were. I knew I was about to lose my virginity. Not to some boy from school but to Andy Pailes, United and England star. It was weird; all the times I'd imagined us together, I'd never imagined us doing this. I'd dreamt about waking up with him in the morning and lying next to him watching him sleeping. But that was all. I felt embarrassed, scared even. But above all, I felt absolutely elated that he should want me this much.

'You are so sexy,' Andy whispered, pulling me down on to the bed. 'That's what makes you so different, you know. You've got absolutely no idea how sexy you are.'

I lay there basking in the glory. Knowing I'd never forget

this moment. The thrill of Andy's heaving, sweating body pressing against me, a mass of taut skin and toned muscle. Every time he touched me a spurt of elation ran through me. He kissed my neck, then my shoulders, working his way down my body and showering me with compliments as he went. He turned me over and peeled off my knickers. 'You've got a great bum,' he said. 'Where did you get a bum like that?'

I smiled, then hesitated for a second, wondering if I should say something, confess I'd never done this before, ask if he had a condom. But I couldn't remember Demi Moore ever stopping Rob Lowe in his tracks. Come to think of it, I couldn't remember anyone in the movies ever mentioning stuff like that. All they said were things like 'Go on, baby' and 'Take me.' And anyway, I knew that if Andy didn't have a condom, I'd let him do it all the same. Just in case I never got the chance again.

His hand slid between my legs, his fingers quick and deft, sending my body into rhythmic contractions. I lifted my head and looked at him.

'Go on,' I said, in my best Hollywood actress voice. 'I'm all yours.'

Afterwards, when it was all over, I lay there, a sticky wet substance trickling down my inner thigh, and wondered why you never got to see how messy it all was in the movies. Or hear the sort of strange squelching noises which had emanated from me.

I looked up at the pictures of Andy and the rest of the team on the wall. Suddenly I felt embarrassed, lying naked squashed up against him on the single bed. Which was weird because I hadn't felt embarrassed while we were doing it. I glanced across at Andy. He was looking at the pictures on the wall too. His face ashen.

I prayed I had been all right, done the right things. I began mentally trawling through all the magazine articles on sex I had ever read. I wished I'd cut them out and kept them now. Stored them in a series of ring binders, like those part-work magazines they advertised on TV. The ones that built up into a 'remarkable collection for you to pass on to your grandchildren'. Although obviously I wouldn't have been able to do that with this one.

I wasn't even sure if I'd had an orgasm. It had felt good. But there hadn't been one little bit which had been better than all the rest, a point where bells had rung or neon lights had flashed. I consoled myself with the fact that Andy had evidently enjoyed himself. What was it he'd said at the end? Just before he had collapsed on top of me and I'd realised that, far from getting going, it was actually all over.

'You are so good, you are so beautiful.' That was what he'd said. And that was all I'd needed to hear.

I pulled the corner of the United duvet over me. I didn't want to get up. I wanted to lie with Andy for ever. Have a cuddle under the duvet, listen to music together, whatever it was other couples did afterwards. But before I could do any of that, Andy got out of bed. He didn't say anything to me. I figured I should get up too.

We dressed in silence, Andy keeping his head bowed. Not looking at me or anything around him. It was strange how putting clothes on was so much more embarrassing than taking them off. I hadn't expected things to feel this awkward, not after what we'd just done. When we got down to the lounge I saw his United shirt lying on the sofa. I hadn't even realised I'd brought it in with me.

'Here, don't forget this,' I said.

'No, you have it.'

'Are you sure?'

'Yeah. You blew your nose on it, didn't you?'

I smiled at him.

'It was all right, wasn't it?'

'Yeah, of course it was.'

I didn't know what I was supposed to do now. How this kind of thing worked. It was like we'd skipped the bit where he asked me out and gone straight to the sex. I wasn't sure if he was going to ask me out now, or whether I should just take it that we already were going out. That it went without saying. It seemed stupid to ask, but I realised he was about to walk away again. And I had to be sure this time.

'When can I see you again?'

'Soon, I'll sort something out.' He didn't sound too sure.

'I'll give you my phone number,' I said, jotting it down on a piece of paper and handing it to him. He put it in his pocket without saying anything.

'Can I have yours, please?' I said. It felt like asking for an autograph.

He hesitated, then took the piece of paper I'd just given him from his jacket pocket, tore the bottom half off, scribbled something on it and gave it to me.

'Thank you,' I said.

I looked at Andy, feeling the tears pricking at the corners of my eyes again. I went to give him a kiss but he moved away. He seemed to be in a hurry. I stood in the doorway, waving to him as he drove off down the road. As I turned to go back inside I noticed two men sitting in a black Escort parked further down the road. One of them was holding something but I couldn't see what it was. As soon as he saw me looking at him he put it down. I shut the door and went back inside. Wondering how on earth I was going to be able to act normal when Mum came home.

I lay in bed, hugging Andy's shirt tightly to me. Certain I could still smell him on it, and still taste him on my lips. I gazed at the pictures of him on my wall. It was weird, if you thought about it. I had a picture of Spandau Ballet on my wall too. And yet I couldn't imagine any of them ever being naked in my bedroom, having sex with me.

I'd lain awake most of the night, thinking about what had happened. It hadn't sunk in yet. I wasn't sure it ever would. A week ago I'd never even kissed a boy. Now I'd lost my virginity to Andy Pailes. *The* Andy Pailes. It was like I'd skipped all the usual stuff, the getting off with lads at school, and gone from nothing to everything in one go. Having sex with someone famous. Someone who meant the world to me. You couldn't get much bigger than that. Part of me was elated, buzzing with the thrill of it all. Yet another part of me felt kind of flat, disappointed almost. It wasn't supposed to be like this. Me lying here, unsure what to do next,

waiting for him to call. I could phone him myself. I'd mem-
orised the number, but I didn't want to appear too desperate,
even if I was. It was better to wait for him. I just wished I
knew whether it would be this morning, tomorrow or the
week after next.

I'd always thought that once you'd had sex with someone, that was it, you were kind of joined to them at the
hip. I'd never expected it to be like this. To not even know
when you were going to see them again. To have all these
doubts and anxieties about the whole thing.

I could be pregnant, for all I knew. Michelle in *East-
Enders* only had sex with Dirty Den once, but she'd got
pregnant. The thought of giving birth frightened the life
out of me (so did the thought of telling Mum I was up the
duff). But there was no way I could get rid of a baby. I
didn't like the anti-abortion people. They'd come to
school once, done a talk and pulled a plastic foetus out of
a shopping bag. Fucking loopy they were. But they'd got
to me. Made me wonder if there had been some darker
message behind Wham!'s 'Choose Life' T-shirts. And if I
was pregnant, it wouldn't be any old baby. It would be
Andy's. So I couldn't possibly get rid of it. Because if I had
his baby he wouldn't have any choice then. He'd have to
love me back.

I needed to go to the loo. I threw back the duvet, catching sight of myself in the mirror. 'Puppy Love', it said on
my nightshirt, above a picture of a spaniel-type thing with
floppy ears and its tongue hanging out. It looked stupid,
like something a ten year old would wear. I wasn't a kid
any more, I was a woman. I should be wearing a sexy

negligée, something in black satin. I'd have to buy one. I didn't want Andy seeing me in some poxy nightshirt.

I padded along the landing. Mum was asleep, I heard her snoring as I passed her bedroom, but I still bolted the bathroom door behind me. As I started to pee, I noticed a strange stinging sensation. It was only then I realised how sore I was. It was like someone had punched me down there; I imagined everything red and puffy. I wondered if it always felt like this afterwards, or if it was only the first time. At least there wasn't any blood on the sheets. I could never have washed them or got rid of them without Mum knowing. The bloodstained knickers had been easy. I'd wrapped them up inside three carrier bags and put them in the outside bin. If Mum noticed they'd gone I could always say I lost them in the changing rooms at school.

I'd just got back in bed when I heard the doorbell go. It was seven thirty on a Saturday morning. No one called at that time. Unless it was the postman, delivering a parcel. But I didn't think we were expecting anything. I lay there for a while, hoping whoever it was would go away. But they didn't. They rang again. That was when I realised it could be Andy. That he might want to see me before he left for the match.

I leapt out of bed, pulled on my dressing gown and dashed downstairs.

'Hang on a sec,' I called to the blurred figure I could make out beyond the frosted glass panel as I fumbled with the lock. The door finally jolted open. It wasn't Andy after all.

'Hello, it's Claire, isn't it?'

I stared at the man on the doorstep. He had a fat, squashed nose and wavy hair that looked as if it was fighting to pull free of his head. I had no idea how he knew my name. I didn't say anything, just nodded.

'Shaun Mackie, I'm a reporter with the *News of the World*. Sorry to trouble you so early, only I need to ask you a few questions about your boyfriend. How long have you been seeing Andy Pailes?'

For a split second it sounded good, hearing Andy described as my boyfriend. It made me feel all warm inside. Then I remembered that this wasn't Frankie I was talking to. It was some reporter who was trying to get Andy into trouble. Instinct took over, telling me to deny everything.

'I dunno what you're talking about.'

'Would you like me to remind you? About Andy's little visit yesterday. We've got photographs, you see. Pictures of him kissing you. And then coming into this house.'

My stomach turned over. What little colour I had drained from my face. My mum was going to go mental. I couldn't work out what had happened. How they'd found out about me and Andy. How they'd got the pictures.

'Nothing happened. He just came in for a chat.'

The reporter was smiling. Like he didn't believe me.

'I take it he knows you're still at school. Did he have sex with you, Claire?'

The churning sensation in my stomach got a whole lot worse. I felt myself going red. The whirring of a camera motor-drive alerted me to the photographer standing at the gate. It was the man I'd seen in the car yesterday. That was what he'd been doing. Taking photos of me and Andy.

He was taking photos of me again now, standing there in my fucking dressing gown. I started to close the door.

'Who is it, Claire?' Mum's voice called from the hallway. I hadn't heard her come downstairs.

'No one,' I said, but it was too late. She came up behind me and poked her head round the door.

'If you're selling something you can go away and come back at a reasonable hour.'

The reporter smirked.

'I'm from the *News of the World*. I'd like to ask you a few questions about your daughter's boyfriend.'

'What are you talking about? She hasn't got a boyfriend. You've got the wrong house.'

'I'm afraid we haven't, Mrs Skidmore. Your daughter's been seeing Andy Pailes, the footballer.'

Mum started laughing. 'In her dreams maybe. Her head's full of silly nonsense. You know what teenage girls are like.'

The reporter took a photograph from a large brown envelope and held it up. It was a bit fuzzy. But you could still make out me and Andy kissing in the car.

'He came to this house yesterday, Mrs Skidmore. He was inside for over an hour. Do you condone your daughter having sex with an England footballer?'

Mum looked from me to the photo, and back to me. As if checking that it really was the same person.

'Claire?'

I looked down at my feet. 'Shut the door, Mum.'

'I really think you should answer, Mrs Skidmore. It's not going to look very good if you don't say anything. Perhaps you could tell me how long your daughter's been seeing him. We understand she was only fifteen when they first met.'

I slammed the door shut and stood with my head leant back against the cold glass, breathing heavily. Desperate to block it all out, make it go away. It wouldn't though. Mum ushered me away from the door and into the living room, looking at me like I was a piece of dog shit stuck to her shoe.

'What the hell have you been up to?'

Her voice was quivering. I'd only ever heard her shout like that once before. The day Dad left home.

'It's not what you think.'

'I've seen the bloody photo, Claire. I want to know what happened.'

'I . . . I met him at court, he gave me lifts home a couple of times. He only came in once. Yesterday, when he dropped me off. It was only kisses and stuff. Nothing else.'

'You must think I was born yesterday. Just came in for a chat, did he? Or a nice cup of tea and a biscuit.'

'I was upset, I needed someone to talk to.'

'You weren't doing much talking in the car.'

'Yeah, well, we got a bit carried away.'

'How far, exactly?'

'It doesn't matter.'

'Yes it does. You're sixteen, for Christ's sake. And he's a bloody footballer. What are people going to think?'

'I don't care what they think. I love him.'

'Don't be ridiculous. You don't even know him.'

'I do. He's given me his phone number and everything. I'm kind of going out with him.'

'Give me strength.' Mum looked up at the ceiling, her whole body shaking. 'He's taken advantage of you, that's what he's done. He's a dirty little bastard.'

The words slapped me across the face. I wished she'd leave Andy out of it. None of this was his fault.

'He's not,' I shouted. 'He didn't sleep with me, OK?'

'That's what you say. I don't know that, do I? And nor does anyone else. If this gets in the papers, you're going to look like a slut. That's what that reporter thought of you. I could see it, the way he was looking at me. Wondering what sort of mother I was, bringing you up to behave like that.'

'Is that what you think of me?'

'I don't know what to think of you any more, Claire. I really don't.'

'That's because you don't know me. You never have done. Andy's the only one who listens to me. The only one who cares.'

Mum threw her hands up into the air. 'For goodness' sake, will you get it into your head. He won't want to know you, not now he's got what he wanted. Believe me, Claire. They're all the same.'

I heard the letterbox rattle and ran back into the hall as a note came through. I picked it up and went back into the living room.

'What does it say?' asked Mum.

'It says to call if we change our minds about talking. It's got the reporter's phone number on it.'

'Well you can put that in the bin for a start.'

I moved towards the phone.

'What are you doing?'

'I'm calling Andy. I'm going to warn him. They might go round there.'

Mum darted forward, standing between me and the phone. I tried to reach it but she grabbed hold of my arm.

'This is going to stop right now. You're not to talk to him, to write to him. Nothing. And if you think you're ever going up that bloody training ground again, you've got another think coming.'

'You can't do that, you can't stop me seeing him.'

'Just you watch me.'

I pulled away from her. 'Why don't you fuck off and stop screwing up my life?'

I heard her burst into tears as I ran upstairs. I'd never sworn at her before. But then she'd never called me a slut before either. I threw myself on to my bed, gulping huge mouthfuls of air as I struggled to take it all in. It wasn't fair. This was the first time I'd ever kissed anyone or brought anyone back to the house, and now it was going to be in the papers. They were going to make me look like a real slag. And it hadn't been like that. It was me and Andy, who I loved more than anyone else in the world. It was special and he was special. Just because I was still at school, it didn't make it wrong. I started crying, huge, heavy tears that plopped on to my pillow. It had all gone horribly wrong. And I had no idea what to do.

I stayed in my room the rest of the day, listening to the radio. United lost 2–1 to Everton. Which meant we were nine points behind them, all dreams of winning the league over. Andy was substituted at half-time. The commentator said he'd had a nightmare, been at fault for both goals, that he seemed to be distracted. I guessed he'd had a visit from the paper as well. I wondered what he'd told them. And why he hadn't called me.

Eleven

'Catherine wheels,' whooped Fiona in delight as she peered inside the box I had just given her. 'Your box has got Catherine wheels. I was only saying five minutes ago that you know the world's in a state when you can't find a decent Catherine wheel in a box of fireworks any more.'

I laughed and shook my head. Fiona's enthusiasm for fireworks knew no bounds. I wasn't sure if it was because Guy Fawkes was a well-known Scots-hater or simply her stubborn refusal to stop behaving like a big kid, but 5 November was bigger than Christmas in the Walker household.

They'd started holding their fireworks parties when Aidan was a toddler. The fact that he was now fifteen years old and therefore wouldn't be seen dead at anything organised by his parents hadn't dented Fiona's enthusiasm or her resolve to continue the tradition.

'You've made a sad lady very happy,' said Neil with a grin.

'Well this should make a sober man very drunk,' said Mark, handing Neil a twelve-pack of lager.

'Thanks. Remind me to invite the two of you around for Hogmanay,' said Neil. 'We shall declare you honorary Scots.'

Mark and I fought our way through to the already packed kitchen where jacket potatoes, chilli and hot dogs were being devoured by the guests.

'Get in quick before the gannets eat it all,' said Fiona.

'Thanks,' I said. 'It smells fantastic.'

'Hopefully it will taste good too. The chilli has the Aidan seal of approval, which is saying something.'

'Where's he gone tonight?' I asked.

'Out,' said Fiona, mimicking her son's gruff voice. 'That's about as much as we get these days from the sullen and secretive one.'

Mark nodded. 'Yep, sounds like a normal teenager to me.'

'I know, but if you could see the kids that hang out on the streets round here you'd understand why we're so worried. Neil knows some of the families. And let's just say he doesn't know them because they're pillars of the community.'

'I went around with some dodgy kids for a bit when I was his age,' said Mark. 'Just to annoy my parents, I think. I soon got fed up of them and went back to my own mates.'

'Yeah, but he's very impressionable. And he's got less than a year to go till his GCSEs. He's supposed to be doing work experience in a couple of weeks but he hasn't even sorted anything out.'

'Why don't you take him into work with you?' Mark asked.

'He wouldn't be seen dead with me. He's at that age when your parents are the most embarrassing people on earth.'

'I'll happily have him with me for a week,' said Mark. 'If you think he'd go for it.'

'Would you really?' said Fiona.

'Of course. Might put him off being a lawyer, mind.'

'No, I think it's a great idea. I reckon he might even go for that. I'll ask him tomorrow. Cheers, Mark.'

Fiona hurried off to get some more potatoes out of the oven. I reached out to stroke Mark's arm.

'Thanks,' I said. 'That was really good of you.'

'I hope he goes for it,' said Mark. 'Be good to have someone to keep me on my toes. Ask lots of difficult questions.' He paused for a second. 'Where did you go on work experience?'

'Hornsey Magistrates' Court,' I said.

'Bloody hell, I pity the poor sod who got you. I bet you gave them a hard time.'

I smiled uneasily. Mark put his arm around me, as if to make clear he'd only been joking. He'd seemed a lot happier the last couple of weeks. More at ease. More confident in our relationship. And I was trying. I was trying so hard to be happy too. But still it hung there in the air. Andy's apparent willingness to rekindle our relationship. And the knowledge that he could call me at any time. I wished I could talk to someone about it. But Mark was obviously out of the question, and Fiona was too close to Mark and not given to discussing emotional affairs of the heart. The only person who might be able to understand what I was going through was Frankie, and I couldn't possibly bother her when she had far more important things on her mind. Emily was at the end of her intensive chemotherapy. They were waiting to hear if it had been a success. And what would happen next. Every phone call from Frankie was more frantic. Every e-mail from Emily more desperate about not being well enough to go to the *Twilight* premiere.

'Come on then,' said Mark, reaching for the plates. 'Let's tuck in, I'm starving.'

'Ladies and gentlemen,' shouted Fiona half an hour later when everyone had been fed and watered. 'If you'd care to take your places on the patio, the main event is about to commence.'

We joined the throng of party-goers huddling together outside as the first rocket went up. Fiona always liked to start with a bang. There was the usual mixture of success-ful fireworks, which gained a cheer from the onlookers and exaggerated oohhs and aahhs, and damp-squib ones presumably thrown in to make up the numbers in the box. I was enjoying Fiona's excitement at the first Catherine wheel when my mobile rang. It was a wonder I heard it above the noise. I guess I was on hyper-alert, as I had been every time it had rung for the past couple of weeks. Won-dering if it would be Andy. Or whether having raised my hopes he'd got cold feet and thought better of it. I grabbed my mobile and looked at the screen. It was Frankie.

'I'd better take this inside,' I said to Mark, hurrying back in through the patio door before answering.

'Hi,' I said. 'Are you OK?' There was a high-pitched sob from the other end of the line, followed by a bang as a rocket went off outside. 'Frankie, what's wrong?'

'Emily's in remission,' sniffed Frankie.

'But that's good, isn't it? That's what you wanted.'

'The doctors say the risk of a relapse is so high because

of this chromosome thing that she's got to have a bone marrow transplant straight away.'

'Oh, Frankie. I'm so sorry.'

'It just goes from bad to worse.'

'You poor thing. What about donors? Can you do it?'

'No. Parents aren't compatible and Joe's not a match. They've tested the kids as well but they're not compatible either. And as I've got no idea where her father is or whether he's got any more children, there's not much I can do. Searching for a Gonzales in Spain would be a bit like looking for a Smith in England.'

'What about that bone marrow register they have?'

'They've checked it for Europe and the rest of the world and it seems there's no match. Apparently that's not uncommon. It's unbelievable, isn't it? The whole fucking world to choose from and nothing for my Emily.'

'So what happens now?'

'We wait and hope that someone compatible joins the register in time. And they won't say exactly how long she's got.'

Another rocket exploded nearby, accompanied by the usual chorus of approving 'oohhs'. It felt wrong, people celebrating, having fun, when someone on the end of the phone was facing losing her daughter.

'Oh God. How's Emily taken it?'

'Pretty bad. She's back from hospital tonight. In her room as usual.'

'I'll e-mail her later. Look, if there's anything I can do to help . . .'

'There is one thing. Although I know it's a lot to ask.

You could register as a donor. They said to ask anyone we knew.'

'Of course I will. I'll ask Mark too. Bloody hell, it's the least we can do.'

'Thanks,' said Frankie. 'We really appreciate it. Anyway, I'd better go. Joe's working and Roberto's scared of the fireworks.'

'Well you take care. Love to everyone. And a big hug from me. If you need to talk . . .'

'I will,' said Frankie.

I slowly made my way back outside. Fiona was lighting a Roman candle. Mark clapped and whooped along with the rest of the crowd as the coloured flares popped up. And I knew that I had to go home straight away. Because all I wanted to do was yell at them to shut up, to show some respect. For a fifteen-year-old girl who might not be around to see Christmas.

'Hi, all set?' I asked when I met Mark outside his offices at lunchtime a couple of days later.

'Yeah, I guess so,' he said, looking decidedly unsure about the whole thing. Admittedly giving a blood sample wasn't my idea of the best way to spend a lunch hour, but I wasn't going to complain when I knew what Emily was going through. Mark had agreed instantly to register as a donor when I'd told him what the situation was. Although he hadn't looked quite so keen when I'd explained it involved a blood test at the local hospital.

'So how was your morning?' I asked as we walked through town, trying to take his mind off what was in store.

'Quiet,' he said. 'So quiet I did some more work on that case. You know, the LawWorks one.' He was representing an arts charity for adults with mental-health problems which faced losing its funding because it had been given notice to leave its premises by the end of the month. 'The landlord of the building is being a complete arsehole. He wants to get planning permission for a commercial use for it. Obviously figures it will be easier with the charity out of the way.'

'Is there anything you can do to stop him?'

'If there is I'm going to find it. The building's got a long history of community use, I'm ploughing through all the planning conditions and deeds at the moment.'

I looked at him. He was really fired up.

'You're enjoying doing this, aren't you?'

'Yeah,' he said, turning to face me with a grin. 'I like sticking up for the little guys against the bullies.'

We walked on towards the hospital, Mark talking enthusiastically about the case. It was great to see him like this: angry and passionate about something instead of appearing as if he was simply going through the motions. He even seemed to forget momentarily where we were heading – until we arrived at the clinic and the colour drained from his face again.

'Are you all right?' I asked.

'Yeah, I'm fine. Hospitals make me feel a bit queasy, that's all.'

I nodded, still not convinced that he wanted to go through with this.

'Look, you don't have to, you know. Frankie would understand.'

'No she wouldn't. I wouldn't understand if my daughter was dying of leukaemia and some wimp didn't want to give four measly millilitres of blood just because he had a thing about hospitals.' It was a fair point. One I couldn't argue with.

'OK. Well if you need someone to hold on to while you're in there . . .'

'Don't worry, I'll dig my fingernails into the nurse. Maybe I can get some blood out of her at the same time.' He was smiling as he said it, but I knew from the colour of his face that this wasn't a laughing matter at all for him. He'd never really explained why he had a fear of hospitals. Just said it was one of those things. It was clearly a big thing, though, for him to look as bad as he did.

'Twenty-six and twenty-seven,' called a disturbingly efficient-looking nurse. We'd been given numbers when we came in. A bit like they did at the deli counter at the supermarket on a busy day. Except we weren't waiting for some pâté or half a pound of Somerset goat's cheese. We were about to be human pin cushions. We followed the nurse through to a small room with two wooden chairs facing various posters about giving blood and HIV screening. I appreciated the NHS didn't have money to spend on flowers or soft furnishings but any attempt to cheer the room up, even a poster of the Simpsons, would have been a help.

I handed the nurse my blood-testing kit which had been sent through by the Anthony Nolan Trust. She scanned the leaflet inside, got the needle ready and made some comment along the lines of being able to do this with her eyes shut. I hoped she didn't mean it literally.

'Right, arm out straight, clench your fist.' I felt the prick before she said anything else. 'OK, that's you done.' Clearly there was no time for pleasantries. Perhaps she was on some kind of bonus depending on how many she got through in a lunch hour. I glanced over at Mark, who was being attended to by the other nurse in the room. If he'd looked pale earlier he looked distinctly green around the gills now.

'Are you OK?' I called over.

'Yes, I think she's drilling for oil,' he said through gritted teeth as the needle was inserted.

I glanced up at the nurse. Not so much as a glimmer of a smile. She whacked a plaster on Mark's arm and went out to call the next number.

I shook my head and smiled as we made our way back along the corridor.

'You're not laughing at the nurse's friendly bedside manner, are you?' asked Mark.

'No, I'm thinking Emily will be so impressed when I tell her about this.'

'What, because we did it for her?'

'No, because of this whole business with the vampires. I'll tell her Edward Cullen took our samples. Might even raise a laugh.'

We were walking through the hospital car park when my mobile rang. My head was still full of Emily. So full that I didn't even think to check the screen before answering, as I'd been in the habit of doing for the past few weeks. I should have, though. To give myself a second or two to prepare.

'Hi, Claire.'

I knew the voice instantly. Had gone to sleep with it playing through my Walkman so many times that I didn't have a doubt in my head that it was Andy. I hadn't actually thought he was going to ring now. Thought maybe I'd read the signs wrong, as I had so often in the past, and he'd simply asked for my number to be polite. Like when people who you haven't seen for years promise to stay in touch if you bump into them in the street, even though you both know damn well you won't.

'Oh, hi.' I looked across at Mark as I said it. He was oblivious, of course, that I was speaking to the person he thought I'd put behind me.

'How are you fixed after work?' asked Andy. 'Only I'm in the area this afternoon. Wondered if you fancied going for a drink?'

I was thrown for a second. Andy Pailes was asking me out for a drink. I had to rein myself back in. Maybe it was nothing. Maybe he was genuinely 'in the area' and was simply being friendly. Or maybe it was the other 'in the area'. The one where you make a twenty-mile detour in order to get there.

'Oh, I see.' I appeared to have been rendered incapable of giving proper answers to questions.

'You can't talk right now, can you?'

I glanced sideways at Mark. 'Er, no. Not really.'

'OK. So, as I don't know any pubs in Rochdale, how about I meet you at the magistrates' court at about half four? Will you be finished by then?'

'Yeah.' I didn't recognise my own voice as I said it. Had

even less idea where the answer had come from. My whole body felt weak, my head was spinning. And it had nothing to do with the nurse with the big needle.

'Great. See you then.'

Somehow, without actually agreeing to anything, other than the time I finished work, I appeared to have arranged to meet Andy for a drink.

'Bye,' I said, trying desperately to stop my voice coming out squeakily, not so much for Andy's sake but so as to stop Mark suspecting anything. And that was it. Andy said goodbye and was gone. Except he wasn't gone. He was everywhere again. Running through every vein in my body. I looked up at Mark. Feeling the need to deny something even though he had no reason to suspect.

'Just work,' I said. And that was it. I had lied to him. It was a slippery slope from here on.

The rest of the afternoon passed by in a blur. It was a bit of luck I had nothing more taxing than a couple of adjournments; I certainly wouldn't have been capable of battling my way through a trial.

'Are you OK?' asked Fiona, as I gathered my things together at the end of the afternoon's session. 'You seem a bit distracted.'

'Do I?' I replied, struggling with the clasp on my brief-case. 'I guess the blood clinic visit threw me a bit.'

'All this business with your friend's daughter must be really worrying. I can't imagine what I'd do if anything happened to Aidan.'

I nodded, feeling bad for using Emily as a cover when

the actual reason for my distraction was Andy. I couldn't tell Fiona that, though. I was hoping she would be gone before Andy arrived. I didn't want the web of deceit spreading any further than it already had.

My mobile beeped a message. I knocked a folder from the top of the pile on my desk in my haste to check it. I hadn't listed Andy's name in my address book in case Mark saw it. Besides, there was no need. I knew the number anyway. I had it listed in my head alongside his home number from twenty-odd years ago. Which had stubbornly refused to be deleted.

'Hi. I'm in the foyer. A'

Fuck. He was early. I had two choices. I could either keep him waiting until everyone had gone or make a dash for it now.

'Right, I'm off,' I said to Fiona as I put the folder back on my desk and grabbed my coat.

'A bit keen, aren't you?'

'Just getting out while the going's good. See you tomorrow.'

I didn't even wait for her reply. I was already out of the door and careering down the corridor. Slowing my pace, I walked down the steps, trying to replace the inner fluster with an outward appearance of calm. I was doing quite well until I saw him. Standing there looking out of the window. His chiselled features marking him out from the round-faced security guards. His expensive-looking winter coat advertising the fact that he didn't belong in Rochdale.

He turned to look at me as my boots clopped down the stairs.

'Wow, get you,' he said as I reached the bottom. 'You're the genuine article now.'

He was right, of course. The last time he'd seen me in court I'd been desperately trying to look like a solicitor. And now here I was. Bulging briefcase in hand and a fully paid up member of the Law Society. And here he was. Still looming large in my life. We were back in court again.

'I guess we've both come a long way,' I said, trying to distance myself from the past. To break the sense of *déjà vu* which was flooding over me.

'Older and wiser, you mean?' said Andy.

'Yeah,' I replied. Although I wasn't so sure about the wiser bit.

'Anyway, good to see you again,' he said, greeting me with a peck on the cheek. I felt my face flush. Was suddenly conscious of the gaze of the security guards. And of my desire to flee the environment which was so tied up with the past.

'You too. Let's make a move,' I said, heading for the door.

'I hope you don't mind me turning up like this,' said Andy, as we headed down the road. 'It's a bit like buses, isn't it? Nothing for twenty-two years then two sightings in a few weeks.'

'Where was your job?' I asked, eager to establish if he really had been 'just passing'.

'Blackburn Rovers. We're doing some work on their new sponsorship deal.'

I nodded. Trying to visualise the surrounding road networks in my head. Pretty sure that there was a quicker way back to Leeds than via Rochdale.

'Here we are,' I said, a few moments later, as we arrived outside the Flying Horse.

'Is this your regular watering hole, then?' asked Andy, holding the door open for me.

'Yeah. Although we don't usually make it here at lunch-time. Or that often after work, come to that. Everybody's busy with their families and stuff, I guess.'

We walked in. It was quiet. Just a few clusters of suits around the tables. I scanned the room quickly in case there was anyone I knew. It was risky coming here, really. But there were so few decent pubs around that I hadn't felt like I had much choice.

'So, what can I get you?' asked Andy.

He had no idea, of course. Because back then, I hadn't even been old enough to drink.

'A dry white wine, please.'

He nodded. 'Sure. You grab a seat. I'll bring them over.'

I made for a small table in the corner and sat down with my back to the rest of the pub. It was ridiculous, really. All the times I'd imagined doing something like this with Andy and, when it actually happened, I was far too worried about being spotted with him to enjoy it. All I could think of was that every time I came here from now on, I would look at this table and immediately be reminded of Andy. He was intruding into my life. On to my territory. Uninvited. Or so I liked to think.

Andy returned with the drinks and sat down opposite me.

'Thanks,' I said.

'Were you with your boyfriend earlier when I called?' he asked, taking a swig from his bottle of Stella.

'Yeah.' I didn't want to go into detail.

'I hope I didn't make things awkward for you.'

'No, not at all,' I said, trying hard not to spill any wine as I raised the glass to my lips.

'I take it he doesn't know you're with me now.'

I didn't understand why Andy was doing this. It was as if he wanted to make me feel even more guilty than I already was. Maybe he was testing me. Seeing if he was still my Achilles heel.

'No, he doesn't. Not that it matters. I mean we're only having a drink, aren't we?'

I was testing him now.

'Yeah. We are. For now, at least.'

'What do you mean by that?'

'You know what I mean, Claire. There can be as many meetings at Blackburn Rovers as you want there to be.'

I looked down, fingering the stem of my glass, scared to look him in the eye in case I gave any inkling of the implosion his words had caused inside. I couldn't pretend it was all in my head any longer. He was right. It was up to me now. And that was the scary bit.

'That's not why I came here, Andy.'

'Why did you come?'

'Because you asked me. Because I've never been very good at saying no to you.'

'So why not just say yes?'

I could feel the word rising up in my throat. I swallowed hard, determined to thwart its progress. While I struggled for enough air to breathe. I glanced over my shoulder as the door opened and a large crowd of people walked in. I instantly recognised one of them from Mark's firm. Larry his name was. Or maybe Lenny. I'd only met him briefly at a Christmas do. But it was enough to make me reach for my coat.

'What are you doing?' asked Andy.

'Look, I've got to go.'

'But you haven't even finished your drink.'

'I'm sorry, OK? I can't stay here any longer.'

'You've seen someone you know, haven't you?'

'What does it matter?'

'It matters because it's getting in the way.'

'It was a bad idea to come here. I wasn't really thinking.'

'So let's meet somewhere else then. Somewhere we can talk properly.'

'I don't know. I need a bit of time to think things through.'

'Fine. Let's leave it a couple of weeks. Why don't you come for Sunday lunch at Salts Mill? Say, the end of the month.'

He was doing it again. Making it seem harmless. Making it hard to say no.

'I can't make it then,' I said. It was a compromise. I wasn't able to say an outright no but at the same time I wasn't going to lie to Mark. Make up some story about where I was going.

'OK. When can you make it?'

'December the fourteenth,' I heard myself saying. The day of Mark's football club Christmas lunch. They always lasted into the evening. I could be there and back without him knowing. It was still wrong, of course. But somehow it didn't seem as bad.

'Sure, no problem. Should be nice and festive. Shall we say about one?'

I nodded, glancing around anxiously as I heard Larry's group move away from the bar.

'I've got to go.'

'OK. I'll see you on the fourteenth.'

'Yeah. See you then,' I said.

I picked up my briefcase and fled. Head down. Eyes firmly on the floor. Not once looking back. Knowing it was wrong to ever look back. But equally scared of what might lie ahead.

Sunday, 13 April 1986

I crept downstairs next morning before Mum was up and dialled Andy's number. I wanted to tell him he was in the clear. That I had denied everything. That it was all going to be OK. I let it ring for several minutes, in case he was still in bed. But he didn't answer. I hated this, not being able to talk to him. It wasn't supposed to be like this. Not now we were going out together. I put the phone down and sat at the bottom of the stairs waiting for our copy of the *News of the World* to be delivered. Telling myself they might not even use the photo. It wasn't really such a big deal, two young people kissing. If I'd been a year or so older, no one would have given a toss.

I heard the garden gate clink and the paperboy's footsteps coming up the path. As the letterbox opened I snatched the rolled-up paper from his hand and unfurled it, steeling myself to look at the back page. There was a photo of Gary Lineker scoring against us and a story about Arsenal sacking Don Howe. I flicked through the rest of the sports pages but there was nothing there, not even a paragraph. A wave of relief ran through me. Andy wasn't going to get in trouble at all. I turned the paper over. The picture of me and Andy kissing stared back at me from the front page.

Above it was the headline, 'England Star in Schoolgirl Shame'. Underneath, in smaller letters, it said: 'Pailes denies under-age sex with teen fan.'

'Fucking hell,' I said out loud. It was there in front of me. In huge bloody great letters, on the front page of a national newspaper. I sat down on the stairs, my hands shaking, unable to take it all in. It didn't seem real. It was like there was another Claire Skidmore, one who had nothing to do with me. The story continued inside, over two more pages. There were more photos too. One of us going into my house and another of Andy leaving afterwards. And a photo of him at his front door which they said they'd taken yesterday. He looked shocked, bewildered. I knew how he felt.

I started reading the story. When I'd finished, I turned back to the front page and started from the beginning again, hoping it would sound better second time around. It didn't though; if anything it got worse. It wasn't the headline I found hard to stomach, or even the quote from an anonymous fan, presumably Susan, saying, 'She tried to come over all innocent at the training ground, but I always knew there was something going on between them.' It was the comments from Andy. The bit where he said I'd never been his girlfriend. That he wouldn't be seeing me again and it had all been a terrible misunderstanding.

I wondered which bit of it exactly I had misunderstood.

They started gathering outside our house within an hour of the paper arriving. The reporter and photographer from the *News of the World* came first. They rang the bell again but I didn't answer. Nor did Mum. I thought they'd go away but they didn't. Soon they were joined by others. Half a dozen photographers with long-lens cameras and bulging bags over their shoulders. And some others, presumably reporters, with spiral-bound notebooks in their hands. Even a bloke with a bloody TV camera with ITN written on the side. Outside our fucking house. Every now and again I peeked at them through the crack in my bedroom curtains. Each time I looked there were more than before. Lined up along the front garden wall. Chatting to each other, having a fag. Waiting for me to show my face. Content in the knowledge they had me cornered. I felt like a fox cowering in its lair. Knowing they could scent my blood. And that if I stepped outside I would be ripped to shreds.

I was surprised Mum hadn't been in. I still had the newspaper by the side of my bed. I guessed she couldn't face it. Seeing what a slut her little girl had turned into. I wondered if Frankie had seen it yet. And if she had, what she thought. I knew she'd be shocked. I hadn't even told her about the blow job. Let alone having sex with him. But at least she'd realise that I wasn't just some schoolkid any more. That I was a proper grown-up. Like her mate Tara.

Most of all I wondered why Andy hadn't answered the phone. Or called me. I needed to talk to him, to explain that I'd never meant for any of this to happen. To sort out what we were going to do. I was worried he blamed me. Maybe even thought it was my doing, some sort of kiss-and-tell thing I'd set him up for. I wondered if he'd meant what he said in the paper, that he was never going to see me again. I knew my Andy wouldn't do that, desert me at the very time I needed him most. But I wasn't sure if he was my Andy. Not any more.

It was halfway through the morning when I heard a commotion outside. People calling out, shouting to someone. I rushed to the window, craning my neck to see if it was Andy, scanning the road for a silver Golf. A second later the doorbell rang. Whoever it was didn't take their finger off the bell. Just left it ringing. I got up and crept to the top of the landing. The letterbox opened and a voice shouted through.

'Claire, it's your father. Let me in.'

I dashed downstairs and opened the door a few inches, standing behind it so no one outside could see me. Dad squeezed through into the hall. He looked as if he hadn't shaved or brushed his hair. His eyes seemed to be flashing about all over the place, like he couldn't get them to focus.

'Hi,' I said, as I shut the door. I wasn't sure what else to say. I didn't have to worry about it, though. Dad seemed to have plenty of things to say.

'Have you seen them out there? Have you got any idea what you've done? I always thought you had more sense than this. What on earth were you thinking of?'

I wasn't expected to answer any of his questions. He didn't provide the necessary gaps for me to do so. And anyway, before I could get a word in, Mum came out into the hall.

'What the hell are you doing here?' she said.

I wished everyone would stop asking questions and actually say something. Dad swung round to look at her.

'I'm trying to find out how my daughter's ended up on the front page of this fucking newspaper,' he said, taking a copy out from inside his jacket and throwing it down on the hall table.

Mum's gaze dropped to the paper. I watched her scan the front page, brow furrowed, eyes bulging, before she looked back at him.

'There's no need to swear.'

Dad snorted and shook his head. 'What's the matter? Worried I might corrupt her? I think it's a bit late for that.'

'Yeah, you're right. You already did that. About four years ago, if I remember.'

Dad looked wounded. If I'd been scoring points I'd have given that one to Mum. But I wasn't refereeing. I was standing in between them, taking each punch squarely on the chin. To try and soften the blow for them.

'You can't pin this one on me, Maureen. You're the one who's supposed to have been bringing her up. Keeping an eye on her.'

'Oh, and I suppose you think I've got nothing better to do than stay at home looking after her all day. It's not as if I need to go out and earn enough money to keep a roof over her head, is it?'

'You could have talked to her. Found out what was going on.'

'And you think she'd have told me? For Christ's sake, Roger, you've got no idea what she's like.'

'I am still here, you know,' I said. They both turned to look at me. Then carried on arguing.

'Maybe if you hadn't encouraged her,' Mum said. 'Got

her all worked up about football, none of this would have happened.'

'I didn't tell her to screw her favourite player.'

'Shut up, both of you,' I shouted.

They turned to look at me again.

'She says she didn't sleep with him,' Mum said.

'And you believe her?'

Mum shrugged.

'Oh, thanks,' I said.

'Did he have sex with you, Claire?' Dad asked. 'It's important that you tell us.'

'Why? So that you can argue about whose fault it is?'

'No. So that if he did, we can report it to the club. I'm sure they'll have rules about players' conduct. And if this started before you were sixteen, well there are laws against under-age sex. You know that, don't you?'

'Course I do. I'm not stupid.'

'You were stupid enough to get caught,' he said.

'So were you,' I replied.

They both fell silent. I knew I'd delivered the knockout blow. It didn't make me feel any better though. If anything, I felt worse.

'All you've done is have a go at each other,' I continued. 'You haven't asked how *I* feel. You don't care what I'm going through.'

'We do. We're just worried that you're protecting him,' Mum said.

'He has got a name, you know.'

'I want you to tell the truth, Claire,' she said.

'OK, I'll tell you. Andy listened to me. He wiped away

my tears. Treated me like a woman. He made me feel more special than anyone else has ever done. And for a little while, an hour or so of my crappy life, he took the hurt away.'

Mum started crying. Dad looked down at the floor.

'I'd better go,' he said.

'That's right,' Mum said. 'Leave me to pick up the pieces.'

Dad looked at her but didn't say anything. He smiled at me. A half-hearted sort of smile. And slipped out the front door.

The commotion started up again outside. I knew they were taking photos of Dad. I could hear him telling them to leave us alone. Mum was still standing there crying. I wanted her to take hold of me. To give me a hug. She didn't though. She went into the kitchen to put the kettle on.

I picked up the phone and called Andy. Still no answer. He must be avoiding me. Two days ago he'd been in this house, telling me how beautiful I was, making love to me. Now he couldn't even bring himself to speak to me on the phone. That was how badly I'd screwed this whole thing up. I needed to talk to someone, I pressed the button and dialled Frankie's number.

'Hello.'

'Hello, Mr Alberti. It's Claire. Is Frankie there, please?'

'Just a minute.'

I heard muffled voices in the background. A woman's voice whispering something. It sounded like her mum. After a long pause he came back to the phone.

'No, I'm sorry. She's not here at the moment.'

'Oh,' I said, not believing him for a moment. 'Can you tell her I called then? I'll be in all day.'

'OK. I'll tell her.'

I went back to my room and sat on the end of the bed, staring at the photo of me and Andy on the wall. It was the first picture we'd ever had taken together. We were both smiling. Like we didn't have a care in the world. It had all been so simple then. If only things could be simple again now. I put my Thompson Twins tape on and fast forwarded to 'Hold Me Now'. I turned it up and sang the words out loud. My voice trembled through the bit about having a picture pinned to my wall and finally broke off when I got to 'tattered and torn'. I turned the tape off, sniffed loudly and wiped the tears away with the sleeve of Andy's shirt.

It was Trevor McDonald who broke the news the next night. In the past I'd always regarded him with affection; a sort of favourite-uncle figure whose friendly smile and soothing tones I welcomed into the living room. And yet here he was recast as the bearer of bad tidings, betraying my trust in much the same way as everyone else had.

'Disgraced England footballer Andy Pailes has been transfer-listed by his club and told he will not figure in the England World Cup squad due to be announced next week.

'United chairman and Conservative MP Roy Brown said Pailes, who is alleged to have had a relationship with a sixteen-year-old schoolgirl, would not play for the club

again. It is thought Brown, who is heading up the govern-
ment's family-values task force, came under pressure from
Prime Minister Margaret Thatcher to take the tough action.

'The news came only hours after the Football Associ-
ation revealed that Pailes would not be considered for
England matches for the foreseeable future.'

It took a good few seconds for everything to sink in,
to process each piece of information, weigh up the impli-
cations and reach a logical conclusion: Andy's career was
finished, I would never see him again – and it was all my
fault.

The howl I let out was enough to bring Mum rushing
in from the kitchen, still brandishing her icing bag. 'What
on earth's the matter?'

'It's Andy,' I said, tears pouring down my cheeks. 'He's
been transfer-listed.'

'Does that mean he'll be leaving?'

'Yeah, he'll never play for us again.'

'Good. Maybe it'll put an end to all this nonsense. Give
us a chance to go back to being a normal family again.'

I wondered what had given Mum the idea that we had
ever been a normal family.

'How can you say that? Andy's the only person I care
about and I've ruined everything for him. He's got to leave
United and he's not going to be picked for the World Cup
squad, and it's all because of me.'

'It's not your fault. He ruined things for himself, so don't
you start feeling sorry for him. Anyway, he can always
play in the World Cup next year, can't he?'

'There isn't going to be a World Cup next year; they

only play it every four years. This might have been his only chance.'

Mum sighed and shook her head.

'For goodness' sake, Claire, this is *your* only chance to get your O levels; that's far more important. Now, I suggest you go upstairs and get yourself ready for school. Because you're not having another day off, even if those photographers are still outside in the morning. We're going to hold our heads up high and get on with our lives.'

I sat on the toilet, staring at the array of air fresheners, odour neutralisers and disinfectants around me. I had never noticed them before. But now that I had, Mum's desire to forget all about it began to make sense. The slightest whiff of something unpleasant and she was there, can of Haze in hand, spraying frantically until the bad odours had dissipated and everything smelt of roses (or forest pine air freshener) again. Only this time she hadn't been able to do it. Because not even her formidable arsenal of ozone-depleting weapons could compete with the *News of the World* and *News at Ten*. So she was burying her head in the sand. Where she couldn't smell a thing.

I wasn't at all sure that living your life by the air-freshener philosophy was a good idea. But I could see that it allowed Mum to exist in a world where anything that caused pain, upset or embarrassment could be obliterated. And I couldn't help being rather envious of that.

I flushed the toilet and turned on the shower. I put the dial to the highest number. Wanting it hot enough to hurt worse than the pain inside. Afterwards I walked back to my bedroom, my skin raw and tingling, my brain struggling to take everything in. Trevor McDonald's words going round and round in my head until they became garbled and made no sense at all, not that they had in the first place. The very idea that Maggie Thatcher had got Andy transfer-listed was bordering on the surreal. I could only presume that it was some kind of divine retribution for me having been disappointed she'd survived the Brighton bombing.

My freshly pressed school uniform was hanging ominously from my wardrobe door. My stomach tightened at the thought of facing the world, of going to school in the morning, of even stepping outside the front door. I wasn't sure I could cope any more. And I didn't see the point of coping when all it would do was get me through another day without Andy.

He was leaving. I was never going to see him again. He hated me now. Probably wished he'd never set eyes on me. Not that I could blame him, after what I'd done. But I knew that however much he hated me, however much Mum and Dad and Frankie and everyone else hated me, they still didn't hate me as much as I hated myself.

'You don't have to do this, you know, Claire,' says Andy, stroking my hair as we sit in Ken's office. 'If you don't want to go through with it, I'll walk away, go somewhere else. You come first, you know that.'

'I know, but I'm not going to let your career suffer because of me. And if this is what it takes, this is what I'll do.'

Andy strokes my cheek with his hand.

'It means the world to me, you know. That you're prepared to do this.'

I shrug. 'It's a small price to pay really. If it means you can stay.'

Andy pulls me towards him and kisses me on the forehead. I know it is going to be hard but I can do this for him. There is a picture of a dove on my wall at home, flying high above the sea. The words on it say, 'If you love someone, set them free. If they come back to you, they are yours. If they don't, they never were.' And Andy will come back, I know that. He will wait for me.

There is a knock and a pensive-looking Ken Benson, dressed in a suit rather than his usual tracksuit, sticks his head round the door.

'Are you ready for this?'

'Yes, boss,' says Andy. 'We're ready.'

Ken turns to face me.

'You're something else, you are. There's not many would be prepared to make a sacrifice like this.'

'You've fought to keep Andy here,' I say. 'This is the least I can do.'

We follow Ken out of the room and along the brightly lit corridor towards United's main conference room. My hand tightens around Andy's. He gives it a quick squeeze. 'Just remember, this will all be worth it in the end,' he whispers.

Ken opens the door and flashes from dozens of cameras explode in our faces as we walk into the room. Andy puts his arm around me and guides me towards a chair, before sitting down next to me. Ken sits on the other side of him.

Andy pulls a sheet of paper out from his inside jacket pocket. I haven't read it but I know what he is going to say. He squeezes my knee under the table and mouths, 'Are you OK?' I nod. He turns back to the sheet of paper and starts to read.

'Claire and I chose to come out and face you today for the simple *reason that we have got nothing to hide. We have been in a relationship for several months now. However, the relationship is not and never has been of a sexual nature. In view of Claire's age, I understand the level of concern which has been expressed about our relationship but I wish to stress that nothing improper has taken place. It is a serious relationship and we are very much in love.'*

He pauses for a second. I feel a lump rising in my throat. I know what is coming next. Andy looks across at me. I nod and he continues.

'However, in order to ensure that there is no further negative publicity for this football club which we both love, we have taken the extremely difficult decision to put our relationship on hold until after Claire leaves school and the World Cup is over. We hope this will serve to demonstrate our appreciation to both Ken and the England manager for their continued support and the strength of our commitment to each other. I wish to stress we will simply not be seeing each other for a few months. We are not splitting up; indeed we have every intention of spending the rest of our lives together. And to that end, I want to give her this.

'I love you, Claire,' he says, pulling a small box from his jacket pocket and opening it. 'Will you marry me?'

The battery of flashes going off blinds me momentarily. But when I blink and begin to see again, there is a ring, a beautiful diamond engagement ring, twinkling up at me. I gaze across at Andy. I had no idea he was going to do this. I am floating in delight, barely able to keep my feet on the ground. He is waiting for an answer. He is smiling, though. Because he knows what I am going to say.

'Yes,' I say, loud enough for everyone to hear. 'Yes, I will.'

Andy kisses me. The flashes go off again. The journalists start asking questions. Whose idea it had been. Whether we have my parents' blessing. Andy deals with them all effortlessly.

'Have you got anything to say, Claire?' asks a young woman scribbling furiously at the front. I look at Andy, waiting for his nod to go ahead.

'Just that I love Andy and United very much. And I'm looking forward to our future together.'

Andy smiles at me. We walk out of the room together, hand in hand.

Twelve

It hadn't been so much of a harvest, more a humane way of putting what was left of my vegetables out of their misery. The truth was the runner bean plants were never actually going to produce runner beans and to pretend otherwise was positively cruel. Equally, any aspirations the carrots had of gracing a dinner plate some time were clearly fanciful. By the time I peeled them there wouldn't really be anything left worth eating. Even the handful of green tomatoes I'd picked would probably never ripen now. But I felt the need to take something home for my efforts, to place them on the windowsill and live in hope of a faint glow of orange appearing on their skin. I remembered watching the film *Fried Green Tomatoes* and wondered if they actually tasted any good like that.

I was still mulling it over when I noticed a familiar pair of size nines hovering on the edge of my patch.

'Hi,' said Mark as I stood up.

I stared at him. His face looked pale and drawn. I felt dizzy. Maybe I had stood up too quickly. Or maybe I was scared that my whole world was going to come crashing down around my ears. Mark must have found out something about me and Andy. Spoken to Lenny at work. It was all I could think of.

'What are you doing here?'

'That's a charming way to welcome me to your oasis of calm and tranquillity,' he said.

'You know what I mean. You never come here. What's wrong?'

He hesitated for a second.

'I had a phone call from those Anthony Nolan bone marrow people.'

He didn't know about Andy. And I felt awful for being relieved when what he was saying was far more important.

'Have you got something wrong with your blood?'

'No, they think I might be a match for someone.'

'For Emily?'

'They don't tell you that. They just said someone who needs a transplant.'

'God. That's all very quick.'

'Yeah, it's a bit like winning the lottery, I guess. You do it but you don't really think it's going to be you.'

I smiled at Mark, who it had to be said looked about as far removed as you could possibly be from celebrating a lottery win.

'So what happens now?'

'I need to give another blood sample at the clinic, a bigger one this time; they've sent me a special kit to post back to them. And I've got to go down to London for a medical at a private hospital on Wednesday.' He looked down and kicked some earth with the toe of his boot. He was trying not to let me see his face. Because he was petrified.

I put my spade down and walked over. Wrapping my arms around him, letting him know he wasn't on his own.

'This is going to be really hard for you, isn't it?'

'You must think I'm a complete wimp,' he said, still not looking me in the eye.

'Of course I don't. Lots of people are scared of hospitals.'

'I can't help it, you see. It's to do with my dad.'

'What do you mean?'

Mark let go of a big sigh. 'He went into hospital when I was eight. It was only supposed to be an exploratory oper- ation but they found something wrong with his bowel, so he had to have another op to remove part of it and they basically cocked it up, which meant he ended up having another major op to try to repair the damage. He was in hospital for nearly six months.'

'God, that must have been hard for you all. Did you visit him and stuff?'

Mark nodded. 'The thing was, nobody explained to me what was happening. You know what my parents are like about talking about anything remotely embarrassing. So I just assumed the worst. I thought he was dying.'

'Oh, Mark.'

He looked up, his eyes moist with tears. All I could see was the little boy inside, frightened and with no one to talk to.

'I remember one time we went in to visit him,' he con- tinued shakily, 'and the old man in the bed next to him, who always used to talk to me and my brother, had gone.

The bed was empty. No one told me he'd gone home so I thought he'd died and that Dad was next in line, because his was the next bed along.'

'And you couldn't even talk to your mum?'

'I didn't want to upset her about it, so I never said anything. Until the day she told me Dad was coming home. I cried buckets. She thought I'd just missed him. She had no idea.'

I shook my head and sighed.

'And that's why you don't like hospitals.'

'Yeah. Stupid really. But I've never got over it.'

'Look,' I said, holding him tightly, 'you don't have to go ahead with this. There's still time to back out if you don't want to do it.'

'I can't, can I? It would be like signing up for the army and then saying you didn't want to go to war.'

'Frankie would understand. I could explain to her about what you just said.'

Mark pulled away and walked across to the other side of the patch, keeping his back to me, trying to hold it together.

'What if it's Emily?' he said. 'What if it's her I match? I can't back out, can I? Imagine how Frankie would feel if I did that.'

'I don't have to tell her.'

'No, you don't,' said Mark, his voice soft but firm. 'Because I'm going ahead with it. Even if it does frighten the hell out of me. I hope it is for Emily, but if it isn't then I still want to do it because someone out there is scared that someone they love is going to die and I might just be able to help them. I know they said it doesn't always work, but it's just about giving someone the chance, isn't it? If it was you, I'd want you to have the chance.'

I stood and stared at him, shaking my head slowly. If I'd heard anyone else's boyfriend make that speech, I'd have been blown away. It wasn't anyone else's boyfriend though. It was my boyfriend. And perhaps it was about time I opened my eyes and saw him for the person he was.

'You're a good man, Mark Parry,' I said, kissing him softly on the lips. 'If I didn't know how insulting you'd find it as a Lancastrian, I'd say there was true Yorkshire grit in you.'

'Thank you for not saying it then.' He smiled.

'I'll come with you,' I said. 'Down to London for the medical.'

'Don't be daft, you don't need to do that. It's only routine stuff and you've got a trial on this week. I'll be fine, honestly.'

'Well at least let me come to the clinic with you for the blood test. Lend a bit of moral support.'

'OK, as long as you promise to tell me some jokes to take my mind off it.'

'Sure. Come on,' I said. 'Let's go back to mine. We're having fried green tomatoes for lunch.'

I waited until Mark had gone to play football the next morning before phoning Frankie. I didn't want to embarrass him by praising his heroic gesture within earshot, or put added pressure on him in case he really was having second thoughts.

'Hi, it's me, how's things?' I asked when she answered. It was weird: all those years apart and here we were, within a couple of months of getting back in touch, reverting to saying 'it's me' on the phone. Just as we used to do.

'Oh, up and down,' said Frankie. 'Mostly down, to tell you the truth.'

'Is that you or Emily?'

'Well, me certainly. It's hard to tell with Emily. She says so little about it. I worry she's bottling it all up inside.' I didn't want to tell Frankie the full extent of what Emily had been telling me. I was sworn to secrecy for one thing. And I didn't want her to feel in any way inadequate as a mother because she wasn't the one Emily was confiding in.

'I know she's talking to Alia,' I said. 'And to Robert, of course.' Robert more than anyone. Hours spent simply looking at him, holding a picture of him, feeling the certainty of his love.

'I understand why it used to drive your mum crazy now,' said Frankie. 'She's not still talking about going to this stupid premiere, is she?'

'There is a plan in existence,' I said. 'Although I can reveal no more than that.'

'Does it involve pulling the wool over my eyes with some limp story about Alia's grandparents' golden wedding party?'

'No,' I laughed. 'I've already warned her not to do that one. It'll be a bit more sophisticated, I think.'

There was a long silence at the other end of the phone.

'She'll be heartbroken, won't she? When she's not well enough to go.'

'I think she'll be OK, actually,' I said. 'I think she kind of knows already. This is simply a game she's playing to take her mind off everything that's going on. She's a hell of a lot wiser than I was at her age, you know.'

'Well that wouldn't be hard, would it?' said Frankie.

'No, I mean her dreams really are just dreams. She knows she's not really going to end up with Robert Pattinson. She's not in the least bit deluded about it.'

'It's crazy, isn't it?' sniffed Frankie. 'Because all I want now is for her to have dreams which can come true.'

I shut my eyes and sighed. Knowing exactly what she meant.

'Mark's tissue type looks like it's a match for someone,' I said. 'They want him to give another sample, go down for some tests.'

There was a brief silence from Frankie's end.

'Really? That's fantastic. Oh Claire. That's the best news I've had in ages.'

'It could be anyone,' I said. 'It doesn't mean it's Emily.'

'I know. But it's just brilliant that he's doing it. That someone, somewhere will have some hope.'

'It's funny. That's exactly what he said. He's terrified, you see. Got a real phobia about hospitals.'

'Well you tell him from me that I think he's a complete star and Joe will probably offer to courier him up a pizza a day for life when I tell him.'

'You'd better not then,' I laughed. 'I'm not sure his waistline can take it.'

'Don't tell Emily yet though,' continued Frankie. 'I think it might be hard for her to take. That someone else is going to get a transplant when Mark only did it because of her.'

'Of course, I understand. I won't say a word.'

'You must be so proud of him,' said Frankie.

'Yes. Yes I am.' And as I put the phone down I realised I meant it too. So the realisation was swiftly followed by a pang of guilt. Because somewhere in my diary was a note of a one p.m. lunch in Saltaire next month. And if I did mean it and I did love Mark, what the hell was I doing agreeing to see Andy again? The first visit had been offi-cially sanctioned. I went because Mark wanted me to. But that was it. It was supposed to be a once-only opportunity. I'd already seen him once behind Mark's back; there could be no excuse for another meeting. Even if Andy's name had been on my laminated card for twenty-two years, it would still be utterly wrong.

Tuesday, 15 April 1986

I woke up with a bellyache. It wasn't just nerves. My period had come on. I felt sad, disappointed. Like I'd let the last bit of Andy slip away. If I'd been pregnant, he'd have had to see me again. We'd have been bonded together for the rest of our lives. But I wasn't. So that was that.

I put the radio on. America had bombed Libya during the night. I couldn't work out why, exactly. Other than that Reagan didn't like Colonel Gaddafi. I didn't like Bryan Robson but I had no intention of dropping a bomb on Manchester. I wondered if there'd be a nuclear war. It was about the only way my life could get any worse. Though I wasn't sure whether being fried alive would actually be worse than what I was about to go through.

I peered through the crack in the curtains. They were still there. Which was stupid, if you thought about it. The world was on the brink of a nuclear war and half of Fleet Street was standing outside my front garden. I wanted to open the window and shout down to them that they were in the wrong place; Colonel Gaddafi didn't live in Potters Bar.

Mum was already in the kitchen when I got downstairs.

Doing her best to pretend that everything was normal. Her normal, not mine.

'Kettle's just boiled.'

'Right.'

'I've done your lunch. It's on the table.'

'OK.'

'I did you cheese and pickle for a change. It's a while since you had pickle, isn't it?'

I didn't waste my breath replying. I popped a tea bag into my United mug and poured water over it, watching the bag being dragged under by the current. I sat silently at the kitchen table, staring into my mug.

'Aren't you having any breakfast?'

'Nah.'

'You have to eat, you know, Claire.'

'Yeah.'

Mum sat down opposite me, stirring her tea frantically, as if paddling for survival. I think I liked it better when she was shouting at me.

'Would you like me to run you to school in the car?'

I was relieved at the offer but didn't want to show it in case she thought it meant I still needed her.

'Yeah. If you want.'

'Just this once, mind. I'm not going to do it every day.'

I hoped there wouldn't be a need to do it every day. Though I was beginning to wonder what level of world disaster it would take to get rid of them.

I finished my tea in silence, picked up my lunchbox and went upstairs to get my bag. I glanced at myself in the bedroom mirror. I was back to being a schoolgirl again. It was like the other Claire had never existed. Except in the photographs in the paper. I took a deep breath and went downstairs.

'All set, then?' said Mum, as if we were popping out for a nice little trip to the shops.

I nodded. I noticed she had her best jacket on. She never usually wore it to work. She turned the latch, opened the door a fraction and then shut it again.

'Now remember what I said. We hold our heads up high. Take no notice of them, OK?'

She was like a general telling the men about to go over the top not to worry about being shot. It was all right for her. She wasn't the one they were firing at. She opened the door and I blinked in the bright sunlight. It wasn't faces I saw. It was a mass of lenses pointing at me. Mum strode towards the car; I followed as close behind her as I could, head down, keeping my eyes on the ground.

'Claire, this way, Claire.'

'Are you going to be seeing Andy again, Claire?'

'Has Andy called you?'

'Have you reported him to the police, Mrs Skidmore?'

'This way, Claire. Over here.'

The barrage of questions and instructions was accompanied by a volley of camera shutters being fired and the whirring of motor drives from the cluster of bodies at the end of the drive. The noise battered against my head. I understood what Princess Di must feel like. Being watched and shouted at like that the whole time. Mum got in the car and leant over to unlock the passenger door. I felt myself shrinking as I stood there, as if my insides had collapsed and the outer shell was about to cave in. I fumbled for the door handle and clambered inside, fastening my seat belt, wishing it could protect me from what lurked at the end of the drive. Mum started the engine and edged forwards towards the waiting photographers. I glanced across at her. She looked flustered. I was trying hard not to cry.

'They're not moving,' she said. 'What shall I do?'

'Just go. Drive straight at them.'

'What if I hit one of them?'

'I don't care. Just go.'

The car lurched forward and the photographers parted, running round to my side of the car. I turned my head the other way but I could still see them out of the corner of my eye. Jostling for position, thrusting their cameras up against the car window, flashes going off again and again. I wondered if Andy would see these pictures in tomorrow's newspapers. Whether he'd look at me and think what a big mistake he'd made. I wished I wasn't wearing my school uniform. It made me look like a kid.

We eased through the gates and turned right on to the road. I could still see them behind us in the mirror. Mum accelerated away. I noticed her hands shaking on the wheel. It was all my fault again.

We didn't say anything to each other during the three-minute journey to school. I think we were both in shock. I could still see the flashes going off every time I closed my eyes. And hear the questions being fired out like a machine gun. Mum pulled up about a hundred yards from the school gates.

'Is this OK?'

'Yeah, thanks.'

'With any luck they'll be gone by tonight.'

'Yeah.'

'If you want, I can come and pick you up from school.'

I imagined what my classmates would say if they knew my mum was waiting for me outside.

'No, it's all right.'

I picked up my bag and opened the passenger door.

'Chin up, eh?' said Mum, managing a half-smile.

'Yeah,' I said as I got out of the car, head bowed.

I watched the blue Fiesta disappear up the road and turned to start walking up towards the school gates. There were no photographers outside. Just masses of familiar faces. Inquisitive eyes and loud mouths at the ready. I knew it was only a matter of time.

'Slag.' I didn't even know the owner of the first voice to speak out. Though I vaguely recognised a fourth-year face. The other lads around him started laughing and pointing. I didn't respond, just kept on walking, wishing I had a Teflon coating instead of an open flesh wound.

The closer I got to the school building, the more people pointed and stared. 'That's her, the one that bonked that footballer,' I heard one girl say as I walked past. I felt a hundred pairs of eyes on my back. I knew what they were thinking. She's nothing special. Whatever did he see in her?

I headed straight for my class room. It seemed the safest place to go. Debbie and Kim were already there. I sat down next to them.

'Awright,' I said.

'Did you hear something?' Debbie said to Kim, looking animatedly around the room.

'Nah,' she replied. 'Nothing worth listening to.'

'That's all right then. What were you saying? Something about that slapper in the papers.'

Some of the lads at the back started laughing. I looked down at my desk. Fixing my stare on a knot in the wood.

'How much for a good knobbing?' shouted one of the boys. He reached into his pocket, produced a ten-pence piece and tossed it towards me.

'What do I get for that, Skidmark? Must be worth at least a blow job.'

Some of the other lads started lobbing coins at me. Kim and Debbie were laughing, egging them on. I thought how unfair it was. I'd spent most of my school life being called a lezzie because I'd never had a boyfriend. Now, after one weekend, they were calling me a fucking prostitute.

'What's going on here?' Mr Butterworth's voice boomed from the doorway.

'Nothing, sir.'

'It doesn't look like nothing to me. Sit down and shut up, the lot of you. I don't want to hear another word out of you.'

When the bell went for first lesson, Mr Butterworth called me over.

'The head would like a word with you, Claire.'

'What about?'

'I think you know what it's about.'

'Now, sir?'

'Yes, now.'

I hurried down the corridor, my shoes squeaking on the newly polished tiles. Mrs Millward, the secretary, looked up as I knocked on the door.

'Go straight in, Claire. Mr Burgess is waiting for you.'

It was weird hearing his proper name. We always called him Birdshit.

I knocked on the door and went in. Birdshit was sitting behind his desk in a large swivel chair. His expression stern. Dark hairs bursting out of his tight collar and bristling under his cuffs.

'Sit down, Claire.'

I did as I was told. I couldn't remember ever being in his office before. I noticed he had a photo of his wife and kids on his desk. It was facing towards me. As if he couldn't bear to look at them but wanted everyone else to know they existed.

'And what have you got to say for yourself, young lady?'

I looked at him blankly. It was a stupid question. I shrugged.

'Perhaps an apology would be a good place to start.'

'Sorry, sir,' I said. I wasn't sure what I was apologising for. It had fuck-all to do with him.

'When we send our pupils out on work experience, we expect them to behave in a way that is a credit to this school. We do not expect them to end up on the front page of a tabloid newspaper.' He paused and looked at me over the top of his glasses.

'No, sir,' I said. Deciding the quickest way out of the room would be to agree with everything he said.

'What's more, we do not take kindly to having the good

name of this school dragged through the mud in this way. Under normal circumstances I would have no hesitation in suspending you. However, in view of the fact that you only have two months left at the school, I am going to allow you to continue as a pupil here in order that you may take the examinations which you have been entered for.'

'Thank you, sir.'

I didn't feel grateful at all. I would have been quite happy to have been kicked out. At least then I wouldn't have had to face going back to my classroom.

'Now I suggest you keep your head down, stay out of trouble and concentrate on your studies. No doubt your mother has already told you this, but I strongly advise that you have no further contact with the young man in question. Do I make myself clear?'

I wanted to knee him in the balls for being such an arsehole. Thinking he had any right to stop me seeing Andy.

'Yes, sir,' I said.

'Good. That will be all.'

I got up and walked out of his office. Mrs Millward smiled again and gestured me towards her.

'The school nurse is in at one o'clock today, dear,' she said. 'In case you need to see her about anything.'

I stared at her, realising she'd read every word in the papers. And that she believed it all.

I went back to my lesson. It was double history. Everyone looked round when I walked in. I sat at the back and kept my head down. It was the same the rest of the morning. I didn't say a word to anyone. Just sat in silence.

Knowing that every time someone laughed, they were laughing at me.

When the bell went for lunch, I let everyone else rush off while I packed my things away as slowly as possible, making sure it was a good five minutes before I left the classroom. I slunk down the corridor towards the canteen. I didn't like the place at the best of times. It smelt of disinfectant and mashed potato, which was strange because I'd never considered that mashed potato had a smell to it before I'd been in there. It was also far too exposed for my liking. The plastic-coated tables were laid out in neat, regimented rows with no more than a few feet between them. And the dining area was fronted by a huge wall of glass, looking out on to the playground, ensuring that no one was safe from prying eyes and pointing fingers, whether from inside or out.

I managed to find an empty table and sat down. Everyone in the canteen turned to look at me. I could see people outside pointing at me as well. And hear a wave of whispers and laughter rolling up from the far end. I eased my lunchbox from my bulging schoolbag, opened the silver-foil package containing my cheese and pickle sandwiches and took a large bite. I chewed it over and over again, but I couldn't seem to swallow. Eventually I spat it out and sat there staring at the mangled mess I'd produced. Wondering whether Andy was able to eat, or whether I'd ruined his appetite too.

The trundling sound of the shutters being pulled down on the canteen brought me sharply back to reality. I was the only one left in the canteen. A dinner lady was standing over me, viewing the remains of my sandwiches with disdain.

'Are you eating them or what, love? Only we've got to get the tables cleaned up and put away.'

'No, it's all right, you carry on. I'm not hungry. I'll put them in the bin on my way out.'

I wrapped the sandwiches back up in the silver foil, squeezing them so tightly that some of the pickle oozed out and dripped on to the floor. The dinner lady tutted, her previously warm expression turning frosty.

'Not content with wasting good food, are you? Got to make a nice mess for us to clear up as well.'

I mumbled an apology before sloping off down the corridor. I started calculating how many school days there were until I'd finished my exams. Getting through one lunch break was bad enough; the thought of surviving thirty-five more was daunting to say the least.

The girls' loos were empty when I pushed open the heavy wooden door. I slipped into the right-hand cubicle, locked the door and fished around in my bag for the slim beige plastic case that contained my spare Vespre. Nothing was written on it to indicate its use; it was its very discreetness which gave the game away. I held one end of my soiled sanitary towel with the very tip of my thumb and index finger and peeled it from my knickers. I looked behind me for the bin, only to discover it was missing, leaving me squatting there, knickers round my ankles, as I considered my next move.

There was a sternly worded notice on the door saying not to flush sanitary towels down the toilet, but short of walking out of the cubicle waving it about, I didn't see I had a choice. I chucked it down the loo, peed on it and flushed hard. The water gushed into the bowl, sending the towel swirling around before disappearing down the U-bend. But as the water rose slowly back up, so too did the towel.

I sighed, knowing I must now wait an eternity while the cistern refilled before I could try again. The main door opened and two pairs of heels clicked into the toilets.

'Fucking hell, it stinks in here. Be quick, will you.'

'Yeah, all right. I've got to do me hair – it was blowing a right gale out there.'

'I know. It was worth it, though. I didn't want her trying to sit next to us in the canteen. Never know what you might catch.'

It was only when I heard the laughter that I recognised the voices. And realised that Debbie and Kim were talking about me.

'D'ya reckon she did bonk him then?' said Debbie.

'Yeah. I bet he wasn't the first, either. I always wondered why she went down to that training ground.'

'I can't work out what that Andy guy saw in her, mind. I mean, he's not bad-looking.'

'He's probably got some schoolgirl fetish thing going on. He looks a bit of a perv to me.'

'Maybe. He dumped her pretty sharpish though, didn't he?'

'Yeah,' said Kim. 'Probably took one look at her fried-egg tits and legged it.'

There was another round of giggles.

'Come on,' said Debbie. 'I'm done in here. Let's go.'

I flushed the toilet again to try and drown out the noise of my sobs. The sanitary towel went down this time. Not that I cared any more. I waited until I was sure Kim and Debbie had gone, then slipped out of the cubicle and splashed some cold water on my eyes, trying to cover up the redness. I tried telling myself it didn't matter. They were only jealous because they'd never been out with anyone older. But a tiny part of me still wanted to run after them, pleading for them to be my friends. I didn't though. Not because my pride wouldn't allow it. But because I was scared it might make them hate me even more.

I turned the corner into my road, my schoolbag banging against my legs. Most of the photographers had gone, pissed off to Libya hopefully. But there were still three left. Leant up against the garden wall, having a laugh about something, probably me. As far as they were concerned I was some silly little groupie who went around shagging footballers. That was what it must look like. I could see that now. As soon as they saw me walking down the road they picked up their cameras and started taking photos. It was like being one of those moving targets at the fairground. I looked down at the pavement, counting the cracks as I stepped between them. The breeze blew my hair over my eyes. I let it stay there. The photographers didn't call out or anything. Just kept on taking pictures. I couldn't believe they hadn't got enough by now.

I opened the gate. Mum's car was parked in the drive. She was home earlier than usual. I hurried up the garden path and let myself in, banging the door behind me. Shutting out the outside world. Mum came out of the lounge. She was fiddling with her rings. She looked like she'd been crying again.

'There's someone here to see you,' she said.

For a split second I thought it might be Andy. Until I remembered there was no way Mum would have let him in. I followed her into the lounge. There was a woman sitting on the sofa wearing a navy suit and wide-rimmed glasses that looked too big for her. She got up when she saw me.

'Hello, Claire. I'm Sergeant Hopkins from the Child Protection Unit.'

I spun round to look at my mum.

'Did you do this? Did you ring them?'

Mum looked away. She didn't say anything.

'I can't believe you called the cops. I thought you were supposed to be on my side.'

'We are on your side,' Sergeant Hopkins said. 'We're here to protect you.'

'I don't need protecting. And I'm not a child.'

'I need to ask you a few questions, Claire. About your relationship with Andy Pailes before you turned sixteen.'

'You wanna get him in trouble, don't you?'

'There are laws, Claire, to protect girls under sixteen. If Mr Pailes did something he shouldn't have, put any kind of pressure on you, you need to tell me. Please sit down, both of you.'

I perched on the edge of the armchair. Mum sat down on the sofa, at the opposite end to the copper. Where me and Andy had been.

'Good. Now the questions I'm going to ask you may be

difficult, Claire, but it is important that you answer truth-fully. I want you to understand that this is a very serious matter.'

I nodded. But I had no intention of hurting Andy any more than I already had done.

'How long have you known Mr Pailes, Claire?'

'Since last summer.'

'And how would you describe your relationship with him?'

'We're friends. Very close. He's the best person I know.'

'And has that relationship ever gone beyond friendship?'

'Only last week. When he kissed me.'

'And nothing at all had happened before then?'

I could see Mum out of the corner of my eye, biting her lip. I decided not to mention the blow job.

'No.'

'OK. So you're telling me there was no sexual contact between you while you were underage?'

'No. Nothing. He's not like that. You've got him all wrong.'

The copper looked at Mum and raised her eyebrows before turning back to me.

'Claire, you do understand that if anything sexual did happen between you, you wouldn't get into trouble. And that you do have a duty to tell me if it did. To protect other girls like you.'

I nodded.

'Right then. We'll leave it there for now. If I can just have a quick word with your mother.'

I went into the hall and listened through the door. I

could hear Mum saying she didn't believe me. But the copper said that without any evidence or a statement from me, there was nothing more they could do.

'Thank you for your co-operation, Claire,' she said, shaking my hand as she came out. 'If you do think of anything else you'd like to tell me, please give me a call.'

She pressed a card with her name and number on into my hand.

'Are you going to interview Andy?' I asked.

'No. Not at the moment. Unless you think we should.'

'No. Course not. I was just gonna ask you to say hi from me if you were. That's all.'

The copper smiled at me, shook her head and let herself out.

Thirteen

Fiona passed me the note with all due solemnity, seconds before the magistrates walked back into court. I nodded an acknowledgement, sat down and opened the piece of paper.

'Mother 'em Maddox is a secret hankie-waver. I have it on good authority that he was spotted morris-dancing at a festival last weekend.'

I pursed my lips hard and stared intently at a crack in the top of the bench to try to prevent the huge guffaw brewing inside me from seeping out. I scribbled furiously on a piece of paper, 'Thanks, you complete cow. How the hell am I supposed to keep a straight face now?' and handed it to her. Fiona read it, nodded slowly as if taking in a complex piece of legal information and filed it safely away in her folder, before turning to the assembled magistrates, including one Martin Maddox.

'Mr Foster is here for the CPS,' she said, 'and Miss Cooper is representing Miss Wilson.'

Maddox nodded, I tried not to imagine the bells jingling as he did so. Instead I looked over at Kaz, who was standing in the witness box, fiddling with her hair.

'You OK?' I mouthed to her. Kaz shrugged. I was aware that her future was hanging in the balance. She had already pleaded guilty to the shoplifting charges. We were only here for sentencing. And although I would have liked to reassure her that everything would be fine, I couldn't. Because I was still waiting to hear if I'd got her the rehab place I'd been chasing for weeks. Dozens of phone calls back and forth between social services, the probation service and a particular rehab centre in York which had come highly recommended. The offer of a place had been due yesterday but had so far failed to materialise. I hadn't told Kaz, of course. There was no point upsetting her at this stage, because even if I did get an offer of a place, there was no guarantee Mother 'em Maddox would go for it. Especially if he'd had a bad day with the hankies.

Nigel rose from his seat next to me, the usual smug look on his face. He'd already told me he was going to ask for a custodial sentence. I hadn't bothered to try to persuade him otherwise. As there was no evidence he had a heart, it was pointless to ask him to use it.

'Your worships,' he began, 'Miss Wilson has pleaded guilty to several shoplifting charges. As you will have seen from the probation reports, she has a long history of previous shoplifting and drug-related offences. I am in no doubt that anything short of a custodial sentence will result in her being back before you within a very short space of time and for that reason urge you to impose the maximum custodial sentence available to you today.'

I rolled my eyes. The trouble with Nigel's approach was that he was so sure of himself he didn't even see the holes in his own arguments. If prison was working for Kaz, she wouldn't keep coming back, would she? I got to my feet.

I was going to adopt a different approach. It was risky and a long shot but it was my best bet. Although it would only work if Maddox truly did have a heart.

'Your worships,' I began, 'I'm going to do something unusual here. I'm going to break the confidentiality clause between myself and my client. Usually you don't get to hear what is said between us in private meetings. Quite right too. But I'm going to tell you what Miss Wilson said to me. Because I think you need to hear it.'

I turned to look at Kaz. She nodded, having reluctantly agreed to what I wanted to do.

'Miss Wilson committed these crimes on purpose. Not, as my colleague from the CPS suggested, because she has a flagrant disregard for the law, but because she wanted to get caught. She wanted to get caught because she wanted to go to prison. Not because it's a soft option but because it's the only place she feels safe. From her dealer, from her drug-using boyfriend, from loan sharks who are out to get her. I know it's hard for us to believe with our nice houses and loving families, but that's the truth. Karen Wilson's life is so awful that she believes she is better off – and safer – inside prison.'

I glanced up as I paused for a second. Maddox was listening intently, a slight frown on his forehead. I was in with a chance here.

'Prison is the only place where she has ever been given any help to come off the drugs which are behind all of her offending. Only unfortunately, the three-month sentences she's received so far aren't long enough to do a proper detox and rehabilitation. So this time she thought she'd muck around, smile at the security cameras, make it look as if she had a flagrant disregard for the law so that you would make an example of her and bang her up for a long time.'

I paused again. Nigel was staring up at me as if I had finally lost the plot.

'I think that's a damning indictment not of Miss Wilson but of our legal system and our society,' I continued, turning to look at Kaz, who was cowering like a rabbit caught in the headlights. 'I think she deserves better than that. I think she deserves a proper chance to build a drug- and crime-free life. And I don't believe prison is actually the best place for that.

'Since the probation reports were prepared, Miss Wilson has been offered a long-term placement at a drug rehabilitation centre in York. It's a good one. One of the best in the country.' I handed Fiona a brochure about the centre and she passed it up to Maddox.

'What I'm asking you to do today is give her that chance. If she ends up back in front of you in a year's time, feel free to make an example of her. But I'm confident she won't let you down. And I'm confident that when you return to your nice homes in nice communities this evening you will sleep more soundly knowing that Karen Wilson is safe and is at last getting the help she needs.'

It was only as I sat down that I realised my legs were shaking. Only as I glanced up at Fiona, her eyes rimmed with red, that I had an inkling of the effect my speech had had on the courtroom. There was silence for a moment before Maddox called Fiona up to the bench. A second later she said, 'The magistrates will retire to consider this matter.' As soon as they did so I went up to Kaz.

'Hang on in there,' I said. 'I've nearly got this sorted for you.' I dashed out of court number three, turned my mobile on and waited for the beep of a message. I was shaking when it came and as I dialled 123 to listen.

'Hi, it's Rob Dangerfield from Turning Point. Regarding the place you wanted for Karen Wilson, I have now confirmed to the probation service that we have one available and advised them to let me know by the end of the day whether she'll be taking it up.'

I breathed a long sigh of relief and scuttled back into the courtroom just as the magistrates were returning, smiling at Kaz as she stood up.

'Miss Wilson,' began Maddox, 'your counsel has given a very moving account of your predicament. Although we were minded to give a custodial sentence, my colleagues and I have decided to impose a six-month suspended sentence on condition you take up the place at the Turning Point drug rehabilitation centre in York.' Karen's face broke into a huge grin. 'May we wish you the very best of luck,' finished Maddox, nodding at me briefly before standing to leave the room. And instantly becoming my all-time favourite morris-dancer in the process.

'Court rise,' said Fiona as the magistrates filed out. I walked over to Kaz, who still appeared to be in shock.

'Have I got the place?' she said.

'Yes, you've really got the place. I just had a call.'

'I dunno what to say. I can't afford to get you anything and I can't even nick you anything now, can I?'

'Definitely not.' I smiled. 'The only present I want from you is to never see you in here again, OK?'

'You've got it.'

'I'll visit you there,' I said. 'See how you're getting on. Have you got your stuff with you?' She nodded. 'I'll speak to the probation service and we'll sort out some transport.'

As I turned to leave the court, Fiona winked at me and walked over.

'Unorthodox, but you pulled it off,' she whispered. 'It's not like me to come over all emotional. You had us all wrung out there.'

'Sometimes you just have to lay it on the line,' I said.

'You know what? I wish Aidan had been here to see that. So he could understand that what you get out of work is what you put into it.'

'Mark says he's been doing really well on work experience this week. Very responsible and showing a lot of interest.'

'Well, I'm glad to hear it,' said Fiona, looking chuffed. 'Maybe there's still time for him to turn things around.'

'I probably shouldn't tell you this,' I said, lowering my voice. 'But as I'm on a roll of breaking client-lawyer confidentiality, I'll tell you something else Mark told me.'

'What?'

'When Aidan's out late at night, he's not hanging out with those dodgy kids. He's seeing his girlfriend.'

'Girlfriend? I didn't know he had one,' said Fiona.

'I know, you're not supposed to. You're his mother, remember. She's got nice tits and a cute arse, apparently. That's what he told Mark.'

Fiona rolled her eyes and laughed. 'Lord, now I have got something to worry about.'

'Not a word, though, remember. You're still playing the dumb parent.'

'And that's exactly what I am,' smiled Fiona.

I was about to leave when I noticed Nigel was still sitting there, shaking his head in disbelief. I walked over to him.

'Sometimes,' I said, 'you don't find the answers in textbooks. It has to come from the heart. I understand the Wizard of Oz can get you one. You have to follow the Yellow Brick Road.' I turned and strode out of the courtroom, a huge bloody great smile on my face.

There was a letter for me on the mat when I got home. I recognised the thick cream stationery straight away. Smith MacGuire used nothing but the best. I put my briefcase down and tore open the envelope. Racing past all the niceties and the 'thank you for coming to the interview' bit to get to the 'I regret to inform you that on this occasion you have not been successful' part. It didn't come though. Instead I read, 'We are delighted to offer you the position of legal executive on a starting salary of £38,000 a year. Please contact our HR department at your earliest possible convenience to advise when you will be able to take up this position.'

I read the letter again just to make sure, but the words remained the same. I'd been offered the job. A plum job at a top city firm with partnership prospects and a salary which dwarfed my present one. But instead of being elated, of dancing around the kitchen in delight, all I could think was that it felt absolutely nowhere near as good as the feeling I'd had in the courtroom earlier.

When Mark came round later after work, I didn't even mention the job offer at first. It was Kaz I wanted to tell him about.

'Hey, that's brilliant,' he said, giving me a hug. 'Sounds like you played a blinder. Do you think she can turn her life around?'

'Yeah. I do. She really wants to. And when you want something that badly I think you make sure you get it.'

'I'd have loved to have seen the look on Nigel's face,' said Mark, sitting down at the kitchen table.

'It was priceless,' I said. 'I suspect that I'll get extra flak from him next time we cross swords, but it will have been worth it.'

'Well I've had a success too,' he said. 'That LawWorks case, the charity's safe; the project's got its funding.'

'How come?'

'I found a condition in the original planning permission for the building, stipulating that part of it had to be retained for community use. The landlord's decided not to sell and withdrawn their notice.'

'That's fantastic. You've completely saved the day for them.'

'Yeah. The project leader was really chuffed. Said some of the group were in tears. Apparently they're busy making me some thank-you piece of artwork.'

'Brilliant.' I smiled at Mark, seeing someone different

standing before me. Someone who appeared to be growing in stature before my very eyes.

'It feels good, doesn't it?'

'What?'

'Making a difference.'

I nodded, knowing I needed to say something.

'I've had a job offer, actually.'

'Smith MacGuire? When?'

'Just now,' I said, pointing to the letter on the table.

'Bloody hell, that's great.' Mark hesitated as he looked at
me. 'Well, it's great that they offered it to you.'

'What do you mean?'

'You don't want it. You might have thought you did, but
now you've got it, you don't, do you?'

'I wasn't expecting it, that's all. It's taken me by surprise.
But I can't say no to a job like that, can I?'

'Why not?'

'It's got everything going for it. Ticks all the boxes. I'd
be crazy to turn it down.'

'You turned down a perfectly good house which ticked
all my boxes because it wasn't what you wanted. That
wasn't crazy. It was the right thing to do.'

'You didn't think that at the time.'

'No. Because like you said I'd got carried away with my
plans and hadn't stopped to think that you might not want
the same things as me.'

'But what's that got to do with this job?'

'I think you're getting carried away with thinking this is
your dream job and you're not stopping to ask yourself if
what you used to want is the same as what you want now.'

I looked down at the table, thrown for a minute by how perceptive he'd become.

'Sometimes you don't know what you want until you try it.'

'And sometimes you don't realise you actually had what you wanted until you've lost it.'

I got up and walked over to the sink, busying myself with filling the kettle. Playing for time while I tried to work out whether Mark was still talking about the job or had moved on to something else. The troubling thing was that I suspected he could be right. Although he had no idea exactly how right.

Everything I supposedly wanted was there for me on a plate. All I had to do was take it. And yet here I was with a sudden yearning to keep the things I had. Because I was seeing them in a new light. Or maybe the light hadn't changed, just something inside of me. I poured our teas and turned back to face Mark. He was sitting at the table, a crumpled envelope in his hand.

'What's that?' I said.

'I got a big letter too today. From the Anthony Nolan people. Confirming I am the best match for the person who needs the transplant. And I've passed the medical, so it's all systems go.'

'What, the actual transplant?'

'Yeah. Apparently there's two ways you can donate these days: the traditional way where they give you a general anaesthetic and take the bone marrow from your pelvis, and some new technique involving blood stem cells, which is much easier and doesn't involve an overnight stay in hospital.'

'So which are you doing?'

'The traditional way. The doctors say it will give the recipient the best chance in this case. So that's what I've said I'll do.'

'How soon?'

'December the fifteenth.'

'Jesus, that's only a couple of weeks away.'

'Yeah. I've got to go down to London the day before. It's a private hospital. I'll only need to stay two nights. Means I'll miss our football club do, but hey, that's not important any more.'

As soon as he said it I realised. The fourteenth was the day I was supposed to be meeting Andy for lunch. My first thought was that it was rotten timing. And then the wave of self-revulsion hit me as I cursed myself for being such a selfish cow. Besides, it was actually brilliant timing because it meant I'd have to cancel. And I knew damn well I should never have agreed to see him again in the first place.

'I'll go down with you,' I said. 'Lend some moral support.'

Mark shook his head. 'No thanks. I want to go on my own.'

'Don't be ridiculous. You can't do that. I'm the one who got you into this in the first place by telling you about Emily. The least I can do is be there with you.'

Mark reached out across the table and took hold of my hand.

'I know you want to and I know I'd want to be with you if it were the other way around. But actually, I really do think it's best if I do this on my own.'

'Why?'

'Because of all the stuff I told you about. It was bad enough you seeing me being pathetic at the blood clinic; what I don't want is for you to see me in hospital, crapping myself before the op.'

'I don't want you to go through that on your own. I want to be there for you. To help you.'

'Then please do as I ask,' Mark said. 'I need to confront my demons on my own. You understand that, don't you?'

I nodded.

'If you can get the time off work, come down on Monday morning so you're there when I come round and I can revel in the glory of what I've done and have someone to help me home the next day. But let me do the first bit on my own.'

I sighed and looked up at the ceiling. I didn't want to agree for two reasons, the first being that I genuinely did want to be with him, to support him through this incredible thing he was doing; the second that I didn't trust myself not to go and see Andy in Mark's absence. Too much time to think about the past, to mull over everything that was on the table, was a dangerous thing. I looked back at Mark. It was what he wanted. I had to go along with it.

'OK, if you insist. But I will feel awful about not being there with you.'

'Well, don't sit about brooding. Go out and have some fun while you get the chance. You'll be stuck playing Nurse Cooper for the rest of the week.'

I smiled the best smile I could muster. And started to worry.

I was still worrying at two o'clock in the morning. Lying next to Mark. Feeling the warmth of his body, the gentle rising and falling of his chest, the familiar light snoring sound he made when he was fast asleep. I swung my legs out of bed, pulled on my dressing gown and padded downstairs to the kitchen to make a cup of tea. I sat down with my mug at the table and flipped open the lid of my laptop. It was annoying, my desire to check my e-mails even at this hour in the morning, but if I couldn't sleep I figured I might as well do something useful with my time.

The only thing in my inbox was from someone whose e-mail address started with em4rob. I smiled and opened up Emily's missive.

So, what do you want first, the good news or the bad news? The bad news is that I'm going to miss the *Twilight* premiere, even though I'll only be a couple of miles away from it. The good news is that it's because I'll be getting ready for a bone marrow transplant on 15 December! They've found me a donor. The match is almost perfect, but there are no guarantees it will work and I've got to have another lot of chemo beforehand. They've given me this massive booklet listing all the things that can go wrong and side effects and stuff afterwards, but hey, what the hell. Someone's given me a chance. And although I'm really gutted about not seeing Robert (Alia's mum won't let her go on her own either), what matters is that I might just be around for the *New Moon* premiere next time. I can't believe that someone I don't even know would do this for me. Would give me this chance. Right now I love them almost as much as I love Robert!

L8ers.

Emily

X

I smiled and wiped the tears from my face as I closed the lid. I wasn't going to reply now. I would speak to Frankie first. Find out if it was OK for me to tell Emily. That it wasn't someone she didn't know after all.

I drank my tea, crept back upstairs and slid back under the duvet alongside Mark.

Sunday, 20 April 1986

The look in Mrs Alberti's eyes as she opened the door was familiar. It was the same look I had been seeing all week. The one of surprise and thinly veiled disapproval.

'Claire,' she said, with none of her usual warmth, 'I'll get Francesca.' No invitation to step inside, no chitchat about how my mother was or how things were going at school. When Frankie appeared in the doorway a few moments later, she had the exact same look on her face.

'You'd better come in.'

It was more an instruction than an invitation and Frankie led the way up to her bedroom without another word. I stared at the bare walls which greeted me.

'You've taken all your United posters down,' I said.

'Yeah, well, it was about time. I couldn't keep them up for ever, could I?'

Frankie looked uncomfortable, seemingly aware that she couldn't avoid the obvious topic of conversation any longer.

'I guess you've had a crap week,' she said.

'Yeah. I was kind of hoping you'd come round, or at least call me back.'

'To say what? Congratulations, you got what you wanted?'

'This isn't what I wanted.'

'No? So how come it's all I've heard about for the past year. How you and Andy were made for each other.'

'I wanted to go out with him. For him to love me back. Not for all this shit to happen.'

'So why'd you have sex with him, then?'

'Who said we did? You're just taking the newspaper's word for it like everyone else.'

'OK,' she said, taking a few paces further towards me. 'Tell me what really happened.'

I looked down at my feet. I could lie to my mum and a copper but not to Frankie. And besides, I wanted her to know.

'We did have sex. Just the once. Unless blow jobs count, I don't know.'

Frankie looked at me like I'd just told her I'd murdered my own granny.

'You dirty slag,' she said, jabbing her finger in the air at me.

I couldn't believe it. I'd expected her to be impressed.

'What d'ya mean? You're the one who told me to grow up. Get real, you said.'

'I meant to stop dreaming about him. Not to go and bloody bonk him or suck his cock off.'

'I don't get you,' I said. 'You've spent half your life going on about how you'd like to screw Matt's brains out. And now you're sounding like the fucking Pope.'

'Yeah, well, it was just words. I was never actually gonna do it with Matt, was I?'

'Oh I get it. You're jealous. Because Andy wanted me and Matt was never interested in you.'

'It's not like that.'

'Yes it is. You're all mouth and no action, you are. And now you're upset because I've done it and you haven't.'

Frankie sat down on the bed and started to cry. I felt a massive pang of guilt.

'Look, I'm sorry it never worked out with you and Matt, OK?'

'It's nothing to do with him.'

'Well what then?'

'You wouldn't understand,' Frankie said, her eyes rimmed with red.

'You always do this,' I said. 'Make me out to be some stupid kid. But I'm not any more. Why can't you see that?'

Frankie was bawling her eyes out now, her shoulders shaking with each fresh sob. I didn't get it.

'I'm the one who should be crying,' I said. 'I came round here because everything's gone horribly wrong and I needed to talk to someone, and all you do is have a go at me and act like some drama queen.'

'You wanna know why I'm upset?' she said, the tears turning to anger as she started jabbing her finger again. 'I'm crying because you've spoilt it all for me. It was safe, me and Matt, you and Andy. Safe and innocent. It was all just a bit of fun, and now you've ruined it, made it dirty.'

'It wasn't dirty. It was beautiful. I love him, you know that.'

'That's bollocks. It was a dirty thing to do. Trust me, I should know.'

'What d'ya mean by that?'

'Nothing.'

'Yes you do. You wouldn't have said it otherwise.'

'All I'm saying is you shouldn't have let him touch you, Claire. You'll regret it. I do.'

'Regret what? You haven't done anything.'

'That's what you think.'

'You never said.'

'Yeah, well, I wasn't exactly proud of it.'

'Of what? You're not making any sense.'

'It doesn't matter now.'

'Yes it does. You can't do this big scene and then say that.'

'OK, you wanna hear it? I'm a dirty slag, just like you.'

I looked down at her, a frown creasing my brow.

'What d'ya mean?'

'Why d'ya think I packed in the tap-dancing?'

'You said it was boring kids' stuff.'

'I had to make something up, didn't I?'

'So why did you leave?'

'I didn't have much choice. Not with him there, leering at me the whole time.'

'Who? Uncle Tony?'

'He's not my uncle, OK?'

'What did he do to you?'

'Fucking hell, do I have to spell it out? He touched me, Claire. In places he shouldn't have. And made me touch him.'

I slumped down on to the bed next to her, holding my head in my hands.

'I'm sorry. I had no idea.'

'No, I know. I didn't tell anyone. Not even my mum.'

'Why not?'

'Because nice little Catholic girls don't let things like that happen to them, do they? And anyway, Auntie Maria was my mum's friend.'

'How long did it go on for?'

'A few months. Long enough to make me feel like a slag.'

'It wasn't your fault, Frankie.'

'Yes it was. I must have done something. Turned him on in some way. Because he didn't touch Connie, or any of the others. He told me that. Said I was his special favourite. It was our little secret.'

'You can't blame yourself. You were only a kid.'

'I still let him do it. I've had to live with that for four years.'

'I wish you'd talked to me.'

'I didn't even wanna think about it. I tried to put it out of my mind. Until I read all that stuff about you and Andy. And it brought it all back again. Made my skin crawl.'

'But this was nothing like that. I knew what I was doing, Frankie. He didn't make me do anything I didn't want to.'

'You don't see it, do you?' she said, standing up, her arms flailing in the air. 'You're still a kid. And he's seven years older than you. He's a fucking pervert.'

'No he isn't. He really cares about me. We would have been going out if all this crap hadn't happened.'

'Oh yeah? So where is he now? Where is your precious Andy Pailes? Called you, has he? Or been to see you? Course he ain't. He got what he wanted and he doesn't give a toss about you. He's no better than bloody Tony.'

I looked at her and shook my head. I was starting to feel sick inside.

'You can't say that. That's a horrible thing to say.'

'It's true. You just can't face up to it. Like I couldn't. I just hope someone doesn't rake it all up again for you years later. 'Cos believe me, it's not very nice.'

I sat there watching the tears streaming down Frankie's face and realised that she was right. It was all my fault. I'd screwed things up for all the people I really loved. It was no wonder everyone hated me. The trouble was I didn't know how to stop, to turn the clock back. Or how to live with myself. I got up and walked over to Frankie. I tried to put my arm around her but she pushed me away.

'I'm sorry, Frankie. I thought I was making everyone happy. Thought that was what you wanted me to do.'

'Yeah, well. You thought wrong, didn't you?'

'I know that now. And I'm really sorry. I don't blame you for hating me.'

'Claire, I don't . . .'

'No, it's all right. I'm going. You'll be better off without me.'

I turned and walked out of the room, down the stairs and out the front door. Not once looking back.

The first thing that hit me when I got home was the smell of the chicken roasting in the oven, reminding me that

Mum had invited Malcolm and my nan round for Sunday lunch. I wasn't sure I could cope with that. I wasn't sure I could cope with anything any more. The radio was playing to itself in the kitchen; upstairs I could hear the sound of the hot-water pipes whistling, confirming that Mum was having her usual Sunday-morning soak.

I hurried into the hall, picked up the phone and dialled the number again, feeling my warm breath hitting the mouthpiece and bouncing back to me as I waited, my hand tightening on the receiver as I heard the ringing tone. He would answer this time; he had to. He didn't though.

I put the phone down, more convinced than ever that Andy must hate me, really hate me, if he still didn't want to talk to me. He had every right to, I reminded myself. After what I'd done to him.

The smell of roast chicken wafted down the hall from the kitchen, wrapping itself around my throat and making me feel slightly queasy. 'Chicken and beans, chicken and beans, chicken and beans,' it taunted me as it swirled around my head. I'd never be able to forget him, I knew that now.

I followed the smell into the kitchen and opened the oven door. The heat hit me square in the face. I felt obliged to stand there and take it though, to suffer a little for Andy's sake. To make some kind of sacrifice.

I pulled the roasting tray towards me, feeling the heat pricking the tops of my fingers through the tea towel. In one quick movement I dragged the tray out and deposited it on top of the hob, watching the plumes of heat rising, turning the pattern on the kitchen tiles behind into a hazy blur.

It was three years since I'd gone veggie. I'd almost forgotten what chicken tasted like. I took the carving knife and prodded the bird. The skin came off easily, rolling back to reveal the white flesh beneath. I took the piece of skin in my hand, holding it between my thumb and forefinger. I licked it first, feeling the grease on my tongue, grimacing as it drizzled down my chin. Then popped it into my mouth, chewing for a few seconds before swallowing hard.

There, I had done it. Done something I'd hated doing, for Andy. I felt a brief spurt of elation before I realised the nasty taste was still there. Lingering on my tongue, seeping into my flesh.

I put the chicken back into the oven and ran to the sink as I started to retch. I could feel the spasms in my stomach. My throat tightening. But nothing came up. It was stuck deep inside of me, with all the other bad stuff; the things I shouldn't have done or said. I was rotten on the inside. And it was spreading, like some giant cancer. Soon it would be out of control.

I had to get out of the house, to breathe some fresh air. And I could only think of one place to go. I dashed up to my room and took the Milk Cup Final tickets from my top drawer. After everything that had happened, I'd decided it was best to stay away. But I realised now that if Andy had been good enough to get the tickets for me, I owed it to him to use them. I took something else out of the drawer as well. The letter I'd written the previous night. The one that explained how sorry I was. How much I hated myself for screwing up his life. I remembered the bundle of letters that had been waiting for Andy on the day I'd gone inside Priory Park with him. All of them from people who thought he was special, who maybe liked to think they were special to him. They weren't, though. I understood that now. They were nothing special at all.

I paused, looking around the room, before grabbing Andy's crumpled United shirt from my bed. I would wear it to Wembley. It was the least I could do.

'I'm going out,' I called in the direction of the bathroom, before bolting down the stairs and out the front door before Mum could stop me. When I reached the post box on the corner I hesitated for a second. And then watched as the envelope slipped from my still greasy fingers and disappeared from view.

Walking up Wembley Way, I tried to blend in with the other fans. It should have been easy enough. I was wearing jeans and a United shirt like everyone else. But it didn't seem to make any difference. I still felt as if I had a huge neon sign above my head proclaiming, 'I'm the girl in the papers, the one that ruined Andy's career, the one you all hate.' I wished I'd worn my United cap so I could have pulled it down over my face and let myself be blindly pushed along by the crowd, up to the twin towers and through the turnstiles.

It was worse still inside. The laughter and the whispers. I caught a snatch of conversation from behind: 'Brown's barmy, if you ask me, getting rid of Pailes instead of having a go at the girl for coming on to him. Stupid slag.'

I felt it like a kick in the stomach. Part of me wanted to turn round and defend myself. But I knew it was pointless. The jury had given its verdict. I was guilty. Obliged to take any punishment thrown at me.

When United walked out on to the pitch, I looked for Andy. Even though I knew he wasn't there. Only his shadow, hanging over everything. I followed the match with my eyes, watching every pass, every header, every tackle. But my heart wasn't in it any more. The magic had gone. It was my fault. I'd wished for too much and had lost everything.

As Matt scored on the stroke of half-time, everyone around me leapt up in the air while my guilt nailed my feet to the ground. I watched them all bobbing up and down in delight, whooping and cheering. And I remembered how good it had once felt.

But although I hadn't felt the usual ecstasy when United scored, I still felt the agony when Forest equalised not long after the restart, and when they scored the winner in the last minute. Maybe I'd known all along that United would lose and had simply come to torture myself. To solemnly watch Forest's lap of honour while all the United fans around me were streaming out of the ground. I was the chief mourner, saying goodbye to a much-loved friend.

It was a long time before I began walking back to the tube station. It was true what they said as well. About it seeming a lot further on the way back when you'd lost. It was raining heavily. The raindrops mingled with my tears and washed them down my face, making room for the next ones.

When I got to the ticket barrier at Wembley Park I had to rummage deep in my bag for my Capital card, searching through the soggy tissues and discarded chocolate wrappers before I found it, stuck firmly to the picture of Andy. The one in the little plastic folder, protecting it from getting damaged or torn. I stopped dead in my tracks, staring at Andy's face smiling up at me. He hadn't known back then, of course. How I was going to ruin his life.

'Are you going through or not, love? We haven't got all day, you know.'

I looked round apologetically at the middle-aged man who had spoken and shuffled to the side of the ticket barrier, letting everyone in the queue which had built up behind me go past. They had trains to catch. They had places to go.

A handful of people were still on the platform when I finally got there, mostly United fans who appeared to have been drowning their sorrows before beginning the journey home. A young man wearing an oversized United bobble hat looked straight at me. For a second I thought he was going to point, to shout, 'That's her, that's the one whose fault it is.' He didn't though; he just smiled knowingly.

'That is one depressed lady,' he said to his friend, nodding in my direction. 'It's all right, love,' he called after me. 'There's always next season.'

There wasn't though. Not for Andy. And therefore not for me. Nothing left to look forward to. I wondered if people felt like this after they'd climbed Everest. That the view from the top hadn't been as good as they'd expected. And that now they'd stood at the summit, there was no place left worth going. Nothing to dream of any more. And without dreams all you had left was reality.

I tried to think of one good thing in my life. One person I loved who didn't hate me, one chance to put everything right, one glimmer of hope on the horizon. I thought for a long time. Nothing came.

I walked to the far end of the platform, past the covered section, and stood letting the rain beat down on me. I wanted it to beat harder, to make me suffer more. I needed a punishment that would fit the crime. Of ruining the life of the very person I loved most in the world.

As I heard the faint rumble of the train on the tracks, I knew what I had to do. It was the only option left. The only thing that would take the bad taste away. And prove how sorry I was for everything I had done. I started running back down the platform, faster and faster as the train came into view. The faces of the other fans flashed past me, as if I was watching them from the train. I heard voices. I couldn't make out what they said, but it was like everyone was talking to me, chanting, urging me to do it.

I stopped and steadied myself for a second on the edge of the platform, wrapping my arms around me as I hugged Andy's shirt, knowing he would give me the strength I needed. I remembered what he had said to me in the car.

'Don't ever stop smiling. You've got a beautiful smile.'

It was all he'd ever asked of me but I hadn't even been able to manage that. I'd let him down. I wouldn't let him down now though. Not this time. I blinked away the tears and stared into the cab of the approaching train, waiting until the driver looked straight at me before forcing a smile across my face. There. I hadn't stopped smiling, see. I could do anything for Andy. Anything at all.

I stepped off the edge of the platform.

Fourteen

'Are you sure about this? I feel awful not coming with you.'

'I told you,' said Mark, taking my hand. 'I want the right to be a complete wuss in private.'

'Well if you change your mind, call me. I'll come straight to the hospital, OK?'

'Sure, but I won't. Come down tomorrow like I said and I can bathe in the glory of it all and you'll have no idea what a fuss I made about the whole thing.'

'Oh I don't know. I think the nurses will probably fill me in on the details.'

Mark smiled and pulled a face at me. He didn't fool me though. I could see how terrified he was.

'Has Frankie told Emily yet?' he asked.

'She's going to tell her this morning. She wanted to wait as long as possible in case there were any last-minute hitches.'

'Like me doing a runner, you mean?'

'You'll be fine.'

'I will now,' he said. 'It makes it easier. Knowing it's for Emily.'

'We still don't know for certain.'

'I do,' Mark said.

I smiled and kissed him on the lips. Knowing it should have made things easier for me too. And feeling wretched about what I might end up doing after he had left.

'Thank you,' I said. 'I think you're doing an amazing thing.'

'It's OK,' he said. 'Just be aware that I'll milk it for all it's worth for years to come.' He grinned as he walked out of the door.

'Text me when you get there,' I said.

He nodded, climbed into his car, waved once and was gone.

I cried as I got ready. Hating myself for not having the willpower to resist. And hating the fact that Andy still exerted such a hold over me, all these years on. Every step towards the train station felt like I was trying to walk the wrong way up an escalator. When the train came I hauled myself on. The journey had begun. I read a book on the way but had no recollection afterwards of the story. Only of seeing the words on the page. By the time I walked across Bradford to Forster Square station I was resigned to my fate and had submitted myself to what was about to happen. I would be carried to Andy. He would be waiting for me. He'd already texted me to ask what train I'd be on. And when I stepped down on to the platform, that would be it. I would be his. Just like I'd always wanted to be.

The train came to a halt at Saltaire station. When I saw him on the platform the grey flecks in his hair threw me for a second. I realised I had been half expecting to see the old Andy standing there. I still wasn't used to the new one. He smiled as he caught sight of me. My body tensed, as if recognising the forces which were at work here. Knowing the destructive qualities they possessed.

'Hi, Claire,' he said as he reached out to touch my arm, bent to kiss me on the cheek. I didn't move this time. I didn't seem to be able to resist any longer. A frisson of excitement ran through me. The familiar churning sensation started up inside. Andy was here. I was not in control any more. 'Good to see you again,' he said. 'How's things?'

I couldn't begin to answer truthfully. To say that actually my boyfriend had just gone down to London to donate bone marrow to my best friend's teenage daughter who had leukaemia and might die if it didn't work. It was all too real, too scary and not part of this at all. I used to be able to talk to Andy. He used to be the only one I could talk to. I realised that wasn't the case any more.

'Fine, thanks,' I said instead.

'Did you hear anything about that job?'

'Yeah, I was offered it.'

'Great. When do you start?'

'I don't. I turned it down.' I'd sweated on it for almost a week before deciding. But the evening after I got back from visiting Kaz at the rehab centre in York, I'd finally written the letter. Mark had been right. It wasn't what I wanted any more. Not at all.

'Oh, why?'

'I guess I realised how much I love what I do now. You know what it's like, you moan and grumble about it like everyone does. But when it comes to leaving, well, it's a different matter altogether.'

Andy nodded. I had no idea if he understood. Or if he was simply being polite.

'So where's Titus?' I asked as we walked across the road towards Salts Mill.

'At home. Safely shut up in the kitchen. I'm afraid his table manners are appalling. I took him for a really long walk this morning to tire him out. He'll be fine.'

We reached the entrance to the mill. Andy held the door open for me. Just as he'd held open another door once before. When we were leaving court. When everything had been about to change.

'Have you ever been here before?' he asked.

'Once, a few years ago. Not to eat, just to look around.'

'It's a great place. It'll be good to have the chance to chat properly as well. Without any distractions.'

I decided to ignore his reference to our last meeting and its rather abrupt conclusion.

'So, are you a regular here?' I asked.

'I often used to come here for Sunday lunch quite a bit. Haven't been for a while.' I guessed he meant he used to come with Jennifer. Going out for Sunday lunch wasn't much fun on your own. I could remember that much.

It was heaving when we got up to the diner, a huge open room with the kitchen on view at the heart of it. We queued for five minutes before a waitress had a chance to show us to a table. Andy pulled the chair out for me before sitting down opposite and smiling at me. The air around us was filled with clatter and chatter. This was clearly a place for talking. It was simply a matter of knowing what to say.

'What are you going for?' asked Andy, after a few minutes of perusing the menu.

'The asparagus risotto, I think.'

'Are you veggie?'

'Yeah, have been since I was a teenager.'

'Oh, right. I don't remember.' He wouldn't, of course. Because we'd never gone out for meals together. It hadn't been that sort of relationship. It hadn't been much of a relationship at all.

'What about you?' I said.

'The salmon fillet, I think.'

'Not the chicken?' I smiled.

'Why do you say that?'

'It used to be your favourite pre-match meal, chicken and beans.'

'Was it?'

'Yeah. You said so, in one of those fact files in *Shoot!*.

Andy laughed and shook his head.

'Jesus. Did anyone actually take any notice of those things?'

'I did,' I said.

Andy looked at me. I wondered if he was seeing the sixteen-year-old me again. Or the one sitting here, beginning to feel I didn't really know him at all.

'Do you keep in touch with any of the United players?' I asked.

'Only Thomo. And only by e-mail, really.'

'What's he doing now?'

'He's a sports physio. He loves it.'

'What happened with his wife?'

'She's fine. She's been in remission for a long time now. Though I don't think he's ever really stopped worrying about it coming back.'

I nodded. Thinking how long ago it all seemed. Almost another lifetime.

'Do you go to any matches these days?' I asked.

Andy shook his head.

'No. My heart's not in it any more. Football got spoilt, didn't it? It's all about big business now. I spend my days negotiating clubs' sponsorship deals and drafting television rights agreements. The actual football doesn't seem to matter any more. How about you? Do you ever go and see United?'

'No,' I said. 'I haven't been since the Milk Cup Final.'

The waitress returned with our wine and to take our order. Cutting through the awkward silence which had descended on the table. Neither of us wanting to talk about what had happened after the Milk Cup Final.

Andy raised his glass.

'To new beginnings,' he said. His eyes were searing into me as he said it. Looking for any chinks in my armour. Any way he could get past my defences to the girl who adored him. Who would have laid down her life for him. Who very nearly did.

I clinked my glass against his but I took only a sip. Everything had been churned up inside. Things which had lain dormant for a long time. All these years I'd dreamt of this. Of seeing him again. Of carrying on from where we left off. But now I was here. And now I remembered exactly where we had left off, I wasn't so sure. My phone beeped twice from my bag.

'Excuse me,' I said, bending to pick it up. I thought it would be Mark, letting me know he'd arrived. It wasn't though. It was Emily.

'Mum's told me. Mark's my donor. I know he is. He's a real live hero. You must be so proud of him. Thanx. Em X'

I put the phone back into my bag and looked up at the ceiling as I struggled to blink the tears away.

'Are you OK?' asked Andy. 'Was that your boyfriend? Is he making this hard for you?'

I stared across at him. Seeing everything so very clearly for the first time. The top of the volcano blew.

'You weren't worthy,' I said.

'Sorry?'

'Of being my idol. You treated me so badly.'

'Claire. I said sorry at the time.'

'And do you think that was enough for all the pain you caused me? You used me. I was sixteen, for Christ's sake. You were lonely and you thought you'd screw me to give your ego a bit of a boost.'

Andy put his glass down, glanced anxiously around the diner in case anyone had heard. A frown creased his forehead. 'It wasn't like that,' he said, his voice soft and low.

'Well, it wasn't far off. You were in my bedroom. The fucking walls were plastered with pictures of you. And you still carried on.'

'I thought it was what you wanted.'

'The Andy I wanted was the one on my wall. The one who would never let me down. Always be there for me.'

'I didn't know it would end up in the papers like that.'

'I know. But you could have given me a bit of support when it did. Instead of buggering off and leaving me to deal with all the crap.'

'It wasn't up to me. The club told me what to do.'

'And you didn't have the guts to stand up to them.'

'My career was on the line.'

'My fucking life was on the line.' My voice broke as I struggled to control the pent-up anger which had festered away for so long. I was aware that other people were looking at us. Thinking we were having some sort of lovers' tiff. Having no idea of the enormity of it all.

Andy looked down at the table, his face long and drawn.

'I behaved like a bastard, I know that. It's been eating away at me all these years. The reason there was nobody serious in my life for so long was you. I knew I could never find someone who loved me as much as you did. You were special, Claire. You really were.'

'Well, you had a bloody funny way of showing it.'

Andy looked up at me, his eyes dark and heavy.

'When you did what you did, I realised what a bastard I'd been. I didn't see how I could put things right so I figured it was best for everyone if I kept well out of the way.'

'I so needed you,' I said, shaking my head. 'So needed to know that you cared.'

'I'm not proud of my behaviour, Claire. But as much as I wish I could, I can't change what happened. Can't make things better.'

'Unless I turn up out of the blue, at a point when you're lonely and feeling a bit down. And you decide to start the whole thing up again.'

'Hey, it was your idea to come and see me.'

'It wasn't. It was my boyfriend's. Mark had the guts to do that, to give me your address and to trust me to come back to him.'

'He's a fool then, isn't he?'

'He's not a fool,' I said, shaking my head and pushing my chair away. 'I'm the fool for taking this long to see how appallingly you treated me. And for agreeing to come and see you again today.'

'You came because you wanted to,' said Andy. 'You want this every bit as much as I do.'

'I thought I did. But I thought wrong. Mark's worth ten of you. I can see that now. And I'm not going to let you screw up my life a second time.'

I stood up, aware that my voice had been louder than I intended. That everybody in the diner was looking now.

'Claire, please don't be like this. Please don't go. Give me a chance to make it up to you.'

'I did,' I said. 'Twenty-two years ago. I lay there for a very long time. You didn't come. Now if you'll excuse me, there's someplace else I need to be.' I turned and strode off past the startled waitress who had just arrived at the table with our meals. I hadn't meant it to be so public, for everything to come out in that way. But now it had, I at last felt free of him.

Tuesday, 22 April 1986

I can hear Andy's voice calling to me. Telling me how much he loves me. Willing me to stay with him. My eyes are shut. I have no idea where I am. Maybe floating somewhere between heaven and earth. I don't care which one I go to, as long as Andy is there.

I drift in and out of consciousness for a while. But Andy is with me all the time. Wrapping himself around me. Love like antiseptic, healing my wounds. Whenever his voice fades, when he seems to be drifting away, I fight harder and bring myself back to him. Closing the gap between us. I draw strength from him. Draw oxygen. Feel him breathing life into me, pumping my heart until I am strong enough to do it myself. I can hear the blood rushing around in my head. Begin to feel a tingling sensation in my fingers and toes. Life flooding back into me.

I am aware that he is holding my hand, asking me to squeeze it if I can hear him. My brain squeezes but the message gets stuck somewhere along my arm. I try to smile. I have no idea whether it is showing on my face. After a while the fog starts to lift but reveals only blackness behind it. I lie still, fearing I have lost him. Until his voice echoes inside my head. The blackness starts flickering. And I realise it isn't blackness at all, but the inside of my eyelids.

With a huge effort I haul them open only for them to fall shut again as the light streams in. Andy responds, the tone of his voice rising, sensing I am nearly there. I wait while my batteries recharge. Then slide my lids half open, letting them get used to the light, before opening them fully. And seeing Andy's face inches from me. His eyes moist with tears but shining brilliantly.

'Hello,' he says. 'I knew you'd come back to me.'

I smile, knowing he can see it this time. I open my mouth to say something but he puts his finger to his lips.

'Rest now,' he says. 'We can talk later.'

I do as he asks. Shutting my eyes then opening them again a second later, to check I still can, before sleeping properly. Knowing I can wake again when I want to.

When I do wake, Andy is still smiling down at me, love pouring from his eyes. I lie for a long time just looking at him. Studying his face. Making sure I know every inch of it so if I slip away again I will be able to see it. Even with my eyes closed.

The rest of the picture around him begins to fill in, shapes, colours and smells. A huge bouquet of lilac and purple flowers stands in a vase at the end of my bed.

'Thanks for the flowers,' I say, not needing to ask who sent them.

'It's OK. It was the least I could do. From now on,' he says, 'I'm not going anywhere. I'm looking after you, that's all that matters.' I smile as I rub my eyes. 'You get some more rest,' he says, stroking my face.

'There's one thing I want you to do,' I say. 'Before I go back to sleep.' I point to the plaster cast on my leg. Andy smiles, picks up a pen from the bedside cabinet and writes in large, sprawling letters across it, 'To my darling Claire, all my love, Andy', and signs a huge kiss after it.

*'Thank you,' I say, smiling while trying to stifle a yawn at the
same time. 'That's made it feel better already.'*

Andy watches as my eyelids slide ever lower.

'Claire,' he whispers. 'I'll love you for ever.'

'I know,' I say, without even opening my eyes. 'I love you too.'

*He sits there for a long time afterwards. I can feel his breath,
warm against my face. And his love enveloping me, keeping me safe.*

It was when I smelt Mum's Yardley perfume that I realised
I hadn't died after all. I wasn't exactly sure what heaven
would smell of but I knew it wouldn't be that. And I
couldn't imagine they'd have any perfume at all in hell.

The initial relief was tempered by an overwhelming
sense of failure at my inability to carry off what should
have been a straightforward suicide. How typical that I
couldn't even get that right.

How much damage I had inflicted upon myself in the
process, I wasn't sure. All I knew was that I was hurting
in a hell of a lot of places. Although considering I should
have been lying in bits on a train track, I realised that, for
the first time in ages, things could have been a whole lot
worse.

But I was still miffed that I hadn't come round to the
sound of the players singing a rousing chorus of 'United
We Stand'. I'd always thought it must be the best thing
about being in a coma – knowing that your favourite stars
would be desperately trying to bring you back to life.

It gradually dawned on me that I had no idea how long
I had lain unconscious. It could have been an hour, a
month or an entire lifetime. I was almost afraid to open

my eyes in case I found myself on a geriatric ward, but in the end, curiosity got the better of me.

It took a few seconds for the world to come into focus and for Mum's face to materialise in front of me. She was smiling a big, watery smile. Beneath it she looked tired and drawn but she didn't appear to have aged significantly.

'What year is it?'

'It's nineteen eighty-six, love. Why? Don't you remember?'

'Yeah, I was just checking. Is it still April?'

'Yes, of course.'

'And what day is it?'

'Tuesday.'

'So I've only missed a day or so?'

'Yes, love, only a couple of days. They've been very long days, that's all.'

I nodded, noticing the catch in Mum's voice. A nurse came over to check on me, smiling, chatting away as if nothing had happened, and went off in search of a doctor.

'How are you feeling?' Mum asked.

'Like I've been hit by a train.' I said it with a smile on my face rather than sarcastically, somehow taking comfort in the familiarity of Mum asking stupid questions. I surveyed the array of monitors around my bed and looked down at my body, much of which appeared to be swathed in bandages or encased in plaster.

'How bad is it?'

'Are you sure you want to know?'

'Yeah, go on.'

'Well, you gave your head a bad bash, although the scans don't show any lasting damage. You've broken your left leg, fractured your collarbone, smashed part of your left arm and fractured a few ribs. The rest is just cuts and bruises. The doctors say you might be left with some scars but you've been very lucky.'

'Right.' I didn't feel particularly lucky, but I knew what Mum meant. The thing I didn't understand was how I'd even survived. But I wasn't sure how to ask without sounding ungrateful.

'So . . . what happened? Why didn't . . . I mean, how come I'm still here?'

Mum gave a long-drawn-out sigh and shut her eyes for a moment.

'The train hit you as you fell but it pushed you into the pit at the side of the track, love; it passed right over you.'

I nodded, trying to picture it all in my head.

'What happened to my shirt?'

'What shirt?'

'My United shirt.'

'I'm not sure. I expect it was in a bit of a mess, like you.'

'Oh.'

A doctor came over and examined me, looked at all the monitors and wrote something on the clipboard on the end of my bed.

'You're going to be fine,' he said. 'No more questions. You need to rest. Try to get some sleep.'

I shut my eyes again, but not before registering the

warmth in Mum's smile. A warmth I couldn't remember seeing before.

When I opened my eyes again Mum was still there, sitting beside me with the same expression, a mixture of relief, anger and guilt, etched across her face. She reached out and squeezed my hand. I noticed that her nail polish was scuffed and flaking. Normally you could see your own face in it.

'Well, you're here, that's all that matters. You gave us all quite a shock.'

I wasn't sure who the 'us' was supposed to refer to, as Mum appeared to be on her own and I couldn't imagine that anyone else would have been particularly bothered about what had happened.

'Your father was in yesterday. He said to give you his love. He brought you those.' She nodded towards a huge vase of flowers that was squeezed on to my bedside cabinet, surrounded by an array of get-well cards.

'Who are they all from?'

'Oh, your nan, Auntie Barbara and Uncle Bob. There's some from your friends at school. Oh and one from Mr Aspland, the newsagent.'

I was confused. I didn't have any friends at school and I hadn't realised Mr Aspland even knew my name.

'So everyone knows, then?'

'Well, yes, it was all over the news again. What do you expect if you go and do these silly things?'

I wondered what other silly things I had done that ranked up there with trying to commit suicide. I supposed Mum meant the Andy thing.

'Has Andy sent a card?'

'For goodness' sake, Claire, don't start all that again. That's what landed you in this state in the first place. When we get you out of here, I'm going to take you on a little break, give you a chance to get away from everything, forget all about it.'

I had visions of another wet week in Great Yarmouth.

'It's all right, you don't need to do that.'

'I do. I need to do a lot of things that I didn't do before. I should have listened, I should have been there for you, I should never have let it come to this.'

Her voice was trembling – as was her hand. I felt I should say something.

'It wasn't your fault,' I said. 'It was just one of those things.'

'It wasn't though, was it, Claire? Teenage girls don't go around throwing themselves in front of tube trains for no reason whatsoever.'

'I couldn't see any other way out. I'd messed everything up. I thought everyone hated me.'

Mum shook her head and looked up at the ceiling.

'Why would I hate you?'

I hesitated before replying.

'Because of what I did with Andy. And because I ran to you that time and told you about Dad, about what I'd seen when I came home from school.'

'You thought I hated you because of that?'

'You never said it wasn't my fault that he left. All you did was give me a Finger of Fudge to eat. It wasn't very much.'

Mum started to cry.

447

'Oh, love. It wasn't your fault. You did me a favour. Stopped me burying my head in the sand, pretending it wasn't happening.'

'You knew about it?'

'I didn't know but I suspected. She wasn't the first, Claire.'

'So why didn't you do anything before?'

'Because I didn't want to lose your father. I loved him so much I wasn't sure I could cope without him. And I knew how much you idolised him.'

'So how come you told him to leave then? After I came to see you.'

'Because he'd hurt you. Because you're the most precious thing in the world to me and I wasn't going to let anyone hurt you like that. And now look what I've done, I've ended up hurting you myself.'

Tears started rolling down my cheeks, dripping on to the crisp white bedsheets.

'I just needed someone to talk to,' I said.

'I know. I should have listened, I should have realised what you were going through. I suppose I didn't want to hear it because I was so scared of losing you . . . scared of you growing up.'

'I do love Andy, Mum.'

'I know.'

'No, I mean really love him. Like . . . I dunno, maybe like you used to love Dad.'

Mum smiled. It was a sad smile. That was when I realised.

'You still love him, don't you? You still love Dad.'

Mum looked down and nodded slowly.

'I know I shouldn't do. But it's not easy.'

'So when I told you about him remarrying . . .'

'It came as a bit of a shock.'

'Is that why you started seeing Malcolm?'

'Partly. It made me realise I've got to get on with my own life.'

'Do you love Malcolm?'

Mum hesitated.

'He's a good man, Claire. There's a lot to be said for that.' She gave a weak smile and tightened her grip on my hand. 'I couldn't have coped, you know, if I'd lost you. I don't know what I'd have done.'

'It's OK,' I heard myself saying, realising how drained Mum looked. 'You haven't lost me. I'm still here. You should go home and get some sleep.'

'Are you sure you'll be all right?'

'I can't do anything stupid in here, can I? Not in this state.'

She managed a smile as she bent to pick up her handbag.

I had been awake a good ten minutes the next morning before I noticed the envelope, the one which had been left on my bedside cabinet by the post lady. It was pale blue and bore a Potters Bar postmark. I asked a passing nurse to open it for me. She ripped the top with her finger and tipped the contents out on to my bed. There was a get-well card and a letter on lined notepaper. The sort of notepaper great-aunts get you for a birthday present. I picked it up with my one good hand and started to read.

Dear Claire,
Hope you're feeling better. You scared the shit out of me, you silly cow. Don't you ever dare do anything like that again.

You never let me finish when you came to see me. I was going to say 'I don't hate you, I could never hate you. You're the best friend I've got.' But you never gave me a chance. I thought I'd lost you, when I heard about what you'd done. I'm so relieved I've got the chance to finish my sentence. I thought I'd do it in a letter. That way you won't get the chance to interrupt like you usually do.

I didn't mean all that stuff I said. I was hurting and I took it out on you. That was mean of me. I know you love Andy. I never loved Matt. He was just a lot safer than a boyfriend.

I told my mum about what happened, to me I mean. It was hard but I feel better now it's out in the open. She cried at first and said I was making it up but I think she believed me in the end. She's been all right since. Just a bit quiet. I don't think she's told Dad. I asked her not to. I'm not going to tell anyone else. Especially not Tara. She's a right gossip.

I'll come and see you soon. Bring you some Cadbury's Creme Eggs instead of all those crappy grapes. I love you and I'm really sorry.
Frankie XXX

I wiped my eyes and put her card right at the front of my bedside cabinet. In the space I'd been saving for Andy's.

Fifteen

I phoned Frankie from the train down to London.

'How is she?' I asked.

'Pretty groggy. The chemo was really tough. But the doctors say she's strong enough. And she says she's ready for the transplant.' A train hooted as it went past. 'Where are you?' asked Frankie.

'On the train down.'

'I thought you weren't coming until tomorrow.'

'Last-minute change of plan. Who's looking after the children tonight?'

'They're with Joe's parents.'

'And where's Joe?'

'Sitting with Emily. We're doing shifts.'

'Will he be OK for a double shift this evening?'

'I guess so. Why?'

'We're going up West, as they used to say in *EastEnders*.'

'Are you crazy?'

'Certifiable.'

'Are you going to explain what's going on?'

'No. Just meet me at Leicester Square tube station in two hours' time. Phone me when you get there because it's going to be packed. Wear your glad rags. Or something black at least.'

'I don't understand. Is this another one of your cunning plans?'

'Sort of. All you need to know is that it's for Emily. Something to cheer her up, OK?'

'OK,' said Frankie, still not sounding convinced. 'But this had better be good, Claire.'

'Believe me,' I said. 'It will be.'

I stepped off the escalator, hurried through the ticket barrier and stopped abruptly outside the tube station. My senses being assaulted by the bright neon lights, cacophony of noise and rancid hot-dog-stall smells of Leicester Square. I'd expected it to be busy, but nothing had prepared me for this. Hordes of teenage girls, all of them dressed in various vampire guises: a uniform of black eyeliner, pale faces and artificially unkempt hair. It was bloody freezing too. The first time for years I'd gone out in stockings and a miniskirt and the chill factor must have been well into the minus figures. I checked my mobile, deciding despite being in central London to keep it in my hand, the level of noise being such that I'd never hear it ring otherwise. I was aware that it was the wrong sort of mobile, of course. The bright young things around me were flashing the latest tiny camera phones around as they took pictures of each other. I was probably the only one here who had a separate camera tucked away in her bag. It was at least digital though. The film one had been left to rest in peace at home.

I turned to watch the crowd of girls behind me, laughing and joking, the thrill and anticipation of it all sparking from their bodies. And then I saw Frankie. Gliding up the escalator in a long skirt and boots, a low-cut top and a flowing black coat. Style oozing from her pores. I shook my head as she approached.

'You really piss me off,' I said.

'Why?'

'You still look bloody hot, even at your age. And I bet you threw it all together in two minutes flat.'

Frankie grinned at me. 'It was pretty much the only decent outfit I had with me. I chucked it in the case in the vain hope we might manage to get out for a meal later in the week. If everything goes OK.'

'Little knowing that I'd be taking you out for a night on the town.'

Frankie rolled her eyes. 'Don't think I don't know what you're up to. I worked it out on the way.'

'Oh,' I said. 'It was going to be a surprise.'

'What, with thousands of teenage girls squealing about their love of Robert Pattinson all over the tube station?'

'Yeah, well. I didn't reckon on it being quite this busy.'

'So I take it that's where we're going,' she said, pointing at the massive *Twilight* sign in red lights above the Odeon across the square.

'You've got it,' I said, taking her arm and starting to march her across the icy pavement to where the crowd had gathered outside.

'And what is the plan exactly?' asked Frankie.

'We're going to get Robert's autograph.'

'Right. Just like all these girls are, you mean?' she said, waving her arm at the throng of devoted Pattinson fans already massed behind the barriers.

'Aah, but we've got an advantage over them, haven't we?'

'What?'

'We're experienced autograph-hunters. We know all the tricks. We were getting signatures from gorgeous guys when they were still in nappies.'

Frankie laughed and shook her head. 'But they're younger and fitter and can probably scream more loudly.'

'Nonsense,' I said as we reached the back of the crowd. 'We'll wipe the floor with them. Now, elbows at the ready, and if any of them protest give them one of your dirty looks.'

We started squeezing our way through, row by row.

'Sorry,' I said to the first girl who blocked my path and refused to budge an inch. 'We've lost our daughters. We think they're somewhere down at the front.' She stepped grudgingly to the side. I started calling, 'Emily, Sophia, where are you?'

'You devious cow,' whispered Frankie with a wicked grin on her face.

'Just remember,' I said. 'We're doing this for Emily.'

Frankie started calling too. 'Emily, don't worry, hon, we're here. Hold on tight to Sophia.'

'The little one's only eleven,' I said to an older girl who was looking daggers at me. 'First time in London as well.' She stepped aside to let us through.

Ten minutes later we were standing triumphantly at the front of the barriers, next to a girl with a 'Bite Me Rob' banner, in a plum spot right outside the cinema. Still pretending to have lost Emily and Sophia but packed in so tightly that having got there, those around us could see it was impossible for us to move.

'What happens now?' asked Frankie.

'We wait.'

'It's freezing my fucking tits off.'

'Sshh,' I said. 'You're supposed to be a responsible mother.'

'We're not very responsible if we've lost our kids, are we?'

I started giggling. Frankie took one look at me and started giggling too.

'I'm so glad I'm not their age,' I said when we finally stopped laughing. 'All that teenage angst and heartache. The pain of unrequited love.'

'What's brought this on?' said Frankie. 'Where have your rose-tinted spectacles gone?'

'I saw Andy today,' I said.

Frankie stared at me hard, as if worried I might be losing it again.

'What do you mean? Where?'

'In Saltaire, where he lives. It's less than an hour from Todmorden.'

'You mean you just bumped into him?'

'No. We had a sort of date.'

Frankie's eyes bulged wide.

'Claire, I'm not getting this. Your boyfriend is lying in hospital about to donate bone marrow to my daughter and you're pissing around with the guy who nearly cost you your life.'

'It's OK. It's not like that. Mark gave me his address. He told me to go and see him. Well, the first time at least.'

'Whoa, you're losing me here. You'd better slow down and explain.'

So I did. I told her everything. From the first glimpse outside his house to me storming out of the diner earlier that day. Frankie stood open-mouthed, sporadically shaking her head.

'I can't believe all this has been going on and you haven't told me about it.'

'I didn't want to bother you, you've had enough on your plate. The last thing you needed was me bleating on about Andy again.'

'You mean you knew I'd say you were being a stupid cow.'

'Well, yeah. Probably that as well. But I had to figure it out for myself. I'm glad I went to see him. He's dominated my life for so long. It feels good to finally have some sort of closure.'

Frankie shook her head again.

'You could have ended up with him. How weird is that? It's like the whole thing went full circle.'

'I know. If you'd told me when I was fifteen that I'd be blowing Andy Pailes out at thirty-eight, I'd have said you were mad.'

'But it is finally over?'

'Yeah. Mark's seen to that. No one's ever loved me that much that they've set me free.'

'Have you told him that?'

'Not yet. I will do later. I'm planning to go to the hospital when we're finished here.'

'He's a great guy, Claire. I know I would say that because

of what he's doing for Emily. But even without that, he's solid gold.'

'Like your Joe then. We did all right between us, didn't we?'

Frankie smiled and gave me a great big hug.

'We did bloody brilliant.'

We had to wait another hour before he arrived. I couldn't actually feel my feet any more. Or my fingers, come to that. The dry ice was pumped along the black carpet laid out in front of us. Lots of people walked past, most of whom I had no idea who they were. The film appeared to have a cast of thousands, but we were only waiting for one man. The flashes went again as a young woman in an off-the-shoulder dress with startled cat-like eyes arrived. I guessed she must play Bella, because the girl beside me hissed in a jealous rage. Then through the ice a tall figure emerged. Black suit, white shirt, hair all over the place. But the eyes. Jesus, the eyes. A thousand girls screamed in unison as he strode towards us. Frankie was one of them.

'Oh my God. He's gorgeous,' she shrieked.

'I told you Emily has better taste than you did.'

'Quick. Where's the picture?' Somehow I managed to yank the poster I'd brought of Robert from my bag and thrust it towards him, pen held out in the other hand. He didn't see it though. His head was bent, and he was busily scrawling signatures on the mass of photos in front of him.

'It's no good,' I said as he started to edge away. 'He's going to go past. You have to do something.'

Frankie opened her mouth wide and screamed.

'I'm a big mamma, Robert, and I want your babies.' He turned instantly, a bemused smile on his face. 'I don't really,' said Frankie, grabbing the poster from me and holding it out. 'I want you to sign this for my daughter. Her name's Emily. She would have been here herself but she's having a bone marrow transplant tomorrow. She worships the ground you walk on.'

Robert scribbled something on the poster before glancing up.

'I hope it goes well,' he said, his voice just audible above the screams which filled the air. And with that he was gone, whisked away to pose for the photographers hollering his name. Only his wild hair visible through the dry ice.

I looked down at the poster, realising that my hands were shaking, and read the words out loud.

'To Emily, live the life you've dreamed of. Love Robert.' Frankie looked at me and screamed again. 'And he's put kisses,' I said. 'Three of them. She's going to love it.'

We stood hugging each other and crying for a long time. Oblivious to the screams and comings and goings around us.

'She's going to be all right, isn't she?' asked Frankie. I nodded and gently wiped the tears from her face.

'She's going to be just fine.'

It was gone nine by the time I got to the hospital. Fortunately they were very relaxed about visiting times. I hurried along the corridor, hoping Mark wouldn't have decided to get an early night. He hadn't though; as I peered through the window of his room I could see him watching Sky Sports on his television screen. I turned the handle and stepped inside. He looked up with a start.

'Hi. You're a day early. It hasn't happened yet.'

'I know. Last-minute change of plan,' I said.

'But you agreed.'

I bent to kiss him and sat down in the chair next to his bed.

'Sometimes people ask you to do something that you know isn't what they really want. Or what they need. You're scared. I'm here for you. It's how it should be.'

Mark nodded slowly and turned off the TV with the remote.

'Thank you. What's with the get-up?' he said with a grin, looking at my boots and short skirt. 'Is that your idea of boosting my spirits?'

'It was my failed attempt at blending in with a bunch of teenage vampire groupies, actually.'

Mark frowned at me.

'I took Frankie to that film premiere Emily wanted to go to. We managed to get Robert Pattinson's autograph. She'll be well chuffed.'

'You're always so bloody competitive. I give her my bone marrow and you have to go one better, don't you?' He smiled.

I looked at him, knowing I had to tell him but not wanting to turn things serious just as he was beginning to relax. It had to be done though. I didn't want to lie to him for a moment longer.

'I saw Andy Pailes again today. He didn't send me packing

last time. Quite the opposite. I'm sorry I didn't tell you before
but I didn't want to worry you.'

Mark's face dropped. He looked as if he was bracing
himself for bad news.

'It's OK. It's over. It's finished now. That's why I'm here
with you.'

'I don't understand. Why would you go and see him
again?'

I sighed and took hold of Mark's hand.

'It wasn't like a normal teenage idol thing. I met him
lots of times. We became friends. Well, more than friends,
actually.'

'You mean . . .'

I nodded quickly. Not wanting Mark to say it.

'Yeah. A couple of times. It was all pretty sordid. Although
of course it didn't seem like that to me at the time.'

'How old were you?'

'Sixteen. Just.'

'Fucking hell.'

'I know. That's what my mum said.'

'She found out?'

I nodded again, looking down at the bed.

'Everyone found out. It was on the front page of the
News of the World. They were tipped off by one of his
teammates.'

Mark raised his eyebrows and blew out. Clearly struggling to take it all in.

'So what happened?'

'He didn't want anything more to do with me. United
put him on the transfer list and England dropped him.'

'And what about you?'

I shut my eyes and squeezed Mark's hand tight.

'I did a really stupid thing. I tried to kill myself.'

I felt the tremors radiating out through Mark's body. His hand went cold in mine. He was quiet for a long time. When I finally opened my eyes he was staring at me, his face unusually pale.

'How?' he managed finally.

'I threw myself in front of a train.'

Mark winced and shut his eyes.

'Fortunately I made a complete hash of it. Ended up in hospital. I was unconscious for a couple of days and pretty badly injured but, well, it was nothing compared to what could have been.'

Mark opened his eyes. A tear ran out of one corner. He shook his head again and again. Something clicked inside his head. 'So your scars. It wasn't a car crash?'

I shook my head, embarrassed at the lie I'd told to explain away the physical evidence on my hip and shoulder.

'Why didn't you tell me all this before?'

'It never seemed the right moment. It's not the sort of thing you can casually come out with. I told David not long after we got married and it kind of freaked him out. I guess I came to the conclusion it was one of those things that was best swept under the carpet.'

'So why are you telling me now?'

'Because I want you to understand why I went back to see him. How deep this all ran. I know I should have told you when you gave me his address. And I feel bad that you had no idea what you were dealing with.'

Mark thought for a moment. 'And what about him? What did he want?'

'I don't know. He's a bit of an enigma,' I said with a smile, remembering the first time I'd said it. 'He's single; he struck me as pretty lonely. Which is probably why he asked to see me again. I know I shouldn't have and I feel really bad about it, but it's like I revert to a sixteen year old in his presence.'

'Did you want to get back together with him?'

'I don't know what I wanted, to be honest. The whole thing with finding the list left me pretty mixed up. But when I saw him today it was like I was seeing him through a grown-up's eyes for the first time. All the anger about how he'd treated me came out. Anger I didn't even know I felt. I told him what a bastard he'd been. I said you were worth ten of him. And I meant it as well.'

I started crying. Mark leant forward and took my head in his hands. Stroking my hair. Holding me as I rocked to and fro.

'It's all right,' he said. 'Everything's all right.'

'You don't hate me?' I sobbed.

'How could I hate you? You're the most precious thing in the world to me and I've just found out that I nearly lost you years before I even met you. I don't care what happened in the past. All that matters is what happens from here on.'

'Good. Because I want to be with you. I've never been more certain of anything in my entire life. I'm sorry I've put you through all this. I know I've been hard work these past few months. But it's all over now. It really is.'

Mark nodded slowly. 'That's all right then. And I'm

sorry too. Because I probably brought it all on by putting you on the spot like that about the house.'

'Hey, you were doing something really nice.'

'Just going about it the wrong way.'

I smiled as he brushed the soggy strands of hair from my face.

'Do you know what?' I said. 'I quite fancy you in those pyjamas.'

'Watch it,' said Mark. 'It's against hospital rules to take the piss out of patients the night before an op.'

'Sorry. I haven't done a very good job of trying to calm your nerves either, have I?'

'Oh, I don't know. You've certainly taken my mind off the transplant.'

'I ought to go and let you get some sleep.'

'What, after coming out with all of that stuff? It'll be going round in my head for hours.'

'Let me sit with you then.' I shuffled on to the bed and snuggled in next to Mark. My hand stroking his leg.

'I'll probably have some more questions,' he said. 'Things I want to know about what happened when it all sinks in a bit.'

'That's OK. There are no more secrets. You can read my diaries when you get home if you want to. I've got a stack of them in the loft.'

'What, and know what was going on inside your head at fifteen? I think I'd rather be blissfully ignorant.'

I smiled. We sat like that for a long time. Both of us thinking. Waiting for everything to settle so we could see what the land looked like after the earthquake.

'I'm glad you came,' he said eventually.

'Good. So am I.'

'You know tomorrow? There's something I'd like you to do for me.'

'Of course. What is it?'

'Keep that outfit on. Something to look forward to when I come round.'

'I love you, Mark Parry,' I said, digging him in the ribs with my elbow. 'I probably shouldn't, but I do.'

Tuesday, 22 July 1986

Every morning I wondered if this would be the day when people would stop being nice to me. If they would think that my broken bones had healed, the scars had faded, I'd left school and was therefore old enough to know better, so they could go back to treating me normally again. I would have understood it if they had done. Part of me would have been relieved; I found the constant concern about my state of mind and the care people took to avoid mentioning anything remotely connected with suicide, depression or trains a bit wearing at times.

But when I went downstairs, Mum was sitting at the kitchen table beaming the same 'Thank God she's alive' smile that she'd been sporting for the past few months. We sat and had breakfast together, Mum making cheery conversation in between each mouthful of toast.

'I was thinking of going into town tomorrow, see if I can find a new sofa for the front room. It's about time we had a change. I don't suppose you want to come with me, do you? To help me choose.'

'OK,' I said, 'as long as it doesn't take long. And you don't drag me to Laura Ashley.'

'Oh no, I wasn't thinking of going there. I was thinking of getting something a bit more modern.'

I tried not to laugh as I took a quick slurp of tea.

'Oh, one more thing,' Mum continued, hesitantly. 'Is it OK if Malcolm comes round for tea this evening? Say if you don't want him to.'

I thought about it for a moment.

'No, it's all right. He can come if he wants to. He's all right, actually.'

I got up from the table and glanced back over my shoulder before I hurried upstairs. Mum had a huge smile on her face. I couldn't remember her ever looking that happy before.

For once, I knew exactly what I wanted from the wardrobe. It had to make me look good but not desperate. My blue summer dress would be perfect. Well, not perfect perhaps, but good enough. I spent ages doing my makeup. Putting on a brave face. When I had finished I stepped back to admire myself in the mirror. The slick of shimmering honey-coloured lipstick stared back at me. It was a long time since I'd seen that. I'd made an effort today, a real effort.

I caught Andy's eye in the mirror. And turned to see not one pair but a dozen others staring down at me from the wall. As they had done every day since Andy had been here with me. He hadn't gone away because I hadn't let him. Mum had threatened to tear the pictures down. But I knew she wouldn't. She was too scared of upsetting me.

I picked up the scrap of paper with the scribbled directions on it and popped it into my bag. Then I floated down-stairs, the cotton dress cool against my bare legs.

'You look nice, love,' said Mum. 'Where are you meeting Frankie?'

'Round hers,' I said. I felt bad lying. But I knew if I told her the truth she'd freak out. And I didn't need a big scene. Not today.

'See ya later,' I called over my shoulder as I pulled the door to behind me. I walked to the end of our road, checked over my shoulder and turned left towards the station.

It was cool in the shade on the platform. I wished I'd brought my jacket. I felt goose bumps climbing up my arms and across my shoulders. I started walking up the platform, as close to the edge as possible. I didn't see the point in confronting something unless you were going to do it head on. A couple of people glanced at me as I walked past. I wondered if they recognised me. If they were rack-ing their brains, trying to remember where they'd seen me before. I was half expecting someone to come and grab my arm as the train came in to the platform. Just in case.

The end carriage came to a halt directly in front of me. I waited while an elderly lady got off, then stepped on board and found myself an empty seat next to the window. It felt weird, travelling in the opposite direction to normal. Away from London. Further into deepest darkest Hertfordshire.

I got off at Welwyn Garden City. It smelt of warm Shredded Wheat. I couldn't understand it until I remem-bered seeing the address on the side of my cereal packet. I hurried up the platform stairs and down again the other

side. The single-decker bus was standing outside the station, engine running. Within a few seconds of me getting
on, the driver set off. As if he'd been waiting specially
for me. The other people on the bus looked like regulars.
Elderly ladies in blouses tucked into elasticated trousers
and mums with fidgeting toddlers on their laps. My age,
clothes and lack of a shopping bag gave the game away. I
didn't normally do this. I had some particular place to go.

The sun was streaming through the windows now. I
could feel the backs of my legs sticking to the plastic seat.
Stretches of green flashed past the window as we started to
leave the rows of neat semis behind. It was another fifteen
minutes or so before the driver called out that we were at
my stop. I peeled myself off the seat.

'Thornley Lane's just there,' he said, pointing to the
other side of the road.

'Thanks,' I said, stepping from the bus, glad to be on my
own at last. I started walking. My feet already sticky in my
sandals. The wetness creeping from under my arms. I hoped
there'd be a cool air dryer in the loos, so I could dry my
armpits Madonna-style. As I drew nearer I felt my breath
quickening. My legs kept walking; I don't think I could have
stopped them if I'd tried. But my steps were less certain. The
nagging doubts in my head grew louder. I wasn't sure it was
the right thing to do any more. Never go back, they said.
But I wasn't going back. I was going somewhere new.

The piece of paper in my hand was shaking when I
looked at it. Left at the bottom and the white gates are
straight ahead. That's what the lady on the switchboard
had told me when I'd rung, pretending to be a loyal fan.

I turned the corner and caught sight of a concrete club-house. It was small and drab. As I drew nearer I noticed the peeling paint on the gates. Even a letter missing from the sign. 'Luton Town Fo tball Club Training Ground' it said. That was what it had come to. I walked through the gates. It was so not United. Even the players' cars were cheaper-looking. My heart started thumping as I caught sight of Andy's Golf. The only familiar thing in the whole place. I stood looking at it for a long time. Remembering being inside. Being with him. Kissing him. And every-thing that had come after it. It seemed like a lifetime ago now. As if it had happened to somebody else. Which, in a way, I guessed it had. When my legs felt strong enough to move again I crept towards the clubhouse, from where I could see over towards the training pitch.

The players were still out there. Though they appeared to be warming down. I picked Andy out straight away. Just by the way he was standing. He had his back to me. It was so weird, seeing him in a Luton strip. Like watching your mum looking after the kids next door. I wanted to shout at him that he'd made a mistake, got the wrong place. He hadn't though. This was where he belonged now. Beggars couldn't be choosers. And as he'd said in the papers, it was very good of Luton to give him a chance to resurrect his career.

I hid behind the wall as the players walked back towards the clubhouse. I didn't want Andy to see me. Not until I was ready. And I hadn't even worked out what to say yet. I had practised it in my head countless times. But now I was actually here, it had all become scrambled. Nothing seemed to sound right any more. A dozen or so Luton fans drifted across from the training area to congregate outside the clubhouse. A girl a couple of years younger than me came and stood a few yards away. She smiled at me; I looked away. I couldn't afford to enter into a conversation. I didn't want my cover blown.

I stood facing away from everyone else. Looking out across the car park. Waiting. A few players came out. I recognised Brian Stein as he walked past. I hoped the others wouldn't think it strange. That I wasn't asking for any autographs. That I wasn't even looking at them.

'Excuse me.' It was the girl's voice from behind me. 'Can you take a photo for me, please?'

I turned round to see her holding her camera out to me. And Andy standing a few feet away from her, wearing a Luton Town sweatshirt and looking at me with wide, staring eyes. I stood paralysed. My mouth opened to say something but no words came out.

'You just press that button,' the girl continued, oblivious to what was going on.

I took the camera from her. As I held it up I could feel it shaking against my nose. I looked through the viewfinder. The girl leant in towards Andy. His hands were firmly behind his back. And he was staring straight at me. His face decidedly pale.

'Thanks,' the girl said.

I handed the camera back to her. Knowing she'd hate the photo, even if it did come out. She moved away and it was just the two of us.

'What are you doing here?' Andy said. It was not the welcome I'd hoped for.

'I wanted to see you.'

'I understand that but this is hardly the place,' he said, glancing over his shoulder.

'Where else could I find you?'

'I'm very lucky to have been given another chance, Claire. I can't afford to screw this one up.'

'Is there somewhere we can go?' I said. 'To talk.'

Andy nodded in the direction of the far corner of the car park, where his Golf was. Beyond it was a low wall, hidden from the view of the other fans and players. I sat down on it a few feet away from him, feeling like a kid all over again. I wanted to touch him but pushed the thought away. I waited for him to speak, to hear what he might say.

'Are you feeling better now?' he said eventually.

People asked you that after a cold. Not a suicide attempt. I looked across at him, frowning.

'I meant have your injuries healed?' he said.

'Yeah, fine, thanks.' I looked away. All the time trying not to think. That the last time I'd seen him was when we were having sex.

'I feel such a shit,' Andy said.

I didn't say anything. I wasn't going to argue and I wanted him to carry on talking. I'd waited a long time to hear what he had to say.

'I couldn't believe it when I heard what you'd done. I thought you were dead at first. And then when I got your letter . . .' He looked up at the sky and shook his head.

'I bet you wished I had died.'

'Don't say that, Claire.'

'Why?'

'Because it's not true.'

'Why didn't you come to see me in hospital then?'

'With all the press outside? They'd have had a field day. Anyway, the club barred me from going anywhere near you.'

'Is that why you didn't ring me, or answer my calls?'

'What calls?'

'I phoned you, loads of times.'

'I wasn't at home. They told me to stay at Skip's. Till all the fuss died down.'

I nodded. We sat in silence for a bit.

'Why did you come here, Claire?' he said at last.

'I wanted to know if I meant anything to you at all.'

Andy sighed and ran his fingers through his hair.

'Look, Claire, I'm not proud of what happened. You're a lovely girl but . . . I never meant for it to turn into, you know, a physical thing.'

I shook my head. This wasn't making sense.

'Oh. So why did it then?'

Andy shrugged. 'I guess I let my heart rule my head again.'

Frankie said it was his prick that he'd let rule his head. But I wasn't going to tell him that.

Andy blew out his cheeks.

'Look, I behaved like a complete bastard. I know that. I was lonely. And I was flattered by your attention. I went out with Annie to get the lads off my back about not having a girlfriend. Then when she dumped me for Clubber . . .'

'You never said she dumped you.'

'I never said she didn't either. You believed what you wanted to, Claire. You idolised me. I realised that when I

473

saw all those pictures in your room. I should have left then.'

'Why didn't you?'

He shrugged again. Avoiding eye contact again. I waited for him to say 'Because I loved you, because I couldn't resist you.' He said nothing. It was my turn to sigh.

'I'm sorry about what happened to you, Claire. Really I am.' He blew out his cheeks again before turning to look at me. I thought he was about to say something else, but he didn't.

We both sat for a bit. I dragged my toe repeatedly across the gravel. After a while I realised my heart had stopped thumping. And that my palms weren't sweating any more.

'You'd better go, before anyone sees us,' I said. And with that I got up, brushed the seat of my dress and walked out of the car park without looking back. Because I knew if I did he would see the tears streaming down my face.

When I got home, Mum was busy in the kitchen preparing tea. I went straight up to my room and slowly, one by one, started taking Andy's pictures down from the wall.

Sixteen

The signed poster of Robert was up on the wall behind Emily's bed when I visited her in hospital the next morning.

'Thank you,' she grinned. 'Mum said it was your idea.'

'My idea but your mum pulled it off. Did she tell you how she got it?' Emily shook her head. 'Ask her later, when it's all over. It'll make you laugh. Or maybe cringe with embarrassment.'

'Was he just as gorgeous in real life?' she asked.

'Better. Your mum's got the hots for him. Just don't tell her I said so.'

Emily giggled. I sat down on the edge of her bed and gave her a hug. Not that there was much of her left to hug. She'd lost a lot of weight. One of the side effects of the last round of chemo. Her hair was starting to grow back. Which was a shame in a way because she'd just get used to having it and it would all fall out again.

'Do you know the best thing about him though?' I said. 'He's just the guy on your wall. It's the best place for him, because that way he can never let you down. Never be a disappointment.'

'I know,' said Emily. 'I wouldn't want to go out with

him. Not really. He can't possibly be as nice as I imagine he is. So it's better that I just imagine.'

I smiled and shook my head.

'What?' said Emily.

'You're so much more sensible than I was at your age. It took me a long, long time to learn that.'

'That guy Andy who you liked. You had a thing with him, didn't you?'

'How do you know?'

'I didn't. I guessed. Something in the way you talked about him.'

'Yeah. I did. I got it all mixed up, you see. The real Andy and the imaginary one. I so much wanted them to be the same person but it turned out they weren't.'

'Did he hurt you?'

'Yeah. He did. I don't think he meant to, but he didn't understand how special he was. Or that the Andy I wanted was the one in my dreams.'

'I can still dream though, can't I?'

'Of course you can,' I said, reaching out and holding her hand.

'All I dream of,' said Emily, 'is being well again. Of being able to go on holiday with Alia next year and taking Sophia shopping when she's older. Of Joe walking me down the aisle one day.'

I smiled and wiped away the tears from her cheeks. 'And all those things can still happen,' I said. 'Your Robert was right. You can live the life you dream of. You simply have to remember that dreams can change and it's important you don't let the old ones get in the way of the new.'

Emily nodded. I passed her a tissue from the box on the bedside cabinet.

'Anyway,' I said. 'Listen to me going on. I must sound like your mother.'

Emily smiled. 'I hope me and Alia are still best friends when we're your age. And I hope I end up with the man of my dreams like you have.'

'How do you know Mark's the man of my dreams?'

'Because you couldn't have wished for anyone better, could you?'

I shook my head. Wishing I'd had half of her wisdom when I'd been her age.

'I'll tell him that,' I said. 'Now you get some rest. Everything's going to be fine. And I'll come and see you again later, OK?'

'OK,' said Emily, still clinging on to my hand. 'Will you tell me all about last night, about seeing Robert? That's what I'll be wanting to hear.'

'Sure,' I said. 'I'll tell you every single detail. Even the bits your mum said not to.'

Emily grinned. I left her lying on the bed. Gazing up at Robert on the wall.

It was a long time before Frankie came down to the waiting room. I'd gone through most of the contents of the drinks machine and still not found anything which tasted good.

She looked tired and washed out. But most of all she looked happy.

'Emily's fine,' she said. 'The doctor said it all went well.

It's just a matter of time now. It will be a while before they know if the graft has taken. And whether her body will reject it.'

She started crying. I wrapped my arms around her and let her sob into my shoulder.

'She'll be fine,' I said. 'She's a tough cookie, like her mother. She's also got more sense than the two of us put together at her age.'

Frankie managed a watery smile. 'What do you mean?' she said.

'All the things I wish I'd known at her age. She's got them all sorted. Knows exactly what's important. Exactly what life's all about.'

'That's good,' said Frankie. 'Maybe, once she comes through this, she'll have a smooth ride, for a few years at least.'

'Just remember,' I said, 'don't you go trying to fix her up with any nice Italian boys.'

'I promise.'

'Anyway, I'd better get over to the other hospital to see Mark.'

'Of course,' said Frankie. 'Will you do something for me?'

'What?'

'Give him a great big kiss from me.'

'Sure,' I said. 'I'd be delighted.'

I peered in through the window before going into Mark's room. The nurse had warned me that he was still a bit groggy but I could at least see him. He was lying on his bed looking like a real patient this time. His face a dull shade of grey. His body lying awkwardly. I slipped into the room and sat down on the chair, pulling it up close to the bed. He turned his face towards me and managed some sort of smile.

'How's Emily?' he asked.

'She's fine. The doctor says it went well. She's in with a chance.'

'Good. Let's hope it stays that way.'

I nodded. 'Oh, and this is from Frankie,' I said, bending to kiss him softly on the forehead. 'And this is from me,' I added, planting a kiss on his lips.

'Thanks. I needed that.'

'How are you feeling?'

'Like someone whacked me over the head, drilled a dirty great hole in my back and took out half of my insides.'

'You were right. You are going to be a lousy patient.'

'I hope you're going to be a good nurse.'

'I'll do my best,' I said. 'But I draw the line at dressing up, OK?'

'Damn, you're no fun at all.'

He lay quietly for a moment. I fiddled with the strap of my watch.

'When you're ready to go home, you're coming back to my place. I'm off until Christmas.'

'You didn't have to do that.'

'No. But I wanted to. Give me a chance to move all your stuff in and get some decorations up.'

'A dog's for life, you know. Not just for Christmas.'

'I know. And that's why I won't be chucking you out in the New Year.'

'But what if you're sick of me by then?'

'I won't be. And your place will be easier to rent out until you find a buyer.'

'What, so we're going to live together?'

'Yep. That's what you wanted, isn't it?'

'Yeah, but I haven't had a chance to draw up a prenup yet, just in case you try to run off with my Chili Peppers albums in ten years' time.'

'We'll be living somewhere else by then.'

'What, with a thatched roof and roses in the front garden?' he said smiling.

'No. Something a bit more sensible but maybe with a bit of character thrown in.'

'Something we both like, you mean?'

'Yeah. With four bedrooms, just in case I change my mind about having kids.'

'Do you think you might do?'

'Maybe. But only if you promise not to buy any of those poxy little Blackburn Rovers romper suits.'

Mark laughed. 'I'll make you very happy, Claire,' he said, reaching out for my hand.

'I know you will,' I said, squeezing it tightly. 'Emily reckons you're the man of my dreams.'

'Must be all those drugs they've pumped into her.'

'I don't know,' I said. 'I have a feeling she's right.'

Acknowledgements

Warmest thanks to the following people: my editor Sherise Hobbs for her professionalism, enthusiasm and for being thoroughly nice to work with; the great team at Headline for all their efforts; my agent Anthony Goff for his expertise, support and advice; everyone at David Higham Associates; Martyn Bedford, for advising emergency surgery on an early draft of Claire's story when I was knee-deep in rejections, helping me turn it around and providing invaluable advice and encouragement over a number of years; Alex Elam for believing in my writing and Claire's story a long time ago; Michelle Hurst for editorial services (with a pink pen) way before I had a book deal, being on the end of the deputy editor's hotline in Grimsby and for bone marrow transplant advice; Rebecca Sutcliffe, Steve Connor and Vincent Carr for legal advice; The Anthony Nolan Trust (www. anthonynolan.org.uk, hotline no: 0303 303 0303), especially Victoria Moffett, Rochelle Roest and Sameer Tupule, for expert medical advice; Amarah Bashforth for being my teenage consultant and telling me everything I needed to know about Robert Pattinson; Lance Little for the great website (www. linda-green.com); Alia Mahon Henson for lending her name and Grainne Mahon Henson for her generosity, the players of Tottenham Hotspur Football Club 1983–86 for putting up with a certain teenage fan's autograph requests (especially Gary Mabbutt for being infinitely nicer than Andy Pailes and a wonderful ambassador for the game); my friends and family for their ongoing support and PR efforts; my gorgeous son Rohan for all his help with my book and for allowing me time off from the Wizard of Oz birthday party preparations to get it finished; and, most importantly, my husband Ian for his unstinting support and belief over a number of years, for getting me out from under the table when the rejections kept coming, promoting my book to the wives and girlfriends of photographers in the north and for working tirelessly on the Emerald City and the Yellow Brick Road sets while I wrote this book. Neither the party – nor this novel – could have happened without you!

The last thing she told me

Linda Green

Even the deepest buried secrets can find their way to the surface . . .

Moments before she dies, Nicola's grandmother Betty whispers to her that there are babies at the bottom of the garden.

Nicola's mother claims she was talking nonsense. However, when Nicola's daughter finds a bone while playing in Betty's garden, it's clear that something sinister has taken place.

But will unearthing painful family secrets end up tearing Nicola's family apart?

Quercus

I Did A Bad Thing

Linda Green

Sarah Roberts used to be good. Then she did something bad. Very bad.

Now, years later, she's living a good life. She works as a local newspaper reporter and lives with her saintly boyfriend Jonathan. She has no reason to think her guilty past will ever catch up with her. Until Nick, the man she was prepared to risk everything for, walks back into her life. And suddenly, what's good and bad aren't so clear to Sarah any more . . .

Quercus

Ten Reasons
Not to Fall
in Love

Linda Green

Jo Gilroy, an award-winning TV news reporter,
gave her heart away once. She won't be making
the same mistake again. Having been dumped by
Richard, the father of her toddler son Alfie, she
returns to work to find she has been demoted
and that Richard is now her boss.

As she tries to pick up the pieces of her shattered life,
she resolves to never fall in love again. But then along
comes enigmatic children's entertainer Dan Brady, who
is a huge hit with Alfie. Just as she wonders if she can
risk opening her heart again, dark secrets from Dan's
past emerge and Jo discovers that he has his own
reasons not to fall in love. Reasons that now threaten
to tear their happiness apart . . .

Quercus